TO PLEASURE A LADY

By Nicole Jordan

TO PLEASURE A LADY

A Novel

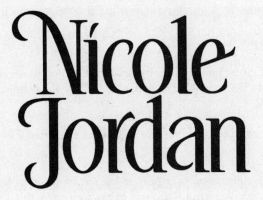

Nicole Jordan

BALLANTINE BOOKS • NEW YORK

A Ballantine Books Mass Market Original

Published in the United States by Ballantine Books, an imprint of The Random House Publishing Group, a division of Random House, Inc., New York.

BALLANTINE and colophon are registered trademarks of Random House, Inc.

This book contains an excerpt from the forthcoming book *To Bed a Beauty* by Nicole Jordan. This excerpt has been set for this edition only and may not reflect the final content of the forthcoming edition.

ISBN 978-0-7394-9177-5

Cover design: Carl D. Galian
Cover illustration: Aleta Rafton

Printed in the United States of America

For Jay:
friend, husband, hero,
with all my love.

Chapter One

❧

I vow the new earl will drive me to distraction, thinking to marry us off like so much breeding stock.
—Letter from Miss Arabella Loring to Fanny Irwin

London, May 1817

Matrimony. The very word was menacing. Yet the new Earl of Danvers could ignore the topic no longer, much to his regret.

"A pity the late earl already met his end," Lord Danvers professed, punctuating his declaration with the slash of a steel rapier. "Otherwise I would have his heart on a spit for the trick he served me, leaving me to play procurer for three wards I never wanted."

His complaint, voiced amid the sounds of swordplay, was met with both sympathetic laughter and skepticism from his friends.

"Procurer, Marcus? Isn't that something of an exaggeration?"

"It perfectly describes my responsibility."

"Matchmaker is a more tasteful characterization."

Matchmaker. What a lowering thought.

Marcus Pierce, formerly addressed as Baron Pierce and now the eighth Lord Danvers, winced with reluctant humor. Although he normally relished a challenge, he would gladly have forgone being saddled with three penniless beauties—and worse, the burden of finding them respectable husbands.

Yet he'd inherited the Loring sisters along with his new title, so he was resigned to discharging his duty sooner or later.

Preferably later.

Marcus had enjoyed thirty-two pleasurable years of bachelorhood, the last ten as one of England's most eligible and elusive marital catches. Since matrimony ranked high on his list of least-favorite subjects, he had put off facing his obligation to his unwanted wards for weeks now.

This fine spring morning, however, he'd finally forced himself to broach the issue while he was engaged in fencing practice at his Mayfair mansion with his two closest friends and fellow escapees of the Marriage Mart.

"But you do see my dilemma?" Marcus asked, executing a swift parry against his equally skilled opponent, Andrew Moncrief, Duke of Arden.

"Ah, yes," Drew answered above the clang of blades. "You hope to marry off your three wards, but you expect to find few takers, given the scandal in their family."

"Precisely." Marcus flashed an engaging grin. "I don't suppose you would volunteer to offer for one of them?"

The duke shot him an eloquent glance as he leapt back to evade a deft thrust. "As much as I yearn to help you, old sport, I cherish my liberty too much to make such a devastating sacrifice, even for you."

"Stubble it, Marcus." The amused drawl came from the sidelines of the salon that Marcus used as a fencing hall. Heath Griffin, Marquess of Claybourne, lounged on a settee as he awaited his turn at practice, drawing idle patterns in the air with his foil. "You're touched in the head if you think to persuade us to offer for your wards."

"They are reputed to be great beauties," Marcus coaxed.

Heath laughed outright. "And spinsters, every one of them. How old is the eldest Miss Loring? Four and twenty?"

"Not quite that."

"But she is said to be a spitfire."

"So I'm told," Marcus reluctantly acknowledged. His solicitors had described Arabella Loring as charming but fiercely stubborn-minded in her desire for emancipation from his guardianship.

"You haven't met her yet?" Heath asked.

"No, I've managed to avoid her thus far. The Misses Loring were away from home when I called to pay my condolences on the death of their step-uncle three months ago. And since then, I've let my solicitors handle all succeeding correspondence. But I will have to deal with them eventually." He sighed. "I will likely travel to Chiswick next week."

The Danvers estate was in the countryside near the small village of Chiswick, some half dozen miles west of London's fashionable Mayfair district, where many of the wealthy aristocracy resided. The distance was an easy drive in a fast curricle, yet Marcus was under no illusions that his task could be dispatched quickly.

"From everything I hear," Drew said as he steadily advanced, "your wards will indeed prove a handful. It won't be easy to marry them off, particularly the eldest."

Nodding, Marcus gave a wry grimace. "Certainly not when they profess to be so adamantly opposed to marriage. I've offered to provide them significant dowries to induce respectable suitors to wed them, but they rejected my proposition out of hand."

"Harbor bluestocking notions of independence, do they?"

"So it would seem. A pity I can't convince either of you to come to my rescue."

It would have been a neat solution to his dilemma, Marcus reflected as he fought off Drew's determined offensive. In addition to inheriting the title of earl to add to his long-held barony, he'd been encumbered with the entailed and impoverished Danvers estate, as well as responsibility for its genteel dependents, three indigent sisters. All three were blessed with impeccable lineage, superb breeding, and enviable beauty, but all were unmarried and getting somewhat long in the tooth.

Their single state was due less to their lack of fortune than to the horrendous scandal in their family. Four years ago, their mother had run off to the Continent with her French lover. Then barely a fortnight later, their father had been killed in a duel over his latest mistress—which had put an abrupt end to any last gasp chances the daughters had of marrying well.

Resolving to give his unwanted wards into more willing hands, Marcus had thought to marry them off by providing them with immense dowries. But that was before he'd discovered how fiercely independent the three beauties were. The eldest sister's letters had become downright impassioned in her appeals for self-rule.

"They are legally my wards until they turn twenty-five," Marcus explained, "but the eldest, Arabella, is already fretting over the constraints. In the past month, she has written me four letters proclaiming that she and her sisters have no need of a guardian at their advanced ages. Regrettably for us all, I am bound by the terms of the will."

Pausing to circle his opponent, Marcus ran a hand roughly through his raven hair. "Truthfully," he muttered, "it would have suited me better had I never heard of the Loring sisters. I never wished for the additional title. I was perfectly content as a baron."

His friends offered him sympathetic but amused looks, which prompted Marcus to add pointedly, "I expect your help in solving my dilemma, you spineless reprobates. Surely you can think of some appropriate candidates I can throw their way."

"You could always offer for one of them yourself," Heath suggested, a wicked gleam in his eye.

"God forbid." Marcus paused to shudder and was nearly skewered when Drew lunged with his foil.

Through much of their boyhood and all of their

adulthood, the three of them—Marcus, Drew, and Heath—had been inseparable, having attended Eton and Oxford together and then come into their vast fortunes and illustrious titles the same year. And after being chased relentlessly by marriage-minded debutantes and barely eluding the traps of countless matchmaking mamas, all three shared grave reservations about the institution of matrimony. Most particularly the sort of cold, convenient union typical of the aristocracy.

Marcus had never encountered even one woman he might want to take for his wife. The thought of being shackled for life to a female he scarcely liked, much less loved, sent chills down his spine. Yet he owed it to his titles, both the new and the old, to carry on his bloodlines, so eventually he would have to marry.

The demise of his bachelorhood, however, would be a long time in coming, Marcus vowed.

Realizing his concentration had been shattered by all this unpalatable talk of matrimony, he stepped back and offered Drew a sardonic salute. "I had best withdraw before you slice me to ribbons, your grace. Heath, pray take your turn at practice."

When the marquess replaced him on the floor, Marcus crossed the salon to a side table, where he set down his rapier and retrieved a towel to wipe his damp brow.

The clash of steel had just resumed when he heard a commotion out in the corridor, coming from the vicinity of his entrance hall. He could only make out every third word or so, but it was clear he had a female caller . . . and that his butler was denying his presence.

His curiosity piqued, Marcus moved closer to the salon door, the better to hear.

"I repeat, Lord Danvers is not at home, miss."

"Not at home or not receiving callers?" the female voice asked pleasantly. "I have come a long distance in order to speak with him. I am willing to search the premises if I must." Her voice was low and melodious but definitely determined. "Where may I find him?"

There followed sounds of a scuffle. Apparently Hobbs was attempting to prevent her from entering the house but losing the battle. A moment later his august servant actually yelped. "Madam, you cannot go abovestairs!"

Picturing the butler blocking the foot of the mansion's sweeping staircase, Marcus found himself stifling a grin.

"Why not?" she queried. "Will I find his lordship abed or in a state of undress?"

Hobbs let out a shocked exclamation before muttering, "Very well, if you insist. I will inquire if his lordship is receiving."

"Pray, don't trouble yourself. Just tell me where he is, and I will announce myself." The dulcet voice paused. "Never mind. I hear swordplay, so I expect I need only follow the sounds."

Marcus braced himself as light footsteps approached along the corridor.

The woman who appeared in the doorway a moment later was striking in her loveliness. Although her tall, elegant figure was gowned modestly in a blue crepe carriage dress, she possessed an unmistakable confidence, a graceful presence, that compelled attention.

A beauty of substance, Marcus realized at once, captivated by the sight.

Despite her unusual height and slenderness, she was curvaceous enough to entice even a man of his jaded experience. Her pale red-gold hair was swept up beneath a bonnet, with curling tendrils spilling around her finely-boned face. He was mainly aware, however, of the pair of keen gray eyes surveying the room, the most intriguing he had ever seen. They were the hue of silver smoke and held an intelligence and warmth that instantly stirred his senses.

Her jaw was set with determination, yet when she spied him, she suddenly faltered. A slight blush rose to her cheeks, as if she realized the impropriety of barging in on three noblemen engaged in a fencing match, all dressed in shirtsleeves and breeches and boots, with no cravats or waistcoats or coats.

Her eyes traveled from Marcus's bare throat to his linen shirt that hung partway open, exposing his chest. Then abruptly, she jerked her gaze back up to his face, as if knowing she'd been caught in a forbidden scrutiny. When he locked glances with her, the color mounted in her cheeks.

Marcus found himself enchanted.

An instant later she appeared to gather her wits and forged ahead with her mission. "Which of you gentlemen is Lord Danvers?" she asked sweetly.

He took a polite step toward her. "At your service, Miss . . . ?"

A vexed Hobbs answered behind her, "Miss Arabella Loring to see you, my lord."

"I take it you are my eldest ward," Marcus observed, concealing his amusement.

Her lovely mouth tightened the slightest measure, but then she tendered him a charming smile. "Regrettably, yes, I am your ward."

"Hobbs, take Miss Loring's pelisse and bonnet—"

"Thank you, my lord, but I don't intend to stay long. I only desire a brief interview . . . in private, if I may."

By now his two friends had paused in their fencing match and were watching his unexpected visitor with avid curiosity. When she advanced into the room, Marcus saw Drew raise a quizzical eyebrow, expressing surprise at her stunning appearance.

Marcus was highly surprised himself. Based on his solicitor's comments, he had expected his eldest ward to be something of a shrew, but the reports of her beauty didn't do her justice. She was, to put it simply, magnificent.

He gave Drew and Heath an apologetic glance. "Would you excuse us?"

Both noblemen crossed the salon with their rapiers, and Heath flashed Marcus a slow grin as he passed, along with one of his habitually baiting remarks. "We will await you in the hall should you need defending."

He saw Arabella stiffen at the quip, but then she laughed, a low melodious sound that once more fired his senses. "I promise not to do him bodily harm."

A pity, was Marcus's first thought; he might have appreciated seeing what she could do to his body.

When they were alone, however, Marcus fixed his ward with a level gaze. He admired her boldness in coming here but knew he should make some show of disapproval if he intended to keep the upper hand with her. "My solicitors warned me about your determination, Miss Loring, but I didn't expect you to flout propriety by visiting me at my home."

She gave a shrug of her elegant shoulders. "You left me little choice, my lord, since you refused to reply to my letters. We have an important matter to discuss."

"I agree, we need to settle the issue of your and your sisters' futures."

Her hesitation was followed by another proffered smile. "I am certain you are a man of reason, Lord Danvers . . ."

Marcus's eyebrow shot up at her obvious attempt to charm him. She was undoubtedly accustomed to twisting men around her fingers, and he felt the effect down to his loins—an effect he instinctively resisted. "Oh, I am quite reasonable ordinarily."

"Then you will understand our reluctance to acknowledge you as our guardian. I know you mean well, but we don't require your assistance."

"Certainly I mean well," he said affably. "You and your sisters are now my responsibility."

A flash of impatience showed in her gray eyes. "Which is patently absurd. We are all past the usual legal age of dependency. Most guardianships end at twenty-one. And we have no fortune to supervise, so there can be no financial justification for your management."

"No," Marcus concurred. "Your step-uncle left you without a penny to your names."

Taking a deep breath, she made an obvious effort at civility. "We don't desire your charity, my lord."

"It is not charity, Miss Loring. It's my legal obligation. You are three vulnerable females in need of a man's protection."

"We do *not* need protecting," she replied emphatically.

"No?" Marcus gave her a penetrating look. "My solicitors are of the opinion that someone ought to take you and your sisters in hand."

Her eyes kindled. "Is that so? Well, I hardly think *you* are qualified to 'take us in hand,' as you term it. You have no experience playing guardian."

Marcus was pleased to be able to refute her statement. "On the contrary, I have a good deal of experience. I've been my sister's guardian for the past ten years. She is twenty-one now, the same age as your youngest sister, Lilian—who is an unruly hoyden, I'm told."

That made Arabella pause. "Perhaps that's true, but Lily was at an impressionable age when our mother deserted us."

"What of your sister Roslyn? By all reports, her uncommon beauty has made her the target for any number of rakes and scoundrels. I suspect she could benefit from a guardian's protection."

"Roslyn can take care of herself. We all can. We have since we were very young."

"But what sort of future can you expect?" Marcus

countered. "Your chances for good marriages were ruined when your parents chose to create their last blatant scandal."

He saw the pain that claimed Arabella's features for a fleeting moment before she forced another smile. "How well I know," she murmured. "But even so, it is not your affair."

Marcus shook his head. "I understand why you resent me, Miss Loring, a perfect stranger taking control of your home—"

"I don't begrudge you the title or estate. What I do resent is your callous assumption that we wish to marry."

That made him smile. "It is hardly callous to offer to find husbands for you. The usual path for young ladies of quality is marriage. You act as if I've gravely offended you."

By now Arabella was clearly biting her tongue. "Forgive me if I gave you that impression, my lord. I know you don't mean it as an insult—"

"You cannot be foolish enough to turn down five thousand pounds each."

"Actually I can—" Suddenly she broke off and gave a rueful laugh. The husky, sultry sound raked his nerve endings with pleasure. "No, I won't allow you to provoke me, my lord. I came here this morning determined to be pleasant."

Marcus found himself staring at her ripe, tempting mouth before he shook himself. Arabella was speaking again, he realized.

"Perhaps you see our decision as inexplicable, Lord Danvers, but my sisters and I do not choose to marry."

"Why not?" When she failed to answer, Marcus hazarded a guess. "I suppose it has to do with the example your parents set."

"It does," Arabella admitted grudgingly. "Our parents were determined to make each other's lives miserable and fought at every opportunity. After the acrimony we witnessed growing up, is it any wonder we have an aversion to arranged marriages?"

Marcus felt more than a measure of sympathy. "I'm familiar with the sentiment. My own parents were scarcely any more congenial."

At his softer tone, she searched his face for a long moment. But then she dragged her gaze away to focus on a pool of sunlight streaming through the nearest window. "In any case, we have no need to marry. We have sufficient incomes now to support ourselves."

"Incomes?"

"If you had troubled yourself to read my letters, you would know about our academy."

"I did read your letters."

She glanced pointedly at him. "But you were not courteous enough to respond. You merely instructed your solicitors to deal with me."

"Guilty as charged. But to my credit, I intended to call upon you next week."

When he smiled winningly, Arabella drew a sharp breath. After a moment, she took another tack. "Come now, Lord Danvers. You don't want responsibility for us, admit it."

Marcus couldn't bring himself to lie. "Very well, it's true, I don't want it."

"Then why don't you simply forget about us?"

"I doubt anyone who has ever met you," Marcus said dryly, "could simply forget you, Miss Loring." When she gave him a piercing look, he sighed. "You are my responsibility now, whether either of us likes it, and I won't abandon my duty to see to your welfare. You'll find I'm not such an ogre. And I'm wealthy enough to fund your dowries."

That made her chin lift. "I tell you, we won't accept your charity. Our academy allows us adequate financial independence."

Admittedly, learning of her academy had roused Marcus's curiosity. "I understand this academy of yours is a finishing school?"

"Of a sort. We teach comportment and manners and correct speech to wealthy young women who were not born to the Quality."

"The daughters of the working class, in other words. How very unique you are, Miss Loring."

Her gaze narrowed. "You are making sport of me."

"Perhaps." Actually he wasn't. He truly thought it admirable that Arabella and her sisters had found an occupation to support themselves, unlike almost every other lady of their station, who wouldn't be caught dead employed in menial labor. But he couldn't help wanting to provoke her, if only for the pleasure of seeing those beautiful gray eyes kindle again.

"And your sisters teach there as well?" Marcus asked leadingly.

"Yes, as do two other ladies who are friends of

mine. Our patroness is Lady Freemantle. It was at her request that we opened the school three years ago. Are you acquainted with her? Her late husband was a baronet, Sir Rupert Freemantle."

Marcus nodded. "I know her. But I'm not certain it is fitting for my wards to be employed at a school, no matter how refined. You realize that as your guardian, I will have to approve your participation?"

Arabella eyed him warily. "I assure you, it is a perfectly respectable endeavor."

"Some would call your opinions bluestocking nonsense."

It was very bad of him to goad her like that, but the pleasure of seeing her spirited reaction was too great to resist.

She seemed, however, to recognize his purpose. "You won't provoke me into losing my temper, my lord."

"No?"

When he took a step closer, she froze, staring up at him as if she found him fascinating. But then she straightened her spine and stood her ground, her gaze direct and challenging. Marcus had the sudden savage urge to sweep her up in his arms and carry her to the nearest bed.

He'd never had such a primal reaction to a woman before—bloody inappropriate, considering that she was his ward.

Arabella drew a slower breath, clearly striving for equanimity, as he was. "I don't believe your mental acumen is impaired, my lord. Why is it so difficult for you to accept that we don't wish to be under your thumb? That we don't want your financial assistance? You are under no obligation to support us."

"The will says differently."

"Then I will hire my own solicitors to contest the will."

"How can you afford it? You don't have the where-withal to contest my guardianship in court."

"Our patroness will help us. Lady Freemantle does not believe that women should be compelled to marry, and she has promised us her support. She is not as wealthy as you, of course, but her father left her a for-tune from his manufacturing and mining enterprises."

"It should prove an interesting contest," Marcus said amiably, crossing his arms over his chest.

His languid smile finally succeeded in igniting her temper. "You cannot force us to accept your settle-ments!"

"No, I suppose not. But once the size of your dowries becomes known, you will have suitors throw-ing themselves at your feet and hounding my door to offer for you."

Her gloved fists clenched as she advanced toward him, her eyes flashing dangerously. "You won't suc-ceed in selling us, your lordship! It is outrageous that grown women are treated as mere property, no better than livestock. We are not broodmares to be hawked to the highest bidder!"

Judging by her impassioned speech, he had struck a nerve. There was fire in her eyes—a fire that filled him with admiration and attraction.

"It seems true after all," he murmured, totally intrigued by the way Arabella was glaring daggers at him.

"*What* is true?"

"That eyes can actually give off sparks. Yours are bright as fireworks."

It was that provocative remark that drove her temper over the edge. The growling sound she made deep in her throat was that of a taunted lioness—a low, dangerous rumble. "I have tried my utmost to remain patient," she began. Marching past him to the table, Arabella swept up his rapier and returned to face him, bringing the tip directly against his chest.

"I was determined to use reason to convince you, and if that failed, I hoped to prevail on your better nature. Evidently you don't have one!"

Utterly fascinated now, Marcus raised his hands slowly in surrender. "I make it a point never to argue with an armed female."

"Good! Then you will promise me that you will abandon this ridiculous notion of marrying us off."

"I fear I can't make any such promise under duress, sweeting."

"You can and you will!"

"No." Despite his fascination, he was not about to be threatened into doing anyone's bidding. But then his gaze fixed on Arabella's face . . . the smooth ivory texture of her skin, her ripe mouth. . . . He was struck with the fiercest urge to kiss her, which was astonishing, since he was not ordinarily a rash man. "Go ahead, do your worst, love."

Clenching her teeth, radiating frustration, she raised the point of the foil to the vulnerable hollow of his throat, but there she stopped.

It was a stand-off, one Marcus was not prepared to endure much longer. When she continued to hesitate, his fingers closed around her gloved ones and slowly, inexorably pushed the tip away from his throat.

Although the immediate danger was over, he kept possession of her hand, shackling her wrist as he stepped closer. His gaze dropped again to the tempting line of her lips.

Her beautiful face was turned up to his, and when she nervously moistened her lips, he fought the fierce desire to capture them with his own.

Despite the warning voice shouting in his head, Marcus found himself drawing Arabella even nearer, pulling her against him, until their bodies brushed. The feeling that sparked between them when he felt the sweet press of her breasts was hot enough to singe him.

Her eyes flared then with a different emotion, while his senses avidly relayed the excitement of touching her.

She felt warm and intensely vital. Intensely alive. Her feminine softness raised every primal male instinct he possessed.

It was all he could do to keep control of himself. "The next time you threaten a man, Miss Loring," he advised in a voice that was suddenly husky, "make certain you are prepared to carry it through."

With another small cry of frustration, she snatched

her hand from his grasp and stepped back. "I will take note next time, your lordship."

Marcus was startled by how badly he wanted there to be a next time. He watched as Arabella tossed down the rapier, where it clattered on the floor.

"You should be glad I am too much of a lady to run you through," she declared. With that she spun on her heel and stalked to the door. But then she paused to shoot a darkling glance over her shoulder. "If you want a battle, Lord Danvers, I promise I will give you one."

Chapter Two

❧

I have finally met the earl and he is even more vexing than I anticipated.

—Arabella Loring to Fanny Irwin

Her gaze was challenge incarnate, a challenge Marcus couldn't resist. When he took a step closer, however, Miss Loring promptly quit the room. He followed her out to the corridor and stared after her, totally bemused.

She brushed past his two friends, who were cooling their heels in the corridor, and crossed to the entrance hall, where his butler hurriedly opened the front door for her.

When she swept out, Marcus suppressed the urge to give chase. Yet the tantalizing encounter had left him hungry for more of her.

"Your mouth is agape, old son," Heath observed, clearly amused.

Marcus clamped his mouth shut, yet he couldn't deny the truth of the accusation. Arabella Loring had left him with all his primal male instincts aroused.

Shaking his head in bafflement, he returned to the salon and proceeded to pour himself a generous ale, then sank pensively onto the leather couch, contemplating his intense reaction to his eldest ward.

His friends followed suit and settled in nearby chairs. Heath was the first to speak. "You didn't tell us Miss Loring was stunning, Marcus."

"Because I didn't know." His solicitors had advised him to expect a beauty, but they hadn't warned him about her vibrancy, her inner fire, or he might have been better prepared to face her.

"She certainly set you back on your heels," Drew commented, his tone edged with sardonic humor. "From what we heard, she threatened to unman you. You were right—you have a virago on your hands."

"No," Heath disagreed. "More like an Amazon or a Valkyrie." His tone was rather admiring.

"I prefer a bit more calm in a female," Drew drawled.

"Not I," Heath replied. "A pity you sent us out of the room, Marcus. I would have liked to witness the fireworks."

Fireworks was exactly what he'd felt with Arabella, Marcus thought, bemused.

"You still look confounded," Drew added more seriously.

Marcus nodded his head in agreement. He'd never before experienced that instantaneous, powerful feeling of attraction. Just being near Arabella had ignited a spark of desire in him.

Which was remarkably novel. He'd known countless beautiful women before. Hell, he'd enjoyed more than his fair share of beauties. So what made his eldest ward so different? The fact that she hadn't fawned over him? That she wasn't eager to please and gratify him as every other woman was?

"Perhaps," he rationalized, "I was just taken aback because she was so unexpected."

"There's no doubt she will prove challenging," Heath said needlessly.

She would indeed, Marcus thought, remembering Arabella's parting declaration of war. Elementally challenging. Irresistibly intriguing. The image of her flashing gray eyes and red-gold hair would be hard to forget.

He took a long drink of ale. Perhaps it wasn't so surprising that his interest had been acutely aroused by an elegant spitfire like Arabella. For months now all his usual pursuits had seemed deadly dull. And he'd been excruciatingly bored by all the women chasing him, ladies and lightskirts alike.

"So just how do you intend to manage the fiery Miss Arabella?" Drew asked.

"Truthfully? I'm not yet certain. I expect I'll move up my visit to Danvers Hall to Monday."

"I would say you underestimated your dilemma in marrying her off to some unwitting dupe."

Marcus laughed inwardly. "No doubt." The task of arranging her a proper match would be harder than he'd imagined. And whoever attempted to court her would have his work cut out for him. "It may be impossible to find a husband for her."

"I'm not so certain," Heath countered. "I imagine any number of men would find her spirit appealing. If she shows half that passion in bed, she would make some man a magnificent mistress."

Marcus shot his friend a scowl. "Mind your tongue, man. That's my ward you're speaking of."

Heath returned a rueful grin. "True, you can't seduce your own ward. A shame she's so well-born.
Wouldn't be honorable. Forbidden fruit and all that."

Forbidden, true, Marcus acknowledged regretfully.
His current connection to the Loring sisters was purely
a legal one, and they were all of an age that they didn't
require a guardian to supervise their every action, yet
he was still responsible for their welfare.

Even so, he couldn't deny that taking Arabella for his
mistress held a definite appeal. He was between mistresses at the moment, since nothing seemed to satisfy
him lately. Slaking his carnal needs in a lush, perfumed
body had held little allure recently—until now.

An image of a willing Arabella in his bed ignited another surge of desire in his loins. The thought of having all that fire beneath him, surrounding him, made
Marcus shift uncomfortably in his seat.

Heath added in a provoking tone, "As I said, you
could always offer for her yourself. It would be entertaining to watch you try to conquer her."

Drew's mouth twisted with a mocking smile. "You
might find it refreshing, having to chase a woman for
a change."

Marcus sent his friends a look of annoyance. "Have
a care, my fine fellows. If you keep ragging me about
matrimony, I'll find a way to make *you* marry my
wards."

"I can understand," Drew replied, unintimidated,
"why the Loring sisters would object to your guardianship. Women like the illusion of pulling all the strings,
making men dance to their bidding. Not being treated

as an unpleasant duty, as you seem to consider your wards."

"I wouldn't find the duty unpleasant at all," Heath mused. "I could enjoy a dispute with the likes of Miss Arabella. What about it, Marcus? You've been complaining for some time about boredom. A battle with her will surely add spice to your life." Heath paused, surveying Marcus over the rim of his mug. "And judging from that glint in your eye, you think so, too."

Marcus nodded. Battling Arabella Loring would be a cure for his ennui, no question. "Doubtless it will prove interesting. I'll find out when I travel to Danvers Hall next week to settle the issue of their marriages."

He didn't know just yet precisely how he would deal with Arabella. But he was keenly looking forward to their next confrontation.

The trouble with bearding a lion in his den, Arabella thought as she climbed into her patroness's plush traveling chaise, was that one risked being eaten. Perhaps she had escaped becoming a tasty meal for Marcus Pierce, the new Earl of Danvers, but her pride had certainly suffered.

As the coachmen whipped up the team to return to Chiswick, Arabella sank back against the velvet squabs and waited for her wits to stop whirling. Lord Danvers had made her so addled for a moment that she'd actually forgotten her purpose in coming.

She'd traveled to London this morning, determined to use logic and charm to make him see reason and convince him to relinquish his unwanted guardianship. But he had completely taken her off guard when she'd interrupted his fencing practice.

It was deplorable, the way her pulse had quickened at her first sight of him. He was tall and athletically built, with thick ebony hair, midnight blue eyes, and the square, chiseled features of a Greek god. But no marble statue had ever made her want to touch it or sparked such brazen images in her mind as he had kindled.

Arabella winced, remembering how his open shirt had exposed part of his muscular chest and the dark hair curling invitingly in the gap. The earl's state of undress, combined with the gleam of amusement in his shrewd blue eyes, had totally disconcerted her. And then she had allowed him to provoke her into losing her temper.

She couldn't imagine what had prompted her to threaten him like that when she had meant to sweetly persuade. It clearly had been a mistake to challenge him, since a man of his ilk obviously relished challenges.

Lord Danvers had shockingly turned the tables on her, rendering her breathless by nearly kissing her. What was worse, she had wanted him to do it! She'd made an ignominious but judicious retreat without attaining her goal, not trusting herself to remain any longer.

The encounter had left her unsettled inside and supremely vexed with herself, not only by her failure but by her foolish attraction to him.

"Silly widgeon," Arabella muttered to herself. "You not only let him get the upper hand, you acted like any other witless female, attracted to a handsome nobleman."

His lordship's superior smugness was just what she had expected. He was a provoking devil, arrogant and highhanded, thinking he knew what was best for them. Yet she couldn't deny his impact was potent. She had felt the fire between them during those few brief moments when they'd been locked together in a battle of wills.

With a sigh of disgust, Arabella turned her head to gaze out the carriage window at the passing countryside.

She should have been better prepared for him. Her good friend Fanny Irwin—whom she had known since childhood and who currently was London's most famous courtesan—had warned her about Marcus Pierce. About his striking looks, his roguish charm, his keen intelligence. As one of the country's most eligible aristocrats, he had enchanted half of England's female population—and bedded a good number of them.

Most women found his sort of rakish charm appealing. But then most women had not had to suffer a libertine father their whole lives long, as Arabella had.

Her new guardian was too blasted handsome for his own good. The thought made Arabella press her lips together in self-reproach. Her mother had sacrificed everything for a handsome face . . . including her own daughters. The wrenching pain of Mama's abandonment still cut like a knife, even after four years.

When Victoria Loring had absconded with her lover, her daughters were left to deal with the resultant humiliation and disgrace. Then to exacerbate matters further, their father, Sir Charles Loring, had gambled away the last of his fortune two weeks later and was killed in a duel over one of his mistresses.

Beyond the emotional devastation of losing both their parents and their family home in one fell blow, the Loring sisters had paid dearly for the scandals in other ways. Arabella had lost her betrothed because of it. Her three-month engagement to a viscount—a man she had sincerely loved—had been quickly terminated, since he wasn't brave enough to defy the vicious censure of the Beau Monde for her sake. His professions of love had proved as ephemeral as cloud wisps, leaving Arabella feeling as if her heart had been broken, just as the poets maintained.

Roslyn, the real beauty of the family, had been denied any sort of respectable future. When her Season ended so abruptly, so did her chance for any suitable marriage proposals. Even more mortifying, she'd been offered carte blanche by three different rakes, infamous propositions that never would have occurred had their step-uncle been a better guardian.

Lilian had had no chance to make a respectable match, either, although she claimed not to mind. Damming up her feelings of anguish and grief, the youngest Loring sister had run a little wild, rebelling against society's strictures and the haughty arbiters of the ton who had repudiated her and her siblings.

Lily had become something of a hellion, much to Arabella's chagrin. She couldn't help but feel guilty for failing to protect her sisters, since she was the eldest.

She'd only been nineteen when their mother abandoned them, but she still felt responsible. Particularly since their step-uncle was such a curmudgeon who cared so little for their welfare.

The seventh Lord Danvers, Lionel Doddridge, had taken them in grudgingly when their family home in Hampshire had been sold to pay their late father's debts, treating them as burdens and objects of charity.

"You'll keep out of my way," he'd warned the moment they arrived on his doorstep. "And you'll behave yourselves, if you know what's good for you. Your mother made herself a byword for scandal, and I won't have you disgracing me as she did."

"You needn't worry, Uncle Lionel," Arabella had responded tightly, speaking for them all. "We have no intention of behaving like our mother."

"Don't call me Uncle! I am no blood relation to you. Victoria was only my stepsister—the result of my father's deplorable second marriage—and Loring had no right to encumber me with the three of you in his will, particularly since he left me nothing to pay for your upkeep. But I am stuck with you, since no respectable gentleman will marry you now."

His declaration had roused a burning anger in Arabella, along with a fierce desire to establish their independence from their step-uncle. But since they were virtually penniless, they had resolved to earn their own livings by putting their patrician upbringing and education to good use.

With the indispensable support of a wealthy patroness, along with the help of her sisters and two genteel friends, Arabella had started an academy to teach the unrefined daughters of rich merchants how to be proper ladies so they could compete in the glittering world of the ton.

Finally, after more than three years of hard work, the school had become a highly successful enterprise, allowing them complete financial independence. Then, dismayingly, their step-uncle died and they were saddled with a new guardian, who had immediately declared his intention of finding husbands for them.

It was frustrating in the extreme, not to mention worrisome. The new Lord Danvers possibly had the legal authority to compel them to stop teaching if he arbitrarily chose. And any husbands he found for them would almost certainly disapprove of their uncommon endeavors.

Moreover, Arabella cringed at the mere thought of subjecting herself to another courtship. She had absolutely no intention of leaving herself vulnerable to the heartache she'd endured four years ago.

Her sisters had entirely different ideas for their futures as well, which did *not* include surrendering their hard-won independence to unwanted husbands. Roslyn was determined to marry only for love, while Lily had sworn off matrimony and men entirely.

"Thank heavens for Winifred," Arabella murmured sincerely.

Their patroness, Winifred, Lady Freemantle, had come from the working classes herself before marrying into the gentry. The middle-aged widow had been an unfailing source of support, not only for the academy but for the sisters' personal lives, including offering her chaise and team for Arabella's journey so she wouldn't have to use her step-uncle's dilapidated barouche.

It was early afternoon by the time the chaise reached the village of Chiswick. Like Richmond farther west, Chiswick had become a fashionable place of residence for the aristocracy during the past century because of the desirable proximity to London.

The carriage passed numerous riverside mansions and villas before turning into the graveled drive of Danvers Hall. The beautiful, stately manor of mellow red brick stood on the tree-lined banks of the River Thames. The setting was lush and green, but the over-grown lawns and landscape resembled more of a jungle. The interior appointments and furnishings of the house, too, were shabby and worn, while the artwork and silver had long ago been sold to pay estate bills.

All but a handful of servants had been let go as well. The remaining staff was led by a butler and house-keeper, an elderly couple who were devoted to the place after having lived there for more than thirty years. They had welcomed the Loring sisters warmly four years ago, even if their step-uncle had not.

When the coach came to a halt before the house, Arabella's sisters came out to greet her.

Roslyn was tall and slender, with pale golden hair, sky blue eyes, and an exquisite beauty that gave her the delicacy of gilded crystal—a laughably false im-pression, since she was the most clever and studious of them all, as well as the most charming. Roslyn would have been far happier had she been born male, so she

could have pursued a scientific career. Instead, her
sharp intellect was wasted on teaching etiquette and
deportment to raw schoolgirls.

Manners and deportment were certainly not Lily's
forte. The youngest Loring sister was a lively hoyden,
far more at home coaching the academy's pupils in
sporting activities and physical skills such as riding
and driving and archery. Curiously, Lily had a bold,
vivid coloring. Her sparkling dark eyes and rich, dark
chestnut tresses made her seem a changeling in her
fair-haired family, while her passionate high spirits
regularly led her into trouble.

Usually her eyes were warm and laughing, but now
they only looked worried.

"Well, what did he say, Belle?" Lily asked as soon as
Arabella stepped down, despite the fact that the coachman and groom could overhear their conversation.

"I will tell you when we have some privacy," Arabella replied, even though she understood Lily's impatience.

When her youngest sister wrinkled her nose in exasperation, Arabella met her middle sister's smiling eyes.

"You must know," Roslyn explained, "how difficult
it has been, waiting for you all day, picturing your interview with Lord Danvers."

"You never could have imagined what actually happened," Arabella murmured inaudibly.

"You should have allowed us to come with you,"
Lily said as they made their way up the steps and
through the front door. "We could have supported
you against the vexatious earl."

"Perhaps I should have," Arabella agreed with a rueful laugh, before surrendering her gloves and bonnet and pelisse to Simpkin, their venerable butler.

Her sisters managed to contain their impatience until they repaired to a small parlor at the rear of the first floor, the only room that had a fire burning in the grate to ward off the spring dampness, which continued their late step-uncle's frugal ways.

"I am sorry to say that I failed miserably this morning," Arabella confessed, not disclosing that she had tried to make her case at the point of a rapier. "I did not handle Lord Danvers at all well—but even so, he was entirely unreasonable."

"He won't withdraw his offer to provide us with dowries?" Roslyn asked in consternation.

Arabella gave a dark smile. "No. In fact, he boasted that we would soon have suitors swarming all over us."

Roslyn pressed her lips together in ladylike annoyance, while Lily gritted her teeth. "So what shall we do to foil him?" she wanted to know.

The new earl's plan to find them husbands had alarmed Lily most of all. Not only was she perfectly happy with the unusual freedom she enjoyed in her current life, she relished working at the academy. And now Lord Danvers was threatening to spoil it all by attempting to make them marry.

The three of them had already discussed possible options in the event Arabella failed to change his mind this morning. There now seemed to be but one way to foil the earl's intentions, and even that would only be a temporary solution.

"I think," Arabella said slowly, "that you will both have to disappear from Danvers Hall for a time. If he can't find you, then he can't coerce you into accepting any suitors he foists upon us."

Lilian looked unhappy. "I still think we should stay and make a stand against him. He needs to accept that he won't be able to coerce us to marry under any circumstances."

"I don't like leaving you to confront him alone, Arabella," Roslyn added.

"I will be all right," she replied, trying to sound confident. "And I would feel more reassured if you were out of harm's way."

Roslyn finally nodded with reluctance. "How long will we have to remain in hiding?"

"Until Lord Danvers can be made to see reason."

"You shouldn't have to fight our battles all by yourself, Belle," Lily insisted.

Arabella smiled. "I know, but I think it best in this instance. You can go and live with Tess for a few days. He won't think to look for you at her house." Tess Blanchard was their dearest friend and a teacher at the Freemantle Academy for Young Ladies, which had been named after their patroness.

"Winifred would undoubtedly take us in," Roslyn suggested.

"Yes, but Lord Danvers is likely to look for you there, since I told him about her ladyship's sponsorship."

When Lily still looked troubled, Arabella gave her an imploring smile. "Lily, promise me that you will go along with my plan for the time being."

"Oh, very well." She threw her arms around Arabella's neck in a brief hug. "But I don't like it in the least. I would rather remain here with you and challenge the vexations earl."

Arabella ignored that comment, for she had learned the hard way that it was unwise to challenge the new Lord Danvers. "I think you should stay with Tess tonight. Lord Danvers will likely call on us soon, and I don't want you to be here when he does."

"How will you deal with him?" Roslyn asked.

"I'm not yet certain," Arabella murmured. As their guardian, he had the right to arrange convenient marriages for her and her sisters, yet she would somehow have to make him abandon his plan. "He is living under the illusion that he can dictate to us, but I will have to show him the error of his thinking."

All her good intentions, however, suffered a serious setback four days later when she spied Lord Danvers riding across a grassy meadow toward her.

"Blast and hang him," Arabella muttered under her breath, abruptly drawing rein. She should have known his lordship wouldn't be happy to cool his heels waiting for her. She had purposely stayed away from home at the appointed hour for the interview he'd requested, determined to make his guardianship as inconvenient as possible. She hadn't expected him to come after her; obviously she had underestimated his persistence.

Her gloved hands clenching on the reins, Arabella hesitated for the barest instant. It was not like her to turn tail and run, yet she didn't trust herself alone with Lord Danvers. It was one thing to meet him when servants were within calling distance; it was quite another to face him alone in a secluded meadow. She had no desire to confront the earl if he was bent on revenge for threatening him at sword point during their first encounter, or for defying his express orders this afternoon.

The lamentable truth was that the handsome devil unnerved her with his lithe, broad-shouldered form, his piercing blue eyes, and his knowing smile. She wasn't certain she could hold her own with him just now.

Or perhaps she had simply turned craven.

Not pausing to further debate the deficiencies of her character, Arabella wheeled her horse and spurred it into a gallop, making for the copse of beech trees in the distance. Any hope that Lord Danvers hadn't seen her, however, died a swift death when she risked a glance over her shoulder. He was giving chase.

Her heart quickening, she bent low over her sidesaddle and urged her mount on. When shortly she reached the beechwood and plunged inside the cool shadows, she was forced to slow her pace to negotiate the low-hanging branches that snagged at her bonnet.

Not so the earl. The sound of hoofbeats behind her told her that he was still pursuing her. When she came out again into another sunlit meadow, Arabella doubled her efforts but knew he was rapidly gaining on her.

Her pulse was hammering in time with the thudding hooves when he drew even with her. For an instant they raced side by side, while her heart pounded with unexpected exhilaration.

Then suddenly he reached out to wrap a strong arm about her waist and pluck her from the saddle as if she weighed no more than thistledown.

Arabella's gasp of alarm turned to outrage when she found herself hauled sideways in front of his saddle and enveloped in his powerful embrace. As she clung desperately to him for balance, her breathless demand, "Let me go, you devil!" was muffled ineffectively against his shoulder and received no reply. Instead of releasing her, the earl merely tightened his grasp.

When he finally brought his mount to a plunging halt, Arabella sucked in a panting breath and lifted her head to glare up at him.

A mistake, she realized at once, for her mouth rested only inches from his. A delicious shock flared through her. She had fantasized about those firm, sensual lips . . . .

Then their gazes locked, and her breath faltered altogether.

The sudden silence seemed deafening. Arabella felt her heart nearly pounding out of her chest, yet this time she couldn't blame her response on physical exertion. Rather, it was because she found herself pressed against his lordship's hard-muscled male body, her heaving breasts nestled against his broad chest.

He sat there unmoving, eyeing her in speculation, and she stared back at him, frozen. When his gaze dropped to her bare throat and then even lower, to her breasts that were thrust prominently upward, she wished she had worn something more substantial than a low-collared muslin gown in deference to the warmth of the spring afternoon. She was acutely conscious of the way her nipples had brazenly hardened at the contact.

He, too, seemed aware of her body's wanton response, for his blue eyes darkened with a sensual gleam.

His voice fell to a languid murmur when he observed, "I had anticipated any number of greetings from you, Miss Loring, but I confess this was not one of them."

Arabella stiffened at his husky, amused tone. "Nor I, my lord. What do you mean, manhandling me in this brutish way?"

The glimmer in his eyes deepened. "Why, I was rescuing you, of course."

"I did not need rescuing!"

"No? I assumed your horse bolted. You would never have been so rude as to deliberately ignore my request for an audience. I arrived an hour ago at the hall to find you and your sisters nowhere in sight."

She had no legitimate reply for that, since her absence had indeed been entirely deliberate.

"You must have forgotten the time," the earl prodded, "for I'm certain you didn't mean to put me to the trouble of searching for you."

Arabella had the grace to blush. "I was previously occupied at the hour you demanded."

"Demanded?" He raised a dark eyebrow. "It was hardly a demand."

"It seemed very much so, since you gave me no choice in the matter."

His gaze dropped to her lips again. "It appears your flight had consequences you never intended." At her puzzled look, he shifted slightly beneath her. "Perhaps you didn't realize that physical exertion rouses a man's blood. And combined with the thrill of the chase . . ."

He let the words hang until she felt the swelling hardness of his loins against her thigh and comprehended his meaning. She had aroused more than his blood, quite obviously!

Regaining her wits, Arabella pressed her hands against his chest, determined to break free. Yet it was too late. His mouth suddenly lowered to capture hers in a kiss.

A slow, devastating, spellbinding kiss.

The unexpectedness of his assault stunned her. She felt light-headed. She couldn't breathe. At the searing heat of it, panic melded with insidious excitement, but she couldn't summon the desire to fight him. Instead, her entire body softened instinctively against him as his lips moved over hers with exquisite pressure. When his tongue delved deep inside her mouth, exploring, she gave a helpless moan.

Marcus felt the same heat surging through him, the same rush of hunger he'd experienced at his first meeting with Arabella . . . only this was more powerful. The sensation rocked him. And her, too, he had no doubt, feeling her shiver of aroused excitement.

He tightened his embrace and deepened their kiss, claiming and wooing, wanting much more of her. His erection throbbed, his pulse pounded.

When at last he broke off to stare down at Arabella, a tangible desire shimmered between them, filling the air. She was profoundly shaken, Marcus knew.

He felt her trembling in his arms as she returned his gaze.

"Let me go," she finally demanded in a hoarse whisper.

"Arabella . . ." he murmured, not wanting to obey.

Her spine suddenly stiffening, she glowered back at him, her eyes sparking with renewed fire. When still he didn't release her, she deliberately drew back her fist and cuffed him on the jaw.

The unexpected blow snapped Marcus's head back and sent stinging pain vibrating through his jaw, making him swear a low oath. His body's reaction was even more primal: He felt the savage urge to kiss her again, to conquer her and prove his mastery.

Arabella, however, took advantage of his momentary hesitation to break free of his embrace. When she attempted to scramble down, he forced himself to let her go this time, grasping her arm solely to help her descend from his horse.

Landing awkwardly, she whirled to face him, as if not wishing to give him any further advantage. Marcus remained in the saddle, scrutinizing her in rueful disbelief.

Once more she had totally taken him by surprise, yet it was his own unexpected response that had startled him more. He'd tried to convince himself that his fierce attraction to Arabella was an aberration. For the past four days, he'd attempted to put her out of his mind entirely. Perversely, he hadn't been able to forget her for a moment.

Instead, all he could think about was meeting her

again, to see if she was as full of life and fire as he remembered.

He had his answer now. Arabella stood there defiantly, her cheeks flushed, her lips wet and softly
passion-bruised, her fists clenched as if she were girded
for battle.

Every inch the beautiful spitfire who had invaded
his dreams the past four nights.

He hadn't intended to take her in his arms just now.
He certainly hadn't meant to kiss her. But he'd been
seduced by the tempting fire of her. The blazing indul-
gence had left him hot and painfully hard. His body
shuddered with the primitive urge to lay her down in
the soft spring grass and take her right there in the
meadow, to bury his throbbing cock deep inside her
delectable flesh, to vanquish her with pleasure.

Worse, their physical clash had only heightened the
mental challenge between them. As he sat staring down
at her, Marcus was struck by two thoughts at once: He
wanted Arabella Loring, more than he'd wanted any
woman in his life. And he couldn't have her.

He wasn't enough of a rake to debauch his own
ward, a young gentlewoman under his protection. The
only honorable way to have her in his bed would be
marriage—

The reflection made Marcus inhale a sharp breath.
Marriage.

No, his conscious mind automatically rebelled. He
had no intention of marrying anytime soon, certainly
not merely to produce an obligatory heir.

But if you want her, a more insistent voice argued,

you will have to put your relationship on a more equal footing than guardian and ward.

Marcus shook his head, scarcely believing what he was contemplating. He was acutely aware that his desire was overriding all his common sense.

Or was it?

If he looked at the situation logically, marrying Arabella was not so irrational. He had wanted to see to her welfare by finding her a proper husband, and he was a better candidate than most. And she was qualified by birth and breeding to be his countess, despite her family's recent history of scandal.

By marrying her, he could also fulfill his duty to carry on his illustrious line. *And* he could honorably satisfy his fierce desire to have her in his bed.

The only important argument, however, was how he felt about chaining himself to her for life in an irrevocable union.

And the answer? The undeniable truth was, Arabella Loring was the only woman he'd ever met whom he might actually *enjoy* having as his wife. And he greatly doubted he would ever find anyone better to fit his needs.

Marcus let out his breath as he came to a decision. Perhaps he'd gone daft, but he intended to propose to his eldest ward.

Still regarding her in bemusement, he offered her a crooked smile as he gingerly rubbed his jaw. "Gentleman Jackson would have admired your right hook, Miss Loring," he remarked, referring to England's greatest boxing champion.

Arabella's mouth pursed with vexation. "How did you expect me to react when you accosted me that way? I was merely defending myself."

At her retort, Marcus nodded in sympathy. "Which you did admirably. And no doubt I deserved worse for allowing myself to get carried away like that. I sincerely beg your pardon."

When she didn't reply to his apology, he dismounted slowly, keeping his eye on her.

Looking around for her own mount, Arabella seemed dismayed to see her horse grazing half a meadow away. She retreated a step, clearly preferring to remain a safe distance from him.

That made Marcus halt. He didn't want to scare her off . . . not that he believed for one minute that she would scare easily.

"I am not accustomed to women running from me," Marcus commented laconically.

"I am certain you aren't," she said, her tone dry.

"Yet you and your sisters appear to be making a habit of it. I'm informed that Roslyn and Lilian have been missing for several days now, ever since you received my missive expressing my intention to call today."

Stiffening, Arabella lifted her chin. "I knew it! Your servants have been spying on us!"

It was indeed true, Marcus reflected. Over the past few days, he'd installed his own staff at Danvers Hall to supplement the two elderly retainers, chambermaid, and man-of-all-work, who tried valiantly but futilely to keep up the large estate. Servants loyal to him, who were willing to make regular reports on his wards. Arabella, he'd been told, had kept out of their way as much as possible, while her sisters were nowhere to be found.

"I wanted to begin setting the Hall to rights," Marcus replied truthfully. "But pray don't change the subject, Miss Loring. I don't doubt that you arranged your sisters' disappearance in an effort to thwart me."

Arabella returned an innocent smile. "They developed a curious case of spots."

"Did they now?" Marcus said.

"Yes. A rash that was obviously a reaction to your intended visit. I worried that it was catching, so I sent them away in order to spare your health."

Marcus laughed. "Come now, Arabella. Can't we agree to sheathe our swords for a time? I don't want a battle with you."

Her determined expression softened a measure. "I don't want a battle with you either, my lord, but you refuse to understand that we won't be married off by a dictatorial guardian."

"I don't intend to marry you off to anyone, I promise. In fact, I mean to marry you myself."

He could tell by the hiss of her breath that he had shocked her almost as much as he had shocked himself. It was incredible, Marcus thought, that he would actually consider the astonishing step of abandoning his precious bachelorhood and marrying his eldest ward.

But his decision felt . . . right somehow.

Now, though, he had to make Arabella see the logic of his proposal and convince her that accepting was in her own best interests.

"You mean to *m-marry* me?" she repeated, clearly not trusting her hearing.

"Yes, marry you," Marcus said genially, becoming more accustomed to the prospect the more he considered it. "I know I've taken you by surprise, my sweet, but I would like to tender you an honorable offer of marriage."

Chapter Three

The new earl is possibly mad as well as vexing!

—Arabella to Fanny

Her speechlessness lasted a dozen heartbeats. "Have you gone mad?" Arabella said finally, her tone wary.

Wry amusement flickered in his eyes. "I assure you I am quite sane," his lordship replied. "I am simply paying my addresses to you."

She started to laugh; she couldn't help it. Here she was, still weak-kneed from the earl's wicked assault on her senses, and now he was deliberately making her head spin with his astounding offer of marriage.

"You wound me, darling," Lord Danvers drawled. "I admit my proposal is unexpected, but I assure you, it is no laughing matter."

Her mirth fading, Arabella raised a hand to her temple. "I cannot believe you are the least bit serious. Lady Freemantle told me you were a confirmed bachelor."

"I was—until two minutes ago. But kissing you had a startling effect on my judgment. It made me realize that I want you for my countess."

She stared at him in bewilderment. "How can one kiss possibly lead you to that conclusion?"

The earl shrugged his powerful shoulders. "It wasn't merely the kiss. There are several reasons you would make a good choice of brides for me. But chiefly . . . I must marry at some point, and you are the first woman who has ever interested me enough to make me contemplate taking the leap."

"But you know almost nothing about me."

"I know enough to think we might be well-matched. Certainly neither of us would ever be bored."

Still stunned, Arabella regarded him for another long moment. "Did you not hear a word I told you in London about my aversion to matrimony?"

"I heard quite clearly. But I intend to persuade you to reconsider."

His confidence took her aback. "You could never persuade me, my lord."

"No?" A smile played across his lips. "You obviously do not know me very well, Arabella."

Now he was beginning to exasperate her. "Indeed, I don't—and I have no desire to further the acquaintance, either. Certainly not as your wife."

"Perhaps you haven't considered the advantages to you."

"Advantages?" she echoed.

"As my countess you will lack for nothing."

"Except the freedom to control my own life. As my husband you would have even greater power over me than you do now as my guardian. By law you would be my 'lord and master,' and I would legally be your possession. I don't want any man ruling me like that."

Lord Danvers grimaced. "I have no desire to *rule*

you, love. I am merely interested in a marriage of convenience."

That struck a painful nerve in Arabella. She had always vowed she would never have a convenient marriage like her parents' bitter union. That she would never marry for any reason but love. "Well, *you* may be willing to abide such an arrangement, my lord, but it has no appeal whatsoever for me," she declared. "My parents married for convenience, and they made each other utterly miserable."

"We needn't have that sort of union," he said patiently.

"We needn't have any sort of union at all!"

At her ardent exclamation, Danvers eyed her thoughtfully. "I would of course make you a large marriage settlement and provide generously for your sisters. I should think you would be grateful that you needn't earn your livings any longer, teaching at your academy."

Arabella took a slow breath, striving for calm. "You obviously don't understand. We don't *wish* to give up teaching. Our employment is not only enjoyable but highly rewarding, besides allowing us the independence to do exactly as we wish."

At her answer, he took yet another tack. "Marriage to me will go a long way toward restoring your reputation in society."

Arabella raised her chin at the reminder of her tarnished social standing. "What of it? I have long since resigned myself to being a byword with the ton. There is a blissful measure of freedom that comes with not having to maintain a spotless character. And as long as we maintain standards of behavior acceptable to our pupils' parents, we needn't concern ourselves with anyone else's opinion."

The earl studied her for a long moment before saying easily, "You might think of your sisters. Don't they deserve a chance to lead the normal life of young ladies of quality?"

His perfectly reasonable question made Arabella feel uncomfortable and a bit guilty, knowing she was rejecting the opportunity to help her sisters. But then she adamantly shook her head. "I *am* thinking of them. Roslyn and Lily feel as I do about matrimony and men. They are just as determined to control their own futures as I am."

He gave her a sympathetic look. "I understand why you hate men. Your betrothed unceremoniously abandoned you once he learned of the scandal your family was facing."

It shouldn't hurt to have that humiliating memory rubbed in her face, since it had occurred four years ago. She was over the despair and heartache by now. But she couldn't forget the painful experience or the harsh lesson she had learned then.

She had foolishly believed she was making a love match. Indeed, she'd only accepted the viscount's proposal because their mutual feelings had blossomed into love. But her joy at falling in love with a man who vowed he loved her had been abruptly crushed by his very public betrayal. Never again would she make *that* mistake.

"I do not *hate* men," Arabella insisted. "I simply have no need for a husband."

"You don't want children?"

The question caught her unawares, and Arabella couldn't repress the stab of regret that went through her. Being unable to have children was an immense drawback to never marrying. The only one, she had come to believe.

"Not enough to suffer a husband," she answered at length.

"I want children eventually," Lord Danvers admitted. "It is my obligation to carry on my family name and titles. But that requires I first have a wife."

"So, you want a broodmare to give you heirs?" Arabella asked archly. "I suspected as much."

"No," he said in exasperation. "I want a companion and helpmate as well."

She found it hard to believe that a rakish nobleman like Lord Danvers was seeking a life companion, but she managed to bite her tongue before calling his veracity into question. Instead, Arabella made herself smile pleasantly. "The polite response in these cases is to express appreciation, so I will thank you for your generous offer, my lord. But I must decline."

"I intend to change your mind."

Her spine stiffened a little at his provoking declaration. When he offered her a charming smile of his own, she felt a responsive flutter in her stomach that she quickly tried to quell.

"I do not see how I can state my position more

clearly, Lord Danvers. I won't marry you for all the spices in India. Is that articulate enough for you to understand?"

He raised an amused eyebrow. "Do you know how many women would be elated to receive an offer of marriage from me?"

"Then apply to any of them. Doubtless they will be deliriously happy to accept. I would not."

Her retort brought a genuine grin to his lips. "I don't want any other woman. I have chosen you, Arabella, and I mean to have you."

Her mouth dropped open. The infernal arrogance of the man!

No longer desiring to continue this impossible conversation, Arabella whirled and headed across the meadow to retrieve her grazing horse.

The earl's next words, however, made her halt in her tracks. "I *could* make you deliriously happy, Arabella. You would enjoy our marriage bed, I have no doubt."

Unsure whether to be offended or amused by his bold declaration, she turned back to face him. "Rather boastful of you, is it not, my lord?"

"It is no boast. You would relish being my lover, I would make certain of it. But the only honorable way for us to be lovers is through marriage."

She was too exasperated to reply—which was likely his intention; he was attempting to keep her off balance by throwing such brazen statements at her.

Her silence made him smile again. "I admit I am intensely attracted to you," he continued, "and you felt it too when we kissed, don't deny it. You were quivering with desire for me."

Color stained Arabella's cheeks. She *had* quivered in his arms . . . although she certainly would never admit it to him.

"Don't be ridiculous," she replied. "It was simply shock at your assault. I could not believe you would act like such a brute. I assure you, I am not attracted to you in the least."

He took a step closer. "Shall I prove it to you?"

"If you dare try, I swear I will box your ears!"

His blue eyes danced with restrained amusement as he reached up to rub his injured jaw. A faint bruise discolored the spot where she had struck him, Arabella noticed. She was ashamed for a moment, until she recalled what had precipitated her struggle— how the earl had hauled her from her horse unceremoniously and refused to release her even after kissing her witless. Or perhaps she had reacted with such desperation precisely *because* he had kissed her witless.

He did not seem intimidated by her threat now, however. "If you were aiming for my ear, love, I take leave to tell you, you missed by a few inches."

He was deliberately provoking her, she knew very well. And his tactics were working. Arabella curled her hands into fists, barely refraining from marching up to him and taking another swing at his handsome face. "You are without a doubt the most infuriating man I have ever met, Lord Danvers."

"Perhaps, but only because I haven't properly exerted

myself to please you. You wouldn't be able to resist me if I seriously tried to woo you."

Her mouth fell open. "Of course I would be able to resist you!"

"Would you care to wager on that?"

At his dulcet tone, Arabella suddenly felt wary again. "What do you mean, wager?"

"How important is your independence to you?"

"I beg your pardon?" Her head was beginning to spin once more from Lord Danvers's unexpected offensive.

"What are you willing to do for emancipation from my guardianship?"

A great deal, was her immediate thought. "Why?"

"I cannot renounce my responsibility for you, but I can have my solicitor draw up a legal document granting you complete control over your own affairs. For you *and* your sisters."

"To what end?"

"To provide me a legitimate opportunity to court you."

"To *court* me? Why the devil would you want to court me? I already told you I won't marry you under any circumstances."

"I want the chance to change your mind. If I cannot persuade you to accept me for your husband in say, a month, I will give all three of you your freedom and make you legally and financially independent of my guardianship. Close your mouth, sweeting," the earl added when she stood there staring at him. "You are much too lovely to be gaping like a landed fish."

Arabella complied, even though she felt completely out of her depth. "Let me see if I understand your wager, my lord. You will give us our freedom if I can resist your 'persuasion'?"

"Precisely."

"You have an astounding faith in your powers of seduction."

His mouth curved. "You could put it that way. In exchange, you must allow me to woo you properly. And if you cannot resist me—if I can make you admit you want me for your husband—then you will have to marry me."

The arrogance of the man, thinking he could seduce her into accepting his offer of marriage! He wouldn't be able to . . . surely.

When she hesitated, Lord Danvers shook his head sadly. "I never expected you to turn craven. You're afraid I will win the wager."

He was purposely goading her again, she realized. "I am not afraid!" Arabella insisted. At least not much. She might be susceptible to his stunning kisses, but there was little risk she would ever want him for her husband, for she planned never to marry. "You won't win, my lord."

"Then you should have no trouble agreeing. After all, I am offering you the chance to gain exactly what you say you want most. Your independence."

"Very well, I will take your blasted wager!"

The glimmer in his eyes indicated his satisfaction and pleasure, which made Arabella almost regret her capitulation. She had let him provoke her into accepting his challenge, despite the danger of her fierce attraction to him.

And yet the stakes were irresistible: Not only could she ensure financial security for her sisters, but they could be rid of the earl's unwanted guardianship for good. He would no longer be a threat to their independence. He would have no right to try to marry them off, or to force them to give up their positions at the academy.

No, truthfully, Arabella reflected, she was utterly delighted for the opportunity to win their freedom.

An entire month was out of the question, however. She was not that confident she could resist the earl's determined seduction for so long—not that she would ever admit her doubts to *him*.

"However," Arabella qualified, "the duration of the wager must be shorter. Two weeks, no more. I couldn't endure your impossible arrogance any longer."

Lord Danvers hesitated the briefest instant before saying, "Done. You drive a hard bargain, sweetheart."

"I must be utterly mad," Arabella muttered.

"No more so than I," he said amiably. "As long as we are discussing terms, I must insist on a sporting chance to win. You will agree to spend time in my company regularly, no less than four hours each day. And it must be at a time of my choosing."

Arabella frowned. "It cannot interfere with my teaching duties."

"Fair enough. I will order my bags packed for an

extended visit and brought to Danvers Hall from London."

It unsettled Arabella to realize Lord Danvers intended to stay at the estate for a fortnight or longer, even though his ownership gave him every right. She quickly shook her head. "You cannot remain at the Hall when I am unchaperoned. You are no blood relation, even if you are our guardian."

"You should have thought of that," he replied wryly, "before you sent your sisters into hiding."

She eyed him with exasperation. "If you insist on living there, I will take refuge with Lady Freemantle."

The earl raised a black eyebrow. "Is that where you've concealed your sisters?" When she declined to answer, he shrugged. "We will have an army of servants to play duenna. My staying there might offend the highest sticklers, but it shouldn't put your reputation at any real risk."

"True," she said, striving to repress the edge of bitterness in her voice. Her reputation was already tainted beyond redemption because of her parents' scandals, so it was pointless to question the propriety of her new guardian living in the same manor house with only a servant staff for chaperones. Besides, if she never planned to marry, it wouldn't matter if her reputation was not entirely spotless, although she couldn't afford a genuine scandal. She had her academy to think of, after all.

Yet she had no doubt her pupils' parents would be awed at her claiming such an illustrious connection as the Earl of Danvers. They wouldn't look too closely at his living arrangements. Nor were the lower classes nearly as judgmental as the gentry, who considered themselves strict arbiters of society.

"You could always bring your sisters home," his lordship suggested in prodding tones.

The notion had already occurred to Arabella. Her sisters' presence would offer her more protection from the devilish earl—but then who would protect her sisters from his machinations?

"I am not that desperate," she said sweetly.

He studied her thoughtfully. "Perhaps it's good that your sisters are away. It will allow us more opportunity to be alone together for our courtship."

The thought discomfited her for a moment, but then Arabella squared her shoulders. She ought to be able to handle Lord Danvers for two weeks. She had every intention of winning his blasted wager.

He must have read the determination in her eyes, for he smiled. "I suspect our wager will prove enjoyable to us both."

To you perhaps, Arabella thought in vexation. No doubt it would be a diverting game for him, trying to make her desire him for a husband.

But perhaps she could play his game, as well. . . .

She was contemplating that intriguing possibility when the earl suddenly changed tacks again. "Come here, Arabella," he murmured, his voice beguiling.

Instinctively, she resisted. "Why?"

"Because I intend to claim another kiss to seal our pact." When she stood stock-still, he prodded gently, "You agreed to let me woo you, remember?"

"I did not agree to let you kiss me."

"But kissing is part of wooing."

"Your sort of kisses are not! No proper suitor kisses the way you do."

The laughter lurking in his eyes was irresistible. "I don't mean to assault you again, I promise. I had in mind something much more pleasurable." His voice was warm, teasing, more seductive than it had any right to be. "Come now, a simple kiss, nothing more. I won't even embrace you. You have my word."

But still Arabella hesitated. He had the most sensual, unsettling gaze of any man she had ever met, and it was supremely dangerous to go anywhere near him. "How can I trust you won't take advantage of me?"

"If I try, I give you leave to darken my daylights."

"I will, you may be certain of it."

"I consider myself duly warned. Now, stop being so missish. It's entirely beneath you."

His lazy, provocative grin made Arabella's pulse quicken alarmingly. She couldn't believe she had let herself be lured into this perilous situation. How was she supposed to resist so charming a rogue?

"Arabella . . ." he said leadingly.

She forced her feet to move until she stood a few steps from him. His eyes were locked on hers; she couldn't think.

When she paused, he closed the distance between them, until they were almost touching. Arabella held herself rigid, caught between dread and anticipation. She couldn't forget the way his muscular chest had felt pressed against her breasts, the strong arms that had crushed her to him, the firm, sensual lips that had taken hers with such fiery heat.

But he merely reached down to capture her hand and bring it to his bruised jaw. His fingers encircled her wrist loosely—and there he stopped.

"Have you ever really been kissed before now, Arabella?"

She blinked at the unexpected question. "Of course I have been kissed. I was betrothed, remember?"

"I'll wager it was a tame sort of peck."

"What does that matter?"

"It matters greatly, if you have nothing to judge by. Your expectations must be severely depressed."

Arabella sucked in a breath; his fingertips had found the bare skin above her glove.

"It's a pity, really."

"What is a pity?" she said absently. She was staring at his lips now, disconcerted by their nearness.

"That you're a virginal innocent, with no experience in passion or physical pleasure."

Her cheeks flooded with color. "Of course I am virginal. I am a lady, despite our family scandal. We are *not* our mother's daughters." This time she couldn't hide her bitterness.

His blue gaze softened. "If you knew the pleasures in store for you, you wouldn't be so quick to swear off men. You have no notion what you are missing."

"And I suppose you are offering to show me?"

"Actually, I am."

"I don't wish you to show me a thing, Lord Danvers.

I only want you to kiss me and be done with it. Would you *please* just get it over?"

"Very well."

He bent his head slowly. Arabella froze, bracing herself for the onslaught. She refused to run this time like a coward. It was supposed to be a simple kiss after all . . .

The trouble was, there was nothing simple about his kiss whatsoever. The caress was a mere brush of lips, true, but his mouth was warm and inviting, and the delicious pressure sent her senses reeling with blazing heat again, made her body shiver with desire. Just like before, when he had left her weak and breathless and helplessly aroused.

Magic, that's what it was. He was working some sort of fiery spell over her.

She was inexplicably disappointed when he lifted his head after the briefest of moments. He was staring at her once more, Arabella saw, feeling dazed.

She raised her fingers to her burning lips as she stared back at him. A flame had kindled in the depths of his blue eyes . . . the same sort of flame that he had ignited deep inside her.

"So it wasn't an aberration at all," he murmured, his voice low and husky.

Arabella tried to gather her wits. "What was not an aberration?"

"Never mind." Satisfaction gleamed in his eyes as he stepped back. "Now, are you ready to return home?"

She shook herself from her daze. "Not yet. I concluded a class at the academy this afternoon and intended to call on Lady Freemantle to make my report. She likes to be kept abreast of every detail."

"I will accompany you there."

"That won't be necessary. Her ladyship's estate is just over the next hill."

He glanced in the direction Arabella indicated. "Then I will send a groom to escort you home when you are through. I don't like the thought of you riding about the countryside alone."

Arabella's expression turned ironic. "I have been doing so for years, Lord Danvers. This is not London. Ours is a completely tame neighborhood, with little wickedness or crime."

"Still, you should have a groom with you. I'm surprised your former guardian was so neglectful."

Arabella felt herself stiffening. "Paupers cannot afford grooms, my lord."

"Your step-uncle could have afforded to supply a male servant for your protection."

Her smile was humorless. "Our step-uncle did not consider us worth the expense."

Lord Danvers contemplated her expression. "Stings your pride to be that dependent, does it?"

"Of course it stings."

"I can imagine."

That made Arabella's lips quirk with true amusement. "I sincerely doubt it. Very likely you have never been dependent on anyone or anything in your life."

He inclined his head, acknowledging the truth of her supposition. "Not since I was out of short coats at least. But in the future, when you are not in my company, I would be obliged if you would take one of my grooms with you."

She cocked her head. "Why should I wish to oblige you?"

"Because I care for your welfare, sweeting."

His easy answer gave her pause. It was the first time in years that any man had cared for her welfare. Their step-uncle certainly had not.

"I will consider it," she conceded.

He grinned at her. "Not willing to surrender an inch, are you?"

"No, my lord," Arabella said sweetly.

"My name is Marcus. If I'm to be your suitor, you should call me by my given name." He raised his hand to her mouth and brushed his thumb lightly over her lower lip. "I will expect you home in time to dine with me this evening. You promised me four hours of your company each day, remember?"

"I remember," she managed to reply, her voice uneven.

Returning to his horse, he gathered the reins and mounted, then sat looking down at her. "Oh, and Arabella, the next time you run from me, you had best choose a swifter horse, for I won't let you off so easily when I catch you."

With that he wheeled his horse and rode away, leaving her to gape after him, her fingers held to her tingling lips.

Chapter Four

❦

I must be mad also, since I just agreed to the earl's wager.

—Arabella to Fanny

Marcus shook his head in disbelief as he rode toward Danvers Hall. He hadn't counted on making an impulsive proposal of marriage to his beautiful ward. Ironic that he would behave so rashly after maneuvering for years to elude the snares set for him by scores of mercenary females. But he'd acted on sheer instinct.

If he had to marry, he wanted a wife like Arabella, and he wouldn't let the opportunity pass to stake his claim to her.

Certainly she fit his requisites for his countess, with breeding and beauty and intelligence to spare. Of more vital importance, she was spirited and fascinating enough to hold his interest long beyond any initial courtship.

Indeed, he couldn't recall ever finding any woman so desirable as Arabella. She would make a delightful lover in their marriage bed, Marcus reflected. Kissing her today had proved irrevocably that the spark of fire between them was no figment of his imagination.

Marcus felt his loins harden at the remembrance of their first embrace. And although their last kiss had been a mere brush of lips, it had still thoroughly aroused him.

He had aroused Arabella just as intensely, he knew. Just not enough to convince her to consider his suit.

Recalling her determined rejection of his proposal, Marcus grinned. Never had he dreamed he would be in this position—having to persuade a lady that she wanted him for her husband. He'd never had to actively pursue any female. Until now, women, like everything else in life, had come easily to him. When he'd played the game of love with his mistresses, it was purely because he enjoyed the challenge of it.

Marcus laughed softly to himself. Arabella would provide him ample challenge, certainly. But her adamant rebuff had compelled him to quickly invent an alternate strategy to woo her, the result being his wager with her.

He had every faith the wager would be a cure for his recent restlessness. He seemed to be suffering from more than simple boredom, Marcus admitted. He filled his days with cards and hunts and boxing mills and races, but his clubs and sporting pursuits couldn't appease the odd dissatisfaction he'd felt with his life of late. Not even the extensive responsibilities of managing his various estates could.

Pursuing Arabella, however, was a goal he could relish. And so was overcoming her resistance. Marcus thought he understood why she was so ardently opposed to marriage. He was confident, however, that he would eventually prevail in gaining her surrender.

Yet he only had two weeks to achieve it.

Suddenly impatient, Marcus spurred his horse to greater speed to return to his newest estate. He had missives to send to London. For the sooner he could devise a romantic courtship of Arabella, the sooner he could declare victory.

By the time she arrived home two hours later, Arabella had pondered the earl's astonishing wager long enough to judge it imperative for her to develop an offensive strategy.

Lord Danvers believed he could seduce her into accepting his proposal of marriage, but while she was firmly resolved never to wed him, she was at a severe disadvantage in their competition, having so little experience in dealing with a nobleman of his stamp.

And he is almost irresistibly seductive, Arabella reflected as she dismounted in the stableyard. Involuntarily, her fingers rose again to her lips at the memory of his devastating kisses. If her melting response this afternoon was any indication, she would be hard-pressed to withstand temptation.

She was eager to begin, however, for she intended to win freedom for herself and her sisters. It might even prove enjoyable, trying to match wits with Lord Danvers.

The first step, of course, was to contrive a plan to foil his seduction. Certainly, if he hoped to woo her, she would have to make him work at it.

She also would have to write Fanny immediately and get her advice. Fanny Irwin was a renowned Cyprian who had once been a genteel young lady herself. She'd practically grown up with the Loring sisters in Hampshire, where they were near neighbors. Even after Fanny had run off at sixteen to make her fortune in London, they had maintained the close friendship.

Since Arabella's broken engagement, Fanny had taught her a good deal about men. Fanny would know much better than she how to rout Lord Danvers.

Meanwhile, Arabella mused, she would be wise to use every resource at her disposal, which meant enlisting help from trusted allies, beginning with her housekeeper and butler.

Feeling an unexpected tingle of anticipation, Arabella left her horse in the stables with one of his lordship's grooms and detoured to the kitchens to meet with Mrs. Simpkin. The housekeeper, who had also become cook when the rest of the staff was let go, regularly prepared tasty if modest meals with the aid of their one chambermaid. And even though three days ago the new earl had installed a dozen servants at the Hall, Mrs. Simpkin still held sway in the kitchens.

If the elderly woman was puzzled by Arabella's unusual request for that evening's dinner, she was too well-trained to show it. But the twinkle in her kind brown eyes suggested a willingness to abet the conspiracy.

"Oh, and Mrs. Simpkin," Arabella added casually, "I would be obliged if Simpkin would remain in the dining room when he waits on us this evening. I would prefer to be alone with Lord Danvers as little as possible."

"I will tell him, Miss Arabella," Mrs. Simpkin said. "Would you also like Simpkin to be present beforehand? Lord Danvers has asked that you join him in the drawing room for a glass of wine before dinner."

"Yes, please," Arabella answered, glad that the housekeeper had readily agreed to aid her cause.

After washing, Arabella dressed for dinner in the most conservative evening gown she owned. Her wardrobe was not extensive, and most of her gowns were outdated and had grown shabby with wear. But upon opening the academy, she'd invested in several fashionable gowns to impress her pupils' wealthy parents. After all, she had her image as a lady of quality to uphold.

When she regarded herself critically in the cheval glass, however, Arabella found her appearance rather dissatisfying. Her empire-waist gown of dark blue silk boasted long sleeves and a high neckline, and thus exposed little of her charms. But her flushed cheeks betrayed her excitement at the prospect of spending the evening in his lordship's company.

How dull her existence had become if his presence could enliven her life so profoundly! Or perhaps it was merely the anticipation of locking horns with the earl as they strove to best each other.

At the thought, Arabella felt herself smile. She had every intention of besting him. She would play his game to win.

Taking a deep breath to calm her nerves, she left her bedchamber to launch her opening salvo in their courtship war.

When she reached the drawing room below, Simpkin awaited her outside in the corridor. The gray-haired, very proper butler offered Arabella the ghost of a conspiratorial smile before preceding her into the room and announcing her. "Miss Loring, my Lord Danvers."

Marcus rose when she entered. His blue gaze raked over Arabella, taking in her reserved attire, but he made no comment other than one of greeting. "Welcome, my dear. I am pleased you could join me."

At his avuncular tone, Arabella gave him a curious glance, but then realized he meant to treat her merely as his ward for the benefit of the serving staff.

"Come and sit beside me," Marcus added, indicating the gold brocade settee that had seen much better days.

Arabella hesitated, reluctant to be seated so close to him. He looked infernally handsome in a blue evening coat and white satin breeches that molded to his athletic form, and an intricately-tied cravat that only enhanced his chiseled masculine features.

Deploring her rapid pulse, Arabella did as she was bid but took the far end of the settee. She caught the pleasant scent of citrus cologne as Marcus settled at the other end. He had evidently shaved for the evening, a disturbing realization since it implied he was taking his courtship of her very seriously.

"That will be all until dinner is served, Simpkin," his lordship said when the butler had poured them each a glass of Madeira. "You may shut the door behind you."

Hiding her concern, Arabella met Simpkin's gaze and nodded slightly in resignation. Already Lord Danvers was scuttling her plan to avoid being alone with him. She was maddeningly conscious of his lithe, powerful body lounging so near to hers.

"Was it necessary to dismiss Simpkin?" she asked when the servant had withdrawn. "It isn't quite seemly for us to be alone together like this."

"Nonsense," Marcus responded easily. "There is no impropriety in a guardian sharing a glass of wine with his ward. And it is indeed necessary, since I need a measure of privacy in order to woo you."

Not having a ready reply, Arabella took a sip of her wine and hid her grimace at the bitter taste . . . along with her satisfaction. Mrs. Simpkin had succeeded in making the brew unpalatable as she had requested.

"About our wager," Arabella began, "I have been thinking. Perhaps we should establish some basic rules of conduct."

"Rules?"

"I suppose *limits* would be a better word. We should define what conduct is allowed and not allowed between us to prevent you from going beyond the bounds of a proper courtship."

Marcus sent her a lazy smile that was full of charm. "Haven't you heard that all is fair in love and war?"

Arabella found herself staring at his mouth. "You know very well our wager has nothing to do with love, my lord. But that is precisely my point. How can I trust that you won't resort to something devious?"

"Because wagers are governed by a gentleman's code. My honor will only permit me to go so far."

Her mouth curved. "That is comforting to know."

"You should not be comforted," Marcus remarked.

"I still have a great deal of leeway within the bounds of the code." He laughed softly at her worried expression. "Never fear, sweeting. I won't do anything to you unless you are completely willing."

Arabella swallowed. "You won't find me willing."

"We shall see. As for rules, I mean to hold you to your pledge to give me a fighting chance to win our wager."

"Yes, but simply because I agreed to let you court me, it does not follow that I must make it easy for you."

"True."

"I intend to do everything in my power to foil you."

His roguish grin made her breathless as he raised his glass of Madeira. "So let the games begin."

As he gazed at her over the rim of his glass, Arabella's heart accelerated in an erratic rhythm. Thankfully, the intimate moment was broken when Marcus took a swallow of wine.

Wincing at the taste, he set his glass aside on a table. "I would never have expected your step-uncle to suffer such inferior quality wine. I will have to rectify that, since I intend to stay here for at least a fortnight. Tomorrow I'll have some casks delivered from my cellars in London."

Arabella's heart sank at the reminder. A fortnight was beginning to seem an interminable length of time. But perhaps she was going about trying to win in all the wrong ways. What if she could simply persuade the earl that he didn't want to marry her? "You know, my lord—"

"Marcus."

"Very well, Marcus. I don't believe you have fully considered what a marriage between us would be like. If you had, you would realize that we wouldn't suit in the least."

"Why not?"

"For one thing, I wouldn't make you a comfortable wife."

His mouth quirked. "What makes you think I want a comfortable wife?"

"Most noblemen do. You want a lady to bear your heirs and manage your household, and to look the other way when you flaunt your mistresses or engage in various dalliances and indiscretions. I could never be so agreeable, my lord."

When Marcus remained silently studying her, Arabella went on. "Lady Freemantle told me a great deal about you and your friends. You are all notorious bachelors." She refrained from adding that her ladyship had a great deal of admiration for the new Earl of Danvers.

"My friends?"

"Your fencing partners last week. Those are your close friends, the Duke of Arden and the Marquess of Claybourne?"

"Yes."

"Well, the stories of your conquests and sporting exploits are repeated in drawing rooms even this far from London. Based on all the tales about you, I can say with utmost confidence that you would not make me a comfortable husband."

He cocked his head at her. "I doubt you want a comfortable husband, any more than I want a comfortable wife. Somehow I can't picture a woman of your spirit settling for a milquetoast."

Arabella gave a soft laugh of exasperation. "That is precisely what I have been trying in vain to make you see. I don't want any sort of husband!"

"You've made that abundantly clear." Marcus relaxed back against the settee. "But allow me to point out that your appraisal of my character is based on gossip and innuendo."

"Perhaps. But I have little doubt you are the same ilk as my father."

"Ah, we begin to get to the crux of the matter." Stretching out his long legs, Marcus laced his fingers over his stomach. "You take a dim view of rakes."

Arabella smiled a little bitterly. "Can you blame me? My father was a philanderer of the first order, and I have no intention of subjecting myself to any husband like him."

"So you condemn me out of hand."

"Is it really out of hand? How many mistresses do you have in keeping?"

A dark eyebrow rose at her impertinent question. "Is that really any of your affair, darling?"

"It is if you expect me to consider your proposal of marriage." When he hesitated, Arabella smiled sweetly. "It is a simple question, Marcus. How many mistresses do you have?"

"None at present."

"But you regularly employ one?"

"I have in the past. Most gentlemen of means do."

She arched an eloquent eyebrow of her own. "I cannot take a blithe view of adultery. I would never tolerate affairs and infidelities from my husband."

"Some men give up their mistresses upon marrying."

"But I could never trust that you would do so, or that you wouldn't relapse, even if you promised fidelity in the beginning."

He held her gaze levelly. "I am not your father, Arabella. And you insult me to put me in the same category."

The sudden intensity of his tone took her aback. "Forgive me," she apologized with a strained smile. "I am only attempting to make you understand why I don't want a marriage of convenience. If your parents had endured a marriage such as mine had, I'm certain you would be just as adverse to repeating their experience."

His mouth twisted sardonically. "As it happens, my parents were much more discreet in their affairs than yours were. But I confess, their experience left me with no fondness for the institution of matrimony." Marcus paused. "Apparently, though, your mother was as guilty as your father of faithlessness."

Arabella's smile faded. "I don't like to speak of my mother."

Victoria Loring's initial transgressions had been nowhere near as severe as her spouse's had been; her single affair had stemmed out of revenge against her husband's countless infidelities. Yet she had committed a worse sin, to Arabella's mind, by abandoning her family. For a moment, Arabella closed her eyes at the dizzying wave of pain that memory conjured up.

Marcus must have seen her expression, for he made a sympathetic sound. "You have not had an ideal time of it, have you, love? First the scandals and being forced from your home, then having to earn your living."

Her eyes opened abruptly, finding his blue gaze alarmingly tender. "You needn't pity me, you know. I have long since gotten over the pain and humiliation." Which was a lie, Arabella added to herself. "In any case, adversity builds character, or so they say."

"You and your sisters have had more than your fair share of adversity."

She managed a shrug. "We were determined to make the best of our lot. The worst part was being dependent on our step-uncle's largess, at the mercy of his whims. More than once he threatened to evict us. But thankfully, we were able to open our academy. It offered us gainful employment so we wouldn't be forced into menial servitude or compelled to wed as our only means of survival."

Marcus's response was forestalled by a discreet knock on the drawing room door. When he bid entrance, Simpkin appeared to announce that dinner was served in the small dining parlor.

Glad to leave off such an uncomfortable subject as her family chronicles, Arabella took Marcus's arm to accompany him in to dinner, an action she regretted immediately. Beneath his coat sleeve, she could feel the warmth radiating from him, could feel the hard muscles flex under her fingertips. The contact did strange things to her pulse.

She was glad to see that their places had been set at either end of the long table, with a significant distance separating the two.

Marcus shook his head at the arrangements, however. "We needn't be so formal, Simpkin. I prefer to have Miss Loring seated beside me."

"As you wish, my lord."

The butler obeyed, hurrying to rearrange the place settings. When Arabella was finally seated to his lordship's right, Simpkin gestured at the two attending footmen to serve the soup course.

When that was done, Marcus nodded. "Thank you, Simpkin. I will ring when we are ready for the next course."

All three servants silently withdrew, without shutting the door at least. Yet the open door couldn't dispel the sense of intimacy Arabella felt at sitting so close to Marcus, or allay her tingling awareness of his nearness.

Trying her best to ignore him, Arabella applied herself to the bland-looking soup, which appeared to be greasy chicken broth with a few pieces of limp vegetables. She nearly choked at the first sip, since it was so salty as to be almost inedible.

After one taste, Marcus shot Arabella a questioning glance and then set down his spoon. Innocently, she forced herself to continue eating her soup.

"So tell me about this academy of yours," Marcus said, his tone curious.

"Why do you want to know?"

"Because I am intrigued by it. And because I want to learn everything about you to aid my courtship." When she grimaced slightly at the reminder, he merely smiled. "You said your academy is something of a finishing school? How did it start?"

Since it seemed to be a safe subject, Arabella was pleased to explain. "Lady Freemantle actually gave me the idea. We became friends after my sisters and I moved here to Chiswick. Winifred was the daughter of a wealthy industrialist, but she married far above her social station and was never accepted by her husband's family or friends. One day she confessed how difficult it had been for her, being the wife of a baronet, enduring all the slights and snubs, and that she wished someone had taught her the proper social graces so she might have competed in Sir Rupert's milieu. I began thinking that there must be other young women in similar circumstances. Most daughters of wealthy magnates are destined to be sold into marriage to gentlemen in need of rich wives, as Winifred was."

"So you proposed establishing the academy?"

"Not at first. When I suggested I might be of help to some of them—advise them on how to fit in to the Beau Monde and make their path easier—I only envisioned taking on one or two pupils. But Winifred leapt at the idea and offered to fund a much larger enterprise."

"But you don't run the academy solely on your own," Marcus said.

"I have significant help. I convinced two of my friends to participate, and one assumed the post of headmistress. They oversee most of the classes, but my sisters and I also teach at least one class a day."

"Not the typical subjects, I collect?"

"No. Most of our pupils have been educated by private governesses, so by the time they come to us, they are usually proficient in sums and globe reading, music and drawing and needlepoint, those sort of genteel accomplishments. But they lack the polish and grace expected of a lady. So for the final two years before they make their comeouts, we instruct them on good deportment, rules of proper conduct, etiquette, and also expose them to the kind of culture and refinement they will find if they marry into the gentility."

"Apparently your academy is a great success. My solicitors tell me you have over two dozen pupils and that there is a long list of applicants waiting for admission."

Arabella smiled. "Yes. We succeeded beyond our wildest expectations. Wealthy tradesmen and merchants are willing to pay huge sums to turn their daughters into refined young ladies. But our academy benefits us, as well. It not only provides us occupation and income but gratification for helping our pupils learn how to deal with society. I personally take great satisfaction in giving young girls more control over their fate. Their birth or breeding might not be of the highest, but they can hold their own in elite circles. And they come to their marriages on more equal footing with their husbands."

"I can well imagine you would find that satisfying," he murmured.

When Arabella gave him a suspicious glance, Marcus returned a bland expression, but he found himself marveling at how much he had enjoyed watching her explain about her academy, her lovely face so animated and expressive. He admired Arabella's passion for her cause. As he absently took a sip from his wineglass, Marcus realized that he hadn't felt that passionate about anything in a long while.

Finding this wine as bitter as the Madeira had been earlier, he immediately set down his glass. "I should like to visit your academy soon."

As he expected, Arabella's wariness increased. "Why would you want to visit?"

"I believe I told you. As your guardian, I will need to decide if I should permit you and your sisters to continue teaching there."

She looked worried for a moment as she anxiously searched his face, but she evidently recognized the teasing gleam in his eye, for her expression relaxed a little. "You are purposely trying to provoke me again, I collect."

"Now why would I do that?" he asked amiably. "Are you finished with your soup?"

"Yes, thank you."

"Good. I can't seem to stomach so much salt myself."

Marcus rang for the butler to clear away the dishes, almost glad for the presence of servants to interrupt his private moment with Arabella, since he was having difficulty controlling his lustful thoughts.

She was near enough that the sweet scent of her rose up to tease his nostrils. And that elegant gown she was wearing made him want to discover what delicious secrets she was hiding underneath.

His imagination could supply some of the details. Her supple, slender body. The ripe curve of her breasts. Her long, elegant legs . . .

Sternly Marcus returned his gaze to Arabella's beautiful face, but it did little to quell his awareness of her. This was the first time he had seen her hair completely uncovered. He had the urge to pull out the pins and see how that red-gold silk would look tangled after their lovemaking.

The erotic thought was arousing enough to make him go hard, and was followed by more erotic thoughts. He could picture shoving away all the china and laying Arabella on the table in order to make a delectable meal of her. She would be far more tasty than the dinner had been thus far. Even more, he wanted her to taste the pleasure he could give her—

But that would have to wait a while longer, Marcus reflected, finally disciplining his errant thoughts. He had promised himself not to rush his fences. This was supposed to be a romantic wooing, not simply a seduction, and he knew it would require much more than physical pleasure to win Arabella over.

It was no hardship, however, to simply share her company. He truly wanted to know all about her. And at least dining together gave them the perfect opportunity for intimacy.

The trouble was, the wine was so acidic as to be undrinkable. And the dishes Simpkin was setting before him looked even less appetizing than the soup had been.

Marcus tasted each one just to make certain: Mashed turnips with no seasonings. Boiled cabbage. And a burnt saddle of mutton that was so dry, it was nearly impossible to chew.

When he realized Arabella was watching him closely, however, Marcus began to wonder at her unusual interest in his reaction.

"As a cook, Mrs. Simpkin leaves much to be desired," he commented casually.

"Oh, do you think so?"

Arabella's tone was perfectly innocent, which aroused his suspicions even further. "Most definitely. If the meals continue to taste so wretched, I will have to send to London for my chef to replace Mrs. Simpkin as cook."

Her response remained blithe. "Do try the mint sauce. It improves the taste of the mutton considerably."

"Not nearly enough," Marcus said satirically, poking his fork at a charred rind. "I think perhaps I should have a few words with Mrs. Simpkin."

Arabella's guileless expression faded. "That won't be necessary, Marcus."

"No?"

"She can do much better than this."

"I don't know that I am willing to risk it. In fact, if she deliberately planned this unpalatable fare, I don't want her in my employ any longer."

His empty threat had the desired effect: Arabella sighed and came to the housekeeper's defense with a confession. "It was not Mrs. Simpkin's fault. It was entirely mine. I asked her to alter her recipes this evening."

Marcus lifted an eyebrow. "You requested that she burn the mutton and spike the wine with vinegar? I suspected as much." He eyed Arabella in amusement. "Let me guess. You're endeavoring to make my stay here as unpleasant as possible in hopes that I will give up on our wager."

"Well, yes," she admitted with only a faint blush of guilt. "And to spoil the prospect of any intimacy between us."

"Since starvation is not conducive to courtship."

"Precisely. But I warned you I would not make it easy for you to woo me. Are you vexed?" she asked sweetly.

Her smile held such satisfaction, Marcus had to grin in return. "Vexed? Not in the least." Exasperated, perhaps. And most certainly fascinated by the beautiful spitfire and her efforts to evade his courtship. But perhaps he could turn her machinations to his advantage . . .

He suddenly rose and held out his hand to her. "Come with me, Arabella."

That wicked smile instantly made her extremely wary. "Come where?"

"You'll see."

When he grasped her hand and drew her to her feet, she had no choice but to accompany him. They swept past a bewildered Simpkin and down the corridor, heading for the back stairs.

"Where are you taking me?" Arabella demanded uneasily.

"To the kitchens to find something more palatable to eat."

"There really is no need—"

"Indeed there is. I insist. You must still be hungry, and I know I am."

Arabella tried to pull back. "I think I would rather starve."

Marcus gave a low laugh. "But I would not. Come along, darling. You don't want to put me to the trouble of carrying you."

Suspecting that he would make good on his threat if she continued resisting, Arabella gave up gracefully.

When they reached the large kitchens, they found Mrs. Simpkin seated at the long wooden table where the servants took their meals, while the maid scrubbed pots and pans at the sink. The housekeeper rose abruptly, looking startled to see them. "My lord! Is something amiss?"

"I would say so, Mrs. Simpkin. The dishes you served tonight failed to satisfy our appetites."

"I can prepare another dinner, my lord—"

"That won't be necessary. You will excuse us, please."

The housekeeper suddenly looked worried. "What do you intend, Lord Danvers? If you mean to punish Miss Arabella—"

"I am merely going to feed her. Now, pray give us

some privacy. Don't be alarmed, I won't harm your mistress."

After a hesitant glance at Arabella, the housekeeper reluctantly left the room, followed by the wide-eyed scullery maid.

Marcus led Arabella to the table and pressed her down onto the bench. "Sit here while I raid the larder."

She obeyed unwillingly. The warmth of the room, combined with the delicious aromas of herbs and cooking, was somehow pleasant, yet she couldn't relax as she watched Marcus search the vast room. It was incongruous to see a tall, lithe aristocrat garbed in formal evening clothes foraging in these domestic surroundings, but it was utterly unsettling to imagine what he had in store for her. He was obviously retaliating in response to her tactics.

He inspected several pantries and then the cellar, gathering items for a feast and returning to deposit his prizes on the table before her. Then he went around the kitchen, putting out all the lamps, leaving only the glow of the hearth fire to provide light.

"What the devil are you doing?" Arabella asked, her voice suddenly uneven.

"I told you, I intend to feed you."

"In the *dark*?"

He smiled at her protest. "Not total darkness. I want to be able to see your pleasure as you savor each bite."

His answer unnerved her, as did his next provocative comment when he settled on the bench beside her.

"This is much more intimate than the dining room, wouldn't you agree?"

This setting was indeed far more intimate than before. Clearly her plan had backfired.

"Marcus, this is hardly proper . . ." she began breathlessly.

His midnight blue eyes gleamed at her. "Hush, sweeting, and take your punishment like a good sport."

She had no choice but to comply, Arabella realized, swallowing the sudden dryness in her throat. She was keenly aware of Marcus's potent masculinity as he leaned nearer, for she could feel his powerful thigh press against hers through her gown. The arousing contact sent heat coiling low in her belly and between her thighs, made her nipples tighten brazenly to hardened peaks.

What was worse, Marcus knew his effect on her, the fiend.

The pressure deliberately increased as he reached into a bowl and drew out a plump strawberry, the first of the season. Next he removed the cloth from another bowl and dipped the ripe fruit in clotted cream, then held the morsel to her lips.

He planned to serve her with his fingers, Arabella perceived.

She tried unsuccessfully to take the berry from him. "I can feed myself."

"But it would not be nearly as enjoyable for either of us. Open your lovely mouth, Arabella, or I will have to kiss it open."

She chose the lesser of two evils, bending forward to bite off the fruit from the leafy stem. The tart-sweet burst of flavor in her mouth was delicious, reminding her that strawberries and cream was her favorite dessert. Yet she couldn't enjoy the flavor, not with Marcus observing her so intently. His lips lifted in a slow, sultry smile as he watched her chew.

He fed her two more berries, until finally Arabella pushed his hand away. "Honestly, I am no longer hungry."

"I am. Hungry for you."

Her heart gave a fierce leap at his low murmur.

"I can imagine how delectable you would taste, love."

Their gazes locked, and Arabella's breath caught in her lungs. She had never felt this aching physical awareness before. Something tangible had kindled between them, and she couldn't look away. She was experienced enough now to recognize the bright spark of desire that flared in Marcus's blue eyes.

A shiver stole through her, even before he raised his finger to draw it along the wet line of her lips. "From now on, every time I watch you eat will be a taste of temptation."

Her breath faltered entirely. Then his fingertips moved lower to touch the pulse quickening at the base of her throat. The tension thrumming between them was nearly unbearable.

Desperate to break it, Arabella surged to her feet. "I must go," she exclaimed, yet she was prevented from fleeing for the door when Marcus caught her hand.

Laughter laced his voice as he protested, "But, darling, you have scarcely eaten a bite."

"I have had more than enough, my lord!"

She snatched her hand from his grasp and escaped to the sound of his soft laughter. Her heart was still thudding moments later when she reached her bedchamber, her body still shivering with heat.

Arabella shut the door firmly behind her, then leaned weakly back against the panel. She was in serious trouble if she could not even withstand her first dinner with Marcus.

She had meant to foil his plan to woo her, but she had done a wretched job of it. Indeed, thus far she had come out the loser in every encounter with him.

Arabella shook her head stubbornly. Perhaps she had lost their initial battles, but she wouldn't lose the war.

Chapter Five

❧

Do take care, dearest Arabella. Lord Danvers is reputed to be impossibly seductive.

—Fanny Irwin to Arabella

The odd sound of sawing woke Arabella the next morning. Prying her eyes open, she glanced at her bedchamber window. The curious noise was coming from outdoors, along with several male voices.

Puzzled, she rose to peer out the curtains and blinked in the bright sunlight. From her bedchamber, she could see the rear of the manor—the gardens and the terraced lawns beyond, which led down to the river. The grounds below were swarming with an army of gardeners, all pruning and clipping and raking years of overgrowth away.

Thoughtfully, Arabella turned from the window to wash and dress. She had risen later than usual since she'd slept poorly. In truth, she had tossed and turned much of the night, images of a certain sensual nobleman inhabiting her restless dreams.

She had just donned a gown of yellow sprigged muslin when she heard a soft rap on her chamber door, followed by Mrs. Simpkin's low voice. " 'Tis I, Miss Arabella. I've brought your breakfast."

When Arabella bid entrance, the housekeeper bustled

in with a laden tray, which she placed on the dressing table. "I suspected you didn't wish to breakfast with Lord Danvers, so I took the liberty of bringing yours here." She had also kindly sent up a dinner tray last night so Arabella wouldn't go hungry.

"Thank you, Mrs. Simpkin," Arabella said with genuine warmth, glad to avoid being alone again with Marcus so soon on the heels of their disastrous dinner. "By the way, who are those laborers in the gardens?"

"They are from London. His lordship sent for them to tidy the landscaping. Oh, and there are a half dozen tradesmen and merchants awaiting you in my accounts room."

Her eyebrows rose with curiosity. "Awaiting me?"

"Yes. Lord Danvers sent to London for them as well. He means to set the manor to rights, to replace all the shabby furnishings and wallpaper and draperies in the house from top to bottom. But he said he wishes you to make all the decisions, since he doesn't know brocade from buckram." The housekeeper returned to the door but paused there to address Arabella again. "I must say it will be good to see the Hall live up to its former glory. And it will be even better to have a mistress here once more." The smile the elderly servant gave her was somewhat secretive. "Perhaps his lordship isn't so disagreeable as we feared."

Arabella wondered what had precipitated Mrs. Simpkin's sudden change of heart, for she'd been as worried about the new earl as his reluctant wards were. But likely the housekeeper was merely grateful that the manor would finally receive some beautifying after the former lord's tightfisted ways.

"Perhaps Lord Danvers isn't entirely disagreeable," Arabella said noncommittally.

"At least he has forgiven me for the wretched dinner last evening."

It had dismayed Arabella to think Marcus would hold the housekeeper responsible for her own actions. "I told him you weren't to blame for the dinner, Mrs. Simpkin."

"I know, but all the same, I don't like to be in his lordship's poor graces." Her brown eyes twinkled. "Thankfully he decided not to bring any toplofty London chef down after all, and he gave me leave to hire a new cook. I will be glad for the respite from the kitchens, I must say. 'Twill be a full-time job to oversee all the maids he instructed me to employ. Simpkin is already hopping to keep up with the footmen Lord Danvers sent from his London house last week." Again the housekeeper paused. "Shall I tell the merchants you will be down shortly, Miss Arabella? They are eager to show you their wares."

"Yes, as soon as I finish breakfast."

Mrs. Simpkin's warning was true, Arabella learned when she had quickly eaten and gone downstairs to the housekeeper's small office. Marcus had indeed summoned an army of tradesmen to refurbish the manor house. There were seven merchants eagerly awaiting her with armfuls of fabric samples and catalogues and sketchbooks.

All of them bowed politely to her, but when they

began clamoring for her attention, Arabella held up a hand. "Pray, give me a moment, good sirs."

Turning quickly, she went in search of Simpkin and found him occupied in supervising the group of new footmen in cleaning and polishing all the lamps in the house.

"Where may I find Lord Danvers?" she asked.

"I believe his lordship is in the study, Miss Arabella," Simpkin answered.

She made her way through the house to the study, where she found the door open. When she entered and spied Marcus, however, she came up short. He was settled comfortably on a sofa, reading the morning papers, which must also have been delivered from London.

The sight of him made Arabella's stomach flutter. He was dressed far less formally than last evening, in a russet-colored coat but no cravat or waistcoat. His linen shirt was open at the neck, showing an immodest expanse of chest, much like last week when she'd interrupted his fencing match.

His slow smile of greeting suggested he understood the affect his casual attire had on her.

"Arabella, what a pleasure," he said, rising. "I confess surprise that you would voluntarily seek me out after hiding from me in your room all morning."

Resolving not to let herself be provoked, she repressed a wry retort and instead asked about his decision to spend what surely would be a fortune. "I don't understand your desire to refurbish the entire house. Why would you go to such expense?"

"This is my home now, as well as yours."

"But you needn't redecorate so completely."

"I think it time, since the furnishings are a century old."

"Is that why you hired so many merchants?"

Marcus shook his head. "I've left the actual hiring to you. And you aren't required to use them all. I only thought to give you a wider choice. You have full authority to decorate any way you wish."

"But why would you allow me so much authority?" Arabella asked in bewilderment.

"Because you undoubtedly have better taste and experience than I, for one."

"This is not simply a way to soften my resistance?"

His sensual smile lit the room. "Of course it is, darling. You know I mean to do everything in my power to persuade you to become my wife."

Biting back amusement, Arabella gave him a measuring glance. "Throwing your wealth around will do little to persuade me."

"But it won't hurt, either. I am not entirely witless when it comes to understanding the female mind. You ladies like to be in charge of a household."

"I am *not* in charge here, Marcus."

"Of course you are. You are mistress here now, and that will continue when you are my countess." When Arabella raised her gaze to the ceiling, he chuckled softly. "I thought you would be pleased by my gesture."

"You have certainly made Mrs. Simpkin happy," she said drolly. "It was clever of you to have increased the servant staff so generously, for there is no surer path to her heart."

"What about the path to *your* heart?" When Arabella refused to answer, Marcus laughed. "Mrs. Simpkin and I have come to an understanding."

"Which means you charmed her into doing your bidding."

"That, and I told her I was courting you. She approves, by the way."

A look of exasperation claimed Arabella's features as she turned and silently exited the room. It didn't surprise her that Marcus would use any means necessary to win the housekeeper's support, for she herself had vowed to employ all her resources to prevail in their wager.

Yet Arabella had to admit she was pleased to see him putting Danvers Hall to rights. The manor was indeed beautiful, and the estate deserved to be worthy of an earl. She only wished Roslyn were here, since her sister had impeccable taste and had been better trained by their mother to fill the role of lady of the manor.

Arabella spent the entire morning with the merchants, appraising the formal rooms of the house and choosing fabrics and furnishings. The task occupied her so intensely that she paid no attention to the passing time.

She was trying to decide between a forest green velvet and blue brocade for the drawing room draperies when Simpkin appeared in the doorway. "Miss Blanchard has called to see you, Miss Arabella."

Arabella raised her head in surprise. "Oh, my word. I completely forgot my class."

It had slipped her mind entirely that she'd been expected to teach at the academy at eleven. Her closest friend and fellow teacher at the school, Tess Blanchard, had no doubt come to see why she had uncustomarily failed to appear.

"Where have you put Miss Blanchard, Simpkin?"

"She is waiting in the entrance hall, since I couldn't find a parlor not covered with fabric and wallpaper swatches."

Arabella was about to leave the drawing room when the butler cleared his throat. "Forgive me, Miss Arabella, but where do you wish me to place all the flowers?"

"Flowers?"

"The ones Lord Danvers had delivered from London. They have been unloaded in the entrance hall at his lordship's request."

Puzzled, Arabella hurried down the corridor, only to find the hall filled with masses of flowers in a breathtaking profusion of colors and scents. There were blossoms of all kinds—lilies and roses and daffodils in particular. Marcus must have raided every flower stall and shop in London, was Arabella's first thought.

Her friend Tess was admiring an enormous vase of red roses but left off when she spied Arabella. "What on earth is going on, Arabella? I was concerned when you didn't appear at school, so I came to investigate, only to find you have sprouted a garden." She sounded half amused but a bit worried also.

"Tess, I am so sorry for missing my class! I entirely lost track of time."

Tess lowered her voice to avoid being overheard. "How are you faring with the vexatious earl, as Lily calls him?"

Glancing around to make certain Marcus was nowhere in sight, Arabella answered ruefully, "Not well, I'm afraid—as you can see." She gestured at the enormous display of flowers. "I believe this must be his notion of a romantic courtship."

"Courtship?"

"Come with me." Arabella drew her friend down the hall to the small parlor so they could be private.

Tess was a beautiful woman, with sable hair and a flawless complexion and figure that were the envy of nearly every lady in the district. She was a year younger than Arabella, yet she had remained a spinster after losing her betrothed in the Peninsular Wars. They'd become fast friends when the Loring sisters moved in with their step-uncle four years before, and grown even closer when Arabella opened the academy. Despite Tess's genteel upbringing that dictated ladies shouldn't soil their hands with menial employment, she had willingly joined as a teacher in hopes that keeping occupied would help her to overcome her sorrow.

Since they had shared so much, Arabella felt no qualms at confessing her dilemma to Tess. "Lord Danvers has proposed marriage to me."

Dumbfounded, Tess stared. "I thought he was trying to marry you off to a total stranger."

Arabella laughed at her friend's expression. "He was. But then he decided to kill two birds with one stone—to be rid of the responsibility for me as his ward and to secure a wife to produce heirs for him at the same time."

"You don't mean to accept him?"

"Of course not. But I agreed to allow him to court me."

She told Tess about the wager and how Lord Danvers had promised to grant her and her sisters their legal emancipation if Arabella could resist his seduction for a fortnight.

"Lily will certainly be pleased to be free of his guardianship, as will Roslyn," Tess said slowly at the conclusion.

"How are my sisters?" Arabella asked eagerly.

"Well enough, considering they have severely curtailed their daily activities so as not to be seen by the earl. Lily is fretting most at being confined indoors, naturally, but even Roslyn is growing restless."

"I can well imagine. Thank you for taking them in, Tess, and for seeing to my class this morning. I know this makes scheduling lessons difficult for you."

"Don't mention it, dearest. You have done more than enough for me these past few years. I couldn't begin to repay you."

"If you don't mind," Arabella added, "I would prefer my sisters remain with you a few days more until we can be certain of the earl's intentions. As long as our wager holds, he will likely leave off seeking to arrange marriages for them, but I don't know him well enough yet to trust him unconditionally."

"Certainly I don't mind," Tess said. "Roslyn and

Lily are more than welcome to stay for as long as necessary. In fact, they are proving invaluable, helping me to make up baskets for the Families of Fallen Soldiers. It's an enormous task, stitching shirts and knitting stockings for so many needy children, and with your sisters' contribution, I should be able to increase the number this year to two hundred." Tess smiled. "Amazingly, even Lily has pitched in wholeheartedly, despite her dislike of sewing, since it is for such a good cause. So tell me about Lord Danvers. Is he the overbearing tyrant you feared?"

Arabella hesitated. She had to admit Marcus was nothing like what she had feared. He might be more than a little arrogant, but he certainly didn't resemble a tyrant. Indeed, he had shown remarkable understanding for a nobleman of his stamp. He had listened intently last evening when she spoke of her academy. And more astonishingly, he appeared to respect her as the mistress of the estate even though her step-uncle had treated her and her sisters as poor relations dependent on charity.

But of course Marcus was showing his most amiable side in order to persuade her that he would make her an acceptable husband.

"No, he is not as bad as we feared," Arabella conceded. "He is rather arrogant and high-handed, as most noblemen are, and accustomed to getting his own way. But I cannot truthfully call him a tyrant."

"I am flattered, sweeting," a lazy masculine voice drawled from the doorway. "Your resounding endorsement warms my heart."

Giving a start at the intrusion, Arabella spun to eye Marcus with reproach. "Did no one ever tell you it is impolite to eavesdrop?"

An amused gleam lit his eyes as he sauntered into the room. "Politeness never won a fair maiden. Moreover, I see no reason to change my methods, since they appear to be working. I am clearly making progress if I've improved your opinion of me so significantly in barely one day. At this rate, we will be married by month's end."

Arabella's mouth twitched with the effort to quell a laugh. "You are indulging in a pipe dream, my lord."

"A very pleasant pipe dream." His provocative look sent the most unsettling shiver of awareness down her spine. "Will you introduce me to your guest? Or do you mean to keep her hidden from me, as you have your sisters?"

She flushed as she finally remembered her manners. "This is Miss Tess Blanchard. Tess, my guardian, Lord Danvers."

Marcus bowed. "A pleasure to meet you, Miss Blanchard. I understand you teach at the Freemantle Academy with Arabella." When Tess arched a cool eyebrow, Marcus sent her a winning smile. "I had my solicitors give me a full report on your school, since my wards are so heavily involved. You are a close friend of Arabella's, I gather."

"I am, my lord," Tess answered, scrutinizing him with interest.

"Then perhaps you might advise me on how to advance my suit with her. I need every advantage I can get."

"You don't expect me to aid the enemy, do you?"

He laughed softly. "You see, that is my dilemma. I have been dubbed 'the enemy' without a chance to prove myself."

When her friend smiled in return, Arabella was amazed that Marcus could charm even Tess, who was extremely wary of rakish noblemen after an unhappy encounter with one in her past.

"Lord Danvers is obviously well-versed in using charm to get his way," Arabella said dryly.

"True," Marcus agreed. "But even my best efforts fail to have much effect on you." He directed his gaze at Tess once more. "Will you stay for luncheon, Miss Blanchard? I hope to persuade you to tell me some of Arabella's secrets."

That won another faint smile from Tess. "Thank you, but I cannot stay. I must return to the academy. I only called because Arabella missed her class."

"I fear that was my fault. I have kept her occupied with my affairs all morning."

When Tess gave her a curious glance, Arabella felt her cheeks warming. "Lord Danvers plans to renovate the Hall and asked me to oversee the work."

"I see," Tess said slowly, although the frown creasing her brow showed a hint of concern.

"Don't worry," Arabella said with an arch glance at Marcus. "I have no intention of becoming Lady Danvers simply because I enjoy decorating his manor."

With Marcus following, she accompanied Tess to the entrance hall, where the forest of blossoms greeted them. Arabella went straight to the vase of roses her friend had been admiring earlier. "Here, pray take these with you, Tess. I know how much you love roses, and you will appreciate them better than I." She turned to the butler, who was waiting by the front door. "Will you have the other flowers delivered to the academy, Simpkin?"

"All of them, Miss Arabella?"

"Yes, all. You may distribute them among our pupils with the compliments of Lord Danvers." She glanced at Marcus with a wicked smile. "I'm certain our young ladies will be grateful that a nobleman of your illustrious station thought to brighten their day. And I don't like to squander such lovely blooms, even though they are wasted on me."

When he inclined his head, acknowledging her slight victory, Arabella felt her pulse leap at his very male smile.

Dragging her gaze away, she ushered her friend outside to her gig to say a private farewell. When she returned, she found Marcus still waiting for her. "Did you wish something of me, Lord Danvers? I should return to the drawing room, where I left our merchants."

"I wanted to invite you to ride with me after luncheon. I thought you might enjoy the exercise." When Arabella hesitated, Marcus added, "I sent for some of my horses in London on the assumption that you and your sisters would appreciate decent mounts for a change. The slugs in your step-uncle's stables are hardly worthy of the name. We can consider a ride part of my daily quota of your company."

She would indeed enjoy riding, Arabella reflected.

And mounted on horseback, she would stand a better chance of frustrating the earl's persistent courtship. "I would like that, my lord."

"Good. Then I shall meet you at the stable at two."

Arabella returned to the drawing room, unable to ignore a tremor of excitement at the prospect of riding on such a lovely spring day, or the more deplorable anticipation of matching wits with Marcus again.

Arabella was not disappointed by either the weather or her new mount. When she reached the stables, Marcus was waiting with a beautiful bay mare for her. He lifted her into her sidesaddle, then mounted a strapping chestnut gelding.

She led the way out of the yard and down the gravel drive to a tree-shaded lane. At the next crossroad, they turned off and set out across the countryside at a leisurely canter, negotiating lush green fields and pastures and glades that flanked the winding Thames River. They finally slowed when they came to the crest of a hill, where they could see a wide valley below.

A pleasant silence had fallen between them. Arabella raised her face to the sun, drinking in the golden-bright afternoon, savoring the rare pleasure of having a spirited horse beneath her and a charmingly attentive gentleman beside her. If not for the wager, she would have keenly enjoyed Marcus's company, she acknowledged.

"Thank you for this delightful treat," she said, patting her mare. "She is a beauty. You clearly have superb taste in horseflesh."

"I buy all my sister's mounts for her," Marcus replied.

"And is she a good horsewoman?"

"The best, since I taught her myself. Eleanor rides neck or nothing, just as your sister Lilian reportedly enjoys doing."

"Lily does indeed ride like a hellion," Arabella replied with a fond smile.

"I should like to meet her and Roslyn one of these days."

She sent Marcus a provocative glance. "We shall see."

"Perhaps I'll invite Eleanor here for a visit. She would enjoy riding here far more than the tame environs of Hyde Park."

"She lives in London with you?"

"In London, but not with me. With our elderly aunt, who acts as her chaperone. Eleanor moved there for her comeout three years ago and chose to stay."

"If you have been her guardian for so long, did you try to marry her off the way you planned to do us?"

Amusement curved his lips. "I wouldn't dream of trying to play matchmaker for my sister. Thankfully there is no need, since as an heiress, she can have her pick of suitors. At the moment, like you she is resolved to remain single—although she has been betrothed twice. Both times she called off the engagement. Our aunt fears Eleanor is earning a reputation as a jilt."

Arabella's eyebrow rose quizzically. "I expect she had a good reason."

"She decided she wasn't in love after all," Marcus

answered lightly. He turned his head to study Arabella. "I am curious about your betrothal. Did you love your viscount?"

Arabella couldn't restrain her wince. It was still painful to remember her former betrothal to George, Viscount Underwood. She had indeed loved him. She'd believed in a future with him, the hope for children.

Realizing that Marcus was waiting for her reply, however, she composed her features to blandness. She was reluctant to answer such a personal question, but perhaps he deserved to know why she had no intention of entertaining his offer of marriage.

"Yes, I loved him," Arabella said, keeping her tone even. "It was the only reason I accepted his proposal, even though it was considered an excellent match and precisely what was expected of me. After my parents' experience, I wasn't willing to settle for a marriage of convenience."

"He obviously didn't love you. If he had, he would never have let the scandal come between you."

She was better prepared this time to hide her wince. "No, he didn't love me," she agreed.

Strangely, Marcus's jaw hardened with something resembling anger. "It was hardly honorable of him to withdraw his suit once you became betrothed."

Arabella gave a dismissive shrug. "True. But I soon realized how fortunate I was that we didn't actually marry, since he didn't love me as he claimed. Our marriage would likely have deteriorated into nothing more than a cold legal union at best." She managed a smile. "In any event, it was four years ago, when I was young and naive. I have grown much wiser since. But you see why I am not eager to repeat the experience?"

Marcus was still studying her closely. "I can see I will have to prove to you that I am nothing like your viscount."

Arabella couldn't help but be amused by the comparison. Her viscount was very little like Marcus. Not nearly as physically attractive or as . . . forceful. George was a *gentle* man, very unlike her powerful, dynamic, libertine father, also—which was primarily what she had found appealing about him. But he had turned out to have little backbone.

"You have nothing to prove on that account, Marcus," she said. "There are few similarities between you."

"You may be sure I won't run at the first hint of scandal."

"No, I can't imagine you running from anything." Arabella gave him a genuine smile. "And truthfully, I have become almost grateful for the scandal. In a way, it liberated us. My sisters and I are able to rule our own lives now"—she flashed him an ironic glance—"or we would if we didn't have an unwanted guardian to contend with."

His intent expression fading, Marcus grinned. "Sorry, love."

"You aren't sorry in the least," Arabella replied lightly. "But as soon as our fortnight is up, I will be rid of you."

"You don't want to be rid of me. You are enjoying our wager too much."

"Am I indeed?"

"Most definitely. You relish the exhilaration of challenging me and matching wits with a worthy opponent."

Arabella arched an eloquent eyebrow. "How can you presume to know what I feel?"

His reply was more serious than she expected. "Because I feel the same exhilaration. One I haven't known in years."

"It must be dyspepsia."

Marcus chuckled. "Come now, admit it. Your life has been deadly dull without me here to enliven it, with only your school to occupy your time."

Arabella regarded him silently, unable to refute his claim. Most of the time her life was oppressively dull, except for the occasional interesting incident at her academy. And she was indeed beginning to find her time with Marcus exhilarating. She would chew nails before she admitted it to him, though.

"You have a highly elevated opinion of yourself, my lord," she said sweetly before gathering her reins. "And I can find far more exhilaration in a good gallop." With her heel, she urged her mare into a canter. "I wager I will reach the Hall before you!" Arabella called over her shoulder.

Marcus found himself grinning at her obvious attempt to avoid any further intimate conversation. But as she galloped away, he took up her challenge.

When she realized he was hard on her heels, Arabella bent over her mare's neck, urging the horse to greater speed. It became a full-fledged race, one that symbolized the fierce competition between them. One they both were determined to win. Arabella set a wicked pace, and Marcus did his best to catch her.

Unlike the last race, however, she was mounted on a swift horse this time, so she managed to win by a nose. Having achieved victory, Arabella slowed her mad dash into the stableyard and drew up laughing.

The bewitching sight hit Marcus directly in his chest before shooting down to his loins. With her beautiful face flushed with warmth and exertion, her lips parted breathlessly, her breasts heaving with exertion, she looked just as she would in the throes of passion, Marcus knew.

The image made his body tighten with desire and arousal. He wanted to pull Arabella off her horse and make love to her then and there. Wanted to sink inside that vibrant warmth—

Unfortunately, they had an audience, Marcus saw as two of his grooms appeared to take their sweating horses.

Denying them the chance to assist her, Arabella slid down from her sidesaddle and turned the reins over with a request to cool off the mare. Marcus did the same with his mount, then followed Arabella to the house.

He caught up to her as she entered the side door. "Will you join me for dinner this evening?"

She gave him a droll glance. "Do you intend to leave me any choice?"

"Of course. We could always complete the remainder

of our four hours later this evening . . . after you retire to bed."

"I wouldn't put it past you," she murmured at his subtle threat to invade her bedchamber.

"Dinner, then?"

Arabella exhaled an exaggerated sigh for his benefit. "Very well. I will join you for dinner. Just now I want to confer with Mrs. Simpkin regarding redecorating the house."

Marcus watched her walk away, admiring the slight sway of her hips beneath the skirts of her riding habit while he mulled over her startling effect on him.

He had to acknowledge that his feelings for Arabella were more potent than desire, and much more complex. He felt a gut-deep exhilaration when he was with her. An excitement that he hadn't known in years. She was all woman, intensely vital and alive, and she made him feel just as vitally alive.

After her confession about her former betrothed, though, Marcus realized more clearly what he was up against. Her suitor's cowardly defection had only compounded her devastation at losing her parents and her home. The bastard's betrayal, even more than her parents' matrimonial battles, had left Arabella painfully gun-shy about betrothals and marriage.

Marcus blew out a slow breath. He hated to think of the hurt and mortification she'd endured at the desertion. But most assuredly he had his work cut out for him if he intended to make Arabella want him as her husband. She would try to foil his courtship every step of the way, just as she'd done this morning when she'd publicly rejected his romantic gesture, giving away his flowers to her pupils. The memory made him smile.

But he wouldn't be deterred, Marcus resolved. He intended to chip away steadily at her defensive armor until she changed her mind about wedding him— beginning tonight. It was time he took the intimacy of his wooing a step further by introducing Arabella to the secrets of sensuality.

A corner of his mouth curved in anticipation. Romancing a reluctant young lady might not exactly be his forte, but the sensual game was one he would win.

Arabella went in search of Mrs. Simpkin to discuss her latest plans for refurbishing the house. Before they began, she asked for a bath in the dressing room she shared with Roslyn, so that by the time she went upstairs a half hour later, a copper tub had been filled with hot water for her.

Undressing, Arabella sank into the tub and sighed at the pleasure. It had been quite a while since she had indulged in the luxury of a long soak.

By the time she finished washing her hair, the water had grown tepid. After toweling off, she put on a wrapper and left her damp hair down to dry. When she came out of her dressing room, Arabella stopped short. Someone had strewn crimson rose petals over the ivory coverlet of her bed.

Marcus, was her immediate thought. The devil must have entered her bedchamber while she was bathing.

It was a novel use of rose petals, Arabella conceded, unable to quell a laugh. The entrance hall had been devoid of flowers when they returned from their ride, but evidently he had saved some of the roses for this latest salvo of his courtship.

She had to admire his inventiveness, and yet . . . he could have been seen by one of the servants, Arabella realized. She glanced at the closed door to the corridor. Their bedchambers were separated by the entire width of the house, since Marcus was occupying the lord's apartments. There could be no reason for him to be on this end of the floor unless it was to visit the music room next door.

Stifling her amusement, Arabella decided that she had to have a cautionary word with him. When she had dressed and come downstairs, she found Marcus in the drawing room.

"Did you leave rose petals on my bed?" she asked as he offered her a glass of wine.

"Guilty as charged. I am wooing you, remember?" When she gave him a measured look, his eyebrow rose. "So you don't appreciate my romantic gesture?"

"Not that particular gesture. It is much too intimate."

He flashed a smile that came close to taking her breath away. "Arabella, darling, we haven't *begun* to become intimate."

Firmly disciplining her senses, she ignored his provocative comment. "But you might have been seen by a servant."

"No. I always take great care to be discreet."

"Marcus . . . you cannot simply enter my bedchamber any time you please."

"I know. But one day soon you will invite me there of your own accord. I like your hair down like that, by the way."

Her expression turned exasperated. "I am not wearing it this way to suit you, but so it will dry."

"I know that, too. Now taste your wine. You'll find it much more palatable than last night's vinegar. It's claret from my own cellars."

The wine was indeed excellent, and Marcus refrained from making any more provocative remarks. Since they kept the conversation to impersonal matters about the neighborhood, Arabella found the interval before dinner rather pleasant. She actually was enjoying being with Marcus by the time Simpkin came to announce that dinner was served.

The meal was delicious—creamed artichoke soup, turbot in lobster sauce, stuffed partridges, braised veal, cauliflower, and currant pudding for dessert.

As the footmen cleared away the dishes, Marcus addressed the butler. "Simpkin, pray send my compliments to Mrs. Simpkin. My London chef could not have done better."

"Thank you, my lord. She will be pleased to know you approve."

When the servants had been dismissed, Arabella glanced at the ormolu clock on the mantel and rose. "This was delightful, my lord, but I believe I have fulfilled my obligation to share your company for today."

"Not quite, love." Reaching up, he gently caught her wrist in his fingers.

She stared down into his blue eyes. "Surely our four hours are up."

"I still have a quarter hour left. Time enough to begin your education."

"My education?"

"To show you what you will be missing if you insist on remaining a spinster."

Her heart started fluttering. "I do not need educating, Marcus."

"You do, Arabella. You badly need a taste of physical pleasure. I want you to understand the connubial bliss you can expect when we are wed. How else can you make such an important decision about your future?"

The suggestiveness of his question momentarily rendered her speechless. When she remained mute, Marcus stood, still holding her wrist. "Come take a stroll on the grounds with me. The gardens should be pleasant, now that they are no longer a jungle."

Arabella glanced at the French doors and swallowed. Dusk had fallen, and a half moon hung low over the horizon, silvering the trees that lined the river. "It is dark outside."

"Dark is perfect for wooing."

"Marcus, I won't go outside with you. Whatever you intend, you can do right here."

"I could, but I don't think you want Simpkin witnessing my advances." When she gave a huff of exasperation, Marcus added cajolingly, "I won't kiss you this time. If I try, you can box my ears again."

"Don't tempt me," she muttered.

He smiled. "Do I tempt you, sweet Arabella? *You* tempt *me*."

"I certainly don't mean to." Pulling her hand away, she strode to the door and drew it open.

Marcus followed her outside to the terraced gardens and then caught her arm. "Let's walk down to the river. It will give us more privacy."

Arabella felt her pulse quicken as he led her down the terrace steps to the sloping lawn. It was unwise to allow Marcus the kind of privacy he demanded, but in all fairness to the wager, she had to provide him the opportunity to woo her. She would have to summon more willpower than she'd shown thus far, however, if she intended to make his seduction difficult.

She could hear the soft ripple of water as they neared the river. When they reached the bank, Marcus drew her behind a chestnut tree. Enough moonlight shafted through the lattice of branches that she could see his handsome face and the midnight blue of his eyes simmering in the dark.

He stood watching her thoughtfully, though, until she finally broke the silence. "What do you intend to do, if not to kiss me?"

He dragged his sensual gaze over her in a lazy caress. "To show you the power of touch."

She didn't like the sound of that. "Marcus . . ."

"I mean only to touch you this time. I want to show you how merely the brush of a fingertip can arouse powerful sensations between a man and a woman."

"I am perfectly willing to believe you. I don't need a demonstration."

Marcus smiled knowingly. "You aren't turning craven again, surely."

His deep gaze had become a dare, which only heightened the quivery little feelings that were rioting deep in her body. "No, I am not craven. I just wish you would hurry and be done with it."

"Patience, sweet Arabella. A proper wooing takes time."

"You only have five more minutes by my calculation."

"Five minutes should be ample time to teach you this lesson."

Arabella tensed as he took her right hand and turned it faceup, yet she couldn't help watching with fascination as Marcus began to trace small patterns on her palm with his fingertip.

When he reached the most sensitive curves, the simple caress made her shiver with awareness.

If she was wise, she would pull away, Arabella knew. Yet she stood immobile with her back to the tree trunk, with Marcus blocking her way. Then he pushed up the long sleeve of her gown an inch to expose her wrist and stroked the delicate flesh there, raising a flush to her skin.

Unnerved, Arabella tried to draw her hand away.

"Be still," Marcus commanded.

"That tickles."

"It does much more than tickle." He lifted his head,

his gaze locking with hers, his eyes containing a gleam of wickedness. He knew precisely how his skilled caresses affected her, the devil.

Arabella clenched her teeth, determined to resist his beguiling touch. The man was too arrogant for his own good.

He left her wrist then and slowly skimmed his fingertips up her arm, over the silk fabric of her sleeve and along her shoulder in a trailing, seductive caress. She sensed the raw power even in this light touch, and when he found her bare collarbone above the high edge of her gown's neckline, she shuddered at the heated rush of feeling assaulting her. The heat only increased when he drew a line down the silky hollow between her breasts.

"Arabella . . ." Marcus warned again when she made to move away.

She swallowed hard, finding it nearly impossible to remain still as he resumed. The truth was, she wanted to be touched this way, wanted him to touch her.

His hand glided upward over her skin, along the column of her throat. "Can you deny how pleasurable this feels?" His voice stroked her senses like velvet, just as his fingers were doing.

No, she couldn't deny the pleasure. His arousing caresses vibrated through her, thrumming at all her nerve endings.

When she didn't answer, Marcus put a languid finger beneath her chin and made her lift her gaze. As she met his dark eyes, her heart thudded erratically, beating a wild pulse in her throat.

He touched her there, pressing faintly against the vulnerable hollow. Then moving higher, he grazed her jawline with his thumb. Arabella quivered at the alluring feel.

His thumb brushed her jaw twice more, his touch lingering and provocative, before wandering with tantalizing slowness to her cheek.

His blue gaze engulfed her as his fingers teased her flushed skin. Arabella couldn't look away. She was too enraptured by his expression and the tender assault of his fingers. She could scarcely breathe as his thumb traced her moist, parted lips, then dipped to penetrate the corner of her mouth.

Her heart beat painfully hard, and for a moment, she wondered if Marcus intended to kiss her. But his hand left her cheek to roam down her throat again, his palm skimming with feathery, delicious sensations, leaving a fiery trail in its wake.

When he drew a seductive finger along the line of her collarbone, her skin burned. Yet he stopped just as he reached the swells of her breasts. Instead, his hands settled with warm possessiveness on her shoulders, and he stepped closer.

Arabella inhaled sharply when he drew her fully against him. His body was warm, hard, strong.

"You said you only meant to touch me," she said breathlessly.

"Holding is part of touching. Don't you like the feel of our bodies pressing together?"

There was an insidious delight in being held against his hard, sheltering body. She could feel the rush of her own blood, could feel the tremors shivering through her. "No, I don't, Marcus."

"Liar," he murmured softly.

To her surprise and disappointment, he released her. Yet he didn't step back. He merely raised his hand to her bodice and feathered the tips of her breasts with the backs of his fingers, making Arabella gasp at the sparks that shot through her. "If you don't like it, then why have your nipples grown so hard?"

It was true, Arabella realized. Her nipples had instantly hardened, betraying her arousal, while her breasts felt heavy and swollen.

And Marcus was doing his best to increase her desire, his knuckles slowly gliding over the silk-covered peaks. Then boldly he cupped one ripe swell, making her knees go weak. Fire radiated from the hand that held her throbbing breast, bloomed between her thighs, shocking her. Fanny had described such powerful feminine feelings as this, but Arabella had never expected to experience them for herself.

She closed her eyes against the pleasure. It was maddening the way Marcus drew out each brazen caress, yet she didn't want him to stop. His touch was so tender, so wicked . . . so right. The sensations left her shaking inside, kindling a heavy ache deep in her lower body . . .

It was some time before she realized his demonstration had ceased.

"Do you understand now?" Marcus asked, his voice husky and low.

Dazed, Arabella opened her eyes. Oh, she understood

perfectly. Marcus had intended to show her the power of a man's touch—of *his* touch—and he had thoroughly succeeded. She was aching with nameless longing . . . aching for *him*.

"I want to return to the house now," she said unevenly, her voice deplorably weak.

At her nonanswer, he gave a satisfied smile. "Of course. I think your lesson is sufficient for now. You'll dream of me tonight, of me touching you like this . . ."

He raised his hand to her throat again, and another frisson of fiery sensation sparked from his fingers to her skin.

Arabella drew back sharply and gave Marcus a dismissive look. But as she slipped past him and turned toward the house on shaky legs, she was very much afraid his prediction about her dreams would come true.

Chapter Six

❧

I promise I will take care, Fanny, even if his kisses are as seductive as you warned me.

—Arabella to Fanny

Arabella did dream of Marcus . . . all night long. But she awoke determined to regain the offensive in their rivalry. As soon as she had washed and dressed, she joined Marcus in the small dining parlor.

He looked surprised to see her as he rose politely from the table.

"To what do I owe this honor?" he asked as he settled Arabella in her chair and returned to his seat beside her.

"I am fulfilling part of my daily quota. I realized that if I must share your company, it would be best to do so in broad daylight."

Amusement glimmered in his eyes. "You realize that won't deter me."

"Yes, but somehow I feel safer."

He surveyed her gown of blue muslin. "Had I known you intended to join me for breakfast, I would have dressed more formally."

He wore no cravat or waistcoat again this morning, Arabella saw, and his shirt was open to his breastbone. She had the most scandalous urge to touch that broad male chest, to feel the muscled flesh she glimpsed beneath the fine cambric.

Instead, Arabella cleared her throat. "Are you occupied this afternoon?"

Marcus raised an eyebrow. "I suppose that depends on what you have in mind."

"I have decided to invite you to tour our academy. You said you wanted to judge whether teaching there is an appropriate endeavor for your wards. Well, this is your chance."

"Then I accept."

"I am instructing a class at four. We usually take tea then, and I thought to use your visit as a learning opportunity for our young ladies. They rarely receive gentlemen callers, so they can practice on you."

His amusement deepened. "So I am to be your test subject."

"I don't doubt you are up to the challenge."

"And you will have protection in numbers," Marcus observed shrewdly.

Arabella smiled. She had indeed counted on that advantage. With two dozen schoolgirls to divert Marcus from his wooing of her, he would have little chance for intimacy, and she would use up much of her obligatory four hours in his company. "There is that benefit, too," she agreed.

"Very well, I will concede to tea if I must. Are you free for a ride this morning?"

She shook her head. "I am afraid I won't have time. I am meeting with the merchants again, and then I am expected at the academy at one. But I'm certain you can enjoy a ride without me. If you will arrive at the academy at half past three, you may inspect the premises before tea."

"I will be counting the minutes," Marcus replied in pained resignation.

Having postponed Marcus's courtship for the time being, Arabella spent a busy morning choosing furnishings for the remainder of the main floor. Later, when she went out to the stableyard, intending to drive herself in the gig to the academy, she found the earl's carriage waiting to take her there.

The afternoon crept by with surprising slowness. Absurdly, Arabella caught herself glancing frequently out the windows in anticipation of Marcus's visit. When his carriage arrived promptly and halted on the gravel drive before the entrance hall, she accompanied the school's headmistress outside to greet him.

"Gentleman caller reporting for duty," he said as he stepped down from his barouche.

Arabella introduced him to Miss Jane Caruthers, the elegant spinster who ran the day-to-day operations of the academy. Allowing Miss Caruthers to lead the tour of the grounds, Arabella remained a few steps behind, yet she found herself watching Marcus intently, surprised to realize how eager she was to have his approval.

Of course, if he saw the good she and her sisters were doing here, he would be more likely to sanction their continued employment. Yet her desire for his approbation was more personal than acquiring his legal consent, she knew. The academy was mainly her creation, her pride and joy, and she wanted Marcus to understand how much it meant to her.

The school was actually comprised of several buildings so as to prepare pupils for the varied experiences they would encounter in high society. Classes were usually held in a large manor house such as one might find on a nobleman's country estate, and a second, more formal mansion that was representative of where the London Quality dwelled. The academy also boasted a large stable and park to practice outdoor skills, and a large dormitory to lodge the young ladies who boarded full-time. The vast majority of the pupils lived in the dormitory, except during summer term when only a handful remained on the premises.

Arabella couldn't hide the little glow of warmth she felt at the tour's conclusion when Marcus praised the facilities.

"Impressive," he said sincerely. "I can see why merchants would want to send their daughters here."

She smiled with pleasure. "The accommodations are excellent thanks to Lady Freemantle's generosity, but our parents appreciate even more the quality of the instruction their daughters receive. Come, let me show you."

When they returned to the "London" mansion, Arabella led Marcus upstairs to a large drawing room, where he instantly became the target of attention of two dozen bright-eyed young females dressed in afternoon finery.

Miss Tess Blanchard rose to welcome him with a

polite smile. When Marcus had bowed over her hand, Arabella stepped forward to address her pupils. "Ladies, I am pleased to offer you a treat today. Lord Danvers has generously agreed to join us so that we might practice the art of properly receiving a gentleman when he calls. We will concentrate particularly on graciously pouring tea and making witty conversation. Miss Blanchard has already arranged the seating, so if you will please take your places, we may begin."

The girls were to take tea with the earl in groups of six while the rest observed. There were servants standing by with tea services and trays filled with scones and crumpets and tiny sandwiches. When Arabella and Tess were seated with the first group, Marcus was announced by a "butler" and shown into the room.

Watching him over the course of the next hour, Arabella couldn't help but admire his fortitude. Some of the girls were painfully shy, and some were crassly bold, but Marcus suffered them all with good grace. It was clear he fascinated them. He held their rapt attention throughout four practice sessions, charming the shy ones and deftly parrying the fawning banter of the flirtatious ones.

And in the third group, when one of the girls sloshed tea all over the lace tablecloth, he calmly withdrew a handkerchief from his jacket and mopped up the spill. Then when Sybil Newstead, a raven-haired beauty who had flirted brazenly with him for the past ten minutes in a transparent attempt to monopolize the conversation, scolded her classmate's clumsiness, Marcus offered the mortified girl an irresistible smile.

"Don't pay Miss Newstead any mind, Miss Fletcher. You have made me feel quite at home. My younger sister Eleanor doused me quite regularly when she was learning to pour. I don't envy you ladies, having to negotiate so many delicate operations. I would be all thumbs."

The scarlet-faced Miss Fletcher flashed him a worshipful look of gratitude, while Sybil Newstead shot him a sullen look of vexation.

Arabella, too, was supremely grateful to Marcus for his kindness, but she waited to tell him so until after the class had ended and Tess had shepherded all the girls from the drawing room.

"That was very well done of you, my lord," she said after the footmen had withdrawn.

"I am glad you appreciate my sacrifice," Marcus replied lightly. "You can't imagine how painful it was, having to fend off a bevy of giggling schoolgirls. I was squirming the entire time."

That brought Arabella's laugh bubbling up. "No one could tell you were the least discomfited."

Marcus eyed her narrowly. "You enjoyed seeing me at such a disadvantage, didn't you, vixen?"

"Only a little." She had indeed expected him to be disadvantaged by the circumstances she had purposely thrown at him, but he had won her admiration instead. "I do appreciate your sacrifice, truly. Our parents will be highly impressed that their daughters took tea with a genuine earl."

His mocking smile was enticing. "Anything for you, my charmer."

Arabella's expression sobered. "Seriously, Marcus, I must thank you for today. You handled our pupils with admirable tact and grace, especially Miss Fletcher."

"I'm pleased to have won your approbation, but you can thank my sister for educating me on how to deal with young ladies." He rose from the settee and offered his hand to Arabella, who also stood. "Allow me to escort you home in my carriage."

For once she was sorry to have to refuse his company. "Forgive me, but I cannot leave just yet. I need to speak privately with Gladys Fletcher to make certain she hasn't suffered any lasting trauma from the spilled tea incident. And I want to have a word with Sybil Newstead as well."

"She is a little witch, isn't she?"

"Indeed. Girls that age can be savage, and Sybil is the worst. She is our wealthiest heiress and our most troublesome, even though this is only her first year. Keeping control of her has been difficult."

"What did she do that was so egregious?"

"What *hasn't* she done? She smuggled three bottles of brandy into the dormitory and made half her schoolmates drunk. She tried to seduce a footman and had him so flustered that he begged to be sent to another place of employment. She ran up enormous bills at her dressmakers, so that her father threatened to withdraw her from school if we couldn't keep a tighter rein on her. Since then we've had to employ a full-time maid to keep a careful watch on her."

Marcus chuckled. "Your other pupils are clearly fond of you. You have an impressive way with them."

"Thank you," Arabella replied earnestly as she accompanied him to the drawing room door. "I try to mold their characters as well as polish their manners, but mainly I strive to give them the confidence to overcome their lack of genteel birth. I don't believe anyone should be condemned simply because her blood is not blue."

"Your radical notions would not sit well with our peers," Marcus said humorously. When they reached the corridor, he paused. "You will have dinner with me this evening?"

Arabella hesitated. "Yes, but I forgot to mention, I have invited our patroness, Lady Freemantle, to dine with us."

Marcus sent her a knowing look. "So you can avoid being alone with me."

She dimpled. "In large part. But also because Winifred is eager to make your acquaintance. She has met you on several occasions, although she doubts that you remember her."

"Oh, I remember her. She is very hard to forget."

"That she is," Arabella agreed. Winifred Freemantle was a large, ruddy-faced woman with a booming voice and an accent that betrayed her lower class origins. "But she is a dear friend."

"And obviously one of your staunchest allies. In that case, it will behoove me to try to impress her. I will have my carriage return here shortly to bring you home."

Arabella nodded before summoning a footman with

instructions to escort Lord Danvers to his carriage. When Marcus had taken his leave of her, she turned the opposite way in order to seek out her pupils, but she still felt that little glow of warmth that had lingered throughout his entire visit.

Her benevolent feelings did not last through dinner.

That evening when Lady Freemantle arrived, Marcus was all attentive charm, and Winifred succumbed to his blandishments like butter melting under a hot sun. By their first glass of wine, he was well on the way to winning her over as an ally.

In his defense, Arabella admitted with grudging admiration, he truly seemed to enjoy her ladyship's company.

Nearly a decade older than Marcus, Winifred treated him with matronly affection, although there was nothing matronly about her heavy-boned, mannish features and coarse manners that were more at home in the stables than an elegant drawing room. But her jovial nature was so warm and infectious that the two of them were soon laughing and sharing tales of their London acquaintances. Much worse, Winifred began confiding in Marcus as if they were old cronies.

Arabella's heart sank as she watched. She had counted on her friend to champion her cause against Marcus, but it was clear before they even went in to dinner that he had made another conquest.

Once again the meal was delicious—sole in cream sauce, fricassee of rabbit, pigeon pie, and Winifred's favorite, a roast of beef, with tarts and syllabub for the sweets. Yet Arabella didn't find the dishes quite as delectable when the subject somehow turned to matrimony.

"My beauty isn't what appealed to Sir Rupert, as you can tell," her ladyship said with frank good humor. " 'Twas the size of my dowry, no mistake. A large dowry can cover up any number of faults in a female, even homely looks."

Marcus sent Arabella an innocent glance. "I had planned to settle a large sum on my wards."

Beaming at him, Winifred bobbed her head in approval. "I knew you were a right 'un, Lord Danvers. I've worried prodigiously about Arabella and her sisters these past few years. But a dowry will make it much easier for them to find husbands."

"Winifred," Arabella protested. "I thought you supported our intentions to remain single."

"No, dear. I want you to have a choice about who . . . *whom* you wed, but you need to marry eventually. That's the only future for a lady of quality."

"I have been trying to tell her so," Marcus said, his eyes laughing.

"You should listen to your guardian, Arabella," Winifred said quite seriously. "Lord Danvers might even be willing to drum up some good candidates for you. Suitable husbands don't grow on trees, you know. With his connections, you might be able to make a good match after all."

"Well, actually . . ." Marcus remarked, "I already have found the ideal candidate for her."

Winifred turned to him with keen curiosity. "Who?"

"Myself. I have proposed to Miss Loring, but she has refused."

Her ladyship looked startled, while Arabella shot him a reproachful glance. She hadn't yet told her friend about Marcus's proposal or their wager, and she regretted that he had brought it up now when she would rather have explained the situation to Winifred in private.

Winifred was still eyeing him in disbelief. "Is that the truth? You *proposed,* my lord? I wouldn't have taken you for the marrying kind."

"I wasn't until last week. I took one look at Miss Loring and was smitten."

Her ladyship's chuckle resembled something of a horse's whinny, while her brown eyes started dancing. "I always heard you were a wicked charmer. I can see why you have a bevy of lovestruck mistresses and admirers all trying to set traps for you."

"Winifred!" Arabella exclaimed again. "It is hardly proper to speak of a gentleman's mistresses at the dining table."

"Now, don't be so missish, dear. You know I believe in plain speaking. And if you want my advice, you could do much worse than to wed his lordship."

"See," Marcus interjected with a provocative glance at Arabella, "even your patroness thinks you should accept me."

Winifred continued as if Arabella wasn't there. "You won't find it easy to win her over, my lord, but don't be discouraged just because she doesn't want you right this minute. Persistence, that's the key. You should take a page from my late husband's book. He practically had to fight off my other suitors, which is why my papa chose him for me—because he admired Rupert's persistence. And even though Rupert only wanted me for my fortune, it turned out to be a good enough marriage. We became right fond of each other." Her eyes suddenly shimmered with tears. "I miss him with a powerful ache sometimes."

She sniffed loudly, then turned her attention to Arabella again. "Which is why, my girl, you don't want to remain an old maid all your life. I know you have your reasons for not wanting to wed, but loneliness is a bleak bedfellow."

With effort, Arabella managed a smile. "I will keep that in mind, Winifred. Now, may we please change the subject? All this pointless talk about marrying Lord Danvers has diminished my appetite."

Arabella was glad when they obliged, but to her chagrin, Winifred was not willing to give up the subject entirely. She brought it up again an hour later when she took her departure. While Marcus waited politely on the front landing, Arabella accompanied her ladyship down the steps to her carriage.

"I think you should seriously consider wedding Lord Danvers," Winifred whispered in a voice loud enough to carry back to the house. "That magnificent specimen of manhood would make you a fine bedfellow, I'll wager."

Arabella felt her cheeks flame, knowing that Marcus had overheard. "That is *not* a wager I intend to take, Winifred."

She was determined to pretend indifference, but when she returned to the house, Marcus stood blocking her way to the entrance hall, his blue eyes alive with humor.

"Don't say it," Arabella warned as she brushed past him.

"Say what, love?" he asked innocently as he followed her inside and shut the door.

"Whatever you intended to say. No doubt you meant to remind me of your superior qualities as a bedfellow."

He chuckled but shook his head. "You malign me unjustly. I merely wanted to invite you to accompany me on a picnic tomorrow."

She gave him a curious glance. "A picnic? I would not have expected you to be fond of picnics."

"I am in this instance, since it's how I wish to spend some of my allotted time with you tomorrow. I'll order a lunch packed, and we'll drive my curricle instead of riding. That way you won't be able to gallop off and leave me to eat your dust."

Arabella hesitated. The prospect of a picnic with Marcus was indeed appealing, even if it afforded him another opportunity to seduce her into accepting his proposal. Yet she *had* agreed to his terms, promising him a sporting chance to woo her. Moreover, she owed him for his kindness to her pupils this afternoon.

"Very well," Arabella replied evenly. "I would be pleased to accompany you on a picnic tomorrow, my lord. For now . . . good night."

When she mounted the sweeping staircase, however, Marcus remained only a few steps behind. And at the head of the stairs, when she turned left toward her bedchamber, he continued to accompany her.

When she was halfway down the corridor, Arabella came up short and gave him a look of exasperation. "What do you mean, following me this way, Marcus?"

"I am merely escorting you to your room."

"I am entirely capable of finding my room on my own."

"Of course you are, sweeting, but I want a moment of privacy with you."

When he took her hand and drew her along the deserted corridor toward her door, Arabella tried nervously to pull back. "Our allotted time was more than fulfilled today."

"I will borrow from tomorrow's allotment."

"You cannot enter my bedchamber, Marcus!"

"I don't intend to."

Although hardly reassured, Arabella ceased resisting, knowing it would do little good.

Guiding her into the adjacent music room, Marcus shut the door behind them and turned to face her. "This should prove adequate."

"Adequate for what?" she asked, her voice suddenly breathless.

"For your next lesson. We won't be interrupted here."

"But I don't need another lesson."

Those midnight blue eyes glinted down from beneath heavy brows. She had only to look into those compelling eyes, gleaming with wicked knowledge, to feel aroused.

"Yes, you do."

Arabella felt her heart quicken alarmingly at the sensual smile that curved Marcus's mouth as he advanced toward her. She retreated a step, holding up her hand to ward him off. "Aren't you aware that when a lady says she doesn't want a gentleman's attentions, it is rude to disbelieve her?"

"Since I never attended your academy, I never learned that particular rule." He caught her hand and halted her retreat. "I mean to educate your senses, sweet Arabella." Raising her hand to his mouth, he pressed his lips to the tender middle of her palm. A soft gasp escaped her at the erotic feel.

"You did this yesterday," she pointed out even more breathlessly.

"No. Yesterday I taught you about the power of touch. Today we'll focus on the power of taste."

"Taste?"

"Kissing, love." His tongue flicked out to lightly dampen her palm, making her gasp again. "I won't use my hands this time. I intend to teach you about kissing using just my mouth, to let you learn the taste of me."

Her heart leapt with excitement. And even though she parted her lips to issue a protest, she couldn't find her voice. The deplorable truth was, she wanted this lesson. She had no doubt that the tame pecks her betrothed had once given her would be nothing compared to Marcus's devastating kisses.

When she didn't reply, he offered her another enchanting smile. Still keeping hold of her hand, he turned Arabella and guided her until her back was pressed again to the wall. Then releasing his grasp, he bent his head.

His warm breath eddied and caressed her lips before he kissed her lightly. His mouth brushed sparks across the surface of hers, jolting her pulse into a wild rhythm, yet Arabella held herself still, fighting the overwhelming temptation to kiss him back.

Marcus lifted his head to study her. "No response? I see I will have to do better."

His dark lashes lowering over his vivid eyes, he bent again, his mouth warm and vibrant as it settled on hers with slow, sure pressure. This time Arabella couldn't keep still, not with all the incredible sensations spiraling through her.

"Open for me, Arabella," Marcus murmured against her lips as she shivered.

His mouth coaxed and beguiled until she did as he bid. Immediately his tongue delved inside, exploring in a sensual invasion that dazed her with pleasure and completely stole her breath away.

It was a long, long moment before she realized he had broken off to ask her a question. "How does that taste?"

Delicious, was Arabella's unspoken reply. The taste of him was exquisite and filled her with a hungry yearning. Her senses dazed, she gazed back at him mutely, grateful to have the wall supporting her back, since her limbs had grown so weak. When finally she licked her lips in response, she saw Marcus's eyes flare.

He took his time, however, when his kiss resumed. This caress was languid and intimate, his mouth mating with hers while his tongue played in a leisurely, erotic dance. Arabella closed her eyes at the surge of desire sweeping through her, oblivious to everything but the movement of his enchanting mouth, his beguiling penetration.

She wanted to whimper in disappointment when at length he ended the kiss, but thankfully, he didn't leave her entirely. Instead, his lips traveled upward, feathering across her cheek to her temple.

"You have the most erotic mouth I have ever tasted," he murmured.

"So do you," Arabella replied honestly.

His soft laugh was a warm burst of breath against her skin. The intoxicating sensation sent a shiver of pleasure rippling down her spine, but when he touched his lips to her ear, drawing the lobe into his mouth, she gave a helpless moan.

"I want to taste your breasts," Marcus added.

His whispered words, so provocative and tantalizing, made her breasts tingle shamefully.

She should pull away, Arabella told herself when she felt his hands moving at her back, working loose the hooks of her gown, but all she could do was stand there quivering, her heart pounding. She watched, spellbound as he drew down her bodice to reveal the rounded swells of her breasts above her chemise and corset. Then he tugged down the edge of her chemise to expose the rose-hued crests.

His eyes flashed at the sight.

"Marcus . . ."

"Hush, you'll like this."

His husky murmur silenced her. Another tremor shook Arabella when she realized he meant to kiss her bare breasts, but she did nothing to stop him.

His gaze burned her as he bent lower, and then so did his breath as it fanned against her tender skin. At the delicate flicker of his tongue against her sensitive flesh, Arabella inhaled a sharp gasp. But when he grazed the tip of her nipple with his tongue, her breath fled altogether.

His teasing, velvet-rough tongue stroked her for a long moment, making her shudder with pleasure. Then with expert skill he drew the soft, swollen bud into his mouth, suckling the aching aureole. A whimper escaped her lips, while her hands rose to tangle in his raven hair. The brazen heat that coiled inside her was almost too intense to bear; it spiraled downward to the pulsing core of her body, weakening her further.

Eventually, though, Marcus shifted his arousing ministrations to her other breast, sucking more powerfully and sending another shaft of fire down to her loins. Stunned, Arabella arched toward him while the muscles of her inner thighs tightened almost painfully.

It was Marcus who drew back this time, however, leaving her hot and wanting.

Pressing his forehead against hers, he held himself rigid, as if straining for willpower. "I had best stop while I still can."

"What . . . if I don't want you to stop?"

He gave a ragged laugh. "God, don't tempt me." Finally he drew a measured breath and stepped back.

"Go to bed, Arabella . . . *Alone*. Before I forget that I'm a gentleman and decide to join you."

She swallowed in an effort to control her jagged breathing, yet it was impossible to recover her dazed senses so abruptly.

As she straightened her disheveled bodice, Marcus opened the door and checked the corridor. "The coast is clear."

His hands moving to her shoulders, he pressed another light, all-too-fleeting kiss on her lips before turning her and sending her from the room.

Still half dazed, Arabella hurried down the hall and slipped into her bedchamber next door.

Her breath was still ragged as she shut herself inside, her nipples jewel-hard, her limbs hopelessly weak. It was a long while before her erratic heartbeat slowed, and even longer before she gathered her scattered senses enough to begin preparing for bed.

Arabella removed the pins from her hair and brushed out the red-gold tresses, then took off her gown, her task made easier because the hooks had been unfastened earlier by Marcus's dexterous hands. When she entered her dressing room, she caught sight of her flushed face in the cheval glass. She looked like a perfect wanton.

Chiding herself not so much for her brazen conduct as her too-easy surrender, she hung her gown in the wardrobe. When she opened the door to the clothespress where she kept her nightclothes and undergarments, however, she froze as the scent of roses greeted her.

Arabella bit back a helpless laugh. Marcus had scattered red rose petals all over her lingerie.

There was no use protesting his wicked intimacy, she knew, for he would claim to be justified in using any means necessary to court her. And she had to admit his methods were effective. Knowing he had been here in her dressing room, touching her undergarments—her chemises, her corsets, her stockings, her nightshifts—brought a flood of sinful images to her mind, including a powerfully potent one . . . of Marcus divesting her of those same garments as easily as he had exposed her upper body a brief while ago.

Her skin flushed with heat as she remembered how he'd drawn down her bodice and kissed her bare breasts, how his wonderful mouth had lovingly teased and fondled her nipples. He'd demonstrated more than just the power of taste tonight; he'd shown her what he would be like as her lover.

At the burning memory, Arabella raised one of the rose petals to her lips, inhaling the sweet fragrance. His devastating kisses just now were his latest lesson in the spark and fire between a man and a woman, and admittedly, the experience had stunned her. He'd not only aroused feminine yearnings she had forcibly buried when her betrothed had deserted her four years ago; Marcus had ignited a desire—no, a *hunger*—in her that she'd never even known existed.

A hunger she couldn't help wanting to explore.

And as she stood there quivering, she heard an insistent little voice whispering in her mind: *What would happen if you gave in to him?*

Wisely quelling the question, Arabella blew out a shaky breath as she began gathering up errant rose petals. The seductive devil was even more dangerous than she had feared. It unnerved her, the lengths Marcus was willing to go to to win their wager, even though she couldn't help but secretly admire his tenacity. He was a man who controlled his own fate, who refused to let anything stand in his way, including *her*. He was determined to wear down her resistance—and he was starting to succeed, blast him.

In her own defense, Arabella reminded herself, any female in her right mind would be thrilled by his romantic wooing, and she was no different. She might have disavowed any prospects of love and matrimony, but she was only human.

The trouble was, the temptation to succumb to his beguiling seduction was growing more irresistible by the moment.

Chapter Seven

✤

*I understand now what you meant about passion—
and why a woman might throw caution to the wind
for a taste of it.*

—Arabella to Fanny

To Arabella's dismay, she succumbed the very next day. She couldn't blame Marcus entirely, however. Her own feminine weakness was as much at fault as his male perseverance.

Admittedly, she was glad to accompany him on an alfresco luncheon in the countryside, for even though she found pleasure in redecorating the house, the outing was a treat that gave her a respite from the demands of the tradesmen as well as her duties at the academy.

She also had to admit that she enjoyed being with Marcus, particularly since he put himself out to be charming as he expertly drove his curricle along the country lanes.

For their picnic spot, he chose a glade beside the river that was open to the sky but protected from prying eyes by chestnut and sycamore trees. After helping Arabella down from his curricle, he spread a blanket on the grass and gallantly led her to it.

When she had settled there, Marcus sat beside her and opened the straw basket to reveal a small feast of roasted chicken and bread and several kinds of fruit. He served her plate, then his, and poured them each a generous glass of wine. As she ate, Arabella sat with her legs tucked under her, her blue muslin skirts arranged demurely around her. Marcus stretched out on his side, his head propped on one elbow.

The warmth of the spring sunshine contributed to the tranquility of the setting. When Arabella was nearly finished eating, however, she purposefully broke the mellow silence. "This is quite lovely, Marcus, but you shouldn't go to all this trouble to court me." She gestured at the feast. "It won't change my mind about wedding you."

Marcus smiled. "If I could endure the torture of taking tea with your pupils, the least you can do is allow me the chance to play the romantic lover."

"True. And I have every intention of fulfilling the terms you set. But honestly, I don't understand your insistence." She regarded him inquisitively. "You know you don't truly want to wed me. You only want to win our wager."

Marcus eyed her over the rim of his glass, contemplating her statement. In fact, making Arabella share time with him each day so he could woo her was no longer solely about winning her agreement to wed him.

He simply wanted to be with her. Wanted her company for the pleasure of having her near. To his genuine surprise, these past few days he'd found himself making excuses to avoid returning to London to deal with his pressing business affairs. He couldn't ever remember that happening with any other woman.

The plain truth was, he felt comfortable with Arabella. He could talk to her and laugh with her as well. He delighted in sparring with her and found himself glad to earn her smiles. He even liked her stubbornness.

Marcus bit back a chuckle, remembering the way her gray eyes had danced with mischief yesterday when she'd made him sit through four rounds of tea with her awestruck pupils. If that was the sort of torment he could expect in a future with Arabella, then he would gladly endure it.

He took a long swallow of wine, acknowledging his remarkable change of heart. The thought of being leg-shackled for life no longer gave him chills. Not if the shackle was Arabella. For the first time in his life, he wanted something more for his future than simply to carry on his titles and estates.

He truly wanted Arabella for his wife.

She wouldn't believe him, of course. She thought his courtship was only a diversion for him. But it was no longer a game. He was wholly determined now to claim her for his bride.

Only during the past hour, however, had he been able to identify why: Because Arabella added a spark of fire to his life that, until now, he hadn't even realized was missing. With her, he felt alive in a way he'd never felt before—lighthearted and reckless and filled with exhilaration.

He felt lust also, of course. And desire. Arabella might be sexually inexperienced, but she was more woman than any of his former mistresses, and he wanted her far more.

A vibrantly sensual woman who stirred his senses.

Now, however, he would do his best to wreak havoc on Arabella's senses. He'd been successful in getting past some of her defenses, but gaining her full capitulation would be difficult. Arabella was still vulnerable to hurt, despite her declarations to the contrary.

A wave of tenderness hit Marcus as he studied her. She had been betrayed by her idiot betrothed, who was fool enough to value his consequence more than her. And after her parents' warlike marriage, she wasn't willing to risk suffering any sort of callous union of convenience.

Marcus knew their own marriage would be very different—far from cold-blooded. But he would have to change Arabella's perspective by escalating the intimacy of their relationship.

He wanted to show her pleasure she'd never even dreamed of, for her own sake as well as the sake of his courtship and his own gratification. She truly had no idea what she was missing by disavowing men. Marcus was convinced that once she understood how pleasurable their marriage bed would be, she would be much more inclined to accept his proposal.

He also knew he would be playing with fire, considering the effort it took to control his own primal urges when he merely touched her. But an urgency was growing in him to win her and put an end to this state of uncertainty.

Resolving to make his next move, Marcus sat up and wiped his hands on a cloth napkin, then took her glass from her and set it aside.

At his unexpected action, Arabella suddenly grew tense. "Marcus, I was not finished eating."

"You can finish later. For now, it's time we proceeded to the next step in our courtship."

"What do you mean?" she asked warily.

"I intend to teach you about lovemaking."

She felt her heart start to pound. "We agreed you wouldn't go beyond the limits of gentlemanly conduct."

"But you want me to."

Arabella opened her mouth to deny it but couldn't.

When she fell mute, Marcus scrutinized her face. "Just because you refuse to marry me, doesn't mean you don't want to experience passion."

His assertion had a significant truth to it, Arabella acknowledged. She couldn't help wondering about passion. But she shook her head. "I won't do anything so shameless, Marcus. I mean to remain chaste outside the marriage bed."

"I can show you about passion without taking your virginity."

"I know." When his eyebrow shot up, she colored a little in embarrassment. "I am not entirely ignorant about lovemaking. A friend of mine told me about the procedure in detail."

Wry amusement curved his mouth. "What sort of friend would foster a proper young lady's carnal education?"

"A close childhood friend," Arabella responded, her chin lifting. "Fanny Irwin. I should think you would know her, since she is currently one of the most celebrated Cyprians in London."

"We have a passing acquaintance," Marcus replied mildly, "although I have never patronized her."

Somehow that casual revelation comforted Arabella. "Fanny is my age, but she is far more experienced than I. She was our neighbor in Hampshire before she left home to make a new life for herself in London's demimonde. We remained fast friends, even though her family disowned her for her wickedness." Arabella smiled a little defiantly. "I continued to acknowledge her during my comeout in London, before our own scandal, and afterward, Fanny was one of the few people who stuck by me and my sisters. She even visited us here on occasion after we came to live with our step-uncle. Fanny told me a good deal about her new life."

"And she satisfied your curiosity about lovemaking?"

"Well, I admit I *was* curious. And when I became betrothed, I asked her what I should expect on my wedding night. So I know in theory what is supposed to happen."

"But knowing in theory is not the same as experiencing for yourself," Marcus said. "Come, admit it. You want me to show you what our wedding night will be like."

At his confident tone, Arabella narrowed her gaze on him. "We will *not* be having a wedding night. And you cannot kiss me witless to convince me otherwise."

When his own eyes narrowed speculatively on her mouth, Arabella realized her mistake. "That was not a challenge," she hurriedly said.

"It *was* a challenge. My male pride is at stake."

"Marcus . . ." she exclaimed as he reached for her.

The smile he gave her was utterly beautiful and utterly maddening. "Let me demonstrate, darling."

Before she could scurry out of harm's way, he pulled her onto his lap and into his arms. Arabella opened her mouth to protest, but he took possession of it with searing deliberation. Clasping her nape in a firm hold, he gave her a lingering, blatantly sexual kiss that heated her blood and set her pulse racing.

She was breathless when Marcus finally broke off to gaze down at her. "You heard your patroness last night, Arabella. Loneliness is a bleak bedfellow."

She licked her tingling lips. "I don't need a husband to ward off loneliness. I have my sisters and my school."

"But those are not nearly as pleasurable. You don't want to remain a spinster all your life."

"I do so."

"No, you don't. You have too much fire and passion in your veins."

He bent his head again, this time brushing her lips with a much more tender kiss. "Don't you want to know what it is like to be fully a woman? What it is like to desire a man? To feel passion and pleasure and physical fulfillment?"

Arabella felt herself wavering, yet her long-held scruples stopped her from yielding. "I cannot make love to you, Marcus! It would be too scandalous."

"If you never intend to marry, what difference does it make if you keep your virginity?"

It was a rational argument, Arabella knew. And the truth was, she did want to know about passion. To know what she was missing in life. To experience the kind of intense pleasure Fanny had claimed was possible between lovers.

Arabella had no doubt that Marcus could show her. And she would likely never have another chance. At least not where she could be assured of keeping any sinful transgressions secret. As her guardian, Marcus was perhaps even more concerned for her reputation than she was, so he would do his best to remain discreet.

While she debated, however, he took the choice from her. Arabella felt herself being lowered to the blanket. Then he followed her down, stretching out beside her, his body half covering hers.

"I mean to use my hands and my mouth together this time," Marcus murmured against her lips. "The power of touch and taste combined."

She pressed her own hands against his chest, struggling for willpower, but he caught her lower lip between his teeth and tugged with soft nips. When Arabella gave a little whimper, his tongue soothed the sensitive flesh before dipping slowly, insistently, inside her mouth.

Finding him impossible to resist, she gave a tiny, shuddering sigh of defeat and returned his kiss helplessly.

His mouth was magical . . . and so was his touch, Arabella thought long moments later. While his kisses enchanted, his hand moved on her throat, then lower, his long fingers stroking her skin as he explored the contours of her breasts beneath the round neckline of her gown.

Shortly Arabella gave a start upon realizing that Marcus had lowered her bodice and chemise to expose her nipples, but the teasing caress of his fingers on her skin soothed her, his palm molding the ripe swells as his hot lips worked their spell. Arabella found herself arching against his touch, seeking more of the delicious pleasure he was arousing in her.

It was some time before he paused in his seduction and raised his head to contemplate her. His gaze was frankly, sharply male as it fixed on her bare breasts, surveying the high mounds crested with rosy nipples.

Arabella felt herself flushing. She was lying there wantonly, accepting his brazen scrutiny without protest. Yet when she made to cover her breasts with her hands, he caught her wrists and held them away.

"No, let me look."

It was arousing in itself, Arabella realized, to have Marcus studying her body. She never would have believed a simple look could be so titillating. The heat of his gaze, combined with the warm sunlight on her skin, made her restless and feverish.

And then his fingers joined his gaze, his knuckles brushing over her tautly straining nipples, dredging a soft gasp from her.

His eyes sparking at her helpless response, he plucked at the tight buds, pinching lightly and then soothing with his thumbs. Arabella nearly moaned at the sweet torment. "Marcus . . . you make me feel so . . ."

"So what?"

"Hot . . . like all my senses are inflamed."

His eyes darkened further. "I know."

He desired her, she knew. The thought gave her a powerfully feminine feeling to combat the vulnerability she felt lying here at his mercy. Determinedly, she returned his gaze, vowing she wouldn't run this time.

His eyes held hers, hot and blue, as he reached for the hem of her gown and drew it up above her knees. Then, very gently, he ran his hand up her stockinged calf to the bare skin of her thigh.

Arabella tensed until Marcus bent his lips to her again. "Just relax, love, and let me caress you," he murmured against her throat as he pushed her skirts higher.

What he asked was impossible, for when he eased her thighs open with his knee, the pressure on the sensitive core of her sent a shock of fire rippling through her.

He touched her frantic pulse with a stroke of his tongue while his hand dipped between her legs to find the wetness there. When she whimpered at his scandalous touch, Marcus kissed her again, a slow, lazy, possessive kiss that had her shivering. At the same time he used his fingers to stroke her, rimming the sleek cleft of her femininity, teasing the tiny bud hidden there.

Completely breathless now, Arabella reached for him and clutched at his shoulders. Her body was feverishly hot, straining against his hand as he continued his delicate ministrations . . . drawing his fingers between her feminine folds, cupping her naked center with his palm. When she began to pant, he drank deeply of her mouth, as if he treasured every gasp she surrendered to him.

And it *was* a surrender, Arabella realized dazedly,

unable to understand why she had fought him for so long.

She was filled with dismay when his kiss suddenly ended, then startled when he unexpectedly transferred his attentions below her waist. Dipping his dark head, Marcus settled his mouth on her inner thigh and began moving upward, tracing the earlier path of his fingers, trailing searing kisses on her skin.

It shocked Arabella when he pushed her skirts above her hips, baring all her secrets, and shocked her more when she felt his warm breath dampen the golden curls at the juncture of her thighs. She trembled violently as she realized his intention. He meant to kiss her there!

At the tender flick of his tongue over her sensitive flesh, she jerked, lifting her hips halfway off the blanket.

"Steady," he whispered, his hands moving to her thighs to hold her down.

His tongue stroked her, probing her folds. Then he drew the swollen bud into his mouth as his middle finger slipped inside her.

The sensation was incredible—his hard finger sheathed in her flesh, his scalding mouth working its magic on her sex.

Her breath coming in hoarse whimpers, Arabella shut her eyes, her head shifting desperately back and forth on the blanket. She was unbearably hot, filled with tension and excitement and wild anticipation.

Her hands clenching spasmodically, she gripped Marcus's shoulders, clinging blindly, seeking more of this fevered pleasure that had caught her up in a maelstrom of desire and frustration. She needed something she couldn't even begin to imagine, something that was clawing at her, tearing her apart.

Yet Marcus wouldn't give her surcease. When she uttered a low, keening moan, the growl in the back of his throat signaled his approval. He continued laving her, caressing her, arousing and teasing and tormenting until she thought she might die from the wild pleasure he had kindled in her.

Then suddenly her senses exploded. Arabella cried out as reality splintered into a thousand sensual fragments of pleasure and her entire world dissolved in pulsing heat.

She was only dimly aware of the passage of time. Even when her pounding heart slowed, she lay there limp and unmoving. Her whole body felt gloriously weak and blissful from the ecstasy Marcus had given her.

When finally she regained her senses, it was to find him stretched out beside her, watching her tenderly.

"See now what you have been missing?"

Yes, she saw very clearly. His lovemaking had stunned her. She'd been overwhelmed by a storm of emotion and sensation.

This was what made sensible women turn insensible, Arabella realized. Yet her insensibility had a great deal to do with Marcus himself. He was undoubtedly a magnificent lover.

"It is no wonder," she murmured hoarsely, "that females fall all over themselves trying to attract your attention."

"I am gratified you noticed."

He smiled lazily down at her, a dark glint in his blue eyes, as solicitously, he drew down her skirts to cover her bare limbs.

Arabella sat up shakily. Something was missing, though. According to her friend Fanny, there was much more to lovemaking than what Marcus had just shown her. She eyed him in puzzlement until it struck her: He had seen to her pleasure but not his own.

Her gaze slid downward toward his hips, where she could see his buff breeches straining across the thick bulge at his groin. "That is all you mean to do?"

His eyebrow rose to his hairline. "You weren't satisfied?"

"No . . . I mean, yes, of course I was. It's just that . . . I understand that it is painful for a man to be aroused without . . . you know."

He laughed softly. "It *is* painful, love—almost excruciating. But I will endure it. You are not yet ready for your next lesson. Now the anticipation will make it all the more pleasurable when I finally make love to you completely."

The prospect of Marcus making love to her completely made Arabella's pulse leap with wild excitement, but she didn't mean for it to happen. Rather than argue, though, she said somewhat shyly, "Would you like me to . . . to stroke you to ease your pain?"

The amused tenderness in his expression grew. "You are all kindness, to be so concerned with my comfort."

"It seems only fair," Arabella said, another blush rising to inflame her cheeks.

"In point of fact, I can deal with the ache myself."

When he reached down to unfasten the front of his breeches, she automatically lowered her gaze again. Her eyes widened as comprehension dawned: Marcus meant her to view his naked loins.

Her breath went shallow as he drew out his long member. Thick and darkly rigid, it jutted out from a sprinkling of crisp black hair at his groin. The sight of that huge, swollen arousal caused her throat to go dry, her stomach to contract.

"I presume you have never seen a naked man before," Marcus remarked.

"No," Arabella rasped.

"Are you shocked?"

Not shocked exactly, she thought dazedly. Despite her genteel upbringing, regardless of the dictates of modesty, she was captivated by the sight of him. Indeed, she would have liked to see all of Marcus naked. She suspected his body was far more beautiful than any other man's. Virile, masculine, hard, corded with lean muscle.

While she stared, he cradled his shaft, running his thumb over the blunt, velvety head. The casually erotic caress made her breath catch.

"You should watch as I pleasure myself," he suggested.

Fascinated, she could do nothing else. Her eyes fixed on his loins, unable to look away, as he cupped the heavy sacs beneath his phallus.

"Of course this would be much more pleasurable

with you," Marcus said, curling his hand around his turgid length and squeezing.

Arabella inhaled a sharp breath when he began moving his hand slowly up and down, stroking himself.

"I'm imagining making love to you right now, sweet Arabella. It's very arousing."

She swallowed hard. It was indeed arousing. She felt a shameful thrill at the intimate picture Marcus painted.

"Can you imagine having me inside you?" he asked as he gripped his heavy shaft harder. When she didn't reply, he raised his head. "I would like very much to be inside you, Arabella."

He met her eyes, held them intently, as deliberately he increased the pace of his strokes. Shortly his face became tense with control, the skin flushed, Arabella saw. The teasing glint in the blue depths darkened into something both primitive and powerful.

Her heart began to pound while an aching tightness coiled throughout her body. She could almost feel Marcus's lengthy shaft gliding slickly between her feminine folds . . .

His jaw locked as his fingers kneaded harder, sweeping up and down his tumescence in swift jerky motions. His breath was harsh and uneven . . . until his climax came abruptly.

Clenching his teeth, Marcus shut his eyes and arched against the explosive release. A low groan escaped him, but as his pulsing seed shot out, he captured the spurting milky liquid in his cupped palm.

Arabella watched, her heart thundering in her ears. Her body felt as if it had suddenly burst into flames with him.

When a moment later Marcus opened his eyes, he smiled. "Regrettably, my little exercise in self-satisfaction is only a temporary solace. I still want you as fiercely as before."

Arabella couldn't find the voice to respond. She was still staring at him, her lips parted, her breath shallow.

He took out a handkerchief from his coat pocket and wiped his hand clean, then quite calmly refastened his breeches. She remained speechless even when he sat up and fastened his gaze on her still bare breasts.

Then he reached up to brush her nipples with his thumbs, making her gasp again. "Now that you know the kind of pleasure you can feel," Marcus murmured, "you will be anticipating our lovemaking with relish."

Before she could deny his prediction, he drew up her chemise and then her muslin bodice to cover her breasts. "However, we don't need to debate the issue now. Finish your wine, sweetheart, so I may take you home. You have another class to give this afternoon, remember?"

"Y-yes . . . I remember."

Arabella shook herself. She did have a class later today, yet her dazed mind had trouble concentrating on such mundane matters when she could still feel the erotic stroke of his hands and mouth on her body, still imagine his hard flesh moving inside her. Marcus had given her a stunning experience she would never, ever forget. . . .

Arabella felt herself frowning as she readjusted her clothing into some semblance of decency. It wasn't his lovemaking that was so troubling, she suddenly realized. It was that for the first time in her life, she could begin to understand her mother . . . why her mother had succumbed to the incredible pleasure an attentive lover could bring.

Of course, *she* would never fall in love and lose her head over a man the way her mother had done, Arabella vowed. She would never destroy her family for the sake of her own amorous gratification, no matter how rapturous.

Her gaze went to Marcus as he gathered up the remains of their picnic.

But at least now, however, she could wholly understand the temptation.

Chapter Eight

❧

I must concede I was mistaken about the earl. He has some redeeming qualities after all.

—Arabella to Fanny

"Roslyn, Lily . . . whatever are you doing here?" Arabella asked when she found her sisters waiting in the academy's reception office where she and the headmistress conducted the business of running the school. "You are not scheduled to teach any classes this afternoon."

"We came to discover how you are faring," Roslyn replied, a look of concern on her lovely face, "and to see if you need our help. Since we couldn't very well visit you at home, we thought this would be the best place. Tess told us the alarming news, Arabella—that Lord Danvers actually proposed to you."

"Yes," Lily agreed, her expression even more troubled. "How in heaven's name did that happen, Belle? The earl has only been here for four days and already you are making outrageous wagers with him?"

Had Marcus only been here for four days? Arabella reflected in amazement. It seemed like far longer.

Debating on how much to reveal, she settled in a wing chair opposite her sisters. "Did Tess also tell you the stakes involved? Lord Danvers promised to grant us our legal and financial freedom if I can manage to resist his courtship for a fortnight. The prospect was too enticing to pass up."

"She told us," Roslyn said. "And we appreciate the sacrifice you are making for us—"

"But we are worried for you," Lily interrupted. There was none of the usual laughter in her warm brown eyes. "Tess says his lordship is sinfully handsome and charming."

And enchanting and irresistible, Arabella thought.

Aloud, she sighed. "Regrettably, he is. But I agreed to give him a fair chance to woo me."

She proceeded to give her sisters an edited account of what had happened between them the past few days, leaving out entirely Marcus's lessons in passion.

"This is our opportunity to win emancipation from his guardianship for good," Arabella concluded.

Lily frowned. "So he doesn't mean to make us abandon the academy or force us to marry?"

"Not if I can win the wager."

"Tess said you found him more agreeable than expected," Roslyn added, "but what sort of man is he?"

Arabella had no ready answer for that. After seeing Marcus yesterday with her pupils, she had to concede that he was someone she could admire and respect. Or so he seemed on the surface. One couldn't fully judge a person's character so quickly. And thus far he was acting the ideal suitor in hopes of convincing her he would make the ideal husband.

"He is indeed much more reasonable than his solicitors' letters led us to believe," she admitted.

"There is no chance the earl will win your wager, is there?" Lily asked, still worried. "He won't convince you to accept his proposal? You have always said you wouldn't risk being miserable in a marriage of convenience, Belle."

Arabella smiled reassuringly. "You needn't distress yourself. I haven't changed my opinion about marriage in the least."

She might not be able to resist Marcus's devastating kisses but she had no intention of wedding him. She certainly wouldn't be so gullible as to let herself fall in love again, and true love was the only thing that could possibly induce her to brave the perils of betrothal and marriage a second time. She was much wiser now, more careful with her heart.

"Do you want us to come home and help you deal with the earl?" Roslyn asked. "We promised Tess we would finish her charity baskets by next week, but your welfare is more important just now."

"Yes," Lily seconded. "Perhaps we *should* come home to support you against the earl."

"Thank you, but no," Arabella replied. "I am dealing with him well enough, truly. And contributing those baskets to the war families means so much to Tess."

She was about to inquire how her sisters were faring when she heard footsteps out in the corridor, then a soft rap on the door. When she bid entrance, the headmistress, Miss Jane Caruthers, entered, followed by a tall, athletic, raven-haired gentleman who was instantly recognizable, even before Jane announced their visitor. "Lord Danvers to see you, Arabella."

Arabella froze as her gaze connected with a pair of keen blue eyes. It unsettled her that Marcus had shown up uninvited at her school, not merely because she had hoped to keep her sisters safely concealed from him for a while longer until she could be certain of his intentions, but because his presence here now badly flustered her.

She couldn't help recalling that two hours ago she was lying in his arms, hot and damp and clinging, while he roused cries of pleasure from her. Arabella flushed at the memory, still feeling the warmth and strength of his hands on her skin, the eroticism of his kisses.

And Marcus, blast him, was clearly remembering too, she realized as their gazes locked for an instant. The heat in his eyes raised her temperature; the intensity of his look made her feel as if he'd put his wonderful hands on her, his sensual, sinful mouth. . . .

Chiding herself, Arabella rose to her feet, while Lily murmured, "Speak of the devil."

"Oh, were you discussing me?" Marcus said blandly, turning his attention to the younger sisters. "You must be my lovely missing wards."

As Jane bowed herself out and shut the door behind her, Arabella stepped forward protectively. Knowing there was no choice, however, she made the introductions.

When she was done, Marcus bowed and treated her sisters to the full force of his devastating smile. "It is a pleasure to meet you at last, ladies."

Roslyn blinked at the sight, while Lily narrowed her

eyes. "We cannot say the same, my lord. We would much prefer that you return to London and leave us alone."

"What my sister means, my lord," Roslyn said more politely, "is that we believe your guardianship to be unnecessary."

"I know you do. But surely you will allow me the chance to prove I'm not the villain you think me."

Rather than succumb to his blatant male appeal, however, Lily determinedly returned his gaze. "You must admit that your actions have been rather villainous thus far. Your solicitors said you intend to find proper husbands for us."

"That was before I came to understand your particular circumstances," he replied mildly.

"It would be extremely unfair to make us give up teaching at the academy, my lord. We have striven for years to make it a success, especially Arabella. And now you are trying to make her wed you."

Marcus's half smile was meant to disarm. "I doubt I can 'make' your sister do anything she doesn't wish to do."

But obviously Lily still saw him as a threat. "Arabella won't be taken in by a handsome face or suave charm, you know."

Marcus shot her one of his roguish half grins. "Of course she won't. She is far too astute for that. Which is why I have endeavored to show her that I have more substance than the typical wealthy nobleman."

When Roslyn eyed him thoughtfully, Marcus continued in the same amiable tone. "I presume you are taking refuge with Miss Blanchard while I am residing at the Hall? Never fear, I have no intention of dragging you both home by your hair. In fact, I am pleased for the opportunity to court your sister in relative privacy—"

Arabella decided it was time to intervene before Marcus could expound on his wicked notions of privacy. "Why *have* you come here, my lord?"

"Why, to offer my services."

"Services?"

"As a dance partner during your lesson this afternoon. I understand you mean for your pupils to practice ballroom etiquette in preparation for the ball the local magistrate is holding on Monday. When I visited here yesterday, Miss Caruthers was lamenting that young ladies can only learn so much from a hired dancing master. So I thought to assist."

Arabella regarded him in surprise. His offer of assistance was beyond generous, considering how torturous it would be for Marcus to suffer another afternoon with a gaggle of schoolgirls.

Of course, he was still attempting to win her favor. Yet she could think of no good reason to decline. Her pupils would indeed benefit from having a real gentleman as a partner. Her sisters usually helped with the ballroom instruction, playing the male roles, but Marcus would be a significant improvement.

"Very well," Arabella said slowly, "if you are certain you don't mind?"

"I don't mind in the least," he assured her. "Your class starts shortly, doesn't it?"

"Yes, in a few moments." Arabella glanced at Roslyn, intent on offering her sisters a chance to escape the earl's focus. "I think we can manage without you this afternoon."

To her surprise, Roslyn shook her head. "I believe I will stay."

"So will I," Lily seconded with a penetrating look at Marcus. "I wouldn't dream of missing it."

Arabella suspected her sisters wanted the chance to observe their new guardian, and to provide her moral support as well. Touched by their concern, she preceded them to the ballroom, where their two dozen pupils were already assembled under the supervision of Miss Blanchard and Miss Caruthers.

Lord Danvers's arrival caused quite a stir. Two dozen pairs of female eyes lit up, not merely at the prospect of dancing with a real earl, Arabella suspected, but of dancing with such a handsome, charming one.

The girls first rehearsed entering the ballroom gracefully, pausing to be announced by the butler, being welcomed by the hosts' receiving line, then how to respond to requests to dance by various suppliants, including how to turn down undesirable partners. When finally they came to the actual dancing, Miss Caruthers moved to sit at the pianoforte to play.

Arabella was about to choose a partner for Marcus when he politely objected. "I would prefer my initial demonstration be with you, Miss Loring."

He had intended this all along, she realized with exasperation. But he allowed her no chance to demur as he took her hand to lead her onto the floor. Her pulse leapt deplorably at his mere touch, for it only reminded her of their tryst earlier this afternoon. And as they faced each other for a contra dance, waiting for the music to begin, Arabella realized she was discomfited for an additional reason: It felt strange to be dancing with *any* gentleman again.

This was the first time since her broken betrothal. In fact, she hadn't been to a real ball since then. Now, whenever she accompanied her pupils to the local public assemblies, she always sat out the dances, since she only attended to act as chaperone and instruct the academy's students. It was more fitting that way and prevented any gossip about a mere teacher not knowing her proper place.

She needed to prevent any gossip now, Arabella reminded herself as she met Marcus's blue gaze, for two dozen young ladies were looking on. She had to forget that passionate interlude with him this afternoon had ever occurred.

For the next few minutes, as he partnered her through the quick patterns of the dance, Arabella struggled to appear composed. His behavior was perfectly proper during the entire dance, but each time their hands met proved a severe distraction. She was usually quite a skilled dancer yet just now she seemed to have grown two left feet.

At the conclusion, Arabella felt absurdly flushed and breathless and so made a point of avoiding her sisters' gazes, knowing they were watching her dealings with Marcus with avid interest.

She was preparing to select another partner for him

when her least favorite pupil, Sybil Newstead, boldly stepped forward. "I should like to be first, Lord Danvers. The other girls don't need the practice, since very few of them have actually received invitations to Sir Alfred Perry's ball. I have, and so has Miss Blanchard." Sybil shot a sly look at Arabella. "Miss Loring has not been invited, nor has Miss Roslyn or Miss Lilian. They are considered too scandalous to mingle with the local gentry."

At Sybil's savage remark, Arabella sucked in a sharp breath, but Marcus responded before she could recover.

Lifting a black eyebrow, he raked the girl with bored scrutiny. "Did no one ever teach you it is impolite to gossip about your betters, Miss Newstead? I would say you don't need practice dancing; rather you need to work on your execrable manners."

Sybil's mouth dropped open, while her cheeks turned red with embarrassment. But Marcus was not done, it seemed. "Take care that you don't annoy the wrong people, for a ball invitation can always be withdrawn. I am acquainted with Sir Alfred, did you know?"

He spoke softly, lazily even, but there was no mistaking his implied threat to have Sybil expelled from local society, as the Loring sisters were.

Arabella stared at Marcus, both surprised and gratified that he had defended her against the girl, even if perhaps he'd been too harsh. It was undoubtedly a lesson Sybil would not soon forget.

Yet there was a more tactful way to teach her that such cruel behavior was unacceptable.

When the girl scowled, Arabella remarked gently, "A lady does not grimace when a gentleman displeases her, Sybil. Nor does she make remarks that can be hurtful to others."

"Yes, Miss Loring," Sybil muttered, her cheeks still scarlet.

"You know that in polite society you are judged by your every word and action. You do wish to be considered a lady, don't you?"

"Yes, of course, Miss Loring."

Arabella smiled encouragingly. "Then perhaps you will be kind enough to allow Miss Trebbs the opportunity to practice first with Lord Danvers."

"Oh, very well." Conspicuously struggling to bite her tongue, Sybil stepped back, but not before flinging Arabella a rebellious look.

Arabella calmly ignored the spoiled girl as the excited Miss Trebbs took the floor with Marcus. But when she herself moved to the sidelines, she caught sight of her sisters' expressions. Lily was simmering with suppressed anger and hurt at Sybil's nasty taunt, while Roslyn was pretending a cool dispassion that hid similar warring emotions.

Arabella shared their feelings. Since their parents' infamy had followed them all the way from Hampshire, they were not received in any of the better neighborhood households—in large part because their late step-uncle had publicly repudiated them for their mother's sins.

It was a bitter pill for Arabella to swallow, not so much for her own sake as for her sisters'. They had learned to accept the inevitable, but still it stung to be shunned by nearly all the local gentry for scandals their parents had created.

Arabella watched the practice sessions with only half her usual attention, and at the end she was distracted enough that she let Marcus usher her into his carriage to take her home when she had meant to avoid being alone with him so soon after their romantic rendezvous.

"So tell me," he said when the vehicle was moving, "why were you and your sisters not invited to Sir Alfred's ball?"

"I should think it obvious," Arabella replied, trying to keep her tone light. "The scandals still haunt us. In this district, no one who moves in higher circles will associate with the Loring sisters—other than Lady Freemantle and Miss Blanchard, of course." She shrugged. "I don't care about myself, really, but my sisters deserve better."

A muscle worked in Marcus's jaw. "I will see to it that you all three are invited to the ball. And I mean to escort you there myself."

She looked at him curiously. She had little doubt he could persuade Sir Alfred and Lady Perry to issue them invitations, but she couldn't understand why he would wish to. "You needn't go to such trouble, Marcus."

"I do need to. I won't have my wards being shunned, especially since you're being condemned through no fault of your own." He was angry on her behalf, she realized.

Arabella forced a smile. "It doesn't matter, truly. We are accustomed to being excluded. In any case, we have nothing appropriate to wear. Our ball gowns are four years out of fashion."

"Then you will order new ball gowns made."

"By Monday?"

"It can be done. I will send for a London modiste to attend you tomorrow."

"Marcus, it would cost a fortune to have gowns made on such short notice!"

"I happen to have a fortune, sweeting. And I can think of no better way to spend it."

This time Arabella shook her head firmly. "We don't need your charity."

"It isn't charity. As your guardian, I am obliged to provide for you."

Hearing the echo of her late step-uncle's complaints at being saddled with their upkeep, Arabella felt herself stiffen. "It is indeed charity, and we won't accept."

Marcus pinned her with a stern look. "Don't be tiresome, love. It is only your pride suffering."

Arabella scowled at him in return. "That is easy for *you* to say. You have obviously never been utterly dependent on anyone. You can't understand the helpless feeling—how humiliating it is to be beholden for every morsel of food and stitch of clothing on your back—"

"No, I cannot understand," he agreed sympathetically. "But your former guardian was a selfish, miserly bastard who deserved to have his teeth knocked down his throat for treating his own nieces like supplicants."

Then perhaps realizing how distressing the subject was for Arabella, Marcus softened his expression. "If you won't accept a new gown for your own sake, then do it for me. My pride is at stake. I won't have my wards dressed in rags. And surely you don't want to appear at a disadvantage in front of your pupils by appearing at the ball dressed in outmoded gowns."

When she hesitated, Marcus prodded, "Come now, confess it, Arabella. You would like to go, if only to prove that you and your sisters are as worthy as the haughty nobs who have scorned you all these years."

She couldn't deny that the thought had appeal. When she remained silent, however, Marcus continued. "I imagine your sisters would find it pleasant to be welcomed back by their peers . . . to take their rightful place in society. And so would you."

She looked away, surprised that Marcus seemed to understand her conflicted feelings. Four years ago, when she'd been disowned by her peers and many of the acquaintances she'd called friends, Arabella had held her head high—defiantly, in fact—refusing to let her life be governed by the fickle denizens of the Beau Monde. Yet there were times when she found herself longing for the kind of acceptance she had enjoyed since birth, before she and her sisters had become social pariahs. Even though she had pretended not to care, she *did* care, probably more than was wise. And she very badly wanted Roslyn and Lily to have the opportunities denied them when their familiar world had come crashing down around them.

Marcus's low tone was unexpectedly serious when he said, "I can see that you and your sisters are accepted in society again, Arabella." Then he caught her hand and made her look at him.

Arabella drew an uneven breath. The warmth in his eyes made it too easy for her to forget that she was supposed to be resisting his overtures. She was oddly touched by his concern, though. His protectiveness brought a strange ache to her throat.

It took effort to withdraw her hand from his grasp. "I would indeed like to attend the ball for my sisters' sake. . . ."

Marcus smiled slowly. "Then it's settled. I will escort the three of you. Have your sisters come to the Hall tomorrow morning to have their measurements taken by the modiste."

Arabella felt her mouth twisting in reluctant amusement as she eyed Marcus. "Only a nobleman would have the confidence to think he needs only snap his fingers to make the world do his bidding."

"Because it's true," he said amiably. "Never underestimate the power that comes with rank and wealth."

"Oh, I do not underestimate it, believe me."

His gaze leveled on her. "You could always accept my proposal of marriage. As Lady Danvers, you would be able to lord it over the entire neighborhood."

Arabella couldn't help but smile, as no doubt he'd meant her to. "That is a delightful notion . . . but even that treat won't tempt me to marry you, Marcus."

"Then I will have to think of some other means of convincing you. I can be quite resourceful when I put my mind to it, you know."

She found herself laughing softly as she turned to gaze out the carriage window. Somehow Marcus had managed not only to banish the dismay she'd felt over

Sybil's spiteful comment, but to lighten her spirits as well. It would be extremely gratifying if he could reinstate her sisters in society as he anticipated.

Hearing her husky laughter, Marcus felt an unfamiliar softening inside him. It was rather humbling to witness Arabella's fortitude. He'd never been subjected to the sort of blatant ostracism she had endured, not even for his most outrageous transgressions. For years Arabella had been unjustly humiliated and scorned for her parents' sins.

But, Marcus vowed, he intended to change that, even before she became his countess. By the time he was through, every high-browed member of the Quality in the district would be making amends to her.

Chapter Nine

✤

I never expected to be grateful to the earl, but I truly am.

—Arabella to Fanny

The next several days passed in a whirl for Arabella. Every available moment was filled with dress fittings and unexpected visitors in addition to ongoing house renovations and her usual classes at the academy.

To her astonishment, she began receiving calls from many of her hitherto disdainful neighbors. The first to appear were Sir Alfred and Lady Perry, who came the very next afternoon to issue a personal invitation to their ball.

Her ladyship practically fell all over herself welcoming the new Earl of Danvers to the neighborhood before she turned to Arabella. "We would be delighted, Miss Loring, if you and your charming sisters could join us for our ball," Lady Perry declared with an enthusiasm that was obviously feigned, since she had always cut the Loring sisters dead whenever they chanced to meet in public.

Arabella refrained from grinding her teeth at the hypocrisy and instead smiled serenely and returned a gracious thank-you.

But because Sir Alfred was the highly respected

magistrate of the district and his wife the acknowledged leader of local society, they set the example for the rest of the neighborhood.

Of course, Arabella knew, none of the gentry dared defy a nobleman of Lord Danvers's rank and consequence, yet it was Marcus's irresistible charm that made them eager to ingratiate themselves. Arabella was frankly awed by his ability to manipulate people into doing his bidding. She watched as time after time he had their callers lapping up his every word. And after the first two days, she no longer had any doubts that his efforts to restore the Loring sisters' social status would be successful.

Since he'd begun conducting his daily affairs from Danvers Hall, Marcus also had numerous visitors of his own, mainly business acquaintances—his solicitors, his estate steward from his family seat in Devonshire, and most frequently, his secretary.

Surprisingly, his secretary brought daily reports on matters concerning the House of Lords. Arabella discovered the fact when Marcus had to travel to London one morning to vote on the latest bill before the House.

When she expressed surprise that he followed the politics of the day, Marcus shrugged amiably. "My conversion to politics has been fairly recent. My good friend Drew—the Duke of Arden—wrenched my arm and convinced me I should take an interest. Drew's theory is that with privilege comes the responsibility of governing."

The revelation gave Arabella food for thought. She

had little familiarity with governmental affairs. Her step-uncle had never taken his seat in Parliament, although she knew that both he and her father had been conservative Tories rather than liberal Whigs, as Marcus professed to be. But it made her realize there was indeed more substance to Marcus than she had ever imagined.

What surprised Arabella most, however, was that he made no more overt physical overtures toward her. Oh, he still required her to spend their allotted time together in intimate dinners, but his lessons in passion had subsided entirely. Oddly, Arabella's relief at the respite was accompanied by an unmistakable disappointment; she had begun to eagerly anticipate the sensual duel of wits between them that usually ended with her flushed and feverish. Yet Marcus never attempted even so much as a kiss.

Instead, after dinner, he usually read aloud to her, or she played the pianoforte and sang. Sometimes they indulged in banter, but more often they simply talked.

He told her about his upbringing, which was typical for sons of the British aristocracy. He'd been relegated from birth into the care of nursemaids, then tutors, before being shipped off to boarding school, and from there, university. He'd seen little of his parents while growing up, since they preferred the delights of London over the country estate of the Barons Pierce in Devonshire, where Marcus had spent the first eight years of his life.

He'd had no close friends until Eton, when he met Andrew Moncrief, the future Duke of Arden, and

Heath Griffin, who would eventually become the Marquess of Claybourne. From the tales Marcus told her, Arabella had the picture of a lonely young boy who'd suddenly experienced the joy of finding "brothers" as adventuresome and reckless and outrageous as he was.

"What of your younger sister?" Arabella asked. "Eleanor is her name, I believe you said?"

Marcus smiled at the mention of his sister. "Eleanor came along unexpectedly ten years after I was born, after I had already left home for Eton. But I saw her whenever I returned on holiday. From the very first, she managed to wrap us all around her finger—Drew and Heath as well."

His expression softened visibly when he spoke of his sister, his stories an indication of their genuine fondness for each other.

He was so forthright in his accounts of his youth that when Marcus questioned her about her own childhood, Arabella answered as honestly, telling him things she had shared with few people other than her sisters and her close friends.

During her girlhood, her family had resided in London each Season and the Loring estate in Hampshire the rest of the year. But no matter the setting, their parents fought bitterly. While in the country, she and her sisters fled out of doors as much as possible, which had resulted in the three of them becoming enthusiastic walkers and excellent riders. And when they were in London, they eagerly escaped into their studies as a distraction from the vitriolic atmosphere Victoria and Charles Loring had fostered.

"Roslyn became downright bookish," Arabella confessed with a fond smile. "She was fascinated by the newest methods of scientific investigation and actually taught herself Latin. But even Lily turned to books for solace. She would pour over historical and geological tomes while dreaming of exploring the world in search of adventure . . . which of course is impossible, given her sex and social station as a baronet's daughter."

"And what of you?" Marcus asked curiously. "Did you keep your lovely nose buried in books?"

"Yes, but not to the extent Roslyn did. And I found my greatest diversion in literature and poetry, not science."

"If your parents disliked each other so violently," Marcus was curious to know, "why did they not simply go their separate ways?"

Arabella had wondered the same thing countless times. "I am not certain. I think they simply took pleasure in hurting each other, perhaps out of revenge for their own misery. My mother once confessed that she had fallen in love with my father shortly after they wed, but the feeling wasn't reciprocated, and his infidelities destroyed any chance her affection might have lasted."

"Then I suppose it's only logical," Marcus said slowly, "that you developed an aversion to unions of convenience."

"I am glad you finally understand," Arabella replied, managing a light tone.

"That doesn't mean you are a hopeless cause, however," he mused. "I won't give up trying to persuade you just yet."

Arabella knew very well Marcus wouldn't give up his pursuit of her until one of them won the wager. He was determined to wed her because he wanted a genteel wife to bear him heirs—although his courtship had definitely changed since the day of their picnic. It was as if he was giving their friendship a chance to catch up to their physical relationship.

She suspected it was a patiently calculated strategy to undermine her resistance. If so, she had to admit it was effective. In truth, she enjoyed the quiet evenings she spent with him. During the day, the house was overrun with modistes and workmen who needed her approval, and with illustrious callers who required her polite attention, so the peace was welcome after the hectic pace of the day. But it was Marcus himself who made the interludes so enjoyable.

He seemed to find them enjoyable as well, and he said as much the last evening before the ball. A comfortable silence had fallen between them as they took tea together in the drawing room while outside a late spring storm spent its fury.

"This is remarkably pleasant," Marcus commented lazily, stretching his long, lithe legs out toward the cheerfully crackling hearth fire. "We might as well be an old wedded couple." Then his amused smile flashed at Arabella. "Although if we were indeed wed, you would not be sleeping alone each night."

Arabella felt her cheeks flush at his suggestive remark. *This* was more like the Marcus she had first come to know. For the past three nights when she retired for bed, he had given her nothing more than a chaste kiss on her fingertips. But even that mild caress had her skin tingling, and she lay awake each night thinking of him, remembering the startling pleasure he had given her the afternoon of their picnic and wondering when he would attempt any repetition.

It would not be tonight, Arabella realized a half hour later, for all he did was wish her sweet dreams, without so much as touching her hand.

His tame dismissal left her strangely dissatisfied—until she scolded herself and resolved to focus her energies on tomorrow's ball rather than on the provoking Earl of Danvers.

The next afternoon Arabella ended her labors on the house early in order to dress for the important event. She and Marcus were to take his carriage to Tess's house to collect Roslyn and Lily and Tess and escort them all to the ball.

Since he had hired an abigail to look after Arabella's wardrobe and to help her dress, it took her less time than usual to bathe and arrange her hair and don her ball gown. When she studied herself in the cheval glass, she was quite satisfied with her appearance.

Her new abigail, Nan, was more effusive. "Oh, Miss, yer a breathtaking sight!"

Her gown was indeed an exquisite confection—silver net over emerald sarcenet that set off her gray eyes and red-gold hair, while the moderately low décolletage and puffed sleeves exposed a fashionable amount of skin.

She was about to go downstairs when Marcus surprised her by sending up a footman bearing a velvet jeweler's box, which contained a delicate emerald necklace and matching earbobs. Arabella hesitated at first to accept such an expensive gift, even though it wasn't improper between guardian and ward. But when Nan cooed over the jewels, she relented enough to try them on and discovered they embellished her gown perfectly.

Marcus seemed to agree, for when she joined him in the drawing room, he stared at her for a long moment before offering her a devastating smile. "That lovely gown and necklace almost does you justice."

"You should not have gone to such expense," Arabella remarked, hiding her flush at his flattery.

"Of course I should have. It was entirely my pleasure."

Marcus himself looked irresistibly handsome in black-and-white evening clothes, and Arabella was keenly aware of him as he helped her on with her satin wrap and then escorted her to his carriage. As they drove the short distance to Tess's house, however, she distracted herself by reviewing for him the names and ranks and relationships of the guests he was likely to encounter at the ball, some of whom had already called at Danvers Hall to make his acquaintance and scrutinize her.

Her sisters and her friend were awaiting them with varying degrees of eagerness, Arabella discovered when they were admitted to the house.

Tess was definitely the most sanguine about attending this evening's ball. She was always welcomed at assemblies and balls, for despite her lack of significant fortune, her birth and breeding were exceptional. And since her mother's family hailed from nearby Richmond, Tess was a great favorite with the older matrons and dowagers in the district.

Roslyn, who looked stunningly beautiful in her new evening finery, maintained an appearance of cool detachment, but Arabella suspected she was keenly hoping the evening turned out well. Roslyn stood the most to gain from their reinstatement, since she was not quite ready to abandon the prospect of having a husband and children someday. And after the mortification of being offered several shameful propositions by various rakes and reprobates, she was more willing than her sisters to accept their new guardian's protection and support.

Lily, Arabella knew, had no desire to associate with any of the disdainful arbiters of the haute ton. Yet even Lily understood how momentous this evening could be to their futures. Thankfully, she had agreed not only to attend, but to make an effort to be charming and ladylike.

"You promised to exhibit no trace of the hoyden tonight, remember, Lily?" Arabella reminded her as Marcus helped the ladies on with their cloaks and wraps.

Lily gave a droll smile. "I remember. You needn't worry, Belle. I would not have endured all those excruciating fittings or primped for hours this afternoon if I planned to spoil our big night."

"Well, the result is splendid."

Lily dimpled before twirling around in her new apparel. "We do look elegant, don't we?"

Arabella had to laugh. While Lilian felt more at home in a shabby old riding habit, she was feminine enough to appreciate a beautiful gown.

Arabella was as pleased with her sisters' ball gowns as she was with her own. Roslyn wore elegant white lace over deep rose silk that set off her fair delicacy, while Lily sparkled in gold-shot tissue over pale gold crepe that accented her vivid coloring. Dark-haired Tess looked just as lovely in lilac lustring, even though her gown was two Seasons old.

When Marcus complimented all the ladies on their appearance, however, Lily's lively good humor disappeared to be replaced by wary politeness as he escorted them out to his carriage.

During the drive, the conversation was amiable enough, with Tess and Marcus upholding most of the discussion. Roslyn was unusually quiet, Arabella noticed. And by the time the carriage drew up before the brightly lit Perry mansion, Arabella herself had developed an unexpected case of nerves. When she felt Tess squeeze her hand in sympathy, she gave her friend a grateful smile and then steeled her spine for the ordeal ahead.

She needn't have worried, Arabella quickly realized. The reception she and her sisters were given by their hosts and the other guests was beyond anything she could have hoped for—all because of Marcus. Judging by the excessive toadying and bowing and scraping the company did for his benefit, one would have thought the Prince Regent himself had appeared in their midst. What a difference his sponsorship made!

Lady Freemantle noticed also, and told Marcus so at the first opportunity, during a lull before the dancing began.

" 'Tis commendable, the interest you are taking in your wards, Lord Danvers," Winifred said, beaming at him in approval.

Standing beside him, Arabella saw Marcus acknowledge the praise with a slight bow. "It is only my duty, my lady."

Winifred snorted. "A pity your predecessor didn't share your sentiments. If Lionel had put out the least bit of effort, his nieces would have had far easier a time of it. Maybe even weathered the scandals their mama and papa incited."

"His neglect was criminal," Marcus agreed. "But I shall do my best to rectify it."

Winifred suddenly gave Arabella a sharp glance. "You should appreciate his lordship, my girl. Your success is now assured."

Just then, Lady Freemantle was hailed by one of her cronies, and she turned away, leaving Arabella alone with Marcus, since her sisters and Tess had drifted off earlier to speak to some other guests.

"I agree, you should appreciate me," Marcus said, amused.

Arabella couldn't help but smile. "Oh, I most certainly do . . . especially for my sisters' sake."

"And what about your own?"

Her expression turned thoughtful as she considered his question. "I am indeed grateful, of course. But surprisingly, the prospect of being reestablished in this illustrious company"—she waved a hand at the crowded ballroom—"doesn't mean as much as I thought it would. I learned to live without the ton's approval for the past four years, and I suspect I can do without it in the future. But for Roslyn and Lily . . . I truly do thank you, Marcus."

Their gazes locked for a long moment, before Arabella managed to tear hers away from his unexpectedly tender one.

"Will you honor me with the first set?" Marcus said, changing the subject.

She shook her head. "Thank you, but I planned to remain on the sidelines tonight with the widows and spinsters as usual. The teachers at the Freemantle Academy are expected to behave with proper decorum and to set a good example for our young ladies."

It was Marcus's turn to shake his head. "It is not improper to dance with your guardian. And you aren't here tonight as a teacher. You are here as Miss Loring of Danvers Hall, the ward of an earl." When Arabella hesitated, Marcus prodded her. "Come, admit it, you would enjoy dancing."

"Well, yes . . . I would. But it should not be the first set. Lady Perry will be heartbroken if you don't lead her out, since you are the highest ranking guest of honor."

"The first waltz, then."

Again Arabella hesitated. She had never danced a waltz with anyone but the academy's dancing master. Once considered scandalous because of the couple's intimate embrace, the waltz had not been introduced from the Continent until two years after her betrothal ended. And the prospect of being held so closely in Marcus's arms worried her a little.

As if he could read her mind, Marcus raised a challenging eyebrow. "Are you being missish again, love? Surely you aren't afraid to waltz with me in public?"

Naturally Arabella couldn't resist his dare, as he doubtless intended. "Certainly I am not afraid. Very well, the first waltz. But I hope you will dance with my sisters as well."

"Of course, I intend to."

Arabella smiled sweetly. "Then as long as you are being so gallant, my lord . . ." From the sleeve of her glove, she drew out a small scrap of paper. "This is a list of our academy's pupils who will be attending tonight. Perhaps you will be so kind as to ask them also."

Marcus took the list and scrutinized it with amusement. "A half dozen simpering young ladies. You are all damned heart, trying to palm me off on your pupils."

Arabella's smile widened. "I am only thinking of their feelings. They will be thrilled to be singled out for your attention."

There was a gleam of laughter in his eye. "You realize this hardly falls under the rules of 'fair play.'"

She raised an eyebrow herself. "I seem to recall you have bent the rules more than once in your own favor, Marcus. And I do still have a wager to win, if you recall. Who knows? One of our young ladies might sweep you off your feet and convince you to abandon your courtship of me."

Her teasing reply made him laugh. "Very well, vixen, as long as you recognize what lengths I'm willing to go to in order to curry your favor. But I will take you and your sisters into supper later."

"Certainly. We would be honored."

If Marcus was reluctant to dance with their hostess, Lady Perry, he gave no indication but soon went in search of her.

Arabella was about to take her usual place on the sidelines with the chaperones when Winifred sailed up to her with an elderly gentleman in tow, whom she introduced as a desirable dance partner. Thankfully, when the orchestra prepared to strike up the opening cotillion, Winifred abandoned her obvious attempts at matchmaking and instead sought out the card tables in the nearby parlor while Arabella took the floor with her partner.

After that she danced with four different gentlemen, and she was gratified that her sisters found suitable partners as well. Their popularity was a far cry from what they'd been accustomed to the past four years.

And then it came time for her waltz with Marcus. Arabella felt a nervous flutter in her stomach as he led her onto the floor and drew her into the proper stance—one hand clasping hers, the other pressed lightly at her waist.

Being held in his embrace was as unsettling as she expected, but her nerves melted a little when Marcus swept her into the lilting rhythm of the waltz.

"You are a remarkably good dancer," Arabella praised him after a moment.

He smiled down at her. "I am gratified you think so. You are quite remarkable yourself."

A warm flush washed over her, making her feel almost light-headed. For a long moment as their gazes held, the rest of the world faded away and only the two of them existed. Eventually, however, the music came to an end.

Arabella was oddly sorry when Marcus bowed to her and turned her over to yet another gentleman. And admittedly, every subsequent dance afterward seemed rather flat to her. Being with Marcus, she had felt almost . . . jubilant.

Then again, Arabella reminded herself, he had that effect on a good number of people, especially the female population. For the next hour, she watched Marcus work his charm on the company. He dutifully danced with every one of her pupils and awed their wealthy parents, much to her gratitude. Such rare attentiveness from an earl would highly benefit her academy, Arabella knew. But the female guests fawned all over him not simply because of his rank and stature but because he was so charismatic and compelling.

He secured a second dance each with Roslyn and Lily, also. It was interesting to watch her sisters' reactions toward Marcus. Roslyn treated him with thoughtful reserve, while Lily was unusually cool. Yet both clearly understood the extraordinary effort he was making on their behalf tonight, as did Arabella.

It had been something of a revelation for her earlier when Marcus had made her question her feelings about her newfound acceptance. The ton's approval was not so very important to her now, she was surprised to realize. She was supremely grateful for her sisters' sake, though. Particularly Roslyn.

After the virtual destruction of their lives four years ago, they each had responded differently: Arabella had become fiercely set on gaining independence. Lily had rebelled outright. And Roslyn had vowed to make her own fate rather than becoming some wealthy gentleman's mistress.

Roslyn's alluring beauty enchanted men of all types, and out of sheer self-defense, she'd become expert at warding off the pestering advances of unsuitable admirers. It warmed Arabella's heart, therefore, to see the legitimate attention her sister was receiving just now from one of their noble neighbors, Rayne Kenyon, the Earl of Haviland.

Lord Haviland was the black sheep of his family who had unexpectedly inherited the title earlier this year. His dark, dangerous looks were a perfect foil for Roslyn's delicate fairness. But despite the fact that they appeared opposites, Arabella suspected that Roslyn had developed a secret tendre for the earl. Her lovely cheeks were flushed now with animation as she conversed with him.

Arabella's delight in seeing her sister's happiness, however, abruptly faded when she recognized the fashionable young buck who had just sauntered up to Roslyn.

Despite his relative youth, Mr. Jasper Onslow was dangerous to any lady's reputation. A rake and a wastrel who urgently needed to marry a fortune, Onslow was one of the scoundrels who had propositioned Roslyn barely three months ago, offering to set her up as his mistress in a cozy love nest in London.

That he dared approach Roslyn now had Arabella bristling with anger and outrage. She had just started across the ballroom floor to intervene when Lord Haviland said something to Onslow that sent the blackguard packing. In response, Roslyn bestowed such a breathtaking smile of gratitude on his lordship that he went completely still, clearly captivated by her expression.

Halting her needless attempt at rescue, Arabella breathed a sigh of relief and muttered "Thank heavens" under her breath.

"Why are you so thankful?" Marcus asked curiously at her shoulder.

With a start, Arabella turned to glance up at him. "Oh, no particular reason," she replied quickly, not wanting to trouble him further with her sisters' affairs.

But he evidently had seen some of the interchange involving Roslyn, for his perceptive gaze lingered on her thoughtfully before returning to Arabella. "You will let me know if she needs my help?"

At his kindness, Arabella felt her heart twist with an odd little ache. "I will, thank you. Fortunately, your assistance appears unnecessary at the moment."

Marcus nodded, apparently willing to let the matter drop. "It is time for supper," he said instead. "Shall we collect your sisters and proceed to the buffet?"

When he offered his arm, Arabella willingly took it. The fare proved delicious, with expensive delicacies such as lobster patties and meringues that the Loring sisters rarely enjoyed. Lady Freemantle and Tess joined their table, so Marcus had five ladies on his hands. Arabella would have invited Lord Haviland to eat with them, except that he had already taken his leave of the ball. Roslyn's private smile, however, suggested that her evening had turned out better than she could have hoped.

Their party was surprisingly jovial, since Winifred kept them entertained with tales of her late husband and Marcus did likewise with stories about the sporting exploits he and the Duke of Arden and the Marquess of Claybourne indulged in. By the time supper concluded, Arabella was feeling a pleasant little glow that had more to do with seeing her sisters genuinely happy for the first time in years than with the warmth of the night or the costly wine she had drunk.

When Marcus escorted her back to the ballroom, however, she came up short, for she had suddenly spied Jasper Onslow again. This time he was showering his attention on her most vexing pupil, Sybil Newstead. From all appearances, Sybil was flirting outrageously with him.

Quickly Arabella glanced around the ballroom, searching for the girl's chaperone, who was nowhere in sight.

Just then Sybil turned and slipped out the French doors that led to the terrace, with Onslow following behind her a moment later.

"Oh, my word," Arabella muttered in dismay.

"What is wrong?" Marcus asked.

"Sybil has just disappeared outside alone with a gazetted rake. Her father will have an apoplectic fit if his precious child is allowed to become the target of a fortune hunter."

She began moving toward the doors, but Marcus detained her with a hand on her arm. "So why is that your concern?"

She eyed him in exasperation. "If it happens while under our care, Mr. Newstead will blame us for negligence and will likely withdraw Sybil from the academy—and other parents could follow suit." Arabella glanced impatiently at the French doors. "That irksome chit has very little sense, but I must save her from herself. I cannot let her ruin herself or our school's reputation."

"Allow me to help."

She hesitated. "Would you mind terribly?"

"If I minded, I would not have offered."

"Very well then, I would appreciate your help."

"Tell me what you know about this fortune hunter."

As he took Arabella's arm and casually strolled toward the French doors, she related something of Jasper Onslow's background—how the young man had run up huge gaming debts in London and often rusticated here at his parents' country estate in order to escape his creditors.

Marcus nodded in understanding, but when they reached the doors, he paused to gaze out at the darkened terrace. Through a part in the chintz draperies, Arabella could see the dismaying spectacle of Sybil locked in a passionate embrace with Jasper Onslow.

"Wait here," Marcus murmured. "I can better handle this alone."

When he stepped outside, Arabella could hear the conversation well enough.

"Ah, there you are, Miss Newstead, I have been searching for you."

Sybil jumped two feet and scrambled to break away from her lover, then hurried to wipe her damp lips while staring at Marcus in evident chagrin. "M-my l-lord . . . how you startled me. . . ."

"I could see that." Arabella could hear the wry smile in his voice when he added lazily, "My apologies if I interrupted anything of import, but you promised me another dance."

When Sybil looked puzzled, Arabella realized they had made no such arrangement, but before the girl could reply, Marcus addressed Jasper. "Sorry, old fellow, but I have prior claim on this little heartbreaker." He held out his arm to Sybil. "Will you do me the honor of dancing with me?"

"Y-yes, my l-lord . . . of course."

Onslow scowled as Marcus led Sybil back inside, while Sybil smiled brightly and shot Arabella a triumphant look as she passed.

Quelling the unexpected prick of jealousy she felt at seeing the girl on Marcus's arm, Arabella caught his eye and offered him a look of relief and gratitude. But it was nearly two hours later before the ball ended and she had the opportunity to express her appreciation personally. When Marcus sought her out on the sidelines, she was moving toward the ballroom entrance doors, where the guests were congregating to claim their wraps and to order their carriages.

"Thank you immensely for rescuing Sybil," Arabella said sincerely. "I will have to keep a closer eye on her in the future, but tonight you averted a potential disaster."

"You are quite welcome." He smiled. "I know how difficult it is for a woman of your independent nature to ask for help from a man, but I am gratified that you need me for something."

"Men are sometimes necessary," Arabella agreed with a smile. "And I admit, you handled Sybil better than I could." She paused. "I also wish to thank you again for being so generous to my sisters."

Marcus shrugged. "It was of no moment. But I mean to claim a reward."

"Reward?"

"Nothing too taxing. I require your attendance in London Wednesday evening."

Arabella sent him a little frown. "In London?"

He smiled crookedly. "Don't look so anxious, sweeting. I merely wish to take you to the theater. I promised weeks ago to escort my sister and aunt to a play at Covent Garden, and I would like you to accompany us. Lady Freemantle has agreed to act as chaperone for you, if you are worried about propriety."

Arabella's eyebrow shot up. "You mean to say that you have already settled the matter with her?"

"Yes, so you would have no reason to refuse. I thought you might enjoy an evening on the town. You have been working much too hard of late."

Arabella felt herself searching his blue gaze. When

was the last time a man had been concerned with her enjoyment? Certainly not her father or her step-uncle. Not even her betrothed had cared enough about her welfare to put himself to this much trouble.

"Come, admit it, you want to attend," Marcus coaxed with a disarming grin.

His perceptiveness was unsettling, but Arabella couldn't deny his offer held great appeal. She did long for an evening in London. The academy was close enough to the city that she and the other teachers occasionally accompanied their pupils to plays and operas so the girls could practice their social graces. But attending the theater with her pupils was not the same as attending with Marcus.

Which was precisely why she should decline. It would doubtless be a mistake to spend an entire evening out with him. But if Winifred were to accompany them . . .

"You cannot use the excuse that you have nothing to wear," Marcus interjected. "I ordered the modiste to make up a dozen more evening gowns for you."

Arabella stared at him in exasperation. "After I expressly asked you not to spend your fortune on me?"

"Precisely, my lovely Belle. I didn't want any argument from you about taking my charity. So say you will come. I want you to meet Eleanor. I expect you will like each other."

Surely it wouldn't hurt to indulge just this once, Arabella told herself. After the intriguing tales she'd heard about his sister, she did indeed want to meet Eleanor. And merely because she accepted Marcus's invitation to meet his family didn't mean she had to accept his proposal of marriage.

"Thank you," she finally said. "I would enjoy attending the theater with you Wednesday evening and meeting Eleanor."

The humorous creases around his mouth deepened. "Good. You have spared me having to browbeat you." He glanced at the diminishing crowd. "I'll order my carriage now if you will locate your sisters."

Arabella watched him walk away, marveling at how persuasive Marcus could be. Yet it was his genuine kindness that brought a strange ache to her throat. Before meeting him, she had presumed him to be nothing but a bored, selfish rake like so many of his peers, but this past week had certainly dashed all her prior assumptions about him.

His kindness was more devastating than all his sensual efforts at seduction—and made him infinitely harder to resist. And far more dangerous.

Arabella was still following him with her gaze when Lady Freemantle found her.

"I would call the Loring sisters' return to society a triumph," Winifred declared with delight. "And you have Lord Danvers to thank for it."

"Yes, we do," Arabella agreed with a smile. "I have already expressed my gratitude to him."

Winifred's gaze narrowed on her. "I think you ought to accept his offer of marriage, my dear. He would make you a good husband."

Arabella felt her smile fading. "Winifred, I know you mean well—"

Her ladyship held up her hands. "I realize you don't want my interference, but it would ease my heart to see you well settled. But that is the last I shall say on the subject for this evening. For now I will take myself home. Give my love to Roslyn and Lilian."

Arabella couldn't help but laugh as Winifred moved away. But when she turned to scan the crowd for her sisters, she found her mind wandering to her friend's comment.

Was it true that Marcus would make her a good husband? More crucially, what kind of marriage might she have with him if she agreed to become his wife and bear his children?

Noblemen of his stamp didn't readily give their hearts, and no matter how much she appreciated his kindness and protectiveness, she wasn't ready to risk the humiliation and pain of opening her own heart again and having it rejected. And without genuine, indisputable, mutual love, she had no desire whatsoever for marriage.

For the first time since his proposal, however, Arabella allowed herself to wonder what a union with Marcus would be like. If she were his wife, she would have a life of ease and comfort, with no financial worries. And she would be given the respect due his countess. As Marcus had pointed out, Lady Danvers would be able to lord it over all their haughty neighbors. Of course, marrying for status and fortune did not ensure happiness, nor could it prevent the kind of misery her parents had endured.

But could their courtship possibly develop into deeper

feelings between them? Or was she just indulging in wishful thinking?

For the most part, she was content with her life. Her school was fulfilling, and she had wonderful sisters and friends. Yet admittedly she was lonely at times and found herself wanting something more. Four years ago, Arabella reminded herself, she had earnestly wanted a husband and family, just as Roslyn did now.

What if she were to seriously consider Marcus's proposal? Could they come to love each other over time? What kind of marriage could she hope to have with him?

More importantly, did she dare risk the hurt she had faced once before? She couldn't deny the thought was a little frightening.

Yet she didn't have to decide now, Arabella reflected. Their wager would last for one more week. When it was over, she could declare her independence from Marcus. But meanwhile . . . what if she were to pretend their courtship was genuine?

She spied her sisters just then, and when they joined her, Roslyn was smiling serenely and even Lily looked pleased by the evening.

"I gather the ball was not as painful as you feared?" Arabella teased her youngest sister.

"No," Lily agreed good-naturedly. "It was indeed more pleasant than I expected. No doubt because everyone was eager to gain the earl's favor."

"But you found him amiable and charming yourself," Roslyn said, laughing. "Come, admit it, Lily, your opinion of the earl has improved significantly."

"True," she conceded. "Perhaps he isn't so very bad after all."

As Arabella ushered her sisters toward the entrance doors, she had to acknowledge that Marcus had risen significantly in her own opinion. Not enough to affect her willingness to marry him, of course. She would have to think long and hard about taking so drastic a step.

But for the next week at least, she could perhaps allow their courtship to be real.

Chapter Ten

It is foolish to let your heart become vulnerable when your dreams have been shattered once before.

—Arabella to Fanny

"Perhaps you will condescend to explain," Drew drawled as Marcus strode into the study of his London mansion the following afternoon, "just what the devil you are up to, Marcus. There are rumors flying about that you are engaged to one of your wards. Pray tell us it isn't so."

"The eldest ward, to be precise," Heath added in a slightly more forgiving tone.

When Marcus had sent his two friends missives yesterday, asking for their company at the theater Wednesday evening, they'd demanded to know why he had avoided them all week. So he'd driven to London just now to spare them the trouble of hunting him down in Chiswick.

The noblemen were waiting for him when he arrived and gave him no time even to sit down before launching into their inquisition.

With a sigh of resignation, Marcus settled on a sofa, prepared for a long debate. "I am not engaged to Arabella at present, no. But it is true that I proposed to her."

Drew stared at him, clearly troubled.

"It is also true," Marcus continued, "that she refused me out of hand. So for the past week, I've been at Danvers Hall, engaged in a campaign to change her mind."

"Have you lost your own mind, old chap?" Heath said after a moment's silence.

"I am touched by your concern for my mental health," Marcus replied dryly, "but I believe I am in full possession of my faculties."

Heath grinned. "Well, I can fathom no other explanation for your demented behavior. You went to Chiswick last week for the purpose of settling your wards' futures, to arrange proper dowries for them so they could entice some suitable marital candidates. It sure as blazes was not supposed to be yourself. I was only jesting before when I ragged you about proposing to one of them."

"I know you were. And at the time I had no intention of offering for Arabella."

"So what in hell's name happened?" Drew asked with grave seriousness. "We knew you were attracted to her, Marcus. But that doesn't mean you should willingly hang yourself in a marriage noose."

"Contain your enthusiasm for me, will you?"

Drew's scoffing sound held impatience. "Come now, you know we can't help but be alarmed and disappointed when you make such a momentous decision that will affect the rest of your life—and ours as well—without so much as a word to either of us."

Marcus smiled faintly. "Perhaps I said nothing because I knew you wouldn't approve."

"You're claiming you actually *want* to be leg-shackled for life?"

"I'm afraid so. Don't look so glum, my friend. I haven't expired. It is only the avowed bachelor in me that has met his demise. It happens to the best of us sometimes."

Drew's gaze narrowed in a scowl. "I never expected it to happen to you—to any of us—for a long time to come."

"Nor did I, believe me," Marcus murmured. "It caught me entirely by surprise."

Heath shook his head in similar perplexity. "It's understandable you would be fascinated by Miss Loring's beauty and spirit, especially if she refused your marriage offer. No other woman you know would dare reject you, so of course you are intrigued by the challenge of pursuing her—"

"It isn't only the challenge," Marcus interjected.

"Then what is it?"

"I finally found someone I could picture as my countess, one who could prove a good match for me."

Drew frowned with deep skepticism, but Heath appeared thoughtful. "If that's true," he said slowly, "then I could almost envy you. I've never encountered any woman whom I considered my ideal match. I suppose you are to be congratulated."

"I believe I am," Marcus replied lightly.

It was no surprise that Heath was willing to regard a foray into matrimony as a potential positive rather than catastrophic development. Heath's effortless charm made him a great favorite with women; he'd just never wanted to be tied down to only one of the adoring females who flocked to him in droves. Yet Heath was the most reckless and daring of the three, and the most open to new adventures, while Drew was the most guarded—and the most cynical.

Just now Drew ran a hand through his fair hair in a gesture of frustration. "You cannot have thought this through clearly."

Yes, he had thought it through, Marcus reflected. But he was acting more on instinct than cold logic.

Arabella brought a much needed spark of fire into his life. She was warm and vibrantly alive. . . .

Marcus smiled as he remembered the laughing gleam in her gray eyes last evening at the ball when she'd handed him the list of young ladies she wanted him to partner. And then later, the grateful emotion in her eyes when she thanked him for rescuing her pupil, her expression soft and giving.

He'd made up his mind then that he wouldn't let her go. His decision, however, was difficult to explain to his closest friends, since they'd never felt such possessiveness toward any woman.

When he remained silent, Drew interrupted his thoughts with a sardonic drawl. "You cannot possibly fancy yourself in love, Marcus."

Love? He wasn't certain he even believed in the emotion. At least he'd never seen a true love match among his acquaintances, although he suspected the possibility did indeed exist.

He had never held out the hope, either, of finding intimacy and affection in marriage, but the prospect was highly appealing—and quite possible with Arabella as his wife.

At the very least, their marriage would be exhilarating. Far from the cold, dispassionate union his parents had known, or the bitterly antagonistic never-ending battle Arabella's parents had reportedly perpetuated.

"No," Marcus said slowly, "I cannot claim to be in love."

"You relieve my mind," Drew said, his caustic tone suggesting just the opposite.

Marcus gave the duke an assessing glance. Drew's convictions would be difficult to sway, he knew. "You will be more relieved once you come to know Arabella, which is why I asked you both to join us at the theater tomorrow night. So you can meet her and judge for yourself. I am taking her to dine at the Clarendon beforehand, with her friend, Lady Freemantle, acting as chaperone."

"Don't tell me you require a chaperone to dine at a public hotel with your spinster ward."

"Under normal circumstances, it wouldn't be necessary, but with her reputation still under the cloud of her parents' scandal, I think it advisable. I mean to reestablish Arabella and her sisters in society, so I'm prepared to do everything that is proper. I've invited Eleanor and Aunt Beatrix to share our box at Covent Garden, so they can also become acquainted with Arabella."

Beatrix, Viscountess Beldon, was Marcus's maternal aunt, and an amiable lady herself. All three men were fond of the elderly dame.

"Why not invite us all to dine at the Clarendon with you?" Heath asked.

"Because I am taking my courtship one step at a time," Marcus explained. "A private dinner with family and friends would be too intimate at this point. I don't want to push Arabella so much that she bolts."

Heath shot the duke an amused glance. "Sounds as if her aversion to matrimony is as fierce as yours, Drew."

"It is," Marcus confirmed. "I had to coerce her just to get her to attend the theater tomorrow night." He glanced between his two friends. "So you will come?"

"I wouldn't miss it," Heath said at once.

"And you, Drew?"

"If I must," he replied more reluctantly.

Marcus smiled. "Good. I expect you both to be on your best behavior. Arabella has a decided distaste for rakes, and all of us qualify to some extent. I want her to see that we do have a few estimable qualities."

Heath raised an eyebrow. "You mean to say that she is a prude?"

Marcus laughed softly, recalling Arabella's enthusiastic reception of his lovemaking. "Not in the least. But her father was a champion philanderer, so she wants nothing to do with men of his ilk."

His friend nodded slowly. "I suppose that is understandable, but you had best take care not to let her turn you into a tame milksop."

"I have little fear of that. Arabella has no fancy for milksops, either."

"What about her two sisters?" Heath asked thoughtfully. "You say they are both beauties?"

"Yes, why?"

"If you find them half as intriguing as your eldest ward, I might like to meet them."

He did indeed find them intriguing, Marcus mused. His second ward was the most exquisite of the three, although he preferred Arabella's earthier appearance— red-gold tresses and flashing gray eyes—to Roslyn's golden princess image. Lilian was as captivating but wholly different from either of her sisters; her bold dark eyes and vibrant chestnut hair gave her a vividness that brought Gypsies to mind.

"The middle sister, Roslyn is an extraordinary beauty," Marcus said, "but a bit on the delicate side for your taste, Heath. The youngest, Lilian, is a true spitfire—more up your alley. Perhaps you might like me to introduce you."

Heath responded with a grin. "I might at that. I have yet to meet the woman who could tame me enough to make me wish to settle down, but one can always hope."

"If you would offer for her, I could be rid of the responsibility for her. What about you, Drew?" Marcus asked. "With her elegance and intelligence, Roslyn might kindle your interest."

"Are you out of your skull?" Drew demanded with a look of mock horror. When Marcus chuckled, Drew skewered him with a glance. "Don't press me, you sorry bleater. It's enough that I am willing to withhold judgment of your new infatuation until I meet her. With any luck, the eldest Miss Loring will have the good sense to rebuff you permanently, so we can return to our normal peaceful existence."

At that cynical comment, Marcus held his tongue, yet he had no desire to return to his normal existence. He was making slow but sure progress in his courtship of Arabella, and he had every intention of wedding her, despite her tenacious reluctance. Arabella was an ideal match for him, even if she refused to see it yet.

His chief difficulty was holding a tight rein on his lust. He deserved an award of some kind for keeping his hands to himself these past few days when he wanted Arabella so badly. It required extreme fortitude to let her retire alone each night, when he would far rather sweep her upstairs to his bed and spend the next fortnight exploring her lovely body and teaching her about passion.

Hopefully, however, his restraint would not be necessary much longer.

Marcus seemed to be intensifying his courtship, Arabella decided as she eyed the large copper bathtub in her dressing room. The tub was appropriately filled with hot water, but much of the surface was covered with pink rose petals. She wondered how he had slipped into her dressing room without being seen by her new abigail, who had taken charge of her elegant new wardrobe.

"Don't those petals smell fine, Miss?" Nan asked

cheerfully. "His lordship asked me to sprinkle them in yer bath."

"Lord Danvers asked you to put them here?"

"Aye, he did. He says you have a fondness for roses, and that petals are good as rosewater to make a body smell sweet."

Well, at least he hadn't tried entering her private apartments himself, Arabella thought with amusement as she undressed and sank into the hot water. In fact, until this maneuver, Marcus had made no intimate overtures toward her in days.

Feeling the petals caress her skin reminded Arabella keenly that she hadn't seen much of Marcus since the ball. He'd spent last night in London on business, and his absence had disappointed her a little, perhaps because she had decided to give his courtship a real chance to develop. She couldn't deny, either, that she had missed his company at dinner last evening.

She also couldn't deny how much she was anticipating the upcoming evening. It would be a delightful treat to dine at the Clarendon Hotel and attend Covent Garden Theater in such distinguished company as Marcus had promised. Arabella was admittedly eager to meet his sister and aunt and his two closest friends. She only hoped she could hold her own with them.

She was glad, therefore, to be able to wear her new evening gown of rose twilled silk and the stunning ruby pendant and earrings that Marcus had sent up. When she studied her attire in the cheval glass, her image gave her pause. She looked very much the regal lady, worthy of being his countess.

Arabella's expression grew thoughtful. Should she perhaps give his proposal earnest consideration after all?

She was even gladder to see Marcus when she went down stairs to find him awaiting her in the entrance hall. At the sight of him, warmth blossomed out from her belly, and she felt her heart flutter rather alarmingly. He looked breathtakingly handsome in a long-tailed burgundy coat, gold brocade waistcoat, and white satin knee breeches. She took his arm gingerly, though, resolved to conceal her pleasure at seeing him again.

It was a lovely afternoon, cool from this morning's rain but with fleecy white clouds floating across the blue sky. They were starting early in order to make the nearly hour-long drive to London.

His coachmen drove them to collect Winifred, who settled beside Arabella with an approving glance. "Your gown is perfect, my dear, and that scent you are wearing is quite pleasant."

Arabella returned a puzzled look, since she was not wearing any perfume.

"It must be the rose petals," Marcus murmured provokingly.

"What rose petals?" the older lady asked.

"Never mind," Arabella said quickly, giving him a quelling glance.

Otherwise, the evening began promisingly enough. Marcus's well-sprung carriage made the journey in relative ease, and from the moment they arrived at the elegant hotel, his party was treated like visiting royalty. They were led to a private parlor, where the staff leapt to anticipate his lordship's every wish and plied them with three delicious courses and a dozen removes. Lady Freemantle claimed to be highly impressed and expressed gratitude to Lord Danvers for the privilege of sharing his illustrious company.

When they arrived at Covent Garden two hours later, Arabella was even more grateful, since without him, she likely would have found the glittering crowd intimidating after four years of being shunned by their supercilious ranks.

The cream of society filled the upper tiers—the lords and gentlemen dressed in formal finery, the ladies dripping in satins and jewels. Since many of them had only come to see and be seen rather than to enjoy the play, the din was quite loud as Marcus escorted Arabella and Winifred upstairs.

His box, Arabella saw when they arrived, was already occupied by two ladies and two gentlemen, who all rose in greeting.

Marcus made the introductions, starting with his Aunt Beatrix, Lady Beldon. The tiny, silver-haired woman had curious bright eyes that reminded Arabella of an inquisitive bird. Without any prompting, Marcus's sister, Lady Eleanor, stepped forward. The raven-haired beauty wore diamonds threaded through her short curls and a smile of welcome as she clasped Arabella's hands warmly. "It is a pleasure to meet you, Miss Loring. My scoundrel of a brother has been keeping you a secret." She sent Marcus a laughing glance.

"He never mentioned a word about you until two days ago."

"Because I didn't wish to frighten her off with your atrocious manners, minx," Marcus said fondly.

"Pah," Eleanor retorted. "She doesn't look the sort to be frightened by anything."

Arabella couldn't help but smile. "At least not by manners. Not after attempting to teach them to scores of green girls for the past three years."

Lady Beldon spoke for the first time. "Marcus told us something of your academy, Miss Loring. I should like to hear about it."

"Certainly, my lady."

Marcus then made known his close friends, the Duke of Arden and the Marquess of Claybourne.

The duke was darkly blond, his tall frame one of lithe elegance, while the marquess was nearly as tall but more powerfully built, his hair a tawny brown. They each responded to Arabella quite differently. Arden offered her a cool bow, but Claybourne was far more welcoming, flashing her a smile of amused charm that reminded her a little of Marcus.

Arabella could see why the three noblemen were the talk of London. They were all striking men, beautiful as sin yet utterly . . . *male*. It was no wonder females were attracted to them in droves. Certainly they drew the rapt attention of the crowded audience now. It seemed to Arabella as if every eye in the theater was trained on their box.

There were two rows of seats, but when Marcus

started to guide Arabella to the nearest chair, his sister intervened.

"Please sit beside me, Miss Loring," Lady Eleanor said. "We can become better acquainted . . . and perhaps compare stories about my brother's guardianship."

Thus, the front row was occupied by the ladies; first Marcus's aunt, then his sister, then Arabella, and finally Winifred. When Marcus and his friends took the chairs directly behind, Arabella felt unusually exposed, especially when she spied a number of the audience whispering behind fans and pointing at Lord Danvers's party.

She soon realized they were gossiping about *her*, although it soothed her pride somewhat to realize she was receiving a few admiring looks of her own from several of the gentlemen.

Lady Eleanor noticed as well. "Don't pay them any mind, Miss Loring. You are merely their latest object of interest. It will blow over quickly." She paused, giving her charming laugh. "At least it always does in my case when I commit some minor infraction."

"Which is far too frequently," Marcus said, leaning forward.

He had allowed ample time before the play started so they could become acquainted, and the initial conversation proved highly congenial. Eleanor managed to keep up a spirited dialogue while subtly interrogating Arabella about her and her family. But as Marcus had predicted, she found herself liking his sister, who on first impression seemed witty and lively with a wicked sense of fun.

She had less opportunity to converse with Marcus's friends, since they sat behind her. The marquess threw in a comment now and then, which was a marked contrast to the duke's conspicuous silence. Arabella had the distinct feeling his grace disapproved of her, although he unbent a little when Eleanor turned to tease him about his glumness. Apparently Arden had scant fondness for Shakespeare, and they were to see a performance of *Richard III* tonight, with one of London's greatest actors, John Kemble, playing the lead role.

It was while the duke was trading quips with Lady Eleanor that Arabella spied her friend Fanny Irwin entering a nearby box on an elderly gentleman's arm. Looking very much the "Fashionable Impure," Fanny was gowned in emerald satin with her upswept ebony hair and her ample white bosom bedecked with jewels.

Fanny sent Arabella a discreet smile, which she returned just as discreetly. They had decided several years ago, for the sake of her academy's reputation, that it wasn't wise for Arabella to blatantly advertise her friendship with a notorious courtesan.

A few moments later, however, she noticed a redhaired lady staring darkly at her from several boxes away. The woman was simply stunning, dressed in an ivory gown whose low décolletage exposed an abundant amount of alabaster skin adorned by diamonds.

Arabella had no idea what she might have done to arouse such enmity from a perfect stranger, but she saw Lady Beldon give the beauty a polite nod of acknowledgment. Fortunately, the curtain rose, and Arabella's attention became caught up in the drama being enacted on stage.

Kemble's performance was truly a pleasure to watch, so the time sped by. At the intermission following Act II, Marcus and the duke rose to fetch the ladies some wine. The marquess offered to act as escort when Eleanor professed a desire to stretch her legs and invited Arabella and Winifred to stroll the halls with her.

Lady Eleanor was hugely popular, they quickly discovered. She was greeted frequently and stopped each time to introduce her new friends.

Eleanor was chatting gaily with an older couple when Arabella spied the stunning, red-haired beauty farther along the crowded corridor. When the lady approached Marcus and offered him a cool smile that held more than a hint of seduction, Arabella felt the strangest urge to scratch the woman's eyes out.

She was scolding herself for her absurd reaction when Winifred noticed her expression. "Don't be dismayed, my dear," her friend whispered. "By all reports their affair was over months ago."

"What affair?"

Winifred hesitated before grimacing. "You may as well hear the tale from me, so you won't leap to the wrong conclusions."

"What conclusions? Winifred, will you please stop talking in riddles?"

She sighed. "Very well, that lady is the Viscount Eberly's very wealthy widow. To put it bluntly, she had a romantic liaison with Lord Danvers years ago when he was still Baron Pierce. Then after her elderly husband obligingly went to meet his Maker, they resumed the relationship for a brief time last Christmas, but it didn't last. She was too possessive and fancied becoming Baroness Pierce, so he broke it off. To my knowledge they have not been seen together since."

Arabella suddenly felt a constriction tightening her chest. "They had an affair while her husband was still alive?"

"Well, yes. But it came to nothing in the end, and I doubt Lord Danvers is the least bit interested in her any longer."

Arabella stared in dismay at Marcus and his beautiful inamorata. She couldn't deny her jealousy, yet her distress was not only because the stunning Lady Eberly had once been his mistress; it was also because Marcus had pursued the lady while she was still another man's wife.

Dragging her gaze away, Arabella lifted a hand to her mouth.

"Are you all right, dear?" Winifred asked in concern.

She couldn't answer just then for the churning in her stomach. To think Marcus had been trying to persuade her to accept his offer of marriage while assuring her that he was nothing like her father, who had harbored no qualms about committing adultery.

"It is nothing," Arabella managed to lie. "Perhaps I indulged in too many rich dishes at dinner. And the theater *is* rather warm. I believe I will return to our box, Winifred."

"Certainly, you should sit down."

She drew a steadying breath as they moved along the corridor, telling herself she had no right to feel such hurt. She had no real claim to Marcus. It was just that she had begun to trust him, to open her heart to him. *You started to believe he was a man you could love.*

She should have known his portrayal of the ideal suitor was too perfect to be real.

But seeing Marcus with his former mistress was a cold awakening to reality. Her father had indulged in countless affairs after marriage, showering his affection on his mistresses, leaving her mother to languish alone in humiliation and resentment and heartbreak, pining after an unfaithful man who could never love her. How could she trust that Marcus would be any different if she wed him?

Arabella felt the hot sting of tears burn her eyes. To think that she had actually attempted to picture herself as his wife. Clearly she had been indulging in pipe dreams. Marriage between them would never work out. She was foolish to have thought it might.

She was an even worse fool to let herself become so vulnerable to hurt after her first wretched experience with love. She had let her emotions become too involved with Marcus, obviously. If she didn't take care, she could end up making the same mistake all over again.

Arabella forced herself to swallow the ache in her throat. At least now there was no longer any danger of her falling in love with Marcus. Her resistance to him had been slipping day by day, softened by his seductive charm and his generosity toward her sisters. But she wouldn't allow it to weaken any further.

Their wager would be over in less than a week. She had only to survive until next Monday and then she could declare her independence from him. Meanwhile, she had to pretend to be unaffected by this new revelation about him.

Her thoughts were so distracted that she nearly ran into Fanny Irwin, who was returning to her own box with her gentleman patron in tow.

"Do forgive me, Fanny," Arabella murmured. "I wasn't watching where I was going."

Fanny surveyed her in concern. "Is something amiss, Arabella?"

She returned a strained smile. "No, I was just woolgathering. It is so good to see you again, Fanny dear."

Her concern evidently allayed, Fanny cast a glance farther down the corridor and then lowered her voice. "We shouldn't be seen speaking together in public, Arabella. Your blue-blooded friends will see you."

Arabella followed her gaze to glimpse Marcus's aunt, Lady Beldon, standing at the door to their box, observing her encounter with Fanny with obvious disapproval.

"It is no matter," Arabella replied. "I have no need to cultivate her ladyship's good opinion."

"But what about—"

"I will write to you tomorrow, Fanny. Winifred," she called over her shoulder. "You remember my good friend, Miss Irwin."

Smiling, Winifred offered a polite greeting. They spoke for a brief moment before Arabella continued on her way. By the time she entered Marcus's box to find his aunt already seated, she was calmer and thinking more rationally, yet she couldn't help reflecting on how right Fanny had been to warn her against succumbing to the earl's seductive advances.

As she settled next to Winifred, though, she realized that Lady Beldon was addressing her. "You do realize, Miss Loring, that it is not proper for a lady to acknowledge a female of that stamp?"

Eleanor entered the box just then and resumed her seat between her aunt and Arabella. "A female of what stamp, Aunt?"

Lady Beldon sniffed. "Miss Loring knows whom I mean."

At the viscountess's censorious tone, Arabella stiffened. Earlier this evening, Lady Beldon had readily acknowledged the promiscuous Lady Eberly. It seemed highly unfair to forgive such wantonness in a married lady while condemning fallen women like Fanny.

But Arabella struggled to keep her tone polite when she replied, "Miss Irwin is a childhood friend, my lady. We grew up together and were as close as sisters."

"That is no excuse for recognizing her now."

Eleanor's curious gaze went directly to Fanny. With a light laugh, she made an obvious effort to smooth troubled waters. "Pah, Auntie, I think you are being too fastidious. Miss Loring should be commended for her loyalty in not cutting her friend."

Her aunt's lips pressed together in a tight line. "I trust I taught *you* how to conduct yourself in such situations, my girl."

Eleanor surveyed the Cyprian thoughtfully. "Yes, you did, dearest aunt, but that doesn't mean I must like it. I expect I would enjoy meeting Miss Irwin. She doubtless leads an intriguing life, with few of the restrictions we unmarried young ladies must suffer."

Marcus returned to the box at that moment, in time to catch his sister's statement. He frowned slightly as he offered his aunt and then Arabella each a glass of wine.

Still vexed at the viscountess, Arabella avoided looking at him as she accepted the glass. "Oh, I agree, Lady Eleanor," she murmured. "I quite envy Miss Irwin her freedom. She is her own woman, in charge of her life. She needn't fret about a guardian controlling her every action."

Casting an arch glance at Marcus, Arabella expected him to respond to her gibe, but Lady Beldon evidently was not finished with her chastisement. She spoke again just as Marcus's two friends resumed their seats behind them. "It is unseemly for a prospective countess to fraternize with lightskirts, Miss Loring. If you mean to have any future with my nephew, you will have to sever the connection with your friend, no matter how close you were."

Although enraged by now, Arabella managed a false smile. "Forgive me, my lady, but I have no intention of severing my connection with Miss Irwin. Instead, I will be severing all connection with your nephew. After next week, he will no longer be my guardian, and I certainly won't continue our relationship by becoming his countess."

Out of the corner of her eye, she saw Marcus's brows snap together. The other occupants of the box had gone silent.

Glancing over her shoulder, Arabella offered the Duke of Arden a brilliant smile. "Does that not relieve you, your grace? You don't wish me to marry Lord Danvers, I imagine."

The duke responded with a repressive arch of one eyebrow. "In truth, I don't," he responded coolly.

The Marquess of Claybourne, on the other hand, looked amused. "I am not yet certain how I feel about Marcus leg-shackling himself to you, Miss Loring. I think I should withhold judgment until I come to know you better."

"Arabella," Marcus interjected brusquely, "we will discuss this later in private."

Her chin rose at his commanding tone, but she could feel his vexation. He had crossed his arms over his chest and was eyeing her piercingly.

"Of course, my lord," she said with feigned sweetness. Leaning toward Marcus, however, she lowered her voice to a harsh murmur. "I don't know what you told your aunt about us, or why she thinks I am eager to wed you—"

His terse reply cut into her reproval. "I told her I had proposed because I didn't want her hearing the rumors from anyone else. I didn't say you had accepted."

"Then you should disabuse her of the notion at

once," Arabella hissed before directing her attention forward again, ignoring how his sister Eleanor was looking between the two of them, clearly aware of the sudden tension in the air.

To Arabella's relief, the play resumed a moment later. She sat through the last three acts, determinedly ignoring the ache in her heart while longing for the evening to be over. All she wanted to do was to go home and indulge in a long bout of waterworks. Except that she suddenly recalled a memory from her youth, of her mother sobbing disconsolately into her pillow after another of her father's infamous indiscretions.

The painful remembrance renewed Arabella's resolve. She would *not* be marrying Marcus when their wager ended. And she most certainly would not be offering her heart to him to be trampled upon.

Her head was throbbing as painfully as her heart by the time the play ended. A disdainful Lady Beldon took her leave with bare civility before sweeping from the box. Eleanor, though, offered Arabella a fond smile and expressed the hope that they might meet again soon.

Marcus's friends differed in their leavetaking as well; the duke treated Arabella with formal reserve, the marquess with good-natured charm.

When half an hour later, Marcus handed Arabella into his carriage, she sank back against the squabs and closed her eyes, wishing she didn't have to speak to him for the rest of the evening.

Winifred apparently sensed the tension between them. Ordinarily she would have nodded off during the journey home, but tonight she kept up a brisk chatter for the entire drive, an evident attempt to defuse the strain. When eventually the carriage drew up before her mansion, Winifred hesitated to get out. "Will you be all right, my dear?"

"Certainly, it is only a short drive home," Arabella answered, even though reluctant to be alone with Marcus, knowing he meant to grill her about her altercation with his aunt.

As soon as the door had been closed by a footman and the coach began moving again, Marcus spoke. "I trust you mean to explain that little outburst of yours?"

Arabella lifted her chin stubbornly. "It was hardly an outburst. And I had sufficient cause to be angry at your aunt's disparagement of my friend Fanny."

Marcus appraised her with a measuring gaze. "She is right, you know. It would be better for you and your sisters to have no further association with Fanny Irwin."

Arabella bristled at that. "Perhaps so, but I will tell you the same thing I told Lady Beldon: I have no intention of cutting the connection. And you cannot forbid me to see her."

"I wouldn't try," Marcus replied curtly.

She was still fuming, however. "Your aunt's attitude galls me. It seems the height of hypocrisy that single ladies are denounced for their sins when married ladies like your former paramour can have countless lovers and even commit adultery but are still received in society."

He regarded her a long moment before finally exhaling. "I suppose you saw Julia."

Arabella forced a taut smile. "If by 'Julia,' you mean Lady Eberly, then yes. I could hardly miss her."

His expression was more sympathetic than defensive. "You needn't concern yourself with her. I broke off our liaison three months ago."

"Oh, indeed, that long ago?" Arabella commented sarcastically.

Marcus's mouth tightened. "I am not a saint, Arabella. I never claimed to be. I'm a man with a healthy sexual appetite."

She gave him an icy look. "I never supposed you to be a saint, but you claimed you were nothing like my father."

"I am not like him."

"No? Then why do you consort with married women, without any consideration for holy wedding vows, just as he did?"

Marcus was silent for a long moment. "My affair with her was a mistake," he said quietly.

"So you say now, when you are trying to persuade me to accept your offer of marriage."

A muscle flexed in his jaw. "I intend to remain faithful to our wedding vows, Arabella. I would not take a mistress once we are married."

"It makes no difference to me either way," she lied. She turned to gaze out the window, trying to ignore the burning in her eyes. She couldn't trust herself to believe Marcus's promises.

Oh, he desired her physically, she knew that much. But carnal desire before marriage was a far cry from fidelity afterward. Their wager was all a game to him. As soon as he won, as soon as the chase was over and he had legally made her his countess, his interests could very well shift elsewhere. And she would be trapped in a loveless, heartless marriage just as her parents had been.

"You needn't be jealous of Lady Eberly," Marcus asserted when she remained silent.

Arabella's tumultuous emotions reached a boiling point and she turned back to stare at him. "Jealous! I am not in the least bit jealous. I don't care if you take a hundred lovers. Your affairs and infidelities are of no consequence to me, since I have absolutely no intention of accepting your proposal."

"Arabella . . ." Marcus said, striving to contain his impatience. "Listen to me carefully, for I will only repeat this once. I won't take any lovers after our marriage."

Her expression remained obdurate. "Well, *I* would! If I did wed you, Marcus, I would certainly have a lover—perhaps more than one. I wouldn't be content to remain at home like a dutiful wife while you catted about all over England."

She saw him go rigid; her brazen declaration had apparently made him nearly as angry as she was.

"You are not taking any lover but me," he said through gritted teeth.

Her chin jutted out furiously. "If I wished to, you couldn't stop me!"

"You don't want to test that theory, sweeting. I could and I would stop you."

Seething now, Arabella clenched her own teeth and

tore her gaze away from him. There was no question now of her losing to Marcus, she promised herself. She would play out the rest of their wager as promised, for she intended to win freedom for herself and her sisters. But once it was over, she would never even speak to him again!

Marcus, too, fell into a simmering silence. It was an effort to keep control of his temper, but he forced himself to wait until they were both calmer to discuss the explosive issue of lovers any further.

The moment the carriage drew to halt in the drive, Arabella opened the door and jumped down before the footman could even lower the step.

Marcus watched darkly as she ran up the front stairs to the house. He followed in time to hear her being greeted by the butler, Simpkin, who was waiting for his mistress's return in the entrance hall, despite the lateness of the hour. When Simpkin offered to fetch her abigail, Arabella shook her head.

"No, don't disturb Nan's rest," she said tightly, throwing a wrathful glance over her shoulder at Marcus. "I can manage alone. I have done so for years."

Without another word, she hurried up the staircase and disappeared down the corridor. A moment later, Marcus heard her bedchamber door slam with enough force to startle the very proper butler into an expression of alarm.

Chapter Eleven

❧

How does a woman keep her heart safe?

—Arabella to Fanny

His own mood fierce, Marcus went directly to the study, where he poured himself a generous brandy in order to calm down.

He could understand Arabella's dismay at learning of his past relationship with his former mistress. After her bitter experience with her libertine father and adulterous mother, fidelity in marriage was a monumental issue for her. But he intended to remain faithful to her once they were wed, and the fact that she doubted his word rankled badly.

It was, however, her vow to take other lovers after they married that enraged him. The thought of Arabella with another lover made Marcus see red.

Gulping a long, burning swallow of brandy, he forced himself to contain his ire. Arabella was not the kind of woman to forswear her marriage vows, and he was far too possessive to ever allow her to. He would keep her so busy in his own bed that she would never even think about wanting another lover.

Meanwhile, though, his campaign to win her had

suffered a serious setback. He would have to intensify his efforts, Marcus knew.

Even so, he could be more tolerant of Arabella's perspective. Her loathing of convenient marriages was based on fear. She was afraid of being hurt again, of being betrayed by a fickle suitor, of making herself too vulnerable to the pain and misery married couples could cause each other. He would have to show her that a union between them would be far, far different than her fatalistic expectations.

He wanted Arabella, had wanted her from the very first, and he would have her. As his countess, his wife, his lover.

Vowing not to be deterred, Marcus drained the last of his brandy and made his way upstairs to his bedchamber. The house was silent since the servants were long abed, but a wall sconce in the corridor had been left alight for his convenience, and so had a lamp in his room.

He shrugged out of his evening clothes, leaving them draped over a chair in his dressing room for his valet to care for in the morning. Not bothering to don a nightshirt since the spring night was only pleasantly cool, Marcus returned to his bedchamber and strode over to the bed, only to come to an abrupt halt.

The covers had been turned down as expected, but a large pile of clothing lay on top, including the rose silk gown Arabella had worn to the theater this evening.

When he caught the sparkle of rubies and the gleam of pearls among the silks and sarcenets, a heavy frown descended on his brow. Arabella had returned all the gowns and jewelry he had bought her!

A folded sheet of vellum rested on the pile. Ripping it open, Marcus read the terse message inside:

> *My Lord Danvers, you may give these to your paramour. I do not require them any longer.*
>   *Your eldest ward, Miss Loring*

Knotting his jaw, Marcus threw on a dressing gown, gathered up her gowns and jewels, flung open his door, and stalked down the corridor to the opposite wing of the manor, where Arabella's bedchamber was located.

He had been extremely patient until now. He had resolved to woo her with tenderness and passion in order to win her surrender.

But since his strategy was obviously getting him nowhere, more drastic measures were called for.

When her bedchamber door flew open, Arabella was sitting at her dressing table, making a desultory effort to brush her hair.

She felt utterly wretched. As a girl, she'd hated witnessing her parents' fights, but she hated fighting with Marcus even more.

Arabella bit down on her quivering lower lip. Her turmoil just now was only more evidence that she'd allowed her emotions to become too involved with Marcus. She had lied earlier when she'd claimed she wasn't jealous of his beautiful mistress. She'd been eaten up with jealousy, proving she was in over her head. She couldn't let it continue—

Marcus's startling entrance made her leap up from her dressing table and whirl to face him.

When she spied him standing there, looking dark and irate, holding her beautiful gowns, Arabella swallowed. She had known he wouldn't be happy that she'd returned her new wardrobe as a symbolic severing of their guardian-ward relationship, but she hadn't expected Marcus to barge into her bedchamber while she was preparing for bed.

As she eyed him warily, his gaze raked over her, taking in her long-sleeved nightshift, her unbound hair, her bare feet. Even though the white cambric covered her completely, Arabella still felt defenseless, so she hurriedly took refuge behind her dressing table chair, using it as a shield.

"Marcus, what do you mean, invading my rooms this way?"

"You misplaced your wardrobe, sweeting."

"No, I didn't. I intended to give everything back to you."

"Well, I won't accept. These garments and jewels belong to you, and you are keeping them." His eyes bored into hers, brightly blue, beautiful, as he strode forward and flung the pile on her bed.

Her hands moving to her hips, Arabella stared back defiantly at him—a defiance that turned to alarm when he advanced on her.

"Marcus, leave my bedchamber at once!"

"I intend to. And you are coming with me."

She tried to elude him, scurrying to the other side of the bed, but he reached her in three determined strides. Bending, Marcus caught one arm behind her knees, the other at her back, and swung her up in his embrace, ignoring her shocked gasp of outrage.

Disregarding her fiercely whispered demands to put her down, he carried Arabella along the dim corridor, past the main staircase.

"Where are you taking me?" she exclaimed when she realized he was heading toward the far wing, which traditionally belonged to the earls of Danvers.

"To my rooms. I'm wooing you, just as we agreed."

"I never agreed to this!"

"Spare your breath, love. I intend to show you what our marriage bed will be like."

Her heart thudding wildly at his declaration, Arabella renewed her efforts to break free, but she couldn't make Marcus release his tight hold.

Moments later, he entered his bedchamber with her, kicked the door shut behind him with his bare foot, and strode over to the massive bed, where he unceremoniously dropped her.

With a sputter of indignation, Arabella came up swinging, intent on boxing his ears.

Before her hand could strike, though, he caught her and dragged her hard against him. The abrupt contact startled her, making her body go rigid.

Arabella drew a sharp breath as she stared up at Marcus. His midnight blue eyes had sparked and darkened with something far different than anger as he held her closely, her breasts pressed against his broad chest, her thighs nestled against his muscular ones.

When he next spoke, his voice suddenly lowered to a husky murmur. "I plan to prove to you that you don't want any lovers but me, Arabella."

She tried to pull back, but Marcus wouldn't let her go. "I do not want you for a lover," she declared in a shaky voice.

"Yes, you do."

"Of all the unmitigated arrogance—"

His mouth came down on hers then, capturing, seizing, his tongue probing deep to duel with hers.

His stunning kiss, however, lasted only a moment before he broke it off.

"You want me, Arabella. You can't deny it."

She did want him, she admitted as Marcus held her even closer. She wanted him desperately. Her breath fled as the fiercest longing swept through her . . . heat and desire and need.

Marcus felt the same longing, she knew, for he had gone completely still. Time suddenly seemed to halt, the very air vibrating with a blazing tension that had nothing to do with their battle of wills. His eyes seemed to burn as they stared down into hers.

Her gaze trapped by his, Arabella stood unmoving.

His expression softening, Marcus reached up to brush her lower lip with the pad of his thumb. "I mean to satisfy you, Arabella. To pleasure you. To show you delights you've never dreamed of."

Passion throbbed between them; her pulse thudded in her ears.

Abandoning any pretense of resistance then, Arabella raised her face to his. "Stop talking and kiss me," she said hoarsely.

That was all it took. Bending, Marcus seized her mouth again, savagely ravishing, and Arabella responded just as fervently. They kissed violently as days of pent-up frustration exploded between them.

In some dim corner of her mind, she felt him guiding her backward toward the high bed. Without breaking the kiss, Marcus urged her down but at the last moment turned and fell back so that she sprawled over him, her hair forming a red-gold curtain around them.

Their mouths remaining locked, he ravaged hers with pleasure. Arabella returned his ardor with all her might, her breath coming in panting gasps. She couldn't get enough of his kisses, couldn't deny the desire and hunger surging through her veins, through every nerve and sinew in her body. She felt frantic, an urgent clamoring need that wouldn't be satisfied by only his mouth. She wanted much, much more from him.

Whimpering, she pressed herself desperately against the strong, muscular male body lying beneath her, suddenly aware that his dressing gown had fallen open to expose his hot, bare skin, his naked loins . . . his swollen hardness that jutted upward to press against her abdomen. Instinctively, her hips ground against him, seeking to get closer.

With a strangled groan, Marcus tore away his mouth from hers. His hands tangled in her hair as he stared up at her. "If you don't want this, then tell me *now*."

She knew what he was asking. Her throat dry, her

breath rasping, her heart pounding, Arabella nodded slowly. "I want this. . . . I want you."

Fire flared in his eyes. Marcus rolled over her, pinning her beneath his weight. Then reaching up, he grasped the delicate collar of her nightdress and ripped the thin cambric to her waist, baring the ripe fullness of her breasts. Before her surprised gasp could even escape her throat, his head dipped to her breasts and he took a taut nipple in his mouth, sucking hard. Arabella nearly came up off the bed at the delicious sensation.

Squeezing the firm mounds together, he lavished attention on her throbbing nipples until she was moaning hoarsely for him. "Marcus . . . please . . ."

His hand reached down between their bodies then, dragging up the hem of her torn nightshift, slipping between her thighs to stroke her pulsing cleft. "Not yet. You're not ready for me yet."

"I am . . . this fire . . ." She was burning with need for him, her very core aching with flaming hunger.

Lifting himself up, he tore her nightdress the rest of the way, then shrugged out of his dressing gown and threw it to the carpet, baring his magnificent, powerful body. Kneeling between her spread thighs, he took her hips in his hands and bent to her.

When his magic mouth found her feminine center, her response was half scream, half sob—a helpless, pleading sound that turned to a keening cry as he ravished her with his sensual expertise, his lips stroking, his tongue plunging in deep. Her hands clenched in his hair as the fire built to a raging inferno, then finally erupted inside her.

When eventually she regained her senses, Marcus was kneeling over her, watching her, his eyes tender, his face taut and flushed with his effort at control.

"Please, don't stop . . . ." Arabella managed to beg in a hoarse whisper.

He went utterly still. For a long moment they remained staring at each other, their gazes locked, time frozen in a moment so sharp, so raw, she could hear his heartbeat, feel the turbulent rhythm echo her own. She knew what caused his hesitation. He was her first lover, her only lover. The next step would be irrevocable.

"Marcus," she whispered again, reaching for him.

His smile was solemn and enchanting, his voice low and hoarse as he replied, "I won't stop."

He lowered his body to hers, covering her, and eased her thighs wider with his. The tenderness in his eyes deepening, he bent to kiss her again. His mouth, which had been fierce and hungry before, gentled from ravishment to tantalizing seduction.

She could feel his hard length probing for entrance. As he pushed inside her a fraction of an inch, Arabella froze, but he brushed her temple with his lips. "Try to relax, Belle. I will be as careful as I can."

With exquisite care, he pressed forward, gliding in slowly, slowly . . . his huge, swollen arousal stretching her flesh, filling her. There was a moment of pain, but it quickly subsided. Arabella felt only a throbbing fullness as at last he sank in the entire way.

Marcus held completely still so she could grow accustomed to his alien hardness, feathering light kisses over her forehead, her cheeks, her lips.

After another moment, he began to move, withdrawing the slightest measure, then pressing in again. Meanwhile his hands were stimulating her breasts, softly kneading, his thumbs stroking the sensitive buds. Arabella trembled, then gasped as another streak of fire ignited deep and low inside her.

She hadn't expected to be aroused this intensely so soon after his last devastating assault on her senses. But to her shock, the inferno began to build within her again. She was suddenly on fire. Marcus's naked skin burned hers, his body setting hers ablaze. Her breath came in short panting bursts as her hips began to move of their own accord, seeking completion from him in a rhythm as old as time.

His breath as tortured as hers, Marcus braced his weight on his forearms and lifted his head to gaze down at her lovely face. He wanted to watch Arabella climax as he took her, wanted to watch her skin flush with passion as they consummated their union for the very first time.

And yet he could feel his control slipping, could feel his need and desire swelling to overwhelming proportions. He struggled to go slowly as Arabella writhed and moaned beneath him, but when she suddenly arched and cried out in ecstasy, he surrendered to his need with a hoarse cry of his own, his body clenching and spasming with the same blazing pleasure she was feeling.

The shattering, searing explosion left him gasping for breath. In the aftermath, Marcus collapsed upon her, trying to spare her the brunt of his weight, and lay there bonelessly as the fire slowly receded.

It was a long while before either one of them could breathe with any semblance of calm. Then slowly, with great care, he pulled out of her . . . flinching when she winced.

"Did I hurt you?" Marcus murmured in concern.

Shaking her head, she gazed up at him with a dazed, dreamy smile. "Fanny told me that lovemaking was supposed to be unpleasant the first time, but it wasn't in the least."

Relieved, he rolled onto his back and gathered Arabella in his arms, drawing her into the haven of his body.

Snuggling against him, she gave a deep, languid sigh. After a time she found her voice. "Is it always like that?"

"Like what?"

"Like fire. Like fiery . . . magic."

He smiled faintly. "Almost never."

She buried her face in his shoulder as if suddenly feeling embarrassed. "You probably felt nothing like magic—"

"You're wrong, sweetheart. I felt it, believe me."

Arabella eased back to peer up at him. "You are just trying to charm me."

His laugh was soft, decisive. "If I had wanted to charm you, sweeting, I would have done so *before* we made love."

His declaration must have reassured her for she closed her eyes again and relaxed against him with another blissful sigh. "I suppose so."

Marcus exhaled as well, relishing the delight of

having Arabella warm and naked in his arms. *Fiery magic* was an apt description, he thought, experiencing a sense of triumph and something even more profound: heartfelt exhilaration. Arabella's passion was as vibrant and exciting as he'd known it would be, and so were the feelings she'd aroused in him. He had never felt more alive with a lover, more satisfied.

Holding her close, he pressed his face into her hair and breathed in her fragrant scent. He thought fleetingly of past lovers—of their seductive charms, the endless ways they'd tried to please him—but not one of them had ever succeeded in arousing such a stark hunger in him without even trying.

A dangerous hunger. His desire for Arabella had made him forget his rational mind, Marcus realized. He'd taken her virginity tonight without any concern for the consequences.

Yet whatever guilt he felt for deflowering her, he was able to reason away. It would have happened when he made her his bride. This was only sooner than either of them had expected. Still, he should have considered the possible repercussions. He could have gotten her with child tonight.

Marcus drew an uneven breath at the prospect of little Arabellas and even little Marcuses. He had always considered the responsibility of fathering children from an intellectual standpoint, if at all. He was resigned to fulfilling his duty to continue his titles and carry on his bloodlines.

The idea of being a father to Arabella's children,

however, not only held immense appeal but roused a profoundly primal emotion in him.

A faint smile curved Marcus's mouth. Drew and Heath would laugh uproariously to hear him entertaining the notion of wanting a family. And to have said family, he would first have to persuade Arabella to wed him. But now there was no question that he would succeed. He would never let her go. Possessiveness had never gripped him so hard.

You are mine now, he thought, stroking her bare shoulder absently with his fingers.

At the caress, Arabella stirred in his arms, then raised her head to glance at his chamber door as if suddenly recalling where she was.

When she uncurled herself from him and started to rise, though, Marcus caught her arm before she could leave the bed. "Where do you think you're going?"

"Back to my room. I shouldn't be here."

He drew her down to lie beside him once more. "You are spending the night with me. We have barely begun to explore the delights of lovemaking."

"But the servants could discover us—"

"The servants have their own wing on another floor. And as long as you return before dawn, no one will see you."

Rising himself, Marcus went to the washstand to fetch a wet cloth. When he returned to wash away the traces of his seed from Arabella's thighs, the enchanting flush that rose to her cheeks betrayed her embarrassment.

He stopped her from drawing the covers over her limbs to conceal her nudity. "Don't hide yourself from me. You have a beautiful body, and there is no shame in my seeing it."

Arabella bit her lower lip but didn't protest his ministrations.

"It's just as well that I destroyed your nightdress," Marcus observed, seeing the smear of blood on the torn cambric. "I would rather not leave evidence that you gave me your innocence. You can throw your shift in the dustbin, or better yet, burn it. I'll give you a nightshirt to wear when I take you back to your room."

"We made a shambles of the bed," Arabella said ruefully as he finished his task and returned the cloth to the wash basin. But when Marcus turned around, she sucked in a sharp breath. Her gaze locked on his loins. He was heavy and aroused—and clearly ready to make love again.

"You are still . . ." Her face flamed even more. "I thought it took hours for a man to . . . recuperate."

Marcus smiled as he climbed back into bed and gathered Arabella in his arms. "Not with the right lover. Not when a man wants a woman as much as I want you."

"Then you mean to make love to me again?" she asked, nestling her head on his shoulder.

"We'll see. You will be tender enough tomorrow as it is."

"It was worth it."

His soft laughter teased her hair. "Then I was right."

"About what?"

"Physically we are highly compatible. We would suit each other very well in the marriage bed."

Arabella felt her defenses leap to life. "Perhaps, but that doesn't mean we would suit in other aspects of marriage. A short while ago, we were fighting just as my parents did. That is hardly the model of an ideal marriage."

"No, but I suspect an ideal marriage would bore us both to tears. Fighting can be invigorating," Marcus said thoughtfully. "Admit it, you found it exhilarating, locking swords with me."

"I found it perfectly wretched," Arabella replied honestly.

"But it was exhilarating to make up," he prodded, a smile in his voice.

Unable to deny the truth of that, Arabella felt a strange turmoil of dismay and contentment ripple through her. Marcus's passion was as thrilling and overwhelmingly wonderful as she had feared it would be. She shut her eyes, savoring his tenderness, the intimacy, the bliss of lying here in his arms like this.

When she wouldn't answer, he eased from beneath her and rolled onto his side so he could gaze down at her. "Why don't we declare a truce for now? No more fighting tonight. Just pleasure."

Arabella hesitated. She didn't want to fight with Marcus. She couldn't regret giving him her innocence, either. But did she want to entertain the scandalous notion of sharing his bed for the entire night?

The trouble was her foolish heart. Could she trust

herself to keep emotionally uninvolved with Marcus if she surrendered to his lovemaking?

At her delay, Marcus bent to place a light kiss on her lips. "A truce, love. For the remainder of the night, we will forget about our wager and just enjoy ourselves."

Arabella bit her lip, telling herself that she shouldn't worry. She couldn't resist his lovemaking, obviously, but now that she was forewarned, she could guard her heart more ardently. She had only to imagine Marcus with his beautiful ex-mistress to bolster her resolve. She wouldn't be so foolish as to fall in love with him if she kept reminding herself of the danger.

"Very well, a truce," she murmured. Reaching up, she slipped her arms around his neck. "So what shall we do with the rest of the night?"

A slow, very male smile curved his mouth. "I suggest we work on your education. Your friend Fanny obviously didn't tell you all there is to know about passion. You know little about my body, for instance."

Taking her hand, he guided it to his loins, letting her touch him . . . his firm, flat abdomen, the long, thick shaft of his manhood, the heavy, swollen sacs beneath. When hesitantly Arabella began to explore his masculine attributes on her own, she discovered his skin was hot and sleek and oh, so arousing.

Her fingers curled around his heated length, squeezing gently. It was burning hot against her palm, hard as steel, throbbing beneath her touch. And when Marcus closed his eyes in obvious enjoyment, his response made her feel powerful and shivery and womanly all at once.

Intoxicated by the sensation, she bent down to kiss him. No, Arabella thought, feeling a searing rush of delight flare through her. Her friend Fanny hadn't told her even a fraction of everything she wanted to know about passion with Marcus.

Chapter Twelve

✾

Are you certain you don't wish to consider the earl's offer? There are worse things than a marriage of convenience to a wealthy, handsome nobleman.

—Fanny to Arabella

Not surprisingly, Arabella rose late the next morning, weary from her lack of sleep but filled with a warm glow from Marcus's enchanting lovemaking. As he'd predicted, her body felt a bit tender, but she couldn't regret spending the entire night with him and experiencing all the incredible delights he'd promised her.

Marcus had shown her pleasure so deep, so blissful, that her senses might never recover.

When finally Arabella finished bathing and dressing and went downstairs expecting to find him at breakfast, she discovered from Simpkin that she had just missed his lordship.

Ignoring her sharp little stab of disappointment, she read the note Marcus had left her, which said he had unexpected business in London but that he would return this evening in time for dinner.

In truth, Arabella realized, she was glad she wouldn't have to face him just now. After the wanton passion they'd shared all through the night, she needed time to regain a semblance of composure.

She felt sluggish and bleary-eyed all morning long—until Simpkin announced that Lady Eleanor Pierce was calling. Wondering at the purpose of the visit, Arabella received Marcus's sister in the morning parlor and was flattered by the warmth of her greeting.

"How delightful to see you again, Miss Loring," Lady Eleanor said with an appearance of genuine sincerity.

Arabella smiled at her caller, who was garbed in a pale blue carriage dress and bonnet that set off her raven curls and rosy complexion to perfection. "I regret you drove all this distance for nothing, Lady Eleanor. Your brother has gone to London for the day."

"Oh, but it is *you* I came to see. I would very much like to become better acquainted with you. I admire you prodigiously—a lady courageous enough to manage her own academy." Accepting the seat Arabella offered, Lady Eleanor sent her a shrewd look. "And any woman who can resist my brother is someone I want to know. I also," she added before Arabella could think how to respond, "wish to apologize for my aunt's officious meddling in your affairs."

Torn between amusement and caution, Arabella took a wing chair opposite her guest. "I suppose I should not have stated my opinions so fiercely."

"You were gravely provoked. I do hope you will forgive Aunt Beatrix. She means well and she has been like a mother to me, drumming proper conduct into my head. But she had no right to rebuke you for not disavowing your friend. Your anger was wholly justified."

Arabella smiled ruefully. "Perhaps . . . but normally

I wouldn't dream of making a public scene. It was very bad of me to dampen the evening for you and your friends."

"But you didn't dampen it for me. I was thoroughly intrigued." Eleanor gave a charming laugh. "I confess I should like to hear more about Fanny Irwin. She is said to be an Incomparable among Cyprians."

"Your brother would not be happy if I shared tales of a notorious highflyer with you," Arabella pointed out.

Eleanor's throaty laughter was engaging. "True. But Marcus doesn't dictate to me, nor does he try to keep me smothered in swaddling clothes the way our aunt does. In truth, he is the best of guardians."

"Is he?" Arabella replied curiously.

"Yes, but he does like to have his way, so I can see how there might occasionally be friction between the two of you, as there appeared to be last night." Her smile turned mischievous. "It is good to foil him sometimes, though. Men deserve to be kept on their toes . . . shaken up now and then. It won't do to let them think they have the upper hand all the time. Don't you agree?"

They shared a congenial laugh, and Arabella found herself relaxing. She liked Marcus's sister immensely.

Eleanor's next comment, however, took her aback. "I confess we were all astonished to learn Marcus proposed to you, since he has always had an aversion to marriage. But now that I have met you, I can see why he acted so precipitously."

Arabella winced. "Lady Eleanor . . ." she began,

determined to put period to any misunderstandings about her future with Marcus. But his sister interrupted.

"Please, we needn't be so formal. Just Eleanor will do. I have yet to grow accustomed to the title of lady, since Marcus's petition to the Crown to raise my precedence to an earl's sister was only recently granted. And may I call you Arabella?"

"Of course you may. But I must tell you, I don't intend to wed your brother."

Eleanor's lively expression turned serious. "I do so wish you would. I would dearly love to have you as a sister. Of course I have Marcus, and Heath and Drew are like brothers to me. But it isn't the same as having other women to talk to and confide in. And I think we could become great friends."

Arabella's mouth curved in unwilling amusement. "Surely you don't expect me to accept your brother's offer simply to provide you with a sister?"

She dimpled. "Well, I suppose not. But I want you to accept for his sake as well. I think you will be the ideal wife for him. Marcus needs a challenge. He would never be happy with a milquetoast bride."

"I am flattered you think so," Arabella said evenly, "but there are many other considerations to take into account when deciding to wed."

"I know," Eleanor agreed. "I have had my share of proposals, two of which I accepted before changing my mind. And truly, I can sympathize with your desire for independence. I feel much the same way—not wanting my life to be controlled by a husband. But Marcus would be a far more lenient husband than most." When Arabella remained silent, Eleanor leaned forward earnestly. "Tell me your other objections so I can plead Marcus's case."

Unable to help laughing, Arabella shook her head. "I applaud your zealousness on his behalf, but honestly, there is nothing you could say that would induce me to wed your brother, or anyone else for that matter."

Eleanor was not deterred, however. "It cannot be that you find Marcus uninteresting. In terms of wit and charm, he is leagues above all my current suitors." Receiving no response to her leading comment, she added, "I confess I am bored to death with my beaux at present, they are so deadly dull. That, or wicked fortune hunters, which admittedly are much more intriguing but too dangerous to toy with, even in fun."

"I don't find your brother dull in the least," Arabella admitted.

Eleanor sent her another perceptive glance. "Despite his reputation as something of a rake, Marcus is not so very wicked—no worse than the typical nobleman, at least. Perhaps you have heard rumors about his former mistresses, but I can assure you, he has no real interest in any of them."

"And I can assure *you* that his mistresses are of no import to me," she dissembled.

"You are wise, then." For the first time, Eleanor looked wistful. "I broke off my first engagement when I discovered my betrothed kept a mistress . . . although I have since wondered if perhaps I made a dreadful mistake. I would not want you to make the same mistake, Arabella, and harbor regrets for the rest of your life."

Other than raising a polite eyebrow, Arabella refrained from responding, but Eleanor seemed not to notice. Instead, she turned her head to gaze out the parlor window, apparently lost in her own somber reflections. "Marcus was very understanding, even when I jilted my second betrothed. He is the very best of brothers. I don't know what I would have done without him when I was a child. Our parents were not particularly . . . warm. I used to live for his visits home from school."

Suddenly shaking herself, she returned her focus to Arabella and summoned a bright smile. "But enough about me. It is you and Marcus I am concerned about. I think he must be smitten with you, since nothing else would induce him to consider matrimony so suddenly."

"Would you care for tea, Eleanor?" Arabella asked pointedly, determined to close the subject.

Finally taking the hint, Eleanor laughed. "Yes, I would, since I am parched. And I promise not to pester you any further just now about wedding my brother."

She waited while Arabella rang for refreshments and returned to her chair, then said lightly, "Whether or not you decide to marry Marcus, I hope we may be friends."

Arabella smiled with true pleasure. "I would like that very much . . . although I doubt Lady Beldon will approve."

"Don't worry about Aunt Beatrix," Eleanor assured her. "I will deal with her. Please say you will visit me in London."

"I would be pleased to. I rarely have the chance to come to town except to chaperone our pupils—an occasional outing to let them practice being in society."

"Then perhaps you can bring them to my aunt's house for tea."

"They would be in raptures over such an invitation," Arabella said honestly.

"And I do hope you will give careful consideration to my brother's marriage proposal—" When Arabella gave her a warning look, Eleanor held up her hands. "But I shall say no more on the subject for now. So tell me about your academy. I find it fascinating that you would take so bold a step."

For the next hour, Arabella explained the workings of the school and answered Eleanor's numerous questions, and then gladly accepted when she offered to help with the academy in any way possible. For the remainder of her visit, Eleanor steered clear of any further mention of her brother, and when she took her leave, merely reminded Arabella of her promise to visit.

Arabella was relieved not to have to defend her position any further. Last night her distress at seeing Marcus's beautiful mistress had cured her of any idiocy in thinking she might be prepared to risk her heart again. But it was not a subject she felt comfortable discussing with a relative stranger like Marcus's sister, no matter how charming and delightful she found Eleanor.

She couldn't even discuss the matter with her own sisters, for then she might have to confess how she had willingly succumbed to Marcus's seduction. Perhaps her surrender had been inevitable, Arabella reflected, given his potent powers of persuasion. And admittedly she was glad that he had awakened her to passion. But her wanton behavior was the worst sort of example for her virginal sisters.

Moreover, she would have to justify to them why she was recklessly courting the danger of scandal by sharing their guardian's bed.

She would also find it hard to explain to them the yearning Marcus stirred in her. Not just the physical desire, which alone was beguiling, but the longing to unlock the mysteries of womanhood. By remaining a spinster for the rest of her life, she would miss the vital experiences most other women enjoyed—husbands, lovers, children. Her last few days with Marcus was her one chance to explore a wondrous world she normally would only be able to dream of.

Tess might understand her conflicting feelings, but Arabella wasn't inclined to burden her friend with such private confidences when Tess was only just now getting over her sorrow at losing her betrothed to war.

No, Arabella decided, it would be much better to keep her affair with Marcus secret.

Avoiding her siblings, however, proved impossible. When Arabella attended the academy that afternoon, Roslyn and Lily caught her daydreaming about her magical night with Marcus. As soon as the class ended, they drew her into a private parlor to question her.

"What is wrong, Arabella?" Roslyn asked in obvious concern. "You were distracted all during your lesson on deportment, and there are circles beneath your eyes."

"Are there?" she asked, feigning nonchalance. "I suppose I got too little sleep last night, since we returned from London rather late." When Lily eyed her with a frown, Arabella added cheerfully, "I am perfectly well."

"You don't look it," Lily replied bluntly. "And you have been extremely secretive of late. You told us you were to attend the theater with Lord Danvers, but you said nothing about meeting his sister and aunt or his noble friends. We had to rely on Winifred to learn of it."

Roslyn's tone was more gentle. "Winifred also said there was a contretemps between you and the earl last night."

"So what happened?" Lily asked.

"Nothing of any consequence." *Except that I wound up in Marcus's bed and relished every moment of it.*

"Then why are your cheeks so flushed?"

With effort, Arabella refrained from raising her hand to her warm cheeks; the true cause of her distraction was not a proper subject for her sisters' tender ears.

"Lord Danvers and I had a disagreement about our future," she prevaricated. "He still believes he can persuade me to accept his marriage proposal, and I was simply setting him straight on the matter."

Both her sisters frowned as they scrutinized her intently. "Should we be worried for you, Arabella?" Roslyn asked.

"Whatever for?"

Roslyn searched her face. "We are concerned that you are becoming too susceptible to the earl. That you may be growing overly fond of him."

"Yes," Lily explained. "We fear you will let yourself fall in love with him, and he will break your heart just like that blackguard Underwood did."

Arabella felt her cheeks flush further. "You needn't worry. I have no intention of falling in love with the earl."

"Are you certain, Arabella?" Lily asked earnestly.

Arabella smiled reassuringly. "There is no reason for you to worry, truly."

"But that dreamy look in your eyes . . . You had that same look the last time you were in love."

"It is merely sleeplessness," she insisted. Her dreamy-eyed look had nothing to do with being in love with Marcus. It was merely that she was so new to carnal relations. Every touch, every caress, was a novel experience; every sensation he made her feel was burned into her memory.

But her heart was safe enough now that she had renewed her resolve to keep it well-guarded.

"I think perhaps it is time we came home," Roslyn said slowly.

Arabella's instinctive response was to object. She didn't want her sisters at Danvers Hall just yet. Not when she still had four more nights with Marcus.

"You need us to help defend you against him," Lily added with conviction. "Tess can spare us, since we have nearly finished sewing all the garments for her war widows and orphans."

Managing a smile, Arabella shook her head. "Truly, there is no need for you to come home. I am capable of fighting my own battles. And the wager is almost over. Only four more days until I will have won."

"And what happens then?" Roslyn asked.

"Why, then we will be free of Lord Danvers and his guardianship, and we can resume our normal lives," Arabella said brightly, determined to disregard the dubious looks her sisters were giving her.

She was indeed perfectly capable of handling her relationship with Marcus on her own, Arabella repeated to herself two hours later when she dressed for dinner. She had every intention of treating him with cool, rational dispassion.

The difficulty was that the moment she saw him, she forgot every bit of her resolve. When he joined her in the drawing room just in time for dinner to be announced, there was nothing cool or rational about her body's response to him. Her heart leapt and her pulse soared, while her skin instantly turned hot at the intimate look he was giving her.

His blue gaze was sensual and very male. That, combined with the low, husky sound of his voice when he merely apologized for his tardiness, stroked Arabella's nerve endings with pleasure and turned her limbs to jelly.

It took all her willpower to greet Marcus in kind and allow him to escort her in to dinner. When she placed her hand on his arm, she actually felt it tremble. They were lovers now, and all her senses were trumpeting the fact.

His behavior was all that was proper, however, no doubt for the benefit of the servants. It was only when the soup had been served and the footmen had withdrawn that Marcus allowed the conversation to become more intimate.

"Simpkin said my sister called on you this afternoon. What did she want?"

"She wished for us to become better acquainted," Arabella answered.

"I confess that worries me."

Arabella gave Marcus a curious glance. "Why would that worry you?"

"If I know Eleanor, she did something outrageous such as request an introduction to your courtesan friend."

Arabella smiled as she picked up her wineglass. "Not quite, but I imagine she would have accepted had I offered. Instead, she made me an offer. Your sister kindly invited me to London to visit her."

Marcus gave her a penetrating look. "I trust you don't intend to introduce my sister into Fanny Irwin's circles."

"Of course not. I have a perfectly good understanding of propriety, Marcus. I merely refuse to be ordered to abandon my own friendship with her, by your aunt or anyone else."

Marcus's mouth quirked. "As long as you don't so-
licit any more of Fanny's advice about lovemaking.
Anything you want to know, I will teach you. We can
continue your education when you come to my rooms
tonight."

Arabella arched an eyebrow. "Aren't you presum-
ing a great deal, expecting me to share your bed tonight?"

"No. I still have to prove that you don't want any
other lovers after we are wed."

She didn't need proof. After Marcus, she was certain she would never want anyone else. But she had no
desire to prolong their futile argument. "The question
is immaterial because we won't be marrying."

His blue gaze narrowed on her. "If you think I will
allow you to stray from our marriage bed, sweeting,
you are gravely mistaken."

Arabella narrowed her own gaze. "I thought we declared a truce last night."

"That was last night. And truce or no, you won't be
taking any other lovers."

There was an unmistakable ring of possessiveness in
his tone, which unaccountably mollified Arabella's
vexation. The possibility that Marcus might be jealous somehow pleased her.

Unwilling to admit it, however, she returned a cool
stare of defiance.

As if realizing how sharp their discussion had become, Marcus suddenly stopped himself and smiled—
a charming, enchanting grin that warmed Arabella
down to her toes. "You are right, love." Taking her

hand, he brought her fingers to his lips for a lingering kiss. "I am supposed to be playing the role of romantic suitor. Pray, let me rephrase. Will you do me the great pleasure of sharing my bed tonight?"

Arabella applied herself to her soup while she pretended to consider his request. "Perhaps."

"You still owe me the better part of four hours of your time today," Marcus reminded her as he lifted his own soup spoon. His voice dropped to a husky murmur. "We can spend it exploring the depths of your sensuality."

The mere thought sent a thrill of excitement and anticipation surging through Arabella. "Very well, since I owe you," she allowed, ignoring the laughing gleam in Marcus's dark eyes.

He knew perfectly well she couldn't possibly refuse such an irresistible offer.

Later, after retiring alone to her bedchamber, she waited another three quarters of an hour for the household to settle down for the night before slipping down the silent corridors to the masters' apartments. Marcus had prepared carefully for her visit, Arabella saw with surprise as she shut the door behind her. Flickering candle flames cast a golden glow about the room, illuminating the massive bed, which was strewn with crimson rose petals.

Her heart melted at the romantic gesture, but it was the sight of Marcus that made her breath falter and her throat go dry. He looked stunningly handsome lounging there on the bed, wearing only a dressing gown. His raven hair was slightly tousled, while his robe was partway open to expose his broad, muscular chest. A chest she had explored at length last night and hoped to do so again very shortly.

Remembering the enticing feel of him, Arabella felt her pulse start to throb wildly. Suddenly weak-kneed, she leaned back against the door for support.

When she hesitated there, Marcus raised an eyebrow, taking in the silk gown she had worn to dinner. "You are still dressed."

"I thought it unwise to risk being seen near your bedchamber in my nightshift."

"True. But you have on far too many clothes. We will have to remedy that at once."

Casually rising, Marcus sauntered over to her. He bent his head and kissed her lips, a slow, lazy, utterly possessive kiss that sent her blood racing. Then he led Arabella to stand beside the bed, where the fragrance of roses scented the air.

Taking his time, he undressed her with tantalizing slowness, starting with her hair, removing the pins one by one, letting the tresses fall in a rippling mane around her shoulders. The candlelight caught the red-gold sheen, turning it to flame and capturing his intent gaze.

"You have the most glorious hair," Marcus murmured, threading his fingers through the silken mass almost reverently.

"Thank you—" Arabella started to say before her reply was cut off by her helpless moan. Marcus had left off caressing her hair and moved his hands to cup her breasts. Even through layers of fabric—bodice, corset, and chemise—she could feel the arousing heat of his palms. Her nipples peaked instantly . . . a fact he evidently recognized, if the sudden darkening if his eyes was any indication.

With a knowing half smile, Marcus drew down her bodice and underclothes to bare her breasts, then lowered his head to feast. Arabella gasped at the erotic feel of his mouth suckling her nipples, the titillating caress of his tongue. Her hands reached up to clutch his shoulders, bracing herself against the delicious sensations he was causing.

"And you have the most luscious body," he murmured between warm strokes of his tongue.

"Do I?" Arabella asked hoarsely, barely able to breathe.

Leaving off his ministrations, Marcus lifted his head to flash her an amused look. "What is this, sweeting? Are you fishing for compliments?"

"No . . . not at all." Color rose in her cheeks. "It's only that I have no way of knowing what a man finds . . . appealing about a woman's body. I don't have the experience to judge."

"Didn't your friend Fanny tell you?"

"She only told me about a man's body . . . what to expect." Arabella glanced down at Marcus. He had purposely let his dressing gown hang open, exposing his nudity. He looked like a very beautiful, very aroused male, intensely vital, intensely appealing. With a smile, Arabella trailed her fingers down his powerful chest to his abdomen. "And I have discovered all on my own that you have a very splendid body."

"I am honored you think so," Marcus said graciously. When Arabella's hand would have moved lower to his loins, however, he caught her wrist. "Not yet, love. If you touch me, I can't vouch for my control."

He undressed her fully this time, removing her slippers and stockings, then her gown and underthings. When she stood naked before him, he shed his robe and drew her fully against him, letting her feel the hard, heated press of his nude body.

His hot breath burned her ear as he whispered, "You can't fathom how I have looked forward to tonight."

Yes, she could fathom it, for she had done the same since the moment she'd awakened this morning.

His lips feathering kisses along her neck, he eased Arabella back upon the bed and followed her down to lounge on his side, his weight braced on one elbow as he continued nibbling at her skin. "I've wanted this for ages . . . making love to you on a bed of rose petals. Ever since you gave away all my bouquets, in fact."

A soft laugh tumbled from her throat as he pressed his warm lips there. When she would have replied, he found her mouth and gave it the same erotic attention, wooing her with laughter and tenderness and incredible sensuality.

It was quite some time before he finally drew back to survey her. "Luscious," he repeated, his appraising scrutiny flickering over her nakedness.

Holding her gaze, he scooped up a handful of rose petals and sprinkled them over Arabella. Then gathering a few more in his fingers, he ran them slowly over her body . . . the swells of her breasts, the curve of her hip, her belly, and lower . . . stroking her woman's mound, the sensitive folds below. Exhaling in a whimper, Arabella arched hungrily against him.

"You're very responsive to my touch," Marcus observed.

"You make me that way."

The rose petals on her skin felt incredibly sensual. The velvet softness caressed her flesh as his hot gaze was doing, making her tremble.

"Marcus, you cannot torment me this way. . . ."

"Yes, I can, angel. I want you senseless from wanting me."

She was already senseless with desire for him, and she wanted him the same way. She wanted to torment Marcus and make him ache with the feverish hunger he had kindled in her.

Struggling for a semblance of control, Arabella raised her hands and pushed at his shoulders, compelling him to roll over onto his back amid the rose petals. She could tell by his look that her unexpected action had surprised him.

"Turnabout is fair play," she said with a faint smile.

"So it is." Marcus lay there, compliant, but his eyes held a bold challenge. "Do you intend to have your wicked way with me?"

"Precisely." She had never felt the least urge to be wicked and wanton with anyone else. With Marcus she felt that way every moment he was near, and often when he was not.

She felt supremely wicked now as the soft candlelight

gleamed tantalizingly over his body. He was beautiful, lithe and strong and totally irresistible.

Suspecting he could see the yearning in her eyes, she gathered some rose petals of her own and dragged them slowly downward over his chest, smiling when he inhaled sharply. Rather than continue caressing him, however, she scattered the handful of petals over him, letting them drift down to his loins, where his manhood stood stiffly erect.

"Roses become you," Arabella murmured, a hint of husky laughter in her voice.

She could tell Marcus was striving to remain still, for his hands curled into fists at his sides. Yet he made no move to stop her. Instead, he watched intently as she knelt above him.

Her hair teasing his skin, she bent and pressed a light kiss to his chest. She could feel the tension in his body, feel his heart thudding beneath her lips. And that was *before* she let her kisses glide lower. When her lips touched him beneath his rib cage, his stomach contracted reflexively.

"Does that hurt?" she asked innocently, raising her gaze to his.

"You know damn well it doesn't hurt," Marcus muttered.

"Then what does it feel like?" When he didn't answer, Arabella caressed the sensitive skin of his inner thigh with her fingertips. "Does it feel pleasurable?"

He gave a low, strangled sigh as her hand curled around his thickly engorged shaft. "God, yes."

Holding him lightly in her grasp, she bent low over

him to let her breath whisper over his skin. His arousal jerked eagerly, and when she pressed her lips to the crest, she made him shudder.

"Where did you learn to do that?" he rasped.

"From you, Marcus. I am only following the example you set me last night."

His ragged laugh turned to a groan. "You are an excellent learner."

Encouraged, Arabella closed her lips over the swollen head, tasting him with her tongue, intent on pleasuring him as he had pleasured her. His entire body went rigid as he fought for control.

His helpless response roused a potent feminine sense of power in Arabella. She had never felt more keenly aware of her senses; the sweet scent of roses, the alluring musk of Marcus's skin, the heat swelling between them, the arousing taste of him. She could imagine him thrusting inside her, darkly male and powerful, as she sucked and pulled gently, coaxing another groan from him.

Savoring the sound, Arabella sighed at the sweet spasm of desire that arrowed down to her loins, deep in her center. She could feel her own secret flesh grow moist and swollen, her blood stirring thickly with excitement.

Marcus had squeezed his eyes shut, while his hands clenched at his sides. His restraint was obviously slipping, though, pleasure eroding his will.

She continued her tender ministrations, wanting to drive him to a frenzy of longing. Her fingers fondled the turgid length of his shaft and the velvety, swollen sacs beneath while she plied him with warm caresses of her tongue and lips. A low, panting growl rumbled up from his throat, and a dozen heartbeats later, his hips rose up to meet her, driving his length deeper into the recesses of her mouth.

His hunger only served to heighten her desire, and she suckled harder, which pushed Marcus to the edge of his restraint.

His jaw knotted tightly, he grasped Arabella's shoulders and pulled her away.

"That is quite *enough*." His voice was harsh and husky, his eyes brilliant with heat as he captured her gaze.

But it is not enough, she wanted to protest. She stared at him in the simmering glow of candlelight, faint with desire for him. She wanted him desperately, longed to feel him deep inside her.

Marcus must have wanted the same thing, for he drew her up to lie upon him so that her thighs straddled his. The melting hunger inside her turned to a relentless ache as his hands settled on her hips and he lifted her, holding the naked core of her poised above his thick shaft.

Bracing her hands on his shoulders, Arabella drew a long, shuddering breath, yearning for the searing pleasure of their joining . . . a breath that sighed out of her as Marcus complied with her unspoken wish. Lowering her slowly, he parted the wet, swollen folds of her sex with his phallus and gently, very gently eased the silken head into her quivering flesh.

Impaled on his hardness, she bit back a soft moan at

the rapturous feel of him, the fullness of his penetration.

And then he began to move, igniting a burst of fire inside her. When Arabella arched her back in response, his hands reached for her breasts, stroking them, teasing her taut, straining nipples. And when she rocked against him, he lifted his hips to meet hers, thrusting his huge, burning shaft into her.

His face was hard with need; the desire she saw there made her chest feel tight as he slowly drove upward again, and then again with more urgency. Her moan turned to a sob, a sound that seemed to enflame him.

Grating out her name, Marcus grasped her hair to pull her face down to his. He kissed her as if he was determined to steal every ounce of willpower she had. Arabella struggled to remain in control, but his tongue plunged into her mouth like the driving rhythm of his flesh sheathed deep in her body. Her inner muscles clutched at him as shuddering tremors began to ripple remorselessly through her.

A keening whimper escaped her throat. She could feel the fire, the all-consuming need, swelling and building.

An instant later, Arabella cried out, convulsing wildly as the relentless waves of pleasure engulfed her entire body.

His control broke then. Marcus's strong body arched helplessly beneath her, guttural groans of release ripping from his throat as he reached his own harsh, powerful climax deep within her.

His arms came around her as she collapsed upon

him. In the melting afterglow, Arabella lay there bone-lessly, still joined to Marcus, her breasts pressed against his sweat-dampened chest, her face nestled in the curve of his throat, their ragged breaths mingling, their frantic heartbeats slowing.

It was a long while before Arabella recovered her senses. Marcus was stroking her hair, a tender gesture that made her sigh.

"I believe you won that round," he murmured hoarsely.

Not moving, Arabella suddenly swallowed hard. No, she hadn't won at all. Once again Marcus had shattered all her control.

Yet that wasn't solely what worried her. It wasn't even that his vaunted powers of seduction had proved so overwhelming. It was that her resolve to remain emotionally indifferent was slipping away with his every sensual caress.

There was supreme peril in letting herself become too attached to Marcus, a warning voice clamored in her mind. She could hear her sisters' worried voices questioning whether she was in danger of falling in love with him. *You need us to help defend you against him,* Lily had insisted.

Perhaps she should have listened, Arabella reflected as she pressed a kiss against the warm bare skin of Marcus's neck. Perhaps she *did* need reinforcements to help maintain her defenses. If she had any hope at all of remaining dispassionate toward Marcus—

A helpless laugh whispered from her lips as she caught herself nibbling on his delicious skin. Even a fool could see she wasn't able to defend herself against him on her own. Not when she was so desperately attracted to his lovemaking.

Just then Marcus shifted beneath her, reminding her that their flesh was still joined in the most intimate way possible. A sweet jolt of fire shivered through Arabella as he captured her face in his hands and brought her mouth to his for another burning kiss.

Most definitely she would be wise to ask her sisters to come home, Arabella decided as she gave herself up to the searing enchantment of his kisses.

Chapter Thirteen

❦

*I can imagine little worse than marriage without love,
except marriage where love is purely one-sided.*
—Arabella to Fanny

When Roslyn and Lily came home the next morning
in response to her summons, Arabella was torn between gratitude and regret. Gratitude because she
would be far safer with her sisters in the house to bolster her defenses. Regret because she would be spending no more enchanting nights in Marcus's bed.

She avoided him at breakfast, and from the moment
her sisters arrived, she kept herself busy with renovations to the second-floor bedchambers.

To Arabella's further gratitude, Roslyn and Lily
didn't press her to explain her change of heart. They
simply remained close to her all day and refused to
leave her alone in Marcus's company.

She was wise to keep away from him, Arabella tried
to convince herself as she and her sisters set out together for afternoon classes at the academy. She didn't
trust herself to be with Marcus and keep her emotions
uninvolved. She had even less faith that she could resist her growing desire for him.

Roslyn and Lily would help save her from herself.

It was better this way, Arabella knew, even though she didn't have to like it.

Marcus admittedly did not like the lack of privacy or having his two youngest wards present to interfere with his courtship of their sister. Nor was he overjoyed when Lilian and Roslyn confronted him in his study shortly after they returned from the academy.

"Arabella has gone upstairs to change for dinner," Lily said gravely upon entering, "but we wished a word with you, your lordship."

Following behind her, Roslyn added more politely but just as seriously, "If you could spare a moment of your time, my lord?"

Setting down his quill pen, Marcus rose from behind his desk and offered them seats near the tall windows. "For my lovely wards, I will make the time."

Though grimacing at his flattery, Lily settled in a wing chair as if forcing herself to behave with proper decorum. Yet she came straight to the point. "We think it best if you stop wooing Arabella, Lord Danvers."

Marcus leveled a curious gaze at his youngest ward as he sat on the sofa across from her. "I collect you mean to tell me why?"

"Because you are too beguiling. You are likely to make Arabella forsake all her good sense. We don't want to see her hurt again by a fickle suitor."

He raised an eyebrow. "I am hardly fickle. I have every intention of marrying your sister."

"But you would not make her a good husband."

Willing himself to patience, Marcus leaned back against the sofa. "So you believe you can judge my qualifications as a husband?"

"You don't love her, my lord." Lily leaned forward in her chair, her dark eyes bright with the glisten of frustration, her expression intent with worry. "Arabella has always been too tenderhearted. Her last betrothed humiliated her and left her heartbroken, and we won't let it happen again. She has been hurt enough."

Lily's distress was obviously heartfelt, Marcus realized.

Roslyn's voice held the same troubled note when she chimed in. "It was very hard for Arabella when her betrothed repudiated her, especially after losing both our parents and our home and having to face the public scorn that resulted."

"From all accounts," Marcus responded, "her betrothed abandoned her at the first test. I am made of stronger stuff."

"Do you love her?" Roslyn asked quietly. "If not now, then could you ever come to love her?"

The question took him aback. Roslyn was eyeing him with her perceptive gaze, which made him feel as if she could see deep inside his mind. But he couldn't reply to her discomfiting question when he himself didn't know the answer.

He had strong feelings for Arabella, certainly. When she wasn't with him, he missed her. And at the prospect of seeing her again, his heart began racing with anticipation. She roused a passion in him that he hadn't felt in years, perhaps never.

But just because he wanted Arabella—and wanted to be with her—didn't mean he would ever feel the romantic love he presumed Roslyn was speaking of.

"I think," Marcus finally said, "that my feelings for your sister should remain private between us."

Roslyn inclined her head in acknowledgment. "Perhaps. But we do not want to see Arabella hurt again."

"I assure you, the last thing I want to do is hurt her."

"But you cannot promise that you won't."

In all truth, he couldn't make any such promise, Marcus reflected soberly, but he would try his damnedest. "I can promise you that if I wed your sister, our marriage will be nothing whatsoever like your parents'."

Evidently Lily wasn't satisfied. "If you make Arabella fall in love with you, you will break her heart. We won't let you hurt her the way Viscount Underwood did."

"There is no chance of that," he replied with all sincerity.

"How can we be certain?" Lily demanded.

"I regret," Marcus said, "that I won't be able to persuade you of my benevolent intentions, but I mean to continue my courtship of your sister."

When Lily continued to stare back at him in frustration, Marcus finally changed the subject. "Actually, I am glad for a chance to speak to you both in private." He paused, glancing from one sister to the other. "Pray, tell me about your mother."

At the mention of their mother, Lily stiffened, while Roslyn looked wary. "What do you want to know?"

"I understand she is living on the coast of France, in Brittany. Have you heard from her recently?"

Lily gave a brittle little laugh. "Not recently. Not in four years, in fact. She hasn't sent us so much as a letter since she fled England with her lover." The hint of bitterness in her tone was unmistakable, and Marcus could tell that Lady Loring was yet another painful topic for Lilian.

"Perhaps she had little chance," Marcus observed. "The war on the Peninsula intensified shortly after she left for France, so communication would have been extremely difficult."

"She could somehow have sent word t us," Roslyn said more softly, "if only to let us know she was safe."

"Your step-uncle never tried to contact her?"

"That is doubtful. Our step-uncle would not let Mama's name be spoken in his hearing. He wasn't willing to forgive her for the disgrace she brought his family name."

"Do you know if she ever attempted to return home to England after the war ended?"

"Why would she?" Lily asked. "She would not have been welcome here."

"What about now? Now that your step-uncle is gone, would you welcome her return?"

"*No,*" Lily answered, her voice quivering with conviction. "I don't care if we never see her again."

Marcus steepled his fingers under his chin as he studied his wards. Roslyn seemed a bit more forgiving of their mother, but he suspected Arabella's feelings were almost as bitter as Lily's.

"Why do you ask?" Roslyn said, watching him again with those shrewd, knowing eyes.

"I am curious," Marcus replied, which was only a partial truth.

He decided it best not to mention the recent turn of events until he had more details to properly judge the situation. His unexpected business in London yesterday had solely to do with Lady Loring. She had written to him a month ago after hearing about her stepbrother's passing, to express her condolences and to extend her felicitations to Marcus on attaining the earldom.

After a long discussion with his solicitors, Marcus had ordered them to locate Victoria Loring in France and provide her safe passage home to England, if she cared enough to come. He wanted to hear her story, since he wasn't wholly convinced she was the black villainess the late earl had painted her. According to Simpkin, who had fulfilled the duel roles of butler and secretary for the former Lord Danvers and had managed all his lordship's correspondence, Lady Loring had written several letters to her daughters over the years, but her stepbrother had burned them without so much as breaking the wax seal.

And if there was the slightest possibility of healing any of the painful wounds caused by her abandonment of her daughters, Marcus couldn't let the opportunity pass. Lady Loring's heartless actions had helped turn Arabella against marriage, and if she could come to forgive her mother, then she might be more willing to accept his own suit.

But he had no intention of sharing his hopes with his wards, in part because he didn't want to risk rousing their disappointment in the event he was wrong about their mother.

His reply evidently did not satisfy Lily, however, for she eyed him intently. "If introducing the subject of our mother is a ploy to distract us from protecting Belle, your lordship, it will not work."

A faint smile curved his mouth. "It isn't a ploy."

Lily continued to scowl as she abruptly stood. "If you dare hurt Arabella, I swear I will make you regret it."

He had no doubt she would keep her word, either, or that her desire to protect Arabella was well-meant.

Politely Marcus rose to his feet. "I will take your warning to heart."

Rising also, Roslyn started to follow her sister from the room, but then she hesitated, looking solemnly back at Marcus. "Do we have your word, my lord?"

"You have my word," he said gravely. "I will do everything in my power to see that Arabella isn't hurt."

His vow seemed to reassure her, for Roslyn nodded slowly and offered him a tentative smile. "For some reason I trust you."

Marcus was touched by her admission. Roslyn might not have declared herself his ally, but at least she was willing to allow him to prove himself.

When she was gone, Marcus frowned, contemplating his next step. He had no intention of hurting Arabella, but there was no way he would give up his courtship.

He had only a few more nights with her and every moment counted.

Dinner that evening was an odd affair, leaving Arabella puzzled by the unmistakable undercurrents between Marcus and her sisters. Lily continued to treat him with wary reserve, but Roslyn seemed to have thawed toward him significantly.

Even odder was the conversation Roslyn carried on with Marcus—asking him about his family history, his tastes in music and literature, his political leanings, the condition of his various properties and estates . . . almost as if she were a protective mother and Marcus a potential suitor for her daughter.

Roslyn's purpose made little sense to Arabella, since her sister was still presumably set against his courtship.

Marcus's response also confounded her. He bore the inquiries with gracious charm rather than the vexation she might have expected. And after dinner, when they all moved to the drawing room, he made a concerted effort to become better acquainted with both her sisters, even Lily.

Arabella herself remained mostly silent, for she knew every word she uttered would be scrutinized by her sisters. And she was far too aware of Marcus's nearness to feel at ease.

For the most part, Marcus paid her little attention the rest of the evening. And he made no attempt for a private word with her, even when it was time to retire to bed. In truth, he had no chance, for Roslyn and Lily accompanied Arabella out of the drawing room and escorted her to her bedchamber, apparently taking their roles as her protectors quite seriously.

Feeling restless and out of sorts, Arabella found herself staring out her window at the moonlit darkness, regretting not being able to sleep with Marcus tonight and wishing she could assuage the urgent longing she felt for him.

Realizing where her foolish reflections had taken her, though, Arabella made a scoffing sound and turned away to undress. She had just removed her evening slippers and started to unbutton her gown when someone scratched on her chamber door.

Disappointment flooded her when she saw it was only her maid, Nan, come to help her prepare for bed, and not the sensual lover who had been occupying her thoughts so obsessively of late.

"You may go to bed, Nan," Arabella said, preferring to be alone. "I won't require your services tonight."

"As you please, Miss Loring," Nan replied with a curtsy, "but Mrs. Simpkin 'as a problem in the kitchen that needs yer attention."

"At this late hour?"

"She said it couldn't wait."

"Very well," Arabella acknowledged. "I will come as soon as I fetch my shoes."

She dismissed Nan and put on the slippers she had just taken off, then left her room quietly so as not to disturb her sisters in the adjacent bedchambers. Their doors were shut, Arabella noticed as she made her way down the corridor to the back service stairs in search of the housekeeper.

When she reached the kitchen, however, she came up short. There was no sign of Mrs. Simpkin. Instead, Marcus was sitting on the edge of the long dining table with his hands braced behind him, looking very much at ease. He had removed his coat and cravat although he still wore his evening breeches.

It was deplorable how her heart somersaulted at the sight of him. Chiding herself, Arabella disciplined her features into impassivity. "Where is Mrs. Simpkin?" she asked, although already suspecting the answer.

"I dismissed her," Marcus said easily.

"So you lured me down here under false pretenses?"

"What did you expect, sweeting? I was compelled to be creative since your sisters are guarding you like mother hawks."

Arabella had to admire his resourcefulness, even if she was the target for it. "My sisters are only acting in my best interest."

"I know they believe so." His mouth twisted. "Lily fears I will beguile you into losing your common sense."

Arabella felt a little stab of dismay. "You didn't tell her about us—"

"Of course not, love. I don't want it known that we sampled the marriage bed before the wedding."

She let that provoking comment pass. "What do you want, Marcus?"

"Simply to invite you to take a midnight stroll with me."

"Why?"

"So I can have some time alone with you. How else can I woo you effectively with your sisters watching my every move? Their presence here at the Hall is putting a significant constraint on my courtship." Marcus cocked an eyebrow. "But that is precisely why you summoned them home, isn't it? Because you fear I am gaining ground with you."

The amused gleam in his eye told her there was no point in denying the charge. When Arabella remained silent, he shook his head. "You didn't think I would be so easily daunted, did you?"

"Regrettably, no. I doubt anything could daunt you."

Casually, Marcus slid down from the table and crossed to where she stood. Arabella felt her pulse quicken at the intimate look he was giving her, at the heat in his gaze that sparked a responsive heat in every part of her body.

"Come with me outside, Belle. We'll walk down to the river."

"I shouldn't," she replied, even as she felt her defenses weakening.

"Craven," he teased softly. His eyes glinted wickedly, making her heart pound harder.

Determined to resist his seductive charm, she lifted her chin. "I am only being wise. You know what will happen if I come with you."

"I know what I *want* to happen. But whatever we do will be solely at your discretion."

Raising his hand, Marcus stroked a thumb over her bottom lip. The frisson of fire that streaked through Arabella at that simple touch made her quiver.

And that was before his voice lowered to a sensual murmur. "A fighting chance to win you, Arabella.

That is all I've ever asked from you. If you lock yourself away in your chaste bedchamber with your sisters as watchdogs, how can I possibly convince you to marry me?"

She felt her willpower wilting. Marcus was devilishly irresistible and he knew it. "My sisters cannot find out," Arabella said finally.

He smiled. "I certainly won't tell them."

"Mrs. Simpkin may suspect what we are about."

"Mrs. Simpkin is very discreet. And she approves of my courtship, remember?"

His thumb dipped inside her mouth, making her breath catch and her wits scatter. Arabella felt the last of her resistance melt away. Marcus was likely to have his way in the end in any case, so she might as well give in with good grace. Besides, what harm could result if she was with him one more time?

"Very well," she said against her better judgment. "I will come with you this once."

The slow smile he gave her was brilliant as he offered her his hand. "Come, we'll sneak out the back entrance in order to foil your sisters."

Arabella couldn't help but laugh. "How dignified for a belted earl to be slinking around his own estate," she said, taking his hand.

"Indeed," Marcus agreed dryly. "But I am forced to employ desperate measures. Now keep your voice down. I don't want anyone to hear us."

He led her out the rear kitchen door, which opened onto the herb garden, and from there to the main gardens. Arabella stifled a laugh as they wended their

way through the neat rows of shrubs and beds of flowers toward the rear of the manor. She felt deliciously
wicked, sneaking out of the house with her lover, yet
she couldn't summon any regrets. All her good sense
had fled, but all her senses had come alive. The night
was lovely, silver-bright with moonlight and fresh
with the sweet scents of spring.

It was her aching awareness of the man beside her,
however, that filled her with anticipation and excitement and need.

When they reached the terraced lawns, Marcus
drew her closer and bent to whisper in her ear. "I feel
like a schoolboy playing truant . . . except that no
schoolboy was ever this painfully swollen."

He guided her fingers to the enormous bulge in his
breeches, and Arabella shivered. Knowing how much
he wanted her roused a pulsing ache between her
thighs and left her breathless with her own longing.

In unspoken agreement, they quickened their pace
until they reached the line of trees that flanked the
river and sheltered them from sight of the manor.
They had to slow as they pushed through a glade, but
the moment they came out into the moonlight again,
Marcus halted and dragged Arabella against him,
seizing her mouth in a fierce possession.

Their kiss exploded in a passionate blaze. The heat
he generated ignited sparks in Arabella's blood, filling
her with savage hunger. She wanted him with a feroc-
ity that shocked her.

Desperate to touch him, she reached down and
fumbled at the front placket of his breeches. Marcus

inhaled sharply at her boldness, but then hastened to help her, almost ripping at the buttons in order to free his rigid length.

It was Arabella's turn to inhale when she saw the dark, pulsing shaft thrust proudly out from his sleek loins.

"Come here," he demanded.

She obeyed, needing no further urging.

Swiftly, he raised her skirts to her waist and cupped the silken curls between her thighs. She was already shamelessly wet for him, and his eyes flared darkly in response. She could see his face in the moonlight—hard, beautiful, taut with desire—and knew the same desire was written on her features as he probed her feminine folds.

Arabella bit back a gasp as he stroked the sensitive bud of her sex and arched against him when he buried a long finger deep inside her. Only the need for discretion kept her from moaning in wild pleasure.

Her response apparently wasn't wild enough for Marcus, though. His midnight-blue eyes smoldering, he insinuated his muscular leg between hers and slid his hands around her hips to her derriere, then lifted her up.

Startled by his unexpected action, Arabella clung to his shoulders for balance.

"Wrap your legs around my waist," he ordered in a rough command.

"Marcus . . ."

He kissed her urgently again, drinking in any protest as his tongue thrust deeply into her mouth.

Below, his arousal penetrated her cleft and forged in with a slow, inexorable pressure. Her body was soft and yielding, accepting the hard strength of his, but even so, Arabella gasped at the searing feel of his claiming.

Marcus captured the sound with his mouth. With his legs braced wide, he anchored her against him and drove in the rest of the way, till he was sheathed deeply inside her.

Arabella trembled in his arms as her flesh swelled tightly around his large possession. It was breathtaking, being filled by him this way. Breathtaking and stunning in intensity.

He held her locked securely against him and began to move his hips, withdrawing and then surging upward, plunging in long, forceful strokes. She shuddered at the impact as he drove himself into her, huge and hard, pumping in a demanding, arousing rhythm while his mouth devoured hers.

His raw desire left her shaken; his hungry plundering made her wild. Moaning, she writhed against him, matching her movements to his with frenzied abandon.

It was hard and fast and thrilling . . . and utterly explosive. The inferno broke over them at the same moment, splintering shards of fiery sensation through them both. Arabella sobbed against his mouth while Marcus staggered at the powerful convulsions, his arms clenching around her. Reeling with desire, he drank in her helpless cries, rendering his own hoarse groans as he poured himself into her.

He was still gasping for breath when she sagged

against him. He thrust into her savagely one last time, then went still except for the racking tremors that continued to buffet him.

They remained fused together for a long while, vibrating with aftershocks. Even when their bodies ceased their wild quaking, Marcus held Arabella tightly, savoring the feel of her.

Finally, though, he eased her to her feet, supporting her with his embrace when she leaned limply against him, too weak to stand on her own.

Marcus's low curse was ragged in the hushed quiet of the night. "Damnation . . . no finesse *again*."

The husky, exhausted laughter that tumbled from her lips touched him even more than her wild response had done, but he couldn't excuse his own wildness. He pressed his lips against her hair in apology for his savagery. "Forgive me, Belle. I haven't lost control like that since I was a callow youth, but I couldn't wait."

"There is nothing to forgive," she rasped against his shoulder. "I couldn't wait, either."

He could hear the laughter in her voice, the pleasure, the contentment, and another fierce stab of desire pierced him.

Then Arabella raised her head and looked up at him, her beautiful face glowing in the moonlight. His heart turned over at the sight.

"I had no idea it was possible to make love that way," she whispered almost shyly.

He'd had no idea, either. He had never made love with such frenzy. The frantic urgency had left him gasping. He'd never felt such bliss with anyone but

Arabella. The satisfaction of making love to her was shattering.

Perhaps it was her inexperience. Every aspect of lovemaking was very new to her, and her wonder and delight made it seem new to him, too. Tonight, however, she had responded to him with an ardent passion that had stolen his breath, his very heart—

Marcus suddenly went very still as the stunning realization shot through him.

He had fallen in love with Arabella. How else could he explain the powerful emotions he felt for her?

The thought jolted him badly; his head was reeling, his heart racing.

Yet he no longer had any doubt. He loved her.

It should have come as no surprise, he mused as he searched her face a little dazedly. Not when he felt such overwhelming possessiveness toward Arabella. Not when he felt such pleasure whenever he was with her. Such contentment. Such simple joy.

No woman had ever affected him as Arabella did; no one had ever come close. She supplied the fire that had been missing from his life.

Drew and Heath would call him mad—and perhaps he was. He'd been smitten, there was no other way to explain the feeling of tenderness and excitement that swept over him when he merely thought of Arabella. He'd never felt this profound need to be with someone the way he did with her.

Marcus inhaled a steadying breath. He hadn't counted on developing an unexpected ardor for his beautiful ward. So now what the devil was he to do about it?

He found himself frowning. Arabella had stormed the defenses of his heart while hers remained still intact. He felt his gut clench, realizing he faced a much greater dilemma than winning their wager. He wouldn't settle for a marriage of convenience with her now. Not when he finally recognized the depth of his feelings.

But winning Arabella's heart would be an even more daunting task than gaining her hand in marriage.

"What is wrong?" she asked when he continued staring at her.

Marcus schooled his expression to nonchalance. She wouldn't believe him if he told her; any professions of love he made would be considered mere blandishments in his effort to seduce her.

"Nothing is wrong," he lied. "I was only contemplating how beautiful you are in the moonlight."

The soft smile that curved her mouth made his heart quicken, but it started racing again when she pressed a soft kiss to his lips.

"I had best return to the house," she whispered, "before my sisters realize I am gone."

No, I won't let you go, Marcus thought fiercely. He was conscious of a savage urge to carry Arabella far away from here, a primal craving to keep her captive, in his sole possession, until she finally agreed to wed him and give him her heart.

Yet force wouldn't gain her surrender, he knew. She didn't trust him enough to love him. Didn't trust him not to hurt her.

Somehow he had to convince Arabella otherwise.

Realizing he needed to give the matter careful consideration, Marcus stepped back and fastened his breeches, then straightened her clothing.

Crushing the urge to make love to her again, he took her hand and led her back through the glade and across the terraced lawns to the gardens.

They entered the house the same way they had left, by the rear kitchen door. Marcus escorted Arabella as far as the back service stairs, where he paused to gaze down at her in the dim light of a wall sconce. He meant to kiss her good night before sending her up to her bedchamber alone, but when he took her in his arms, a noise above him made him halt.

Looking up, Marcus cursed silently.

Arabella's sisters were waiting for them at the head of the stairs, and neither appeared happy. Roslyn's expression was troubled, while Lilian looked dismayed.

"See, I told you Belle was in danger," Lily said, her voice low and hoarse and despairing.

Chapter Fourteen

✤

What fools we females can be, letting ourselves be seduced by a charming address and a handsome face.
—Arabella to Fanny

Protectively, Marcus stepped in front of Arabella, but she wouldn't allow herself to hide behind him.

"Good night, my lord," she murmured, slipping past him.

He caught her arm. "If you need me—"

"Thank you, but I had best speak to my sisters alone."

Aware that she had badly disappointed them, Arabella mounted the stairs to the second-floor landing. Both Lily and Roslyn followed her down the corridor to her bedchamber and closed the door behind them. The strained silence that ensued did not last long.

"How could you, Arabella?" Lily demanded unhappily. "Sneaking out with the earl for a midnight tryst. You have been kissing him, haven't you? Your hair is disheveled and your mouth is red and bruised."

Indeed, she looked a perfect wanton, Arabella realized when she glimpsed her reflection in the cheval glass. She bit her lower lip in chagrin. At least the damp, tender ache between her thighs wasn't visible.

Her muteness only distressed Lily more. "Just how far has your affair with Lord Danvers gone, Belle?"

She could feel heat searing her cheeks. She had no desire to confess that she had not only given her virginity to Marcus, she'd spent the last three nights making mad, passionate love with him.

Before Lily could press her further, however, Roslyn intervened in a gentler but just as troubled tone. "We are worried for you, Arabella. You are exhibiting all the signs of a dangerous ardor. We don't want you to be hurt again."

Arabella grimaced. "You needn't worry, truly. I won't let myself fall in love like last time."

"But you could still be hurt," Roslyn pointed out. "Think carefully, Arabella. If you continue in this vein, you may have no choice but to wed Lord Danvers. You cannot afford to create a scandal—not unless you are prepared to see our academy's reputation suffer. If your indiscretions become known, marriage to him will be your only course."

Disliking to acknowledge that possibility, Arabella swallowed hard. She had deliberately ignored the risk of scandal for the momentary pleasure of being with Marcus.

"Yes, please *think,* Arabella," Lily pleaded. "You don't want to be forced to wed him to save your reputation."

"Even worse," Roslyn added softly, "is the prospect of being locked in a union like Mama and Papa were. If the earl doesn't love you, he could make your life a misery the way Papa did Mama."

"I know," Arabella murmured. "My behavior has been reckless. But it won't happen again."

"I hope not," Lily said, true distress in her voice. "If you don't take care, he will seduce you. Surely you don't want to wind up like Mama, falling under the spell of a charmer, lusting after a man to the detriment of your entire family?"

The notion struck Arabella like a blow. *Was that what she was doing?* She stared at her youngest sister in dismay. It appalled her to think that she might be following in her mother's footsteps.

"Has it come to that, Arabella?" Roslyn said more quietly. "Are you letting your heart overrule your head, like Mama did?"

Arabella shook her head earnestly. "My heart is not involved. I have known Marcus barely a few weeks. That is too short a time to develop any lasting ardor."

"You may not be able to help yourself," Lily asserted. "Doubtless he is counting on your feminine weakness, trusting that he can make you fall in love with him. He is playing on your physical desires—and he is clearly succeeding."

Arabella couldn't refute the charge; she had warned herself of the same thing countless times. She raised a hand to her temple. "I won't deny that I feel a physical attraction for him, but it is only passion I feel."

"Then you had best keep away from him entirely," Roslyn advised. "Passion is not a sound basis for marriage. Passion can burn out quickly, and then what is left?" Roslyn hesitated, gazing at her sympathetically. "It might be different if there were any chance you could come to love each other."

Roslyn's advocacy of love was not surprising. She

was not set against marriage as Lily was; she just felt strongly that love must come first if a union was to have any chance of truly prospering.

"There is little chance of that," Arabella replied. "He doesn't want a love match. He only wants a marriage of convenience with a proper wife to breed him heirs."

"Then you should end your courtship now."

"Yes," Lily seconded. "You don't dare risk falling in love with him, Belle. Love can turn you into an utter fool, blinding you to all else."

Arabella nodded in agreement. Roslyn was the wisest of the three of them and could be counted on to analyze the situation rationally. Lily, on the other hand, was speaking from sheer emotion. Despite her hoydenish ways, she was the most sensitive Loring sister and had been hurt most by their mother's abandonment.

Yet Arabella shared Lily's feelings in this instance. Love made a woman much too vulnerable and susceptible to lunacy. She well knew the pain love could cause, both from her own experience and from her mother's. Victoria Loring had fallen in love and destroyed her family because of it. . . .

"You are right, of course," Arabella murmured.

Evidently Lily wasn't convinced of her sincerity. "We can try to help you resist him, but only you can crush your feelings for him before they go too far."

"I know." She couldn't—*wouldn't*—permit herself to fall in love with Marcus. She squared her shoulders. "You needn't worry about me, Lily. Our wager ends on Monday—only two and a half more days."

"Hang the blasted wager!" Lily declared. "You have to call it off immediately. It is not worth the risk."

She couldn't call off the wager now. Not when she was so close. She had her sisters to think of as well as herself. Their independence was also at stake. If she lost the wager, Lily and Roslyn would suffer for it.

Taking a deep breath, she gazed solemnly back at them, filled with new resolve. "No, truly. I promise I will keep away from Marcus from now on. No midnight trysts . . . no trysts of any kind. I won't allow myself to be alone with him ever again."

It was a promise she was determined to keep, Arabella vowed to herself. The reminder of their mother's behavior had had a chilling effect—and she had absolutely no intention of losing her heart the way her mother had done.

She managed to hold to her promise for the better part of the next day. Knowing Marcus had an afternoon appointment in London on a political matter but not wanting to risk encountering him beforehand, Arabella eschewed breakfast and left Danvers Hall early with her sisters to take refuge at the academy. There, she distracted herself the entire morning by listening to musical performances.

The afternoon passed much more slowly, since it was Saturday. With only a half day of lessons scheduled, the young ladies were allowed the afternoon free to do whatever they pleased. Most chose to go shopping in the village, which left the school unusually quiet.

Despite Arabella's best intentions and her sisters' attempts to divert her, Marcus occupied her thoughts far too often. Thus, she accepted readily when Roslyn and Lily suggested they take an early tea with Jane Caruthers, the spinster who ran the school's daily operations. When Tess Blanchard elected to join them, the pleasant interlude became reminiscent of the early days before they opened the academy, when the five of them had regularly gathered to discuss plans.

Afterward, the ladies repaired to the dining room, where their pupils were partaking of their own tea. They had barely settled when Jane was summoned away by the housekeeper, Mrs. Phipps.

A short while later, Arabella also found herself approached by Mrs. Phipps, who whispered urgently, "Forgive the interruption, Miss Loring, but Miss Caruthers asks to speak with you in private."

"Very well, where is she?" Arabella asked.

"The dormitory. Miss Newstead's room."

When Arabella eventually mounted the stairs to Sybil Newstead's bedchamber, she found Jane wringing her hands.

"Sybil has disappeared," was Jane's immediate pronouncement, "and I fear she has left the grounds."

Arabella frowned. Sybil had not come down to tea, but that in itself was not alarming, since one of her schoolmates had claimed she had taken ill and was resting in her room. But obviously the girl was not in her bed.

Tess joined them as Arabella asked Jane, "What makes you believe she has left the grounds?"

"Her bandbox is missing, along with several of her best gowns. And the maid we set to watch her has disappeared as well. No one but Caroline Trebbs has seen Sybil since this morning."

Arabella's frown deepened. The two girls shared this bedchamber, and Caroline had been the one to report Sybil's illness.

"I think we had best talk to Miss Trebbs," Arabella said, "before we draw any rash conclusions."

She kept her voice calm but felt a niggling uneasiness in the pit of her stomach. Sybil Newstead was capable of most any indiscretion, although why she would have run away was puzzling. As for the maid, Sybil could possibly have bribed the servant to look the other way, although it would be worth her position—

"Do you think she might have eloped?" Tess asked, clearly worried.

Arabella's uneasiness turned to alarm. "Dear heaven, I hope not." But that would be one rational explanation for Sybil's disappearance.

When Jane went to fetch Caroline Trebbs from the drawing room, Arabella waited with Tess impatiently. Her mind raced as she tried to recall observing any unusual behavior from Sybil recently—an exercise in futility, Arabella knew. She had paid little attention to any of her pupils this past week, she had been so busy being wooed by Marcus. But for an elopement, Sybil would have to have a suitor—

Her alarm twisted into a knot of dread as the answer struck her: *Jasper Onslow*. She had caught the notorious rake stealing a kiss from Sybil on the balcony at the

Perrys' ball. A wastrel like Onslow might be desperate enough to lower himself to marry a mill heiress for her vast fortune. But had Sybil gone willingly? Her missing gowns suggested that force hadn't been necessary. . . .

Arabella's whirling thoughts were interrupted when Jane returned with Caroline. Miss Trebbs was a plump, plain-looking girl. When she entered the bedchamber with obvious reluctance, the guilty look on her face spoke volumes.

Arabella didn't waste time with polite queries. "Caroline, we need you to tell us where Sybil has gone."

Bowing her head, the girl mumbled something unintelligible.

"She took you into her confidence, didn't she?" Arabella pressed, striving for patience.

"Y-yes, Miss Loring. . . . But I promised not to tell. Sybil said she would cut out my tongue if I b-breathed a word to anyone."

Arabella drew a slow breath. "We won't let her harm you, Caroline. Please, we need you to tell us what has happened. She could be in danger."

It was another long moment before Caroline said in a rush, "Sybil is not really in danger, Miss Loring. She went to Gretna Green."

Jane let out a low moan, while Tess met Arabella's eyes with similar dismay. Sybil apparently had eloped to Scotland with her fortune hunter suitor, just as they feared.

"Did she go with Mr. Onslow?" Arabella asked.

Caroline's jaw slackened as she stared in surprise. "How did you know?"

"Never mind. Just tell us what she planned. It will take at least three days for them to drive to Scotland, perhaps more. What arrangements did they make? When did they leave?"

"Shortly after classes let out . . . when we went shopping in the village. Mr. Onslow met us there with his carriage."

"How did she intend to deal with her maid?" Tess asked. "I doubt Martha would simply have let Sybil elope without protest."

Caroline hung her head, as if ashamed. "Sybil knew Martha wouldn't keep quiet, so she made her come with them. They planned to set her down further on tonight, to make her way home by mailcoach tomorrow. And I was to cover for Sybil this evening by saying she was ill. She thought the soonest anyone would miss her was tomorrow after church."

"Yet Mrs. Phipps," Jane said tightly, "began wondering where Martha had gotten to, and so she searched this room and found Sybil's belongings missing."

"Yes," Caroline whispered. Her gaze returned to Arabella. "I am so very sorry I lied, Miss Loring, truly."

Arabella bit her tongue to keep from lashing out at the girl, but Jane didn't. "This could ruin us," she muttered. "Mr. Newstead will be outraged—"

But Arabella didn't want to discuss the academy's business before one of their pupils. "Caroline, I wish you to return to the dining room for now. And please don't say a word to any of the other girls."

"I won't, I swear it."

Jane had had enough of patience, however. "Young ladies do *not* swear, Miss Trebbs."

"Yes, Miss Caruthers . . . ah, no, Miss Caruthers. . . ." With quivering meekness, Caroline gave Jane a wide berth as she crept from the room.

Arabella looked at her two friends in shared dismay, excruciatingly aware of the scandal that threatened them. If they allowed one of their wealthy young pupils to fall into the clutches of a fortune hunter, marriage or not, no parents would ever trust the academy again with their daughters.

Even worse, Sybil could suffer more than a loss of her reputation. By eloping with only a maid for protection, she risked ravishment. No matter how vexing the girl was, she didn't deserve that fate. And regardless, her entire future was at stake. If she was merely witless enough to let herself be seduced because she fancied herself in love, she was making a grave mistake, since Onslow was not the kind of man to cherish anyone but himself. Sybil was unlikely to relish life as his wife.

Arabella hated to think of any innocent young girl at that bounder's mercy, even the troublesome minx Sybil. Besides, she thought grimly, Sybil was supposed to be under *her* protection. It was her responsibility to keep her pupils safe, and it appeared that she might have failed.

"We must stop them somehow," Tess said, stating what they were all three thinking.

"But how?" Jane asked.

"I will go after them at once," Arabella replied, putting a hand to her temple as she thought madly. "They have nearly four hours' head start, but they will likely put up at an inn tonight. I cannot see Sybil suffering the inconvenience of sleeping in a carriage. If I drive through the night, I may be able to catch them."

"But you will need help," Tess pointed out. "Would Lord Danvers be willing to accompany you?"

Arabella nodded. "I'm certain he would, but he is in London for the day, and I expect he took his coach since it threatened to rain this morning. I will ask Lady Freemantle to loan me her coach and several stout footmen as well. They should be able to help me convince Mr. Onslow to abandon his designs on Sybil."

"What if he has already . . ." Jane broke off, her face turning red.

Arabella understood the question, but Tess spoke first. "Already claimed her virtue?" she supplied. "Sybil would be an utter fool to let him touch her before they were properly married, and she is cunning enough to keep the upper hand until then."

"He may be dastardly enough to force her," Arabella observed.

"Perhaps, but I don't think he will risk it," Tess said reassuringly, "since Sybil is just stubborn enough to refuse to marry him if he tried to coerce her. No doubt she sees an elopement as an adventure and hasn't properly considered the full consequences. She thinks her father can be persuaded to accept him for her husband. Onslow may be a rake and a wastrel, but he is considered a gentleman in most circles, and would be a fair catch for a tradesman's daughter."

Jane's mouth twisted in a mournful grimace. "But

even if Mr. Newstead eventually accepts the marriage, our academy will never recover from the blow."

"I know," Arabella said grimly. Everything they had striven for during the past three years would be ruined.

When she remained silent, Tess searched her face. "Wouldn't you prefer to wait for his lordship to return?"

She would indeed prefer to wait for Marcus, but she didn't have time. "I must leave right away, Tess. If we hope to keep the elopement quiet, I will have to bring Sybil back before anyone discovers she is missing."

"Perhaps I should come with you," Tess offered.

"I think it best if I go alone," Arabella responded. "My absence from the school won't be remarkable, but if both of us are gone, it will be noted. Roslyn and Lily should remain here also and attend church tomorrow as usual to keep up appearances."

"So how do we explain Sybil's absence?" Jane asked.

Tess answered that question. "We can say she became ill, and that Arabella took her to London to see Lady Freemantle's personal physician."

"That should suffice," Jane said. "Assuming you can find Sybil and prevent the marriage."

"Oh, I *will* find her," Arabella said with determination. She had no intention of letting the exasperating little chit ruin herself or the academy. "And I will keep them from marrying, even if I have to order Winifred's footmen to overpower Onslow so I can drag Sybil home by her hair."

With no time to waste, Arabella found her sisters and managed to gain their approval of the plan. Although reluctant to let her go alone, Roslyn and Lily clearly understood the need for discretion and agreed to remain behind and support the pretense they'd concocted.

Next, Arabella quickly drove the gig to the Freemantle estate. She hoped to leave as soon as she could borrow Winifred's coach and footmen, but she hadn't counted on her friend balking.

After listening to Arabella's request, Winifred shook her head adamantly. " 'Tis a demmed fool thing even to consider, my dear, you chasing after them alone. You need to let Danvers handle the matter."

"He is not here to handle it, Winifred," Arabella said, taken aback by her refusal. "He is in London."

"Then you should wait for his return."

Arabella tried to quell her impatience. "I cannot wait. Sybil is in my charge, Winifred. I am responsible for her well-being. She could be in real danger."

"And you could be putting yourself in danger if you follow her. You should rely on Danvers to help you. He is your guardian, after all."

"Not for long. By next week, he will be obliged to grant my sisters and me emancipation from his guardianship. But that is entirely beside the point."

Winifred gave her a stern look. "You cannot go gallivanting off across England all alone without protection, Arabella."

"I will have your coachman and footmen to protect me."

"Lord Danvers would do better than a score of servants."

Doubtless he would, Arabella silently agreed. She

desperately wished Marcus were here to help her. On the other hand, she had no desire to be cooped up in a closed carriage with him for who knew how long, since it would prove a severe test of her willpower.

Regardless of her own wishes or reservations, however, she didn't dare delay.

"I don't intend to stand here arguing, Winifred. If you won't help me, I will hire a carriage at the posting inn."

Impatiently, Arabella turned on her heel, but was stopped by Winifred's protest. "Oh, very well, you may have my coach and servants. But if you wind up getting in over your head, my dear, you cannot say I didn't warn you."

"I won't," Arabella promised.

A quarter hour later, she sank back against the velvet squabs as Lady Freemantle's coachman whipped up the team of horses. Five strapping grooms and footmen served as postilions and outriders, allowing Arabella to breathe a sigh of relief as she finally set out in pursuit of the eloping couple.

What Sybil had done was deplorable, Arabella reflected, but despite her anger and dismay at her errant pupil, she could sympathize to some extent.

After all, the girl was not so different from herself, unable to resist a seductive suitor.

Her relief lasted only a few hours. The coach made good time at first, heading directly for the nearby town of Hammersmith, where five main roads converged, and reaching north London and the main road to Scotland before dark. After that, however, they faced numerous delays, since they paused at each posting house to inquire after the fleeing Sybil and her scoundrel of a suitor.

To protect the chit's reputation as well as her own, Arabella fabricated a tale about Sybil being her cousin, claiming they were making an urgent journey home since Sybil's mother was gravely ill. Regrettably, though, none of the ostlers or innkeepers remembered seeing a raven-haired young lady, with or without her maid or gentleman escort.

When night fell, Arabella's coachman had to slow the pace considerably, for the moonlight was greatly diminished by thick black clouds scudding across the sky. Then when they stopped briefly at a posting inn to change teams, other travelers warned that a fierce storm was brewing up ahead, directly in their path.

The warning proved all too true. The roiling clouds quickly turned ominous and soon gusts of wind began buffeting the coach, rocking Arabella inside. She could smell the heavy scent of rain in the air long before she heard the first drops strike the rooftop.

The thunderstorm hit full force a half hour later, lashing them with a blinding rain punctuated by frequent bursts of lightning and rolling cracks of thunder.

The danger grew even worse when the coach wheels started to slide precariously. The road had turned treacherous with mud, and Arabella found herself clutching the strap just to keep from being thrown off the seat each time the coach lurched over a rut.

Tension filled her and didn't ease when she felt the vehicle slow to a halt a few moments later.

When the coachman drew back the small driver's panel to speak to her, he had to shout to be heard over the pounding rain. " 'Tis no use, Miss Loring! We 'ave to take shelter till the storm passes."

Arabella nodded grimly, knowing they had no choice but to call a halt to the search tonight. Even if they avoided being struck by lightning, they risked serious accident and even injury from losing a wheel or turning over in a ditch.

"Can we make it to the next inn and put up for the night?" she shouted back over the din.

"Aye, there's the Duck and Bill up ahead a mile or two. But I canna keep the team calm much longer."

As if to emphasize his point, the heavens erupted again: A glittering bolt of lightning lit up the night with garish white, followed by an enormous clap of thunder, which sent the frightened horses plunging wildly ahead.

"Do your best," she urged, grabbing the strap again as the coach lunged forward.

Thankfully the coachman wrestled his team to a halt, but another delay ensued while the two postilions climbed down to hand-lead the jittery horses through the engulfing tempest. It was heavy going, slogging through the mud and driving rain, and they only managed a snail's pace.

Pitying the poor servants and animals who were exposed to the violent storm, Arabella muttered a frustrated oath. No doubt Sybil was tucked snugly in bed at an inn, sleeping soundly, while her pursuers were risking life and limb to chase after her.

By some miracle the coach made it safely to the Duck and Bill and limped into the deserted stable yard. The rain still came down in torrents, though, and when the coach door was opened by one of her footmen, it was slammed back by a gust of wind with enough force to take Arabella's breath away.

Although she drew her hooded cloak tightly around her, by the time she made it inside the inn, she was drenched and shivering. But the innkeeper and his wife were eager to accommodate her, promising to see to her servants and horses and offering Arabella the last empty bedchamber. There was no private parlor available, since the inn was nearly full with stranded travelers.

She explained her lack of baggage similarly, by saying she hadn't planned on stopping overnight, and giving the same tale as before about her aunt being critically ill. When she asked after her "cousin" Sybil, however, Arabella was gratified to hear that a couple matching Sybil's and Onslow's descriptions had changed horses and taken supper there some three hours earlier, which at least gave her confidence that she was on the right track.

The innkeeper's wife led Arabella upstairs to a small but cozy bedchamber and lit the fire in the hearth, then left promising to bring her some supper and hot mulled wine shortly. Soon a welcoming blaze burned brightly enough to take the chill from the room although not from her bones.

Arabella removed her sodden cloak as well as her mud-caked shoes and stockings and arranged them before the fire to dry. Yet she couldn't sit still. Instead, she paced restlessly before the hearth, feeling utterly impotent. The storm had spoiled her plans to reach Sybil tonight. Now she could only hope that the elopers had been delayed by the dreadful weather as well—and even if not, that she would catch up to them sometime tomorrow.

After a while, however, the lack of activity sent Arabella's thoughts wandering down a different path, and she found herself dwelling on her own predicament, namely her wager with Marcus.

Rubbing her chilled arms as she stared down at the fire, she wondered if he would demand more time to win, since she hadn't allowed him to share her company at all today and might not be home by tomorrow. And from there, she started remembering their moonlit tryst last night . . . how Marcus had taken her standing up, the searing passion—

Realizing where her errant reflections had taken her, Arabella gave a snort of vexation and turned away from the hearth.

Suddenly a wave of exhaustion claimed her. Since there was nothing more she could do this evening, she decided she might as well try to sleep, although the noise from the storm would likely make that difficult. Rain beat against the shutters, while the wind moaned around the eaves.

Trying to ignore the bluster, she removed her gown and petticoats and corset, intending to sleep in her shift, since she had no nightdress. She had just drawn a quilt around her to keep warm when she heard a soft rap on the door. Expecting that the innkeeper's wife had returned with her supper and wine, Arabella crossed the room in time to hear the woman call out: "Yer ladyship? Yer 'usband is come."

Husband? Arabella thought with puzzlement.

Pulling the quilt more tightly about her, she opened the door partway to peer out.

Her eyes widened first in surprise, then elation. Marcus stood there in the corridor, his wet ebony hair plastered to his head, the capes of his great coat dripping with rain, his top boots coated with mud. The leather saddlebags he'd slung over one arm were also soaked through, as was the tall beaver hat he carried.

When he offered her a cool smile, Arabella drank in the sight of him, realizing that he had somehow ridden after her. Odd how seeing him not only filled her with gladness but made all her weariness and misery suddenly evaporate.

"Ah, there you are, my dear," he said, pushing the door open and strolling past her into the room. "I am pleased I finally caught up to you."

Chapter Fifteen

❧

It is deplorable, how few defenses I have against him.
—Arabella to Fanny

After tossing his hat and saddlebags on a table, Marcus turned to survey Arabella's beautiful face with a cross between anger and relief. Relief that she had made it safely through the fierce storm and that he had managed to overtake her. Anger because she had set out on a potentially dangerous mission by herself, with no thought to her own safety.

At least she didn't refute his claim of being her husband in front of the inn's proprietress. Evidently Arabella understood the necessity of endorsing the lie to protect her reputation, for she offered him a smile of welcome. "I did not expect you to follow me, dearest."

"I disliked you making such a long journey alone without my protection, love," Marcus replied tersely.

"But I had no wish to put you to such trouble."

When his gaze narrowed on Arabella, her luminous gray eyes returned his regard steadily.

A throat being politely cleared reminded Marcus they were not alone; the proprietress lingered just outside the bedchamber door.

The woman indicated the tray she carried. "I've a pot of hot mulled wine for 'er ladyship, m'lord, and some supper."

"Set it on the table, if you please," Marcus instructed.

"I can bring more if ye wish."

"That won't be necessary. I'm certain my wife is willing to share."

"Of course," Arabella agreed pleasantly.

Entering the room, the proprietress set the tray down next to his saddlebags, then turned to go. "If ye'll put yer boots outside the door, yer lordship, I'll have 'em cleaned and polished by morning."

Marcus shot an impatient glance down at his ruined boots. "I doubt anything can save this pair. But I would ask that you have breakfast ready by dawn. We want to make an early start in the morning."

"Aye, m'lord." With a curtsy, the innkeeper's wife withdrew and shut the door behind her, finally leaving Marcus alone with Arabella.

"I am waiting for an explanation, sweeting," he said in a dangerous voice.

"Explanation?" she repeated, puzzled.

"Lady Freemantle told me about the elopement and your plan to try and stop it. What I want to know is why you didn't wait for my return."

Her eyes widened at his angry tone. "I had no choice, Marcus. The situation was too urgent. Onslow could very well seduce Sybil. Even if he marries her, it cannot possibly be a sound marriage."

"That is no excuse for you to risk your own safety."

Arabella stared at him. "I cannot believe you are angry at *me*! I am worried my pupil will be ruined by a rake, Marcus. She is my responsibility."

He strode over to her. "And you are my responsibility." Capturing her chin with his fingers, Marcus compelled her to look at him. "As long as I am your guardian, I'm obliged to see to your safety. And guardian or not, I'm not about to let any harm come to you. If you are in trouble, I expect to help."

Her chin rose stubbornly. "I am perfectly capable of handling Sybil's rescue."

"That is debatable, but I don't intend to let you fight this battle on your own."

"I am not on my own! I brought an army of servants with me for protection."

"So you plan to get into a physical brawl with Onslow?"

"If I must in order to force him to relinquish Sybil."

"That seems foolish when there are better ways to convince him."

Arabella's lips pressed together tightly as they stood nose to nose, glaring at each other. But then her expression suddenly softened. "You are right, of course. I don't wish to use brute force. To be truthful, I am relieved you are here. I was not looking forward to dealing with Onslow by myself."

"I should hope not."

A frown creased her brow. "I have to stop him, Marcus. Even if Sybil comes through unscathed, an elopement will destroy our school's reputation."

The distress in her tone was obvious, and some of

his wrath dissipated a measure. "You still should have called on me."

"Perhaps so." Her mouth curved. "Truly, I will be grateful for your help." When he didn't reply, her gaze traveled downward, over his sodden greatcoat. "You rode on horseback through that dreadful storm?"

"Unfortunately yes, since a carriage would have been too slow when you already had a two-hour head start."

"I am sorry you had to suffer such a miserable experience."

Marcus gave her a quelling look. "If you are trying to soothe my ire, it won't work."

"No?" Arabella gazed up at him, a half smile playing on her lips. "Perhaps if you were warmer, your temper would be cooler. You should remove your wet coat and drink some hot wine. You must be totally chilled."

Finding no rational reason to argue—even though perversely wanting to—Marcus shed his soaked greatcoat and hung it on a wall peg to dry while Arabella moved over to the table and poured some hot mulled wine into a mug. She brought it to him, then returned to the hearth to warm herself before the fire.

Marcus sipped the wine while observing her. Her damp hair, which spilled around her shoulders and curled in drying wisps around her face, glowed bronze in the crackling blaze.

His gaze traveled downward to Arabella's bare feet, which peeped out from beneath the quilt she held around her shoulders. Wondering if she was naked beneath it made him instantly hard, despite the fact that his body felt half frozen from the frigid weather.

Disciplining his lust, Marcus carried the mug over to her. "Here, drink. You look as cold as I feel."

Arabella took it and sipped while gazing up at him. "Marcus, I would have gladly asked for your help had you been home."

In the face of such an apology, he knew it would be churlish to continue berating her. After all, she was only trying to protect her reckless pupil as well as her academy. Everything Arabella and her sisters had worked so hard for during the past three years was in jeopardy.

And in truth, he couldn't deny his admiration for her. He was worried for her safety and vexed as hell that she would endanger herself by flying to the rescue of her wayward student, but he had to admire Arabella's mettle, putting herself at risk to protect the young girls in her charge.

Not that he would admit it to her just now, Marcus decided. Arabella was too independent as it was.

She was still watching his face, as if gauging the depth of his anger. Finally she said in a soft, imploring tone, "I don't want to fight, Marcus. Do you?"

"No," he replied gruffly, his temper still inflamed after chasing after her for hours.

"Perhaps we should call another truce."

Marcus gave her a long look. "What did you have in mind?"

Casting a glance at the single bed, Arabella swallowed. "As you said, we're both chilled to the bone. We can warm each other."

It was a clear invitation to make love to her. The

prospect had the effect of pacifying his foul mood to a degree. It was the first time Arabella had made the advances in their relationship.

"Very well, a truce," Marcus said more calmly.

Draining the last of the wine, he set the mug aside and began to strip off his clothing, starting with his coat and waistcoat and boots. Tossing aside his cravat, he took off his shirt and breeches and drawers and hung the garments up to dry.

Completely naked now, he blew out the flame of the candle sitting on the table, leaving the bedchamber lit only by the warm glow from the fire.

As he crossed to Arabella, she let the quilt fall from her shoulders. Marcus halted in his tracks, his breath caught in his throat. Firelight betrayed her beauty through the filmy cambric of her chemise, while her hair spilled down in a glorious, rippling mane of flame.

When he moved to stand before her, she gave a soft laugh.

"What is so amusing?" he asked.

"This. Our pretense of being husband and wife." She reached up to touch his lips with her fingertips. "Isn't this what you have wanted all along, Marcus? To be able to call me your wife?"

It was exactly what he wanted. As he stared down at her, his anger and frustration eased away, to be replaced by desire and fierce tenderness. He was still a little stunned by the realization that he loved Arabella. But he knew now that it wasn't a passing fancy or a reckless obsession.

This feeling was deeper, more profound. Arabella

was the woman with whom he wanted to spend the rest of his days. He felt a burning need for her deep inside him. A heat and hunger that craved to be sated . . .

Holding her gaze, Marcus stepped even closer. He intended to brand her with his possession. To make her accept that she belonged to him. To make her feel the same primal need he felt.

With that silent vow, he reached for Arabella, divesting her of her chemise and drawing her naked into his arms. For a long moment he simply held her against him, the chill of their bodies mingling, the heat of their gazes melding.

He could win her body, he had little doubt; it was her heart he wanted now.

His own heart beginning to pound, Marcus lowered his mouth to kiss her gently, a sweet mating of skin, of breath, that gave little sign of the savage desire that raged through him. Yet as his lips met hers, a new emotion assailed him.

He had never experienced this particular novelty before, making love to the woman he loved. And it was a remarkable feeling.

Keeping their mouths fused, Marcus drew her to the bed and fell back upon the sheets, pulling her with him.

Arabella willingly sank into his embrace, her body fitting itself to his magnificent form as if she were made for him. Aching with need, she returned Marcus's kiss measure for measure, her fingers clutching in his hair as she blindly sought the rapture he promised.

Making love to him again was unquestionably a mistake, yet she couldn't deny herself the pleasure of being with him one last time. She wanted him with a longing that was almost frightening.

When the need grew too intense to bear, he took control back, rolling over her and pinning her arms above her head as he spread her thighs with his own. She opened eagerly to him as he thrust deep inside her.

Her heart pounding, she gazed up at him in the golden firelight, at his handsome face that had grown dark with desire. "I have no willpower when I am with you," Arabella whispered hoarsely.

"A damn good thing," he rasped, satisfied, "since I have none with you either."

He began to move then, vital and strong, filling her with his passion, with his hunger. In only moments she was sobbing . . . and then the climax came, as beautiful and as shattering as any of their lovemaking that had gone before. She cried out with ecstasy as she convulsed around him, while Marcus shuddered and groaned with the same overwhelming force.

Afterward, Arabella lay panting beneath him, unable to move. She wanted him to stay inside her like this forever, wanted this bliss to last. Marcus filled the emptiness inside her, made her feel complete.

At length, though, he eased onto his side and drew her back into the curve of his body. His arms came possessively around her from behind and held her tenderly as he twined his legs with hers. Arabella could feel the powerful beat of his heart at her back, while her own heart thudded with the chaotic emotions churning inside her.

She was frightened to realize how *right* it felt to be with Marcus. Arabella shut her eyes. She wanted him far too much, wanted to be with him far too much. It was deplorable, how glad she had been to see him. It was even more deplorable that she almost regretted their wager was nearly over.

She pulled a sharp breath and shivered.

"Are you cold?" Marcus's husky voice broke the silence between them.

"No . . . not any longer."

He was stroking her bare arm, his touch soothing and comforting now rather than arousing. His protective tenderness was even more dangerous than his passion, she realized, for it made her acknowledge the tenderness that tugged at her own heart.

She urgently needed to find Sybil, Arabella knew. There was no way she could hold out against Marcus if she had to travel alone with him all the way to Scotland, for continuing this tender intimacy would leave her utterly defenseless and more vulnerable than ever.

As Arabella had hoped, they set out in the Freemantle coach at first light the next morning, in pursuit of the elopers. Speed was of the essence, since Marcus believed Sybil and Onslow had likely been far enough ahead yesterday to have missed the worst of the storm.

Much to Arabella's frustration, though, her coachman could only achieve a snail's pace. After the downpour, the roads were a morass of mud, and even Winifred's well-sprung coach had difficulty keeping purchase as it rattled and splashed and bucked over innumerable ruts and potholes. The day was chill and gray, adding to Arabella's anxious mood.

She also felt a little stab of alarm when shortly after leaving the inn, Marcus drew a brace of pistols from his saddlebags to check the priming.

"Marcus," she said uneasily, "you don't mean to challenge Onslow to a duel, do you?" Her father had been killed in a duel, and she shuddered to think of resorting to such violence.

"No, I won't call him out," Marcus returned wryly. "A duel would draw too much attention to the situation. We need to prevent a scandal, not cause one."

A grimace claimed Arabella's features. "Yes, exactly."

"I don't intend to use these, but I want to be prepared for any eventuality."

She clung to the strap as the coach bounced over another rut. "Good. I don't want to even consider shooting him. However, if we are forced to make Onslow see reason, I admit I would be more than happy for you to use your fists."

Marcus sent her an amused glance. "Out for blood, are we?"

"Quite," she muttered.

"I expected you to be more enraged by that troublesome Newstead chit. She's likely the instigator of the elopement, wouldn't you say?"

Arabella sighed. "That is highly possible. Sybil is outrageously spoiled and thoughtless. But I don't consider her irredeemable. I will have to bring her back safe and sound, and with no one the wiser as to her elopement. Particularly her papa."

"We will find them eventually," Marcus reassured her.

"I only hope it is in time," Arabella said fervently, trying to stem her anxiety.

Miraculously, her hope was answered an hour later when they came across a closed carriage on the side of the road, canted at an unnatural angle from having lost a wheel. Praying the vehicle belonged to Onslow, Arabella held her breath while Marcus investigated. There were no signs of horses or coachman or passengers, although the boot held a valise containing three lace handkerchief's bearing Sybil's initials.

Arabella didn't know whether to be relieved or alarmed.

"They might have walked to the next posting inn," Marcus suggested, "in search of a wainwright to repair the wheel."

She shook her head. "I cannot see Sybil traipsing along the road any distance. She likely would have waited here in the carriage for the servants to handle the problem."

"If so, she would have been caught in the storm. . . ." Marcus glanced around, searching the countryside. "There." Beyond a grassy field stood the ruins of an old hay barn with the roof half missing. "They might have taken shelter in that abandoned barn."

Arabella sent him an admiring glance as he retrieved his pistols from the coach, knowing she never would have thought to look in a wayside barn for the elopers. Nor had she thought to come armed. She was indeed very grateful to have Marcus along.

He handed one pistol to her coachman and carried the other himself as he took Arabella's arm to help her negotiate the uneven, slippery ground. With the grooms following, he led the way across the field toward the crumbling barn.

They were still some dozen yards away when Arabella heard voices raised in argument. A surge of relief washed through her as she recognized Sybil's plaintive utterances. Gesturing for her coachman and grooms to wait, Arabella glanced up at Marcus. "Let me speak to her first, please?"

"Very well," he agreed, although he remained close behind her and kept his pistol at the ready.

She quickened her pace but came to a halt when she reached the large barn door that hung drunkenly on its hinges.

In the gloomy interior, she could see Onslow pacing the floor impatiently. Sybil was nowhere in sight, but her shrill voice floated over the edge of the loft above, declaring both her presence and her unhappiness as she carried on about what a cruel man Mr. Onslow was.

Onslow gave a visible start when he spied Arabella, but to her surprise, an unmistakable look of relief swept over his face. He came up short, however, when he saw Marcus standing directly behind her, holding a pistol.

His face paled, but then he squared his shoulders and strode determinedly forward. "Miss Loring," he said fervently, "you cannot know how grateful I am to see you."

At his greeting, Sybil's tirade stopped abruptly; a heartbeat later, she peered over the loft's edge, searching the gray gloom below. "Oh, Miss Loring! Thank heavens you have come to rescue me. That villain abducted me!"

Onslow shot a scathing glance upward at the girl. "Abducted you! I did no such thing."

"You refused to take me home when I asked you to! What is that if not abduction?"

"I refused because we were in the middle of a thunderstorm, you demmed little twit!"

Her face contorting with fury, Sybil rose to her knees and planted her hands on her hips. "There is no need to curse me, you . . . *fiend*! If you were not such a nip-cheese, you would have hired a coach with better wheels. And decent springs! I vow I am black and blue from being tossed about all day yesterday."

"The coach I hired was perfectly adequate. It was only ill-luck that the wheel broke. And you cannot blame me for your stubbornness. You could have been warm and dry at an inn, but no, you refused to dirty your slippers to walk to the next village."

"Of course I refused!" Sybil screeched. "I didn't wish to be seen in public in such a bedraggled state."

She did indeed look bedraggled, Arabella thought. Her raven hair was disheveled and littered with hay, as was her pelisse. And no doubt she was cold and hungry.

Before Arabella could speak, though, Sybil went on

ranting at Onslow. "Nor did I wish to spend the night alone with you without even my maid to act as chaperone! But no, you insisted upon leaving Martha at that posting inn twenty miles back because you were too closefisted to spend a few more shillings to put her up for the night."

"It was *your* idea to dismiss your maid and send her home! And the storm was hardly my fault."

Onslow glanced apologetically at Arabella. "We did not intend to spend the night here, Miss Loring. My coachman was supposed to return last night with a new wheel, but then the gale struck, so we were forced to take shelter here."

"It was still inexcusable of you to treat me so abominably!" the girl sputtered. "You made me sleep in a *barn*!"

Arabella quelled a smile. Sybil's indignation might have been amusing if the situation were not so serious, but at least the girl was regretting her rash action in eloping with Onslow, since he apparently couldn't afford to keep her in her accustomed luxury.

Summoning a stern expression, Arabella moved farther into the barn. "Sybil, pray quit shouting and come down here."

"I will once that villain leaves."

Onslow raised his gaze to the crumbling roof, as if pleading to Heaven for deliverance. "Thank God you are here, Miss Loring. You can take that vixen off my hands."

"Yes, thank God, Miss Loring," Sybil seconded. "I was a fool to ever think I wanted to wed Mr. Onslow.

He deceived me so dreadfully. I am quite convinced now that he was only after my fortune all along."

At that superfluous assertion, Arabella stifled the urge to utter a sardonic reply and merely repeated her command. "Sybil, come down this instant."

The girl disappeared for a moment, then eased over the loft edge to descend the rickety ladder, a maneuver which was made more difficult since she had a bandbox with her and refused to drop it.

While Sybil slowly made her way down, Arabella turned a withering gaze on Onslow. "You should be ashamed of yourself, Mr. Onslow, preying on young innocents."

"I assure you, ma'am, Miss Newstead is no innocent," he muttered. "She is a viper masquerading as a female."

Arabella felt her hands clench as she fought the urge to do him physical damage.

As if reading her mind, he held up his own hands in surrender. "I never touched her, Miss Loring, I swear it. Thankfully I came to my senses in time. I couldn't bear two days being wed to that spoiled little she-devil, let alone a lifetime."

Arabella felt another surge of relief that Sybil was still virginal. At least that disaster had been averted. When she shared a thankful look with Marcus, he stepped forward.

Nervously Onslow retreated a step. "M-My lord . . ." He eyed the pistol in alarm. "You w-won't shoot me, will you?"

"Not if you take yourself out of my sight in the next ten seconds."

"Yes, of c-course. . . ."

He started for the door, but Marcus stopped him. "Oh, and Onslow, when your carriage is repaired, you will continue on your way to Scotland, where you will make an extended stay. If you show your face anywhere near Chiswick again—and if I ever hear of you attempting to repair your fortunes by eloping with an heiress—you will be meeting me on the dueling field and swallowing a bullet. Nothing will save you. Do I make myself clear?"

His tone was cool and deadly, and Onslow clearly believed him, for his face turned stark white. "Perfectly clear, my lord. But you needn't worry. I have learned my lesson, I swear it."

When Marcus gestured with the pistol toward the door, Onslow ran out of the barn as if the little she-devil herself were on his heels.

In the ensuing silence, Sybil came to stand beside Arabella, her head bowed humbly. "Oh, Miss Loring, can you ever forgive me?"

Unable to believe such meekness, Arabella eyed the girl narrowly. "I cannot think of any reason I should."

"I made a dreadful mistake, thinking I wanted to wed that dastardly fortune hunter."

"You did indeed," she replied tartly. "Have you no sense whatsoever, Sybil?"

Awkwardly, the girl twisted the strings of her bandbox. "I thought it would be romantic to elope."

"And you didn't think about the future at all. You didn't consider what would happen to you two days from now, much less twenty years." Arabella's tone softened. "Marriage is a risk under the best of circumstances. Because of your reckless impulsiveness, you could have suffered for the rest of your life."

With that, Arabella turned to leave the barn.

Sybil hurried after her, carrying her bandbox. "You won't tell Papa that I almost eloped?"

"I am still debating that question."

"Please don't tell him, Miss Loring! Papa will be furious enough to withdraw me from school, and I don't want to leave. My comeout isn't until next Season."

Arabella said not another word until they reached the road. "Get in," she ordered Sybil as a groom hastened to open the door to the Freemantle carriage.

Mutely, the girl obeyed. Entering after her, Arabella settled next to Sybil, while Marcus stowed her bandbox in the boot and the coachman transferred her valise from Onslow's broken-down vehicle. After a brief discussion about driving to the next intersection so as to have the space to turn the coach around, Marcus joined them inside.

The coach was moving before Sybil spoke again in an imploring tone. "Please, Miss Loring, don't tell my father. If I have to leave the academy, I won't be prepared for my comeout next Season. I will behave with complete circumspection from now on, I swear it. I will be a perfect angel."

Arabella raised a cool eyebrow. "And what reason do I have to trust your word after this?"

The girl looked despairing. "I know I have been exceedingly foolish, Miss Loring, but I hope you can find it in your heart to forgive me." There was a note of sincerity in her voice that rang true. "*Please*, can't we keep this between us? I *beg* you."

Arabella waited a long moment before she shrugged as if coming to a decision. "Very well, we will keep it between ourselves—if that is even possible at this juncture."

The coach slowed just then in order to change directions, and a short while later they were heading back toward London.

"Will you take me back to school?" Sybil asked, her tone still subdued.

"Not immediately. You will stay with Lady Freemantle for a day or two. We'll say that you became ill and that I took you to London to see her ladyship's physician. You will recuperate at her house for a time. If Lady Freemantle publicly vouches for you, that should be enough to scotch the worst gossip and prevent any permanent damage to your reputation."

"Oh, *thank you*, Miss Loring."

Arabella sent the girl an arch smile. "You may not be so thankful once you spend time living with her ladyship. She won't be as forgiving of someone who thoughtlessly jeopardized our academy. I doubt you will find the experience pleasant."

Arabella caught the amused gleam in Marcus's eye and quickly looked away. On the one hand, she was enormously relieved to have found Sybil. Her most immediate problem was solved—or it would be if they could conceal the truth of the elopement. And the vexing chit would likely think twice before causing any more serious trouble.

On the other hand, there was still the much larger problem of Marcus to be dealt with.

Arabella bit her lower lip as she gazed out at the passing countryside. At least Sybil's company saved her from the temptation of any further intimacy with Marcus.

She still felt the urge to throttle the girl, but even so, she was very glad for her presence until she could make it home to her sisters.

Chapter Sixteen

I am ten times a fool for letting myself fall in love again.

—Arabella to Fanny

It was late afternoon by the time they were able to settle Sybil with Lady Freemantle and return to Danvers Hall in her ladyship's coach. Alone with Marcus on the drive home, Arabella was very aware of him sitting beside her. The nerves twisting her stomach tightened further when the carriage rumbled to a halt before the manor, for she felt his penetrating blue gaze appraising her.

"Thank you for helping me rescue Sybil," she said to break the tension.

"Don't regard it. I was glad to oblige."

Pushing open the door, Marcus descended and then handed Arabella down. At his mere touch, she felt herself shiver with desire. Thank heavens their wager was nearly over. She had only one more evening to get through.

"Forgive me if I leave you so abruptly," Arabella murmured. "I need to find my sisters and set their minds at ease about Sybil."

"Of course," Marcus said mildly as she preceded him across the gravel drive to the front steps. "But I would like to speak with you privately before dinner. Why don't you join me in my study in an hour?"

"Very well," Arabella replied before hurrying into the house.

As she expected, her sisters were on the lookout for her arrival, for they met her in the entrance hall.

"So, were you successful?" Roslyn murmured, obviously anxious to hear the news but not wanting to broadcast the purpose of the journey to all the servants.

"Thankfully, yes," Arabella replied. "I will tell you about it if you accompany me upstairs."

Lily eyed Marcus with a measuring frown before turning to follow Arabella up to her bedchamber, where she recounted the events of the past day, leaving out the fact that she had spent the night in Marcus's arms.

But once reassured of Sybil's safety, her sisters turned their concern on her.

"Are you all right, Arabella?" Lily asked, clearly troubled. "I regret we weren't with you to protect you from the earl. If we had known he meant to set out after you, we would at least have tried to accompany him."

"I am perfectly fine," Arabella assured her.

"I do hope you were able to resist him."

She tried to quell the flush that rose to her cheeks. "I managed well enough," she equivocated. "And thankfully, I won't have to worry about the earl after tomorrow. He has asked to speak to me before dinner this evening. I expect he wishes to discuss the resolution of our wager."

"And what do you mean to tell him?" Roslyn asked.

Arabella summoned a smile. "Why, that I have won, of course."

Roslyn regarded her thoughtfully, but Lily looked relieved. "Good," Lily said emphatically. "He needs to understand there is no chance you will marry him."

"No, there is no chance."

Comforted, her sisters rang for her maid and left Arabella alone to bathe and dress.

Arabella spent the time carefully preparing her speech to Marcus, but an army of butterflies were marching in her stomach when she finally went downstairs in search of him.

She found him in the study, seated at his desk. He was busy writing a letter, but he set his quill pen down as soon as she entered.

His expression softening with a smile, Marcus rose and came around the desk to greet her. At his advance, Arabella stopped abruptly.

Marcus halted to eye her with curiosity. "Why are you so nervous, sweeting? I won't pounce on you."

"I am not nervous, precisely."

"Then why are you standing near the open door as if you're prepared to flee?"

"I don't trust myself alone with you, if you must know."

He smiled again and lowered his voice. "I don't intend to make love to you just now, Arabella. Not when we need to have a serious discussion. Now shut the door so we won't be overheard."

Obeying with reluctance, she risked moving farther

into the room. "I presume you mean to discuss your plans for tomorrow, Marcus. Will you be returning to London?"

He cocked his head. "Why would I return to London?"

"Because our wager will be over then. You wagered that you could persuade me to accept your marriage proposal if I allowed you to court me for two weeks. Well, the two weeks end tomorrow afternoon, and I will have fulfilled the terms we agreed on."

A pregnant pause followed her observation. Taking a step backward then, Marcus leaned his hips against the desk. "Come here, Arabella."

"Why?"

"Because I asked you to."

Warily she crossed to stand before him.

Holding her gaze intently, Marcus reached down to take her hand and draw her closer.

Arabella's breath caught in her throat as a frisson of heat raced through her body. Summoning all her resistance, though, she pressed her palms against his chest. "What do you think you are you doing, Marcus?"

"I am renewing my addresses to you."

Arabella swallowed. "You needn't make me another proposal. There is no point."

"I beg to differ. Our circumstances have changed a great deal since I made my first offer of marriage to you."

"Not enough to matter."

Marcus raised an eyebrow. "No?"

She managed to gain her release without struggling, which surprised her a little. "No," Arabella repeated as she backed away. Then forcing herself to stop retreating, she launched into the speech she had prepared. "Marcus . . . I would like to thank you sincerely for all you have done for me and my sisters, and Sybil as well. It was very kind of you to take such an interest in our welfare. But your guardianship is almost over. After this you will no longer be responsible for us."

"I don't want to relinquish responsibility for you."

"But you must if you mean to honor our bargain."

His blue gazed fixed on her, searching her face. "Oh, I will honor it, but there is one small problem."

She eyed him cautiously. "What problem?"

"I still want to marry you, Arabella, only my reasons have changed. I don't want a marriage of convenience any longer."

"Then what do you want?"

"A love match," he said softly. "I want a real marriage with you . . . because I love you."

Arabella sucked in a startled breath. Her stomach suddenly coiled in knots at his unbelievable announcement. "You don't love me, Marcus," she finally found the wits to respond.

Amusement gleamed in his eyes at her skepticism. "Ah, but I do. Love is a new experience for me, you see, so it took me a while to understand what was happening to my heart. But I haven't been the same man since you challenged me in my parlor with my own rapier."

When she remained mute, Marcus continued. "I knew you fascinated me, that you constantly plagued my thoughts. But until the first time I kissed you, I never realized why. It's because you make me feel alive, Arabella. A precious commodity for a man of my jaded experience."

"You . . ." The word came out so hoarsely that Arabella swallowed and cleared her throat. "You only consider me interesting because I speak my mind to you. Because I don't toady to you like every other female of your acquaintance."

"That is part of your attraction, true, but the far more profound effect is how you make me feel."

Her heart racing in consternation, she took another step backward. "You don't love me. You are only saying that to win our wager."

A crooked smile forming on his lips, Marcus shook his head. "Sorry, angel, but you cannot tell me what I feel. I love you rather deeply, in fact. And our wager has nothing whatsoever to do with it."

Arabella felt herself pale. She didn't believe Marcus truly loved her. She couldn't let herself. She had been down this painful path before, a suitor professing his love for her. She clasped her fingers together protectively, and realized her palms had turned clammy.

"My betrothed claimed he loved me," she finally murmured, "and I was foolish enough to believe him. I won't be so gullible again, Marcus."

She saw his lips press together in vexation. "How many times must I say it? I am *not* your betrothed."

When she winced at his sharp tone, he inhaled a

slow breath. "I understand why you find it hard to trust my declaration, Arabella, but I promise you, this is no subterfuge to gain your capitulation. I love you. I want to marry you and to have children with you. I want to spend the rest of my days with you, making you happy."

Arabella stared back at Marcus. "Whatever you feel for me is only temporary, I'm certain. You will get over it soon enough—"

"No, I won't get over it. What I feel is real, and I have no doubts that it will last. It *is* love, Arabella." He paused, studying her intently. "From the terrified look on your face, you don't yet return my sentiment. But that is no matter. Someday you will come to love me in return."

"*No,*" she whispered. Yet her response wasn't a denial of her future feelings; it was a stark realization of her present ones. She already did love Marcus. Dear heaven, what had she done?

Her heart suddenly pounded in her chest; she couldn't breathe. "No," Arabella repeated in a rasp. How could she have been so foolish as to fall in love again?

There was true fear in her voice now, which made Marcus go still for a long moment before he crossed the room to her. Arabella could feel herself trembling as he stood gazing down at her.

"What must I do to convince you?" he said finally, quietly.

She shut her eyes, her chest filled with panic. She had vowed to keep her heart safe from Marcus, but she had failed miserably. Like an utter fool, she had made the exact same mistake as four years ago. And the end result would likely be the same.

How had she refused to recognize her feelings for Marcus until now, when it was too late to protect herself? For days she'd clung to the conviction that their relationship was purely physical, that she could resist feeling anything deeper for him. But all the portents had been there. She just hadn't wanted to face them. With every kiss, with every caress, she had fallen deeper under Marcus's spell. She loved him. Heaven help her.

Now she could only hope to try and conquer her traitorous feelings before she suffered even more agonizing hurt than before.

Struggling for calm, Arabella steeled her shoulders and forced herself to wipe all expression from her face. She refused to repeat history, trusting in a man's love, loving him in return, only to have her feelings betrayed, her faith shattered. "I repeat, Marcus, I appreciate everything you have done, but when the wager is over tomorrow, I will have won. I will not accept your marriage proposal."

Frustration claimed his features as he took a step closer, but she spoke again before he could. "Please believe me. I have no desire to marry you."

He shook his head slowly. "I think you are deceiving yourself, Arabella. You feel every bit of the same fire I feel. We have a remarkable passion together—"

She deliberately interrupted. "What if we do? Passion is not a good basis for marriage. And even if it were, it is entirely beside the point. The question now is, do you intend to honor our wager?"

His jaw tightened. "Certainly I do. I am a man of my word." Marcus gestured toward the desk behind him, at the letter he'd been composing. "I've already written my solicitors with instructions to draw up a contract for your emancipation from my guardianship. You and your sisters will have your freedom regardless of whether you marry me. I don't want your decision to be contingent upon anything but your feelings for me."

"Then I will look forward to hearing from your solicitors."

They stared at each other for a long moment, but when the tense silence drew out, Arabella found the voice to say calmly, "You may as well leave tomorrow, Marcus. There is no reason for you to stay here any longer."

"It appears not." The deep blaze in his eyes told her that he was suddenly very angry. His words were clipped when he said, "Don't worry, sweeting. I'll return to London tonight."

Arabella regarded him silently, not crediting that Marcus had capitulated so easily. And of course, he hadn't.

His hands rising to her shoulders, he hauled her close and brought his mouth down to kiss her—a hard, irate meeting of lips that was more punishing than loverlike. Even so, it instantly stirred heat and hunger deep inside Arabella.

When finally Marcus broke off and drew back his

head, his eyes were glittering with anger and triumph. "You feel the same passion I feel, but you aren't willing to admit it because you're letting fear drive you. I won't hurt you the way your bastard betrothed did, Arabella . . . but I can't force you to believe that."

"No, you cannot," she replied shakily.

The muscles in his jaw clenched again, but Marcus managed to restrain his ire other than to say tightly, "My solicitors will be in touch."

Returning to his desk, he snatched up his letter, then turned on his heel and crossed to the door. Flinging it open, he strode forcefully from the room without looking at her again, leaving a profound silence in his wake.

Swaying, Arabella moved over to a chair and sank down, her hand held to her breastbone, where a relentless fist squeezed her chest. She wouldn't let herself believe what Marcus had claimed, even though a part of her dearly longed for it to be true.

I love you. I want to marry you and to have children with you. I want to spend the rest of my days with you, making you happy.

The remembrance made her throat ache—

Stop this ridiculous sentiment at once! Arabella berated herself. Marcus didn't love her. He had walked out without attempting to change her mind, without even demanding to play out the final day of their wager. How powerful could his feelings for her be if he hadn't even bothered to argue with her?

She had wanted to argue with him. She had wanted to call him back and tell him how she felt for him.

At the painful wrench of her heart, Arabella squeezed her eyes shut. What idiocy! She should be glad she had deliberately sent him away before she risked even greater hurt than last time. Yet no amount of rational logic could explain the dreadful ache inside her, the hollow sense of devastation.

Trembling, Arabella wrapped her arms around herself. What was wrong with her? It was absurd to feel moisture burning in her eyes. Absurd and deplorable. She *despised* tears. Other than to mourn her father's passing, she had never cried during the terrible scandals her parents had caused. She had borne the painful loss of her mother and the public repudiation by her betrothed without once giving in to tears. She had stoically endured the humiliation, the rejection and poverty that had followed. So why did she feel so desperately like crying now? She was free of Marcus. She should be overjoyed that the threat was over.

Yet it seemed an empty, bitter victory.

It was then that she heard Lily's muttered oath behind her. "Did the earl make you *cry*, Belle? I swear, I will draw and quarter him!"

Arabella dashed frantically at her eyes and summoned a weak laugh as she looked up at her youngest sister. "It is not ladylike to swear, Lily. And it is certainly not polite to threaten to dismember an earl."

"I don't give a fig! I will murder him for hurting you."

Easing Lilian aside, Roslyn bent over Arabella and took her hand. "She doesn't mean it. It is just that we hate to see you in such pain."

"I will get over it."

I *will*! Arabella vowed fiercely, although she knew it would be a long time before it happened, if ever.

Chapter Seventeen

❧

Can I believe Marcus when he says he loves me? Do I dare to trust in love again?

—Arabella to Fanny

Dismayingly, the pain did not relent. Nearly a full week after Marcus's acrimonious departure, Arabella still felt the residual effects, despite her every effort to the contrary.

The weather on this Saturday afternoon was perfect—lazy and bright with sunshine—and yet a stark contrast to Arabella's dour mood. The academy's pupils were enjoying an outing at the Freemantle estate, some playing Pall Mall on the lawns with Roslyn, others rowing boats on the ornamental lake, supervised by Tess and Lily, and still others plucking flowers from the gardens and making wreaths to adorn their hair and bonnets under the guidance of Jane Caruthers. A sumptuous tea would follow later, held under the elm trees and presided over by Lady Freemantle.

Arabella took little pleasure in the treat, however. Instead, she withdrew to the shade of an elm, where she could nurse her melancholy in private and halfheartedly watch the frolic on the lake. When the girls began playing tag with the rowboats, splashing each other and frequently erupting in shrieks of delighted laughter, she was surprised that Tess Blanchard joined in.

Arabella roused herself from her morose thoughts long enough to smile. It was good to see Tess laughing and enjoying life for a change, since she'd been in mourning for the past two years. Before her engagement had ended with the death of her betrothed in the terrible Battle of Waterloo, no one had been more lively and high-spirited than Tess. That she was now showing some of her once customary gaiety suggested that she finally had resolved to rejoin the living.

Perhaps a quarter hour later, Tess tore herself away from the lake battle and made her way, breathless with laughter, to where Arabella sat all alone.

"I have come to recruit you to our side, Arabella," Tess said, extending her hands down as if to pull Arabella to her feet. "We need you for reinforcements."

Arabella returned a wan smile. "Thank you, but I have no desire to become drenched, as you are. I endured more than enough soaking last week when I chased after Sybil in an atrocious thunderstorm."

Tess cast an amused glance over her shoulder to eye Sybil, who was primly wandering the gardens under the strict dictates of Lady Freemantle. "Your sacrifice was obviously worthwhile. Sybil's reputation was saved along with our academy's. Even better, she is so disquieted by the possibility of being expelled that her behavior has become perfectly angelic. I vow I don't recognize her anymore." Tess returned her attention to Arabella. "Come now, the sun is warm enough to dry your gown quickly. I won't allow you to mope on such a glorious day."

When Arabella refused to respond, Tess frowned and sank down to sit on the grass beside her. "What is wrong, dearest? You have been perfectly miserable ever since Lord Danvers left for London."

Wincing, she looked away. It was vexing to admit how wretched she'd felt since Marcus left. She had hoped her life would return to normal, but her hopes had proved futile, since everywhere she turned, she found reminders of him. Her misery was compounded by the fact that she hadn't heard a word from him *or* his solicitors in all that time.

"Perhaps I am sickening with an ague," Arabella prevaricated.

Tess gave her a penetrating look. "Perhaps you are lovesick."

Unable to deny the charge, she returned a humorless laugh. "Is my condition so obvious?"

"Your unhappiness is obvious, at least." Tess's gaze searched her face. "But are you certain it is love you feel for him, Arabella, and not just a powerful physical attraction? It isn't merely infatuation?"

She had little doubt of her feelings for Marcus, Arabella reflected, but it would be good to talk about her dilemma with someone who could understand. Tess knew about true love, since she had been sincerely in love with her betrothed. "I believe it is love, but how does one tell?"

Her friend's gaze grew thoughtful. "The signs are usually recognizable. When you love a man, he becomes the center of your world. You yearn to be with him, and when you are not, he is constantly on your mind. He brightens your day. His simplest touch sparks passion in you . . . a tender look fires a warmth in your heart. Life feels *empty* without him." Tess paused. "Is that how you feel about Lord Danvers, Arabella?"

Gazing down at her clasped fingers, Arabella nodded. That was *precisely* how she felt about Marcus, including the emptiness. Since he'd been gone, the hollow feeling inside her chest was a relentless ache that wouldn't go away.

"You miss him sorely, don't you?" Tess prodded in a sympathetic tone.

"Yes." She missed him dreadfully.

"So what do you intend to do about it?"

Arabella gave a helpless laugh. "I don't know."

"Do you think he might love you in return?" Tess asked.

"He claimed he does."

Tess stared. "Lord Danvers actually told you he loves you?"

"Yes . . . last week, just after we returned from rescuing Sybil. But I wouldn't believe him. I feared he was just saying so to persuade me to accept his proposal."

Her friend hesitated. "Arabella, he doesn't strike me as the kind of man to declare his love without meaning it. I doubt he has ever made such a confession to any other woman."

"No, I suspect not."

"So how did you respond to his declaration?"

She flushed at the memory. "I'm afraid I panicked.

That was the moment I realized I loved him, and I was suddenly terrified. I told Marcus that I had won the wager and wouldn't marry him. That he would be better off leaving at once."

"So that is why he left Danvers Hall? You drove him away?"

"Yes."

"Well," Tess said slowly, "it is not too late to mend matters. Not if you love each other."

The stab of panic returned to lodge in Arabella's chest. "But that is the problem, don't you see? I can't be certain of his love. And even if he does love me a little now, how do I know his feelings will last? There is nothing more hurtful than loving someone and not being loved in return. I know because I have experienced it."

Tess shook her head. "Viscount Underwood was clearly not worthy of your love, but I believe Lord Danvers is. You must think so too, or you would never have allowed your affection to go so far. Isn't that so?"

"Yes."

"Do you love him as much as you loved Underwood?"

"Much more." Her love for Marcus was far stronger than her first love had ever been, which meant the devastation would be far greater if it turned out to be one-sided.

"Then perhaps you should accept his proposal," Tess said.

Arabella sent her friend a despairing glance. "Marriage would only make any disparity worse. My mother loved my father initially, and look where their marriage ended."

"But from everything you have told me, your parents were a terrible mismatch. You and Lord Danvers are much better suited."

"Why do you say so?"

Tess smiled. "I have seen you together, the way you are with him. The way you look at each other. A fire lights in your eyes when you look at him, did you know?"

It was Arabella's turn to stare.

Tess went on. "As surprised as I am to admit this, I think he could be the ideal match for you. You would always keep him challenged and interested, and he would do the same for you."

Arabella shook her head in denial. "I cannot be sure of that."

"No, I suppose you cannot. But we can never be sure of anything in life, Arabella. And the chance for love is worth the risk of being hurt. Do you really want to give up hope for your future because of what happened in the past?"

Twisting her fingers in her lap, Arabella looked away. Marcus had accused her of letting fear rule her, and she knew it was true; she feared being hurt again. But she was already hurting dreadfully. How could the pain be any greater than what she felt right now?

When she remained silent, Tess asked quietly, "If you could be certain he loved you, would you marry him?"

"Yes," she finally murmured.

Tess sighed. "Well, you will have to decide for yourself, but I don't think you will be happy without him. And I don't think he will wait forever for you to make up your mind." Climbing to her feet, she gazed down at Arabella, her voice softening. "I believe you should take the risk and accept his proposal, Arabella. True love is too precious to waste. I would give anything to have that chance again."

Turning away, Tess left Arabella struggling with her warring emotions.

True love is too precious to waste. If that was so, then she would be an utter fool to let her fear of being hurt again prevent her from seeking happiness with Marcus.

Wanting privacy to settle her agitated thoughts, Arabella departed early for home before the tea even began, leaving her sisters and Tess to supervise the event. When she reached the Hall and spied a carriage bearing the Danvers crest standing in the drive, her heart leapt. Marcus had returned!

She tried to keep her eagerness under control as she drove the gig around to the stables and turned it over to a groom, yet she found herself hurrying toward the house.

Simpkin met her in the corridor to take her spencer and bonnet and to announce a visitor. "Lady Loring has called, Miss Arabella."

Arabella froze, not certain she had heard correctly. "My *mother* is here?"

"Yes. I have put her in the small salon."

She felt the color drain from her face. When she

swayed dizzily, Simpkin instantly became concerned. "Are you unwell, Miss Arabella?"

"No. . . . I am just . . . surprised." Although *shocked, dismayed, bewildered* were more descriptive of her feelings.

To think her mother had come to call after all this time. What in heaven's name did she want? And where had she come from? Four years ago Victoria had reportedly fled with her lover to the coast of Brittany in France, near Brest, when Britain was still at war with France. Travel was perilous and any communication between the two countries was unpredictable at best. But they'd heard nothing more about her, not even after the long war ended with Napoleon's abdication the following year.

Her footsteps hesitant, Arabella walked slowly down the corridor to the salon and paused on the threshold to observe the familiar stranger seated on the settee.

She was unmistakably a lady, fair-haired and elegant. In looks, Victoria most resembled Roslyn, with the same golden delicacy and aristocratic bearing. And she was still quite beautiful. Even though she had borne three children and endured a scandalous widowhood, the years had been kind to her.

At the sight of her, a chaos of emotions flooded Arabella, along with a rush of painful memories. Then Victoria looked up, her expression hesitant, vulnerable . . . even fearful.

Reflexively, Arabella felt her hands clench with anger and bittersweet happiness. She had never forgiven her mother for abandoning her and her sisters and leaving them mired in scandal. And yet some part of her was overjoyed to see Victoria again.

Trying to remain calm, Arabella entered the room but kept her distance. When her mother simply watched her warily, she broke the taut silence. "What brings you here, Mama?"

"You, of course," came the quiet answer. "I wanted to know how my daughters are faring."

Arabella couldn't keep the bitterness from her voice. "After four years without even a word, you suddenly care how we are faring?"

"I have always cared. It is wonderful to see you again, Arabella." Victoria patted the seat cushion beside her. "Will you come and sit with me?"

"I prefer to stand, thank you."

A small, sad smile twisted her mother's mouth. "I knew you would not forgive me. I told him so."

"Him?"

Victoria sighed. "Lord Danvers."

Arabella's brow furrowed. "What does he have to say to the matter?"

"He is the reason I am here. His lordship sent a ship to France this week to escort me home to England. His secretary met me in Dover yesterday, and his carriage brought me here today."

Marcus had hunted down her mother in France? Arabella wondered, a little stunned. "Whatever for?"

"Because he has hopes that I can reconcile with my daughters. At the very least, he is determined that I explain . . . and apologize to you for what I did."

Her eyes widened as she stared at her mother. "What explanation could you possibly give that would excuse abandoning your children the heartless way you did? You walked out of our lives, Mama, without even a single word of farewell, and then left us to deal with Papa's death all alone."

"I am so very sorry, Arabella."

Her mouth tightened. "Isn't it a bit late for apologies? It all happened a long time ago, so I'm not certain there is any point in even discussing it."

Wincing, Victoria held up a hand. "Please, won't you at least listen to my side of the tale?"

"Very well," Arabella said finally.

"You had best sit down. It is a long story."

Reluctantly, she moved to claim a wing chair across from the settee. Her mother searched her face for a long moment before finally saying in a low voice, "Truly, I am sorry for ruining your life, Arabella. I never meant to hurt you and Roslyn and Lilian."

"But you did, Mama." A savage ache tightened her throat. "More than you can imagine. We were all devastated by your leaving, especially Lily. She cried for *weeks* afterward."

"I . . . know. I should have considered how my conduct would have affected you. I should have put my daughters first. But once I took the first step, my actions became irrevocable."

"I don't see how."

Victoria bit her lower lip. "You have to understand how bitterly unhappy my marriage to your father was."

"Oh, I *understand*," Arabella responded. "How

could I not after watching you and Papa fight so savagely for so many years? But your unhappiness hardly justifies adultery."

Victoria winced again as if from a blow. "Perhaps not, but I was terribly lonely. I am sure you know that your father kept a series of mistresses."

"I could hardly be ignorant of the fact," Arabella said, her tone acrid.

"Charles once was discreet about his affairs, but when he began flaunting his mistresses in my face, I couldn't bear it any longer."

"So you took a lover because you wanted revenge."

"It was not that simple, Arabella. I suppose I wanted revenge, but mostly I wanted . . . intimacy. I met Henri Vachel in London. He had come to England as a boy, after his parents were guillotined during the Terror. His mother's family was English, so he lived with them in Surrey. Henri was so gentle and kind. . . . After your father's neglect, it is not surprising that I responded to him."

When Arabella remained silent, Victoria plowed ahead doggedly. "When your father found out, he was furious about being cuckolded. It was perfectly permissible for *him* to make a mockery of our marriage vows but not his lady wife. Charles demanded that I leave England and never show my face again, and he threatened to kill Henri if I didn't. I knew he would, Arabella."

She gave a skeptical frown. "That is not what Papa told us. He said you developed a violent passion for your lover and fled to France to be with him."

"Of course Charles would claim so, since he wished to make me the villain. But it wasn't true. I didn't love Henri. Not then. And I only left because your father compelled me to do so."

Crossing her arms defensively over her chest, Arabella stared. "Papa was killed two weeks later in a duel, Mama. You could have returned to England then."

"No, I could not," Victoria said with regret. "Because of the war it was months before I learned I was a widow, and by then my stepbrother had guardianship of you. Lionel was so enraged with me, he refused to let me return. He vowed to withdraw his financial support for you and your sisters—to throw you out into the streets—if I didn't keep away so that the scandal could die down. In any event . . . I thought you were better off without me after the disgrace I caused."

Arabella's resistance softened a little. Was it possible Mama hadn't completely turned her back on her daughters after all? It was at least believable that their step-uncle had threatened to drive them from his home, since he had never wanted responsibility for them in the first place. But that did not wholly absolve her mother's deeds. "You could have written, Mama."

"I did. Every week for a full year. Henri used his smuggling connections to have my letters delivered from France. But I never knew what happened to them until just recently. Lionel burned them all."

"How can you possibly know that?"

"Your butler, Simpkin, told Lord Danvers. Danvers questioned him quite carefully about the matter. Lionel flew into a rage each time one of my letters arrived and threw every one in the fire. If you don't believe me, you may talk to Simpkin. He can confirm that account. Lionel hated me so much by then that he cut off all communication with me."

That version of events had a ring of truth to it, Arabella admitted. The elderly butler and housekeeper had served her step-uncle at Danvers Hall for decades and so would have been privy to much of the late earl's affairs.

Her thoughts whirling as chaotically as her disquieted emotions, she stared at her mother, wondering if she dared believe the rest of her tale. Had Victoria's abandonment of her daughters truly been out of her control? Because she had been banished from England, first by her husband and then by her stepbrother? If so, then was it also possible their father had lied to them all along about Mama's devotion to her lover?

Keenly troubled by the notion, Arabella cleared her throat, but her next question still came out hoarsely. "You said you did not love Monsieur Vachel at first. What did you mean by that?"

Victoria's smile was less bleak this time. "Our liaison was only physical in the beginning, but my feelings for him grew over time. Henri stood by me when I had nowhere to turn. He not only offered me protection but shared my banishment, taking me to his father's home in Brittany. Not many men would have been so caring and unselfish. In the end, I came to love him. I couldn't help myself. I . . . married him eventually, Arabella. I am no longer Lady Loring. I am simply Madame Vachel. You have a stepfather."

Arabella fell silent. It seemed strange to think of her mother as remarried. But she was more disturbed by Victoria's other revelations. All this time she and her sisters had been led to believe that their mother deserted them because she fell madly in love. But apparently that wasn't true. Victoria hadn't lost her head because of love—

Her thoughts were interrupted just then by her mother asking in a small voice, "Do you think you could ever come to forgive me, Arabella?"

Arabella looked away. She was dismayed to think she had misjudged her mother all this time. Even more dismayed to imagine what Victoria had endured these past few years. Yet the pain of losing her was still very real. All the sorrow and anger and bitterness could not instantly be healed by learning there had been extenuating circumstances that made choosing her lover over her daughters more explicable.

"I will have to think about it, Mama," Arabella finally said.

"Of course you need time to digest what I have told you. And I will understand if you cannot find it in your heart to forgive me . . . if you want me to leave." Her shoulders hunched as if braced against a blow, Victoria murmured quietly, "I will return to France for good if you wish me to."

"I am not certain what I want." Arabella raised her hand to her temple. "I cannot decide anything just yet. I must talk to Roslyn and Lily first."

"I would like to see them," Victoria said hesitantly.

Not wanting to increase her mother's misery, she

kept her voice soft when she replied. "It's possible they may not wish to see you, Mama. Lily is very hurt, and so is Roslyn."

"I . . . understand." She twisted her fingers together helplessly. "If you choose to reach me, I will be staying at the Red Boar in Chiswick. Henri came with me to England, and we intend to remain there for a few days before traveling to Surrey. Henri wishes to see his family there."

When her daughter didn't reply, Victoria slowly rose to her feet and moved to the door. There she paused with her head bowed, the picture of pain. "God bless and keep you, Arabella."

Arabella's heart wrenched at the quiet agony in her mother's voice, and when Victoria exited the salon without another word, she couldn't bear it.

Jumping up from her chair, Arabella hurried after her, calling out to her. "Mama?" When Victoria halted and turned, she added softly, "I will plead your case with Roslyn and Lily and try to make them understand."

Her smile was bittersweet. "That is all I ask."

Watching as her mother disappeared down the corridor, Arabella remained standing there for a long while, her thoughts in turmoil, her emotions running the gamut from dismay to hope as she considered the question of forgiveness.

Certainly Victoria had made significant mistakes. But she had also been wronged by her husband and her stepbrother. And she genuinely regretted hurting her daughters.

Perhaps that was all that truly mattered. That Mama *cared*.

She would have to make her sisters see that, Arabella decided finally as she headed to her bedchamber to await their return.

The chance to get their mother back was too gratifying to pass up.

Lily turned stark white when Arabella broke the startling news about their mother's presence in Chiswick, while Roslyn, after a stunned moment, grew solemn and thoughtful. But they both listened carefully as Arabella related every detail of her conversation with Victoria and argued for forgiveness.

Their ardent, highly emotional discussion lasted well into the evening. As Arabella expected, Lily was the hardest to convince, yet she seemed concerned more for Roslyn than for herself.

"Have you truly considered the ramifications, Rose?" Lily implored. "The scandal is likely to be resurrected, just when we have finally begun to live it down. It matters little to me, since I never intend to wed, but if you want to marry, then welcoming Mama back will undoubtedly hurt your prospects of making a good match."

Roslyn nodded slowly. "Perhaps so, but I think it is a risk I must take."

In the end, they all decided to relent. Victoria was their mother and they wanted her back in their lives, regardless of what she had done in the past, or what it might cost them in the future.

The hour was past eight o'clock by the time Arabella ordered the old Danvers carriage made ready to take them to the nearby Red Boar Inn where their mother was staying. They spoke little on the way, and when they reached the inn, Lily lagged behind. Thus, when they were shown into a private parlor, Lily was closest to the door when it slowly opened a short time later.

Victoria stood there on the threshold, as if afraid to enter. One by one, she met each of her daughters' gazes, until Arabella broke the tense silence. "We are glad to have you back, Mama."

With a shuddering sigh, Victoria covered her face with her hands for a moment, before reaching them out to her daughters. "Oh, my dearest girls . . ."

Lily gave a small sob and flung herself into Victoria's arms. She embraced her two older daughters next, and soon they were all laughing and crying.

It was some time before Arabella realized they were not alone. A gentleman had joined them, shutting the parlor door quietly behind him.

Eventually Victoria calmed herself enough to recall her manners and introduce her new husband. Dark-haired and dark-eyed, Henri Vachel seemed a somber man, but he hovered protectively near Victoria, and Arabella liked him the better for it. He looked relieved when Victoria smiled and told him he could return to their bedchamber to allow her privacy with her daughters.

When Monsieur Vachel had withdrawn, they settled in chairs around the hearth. The tears and apologies that followed made for a poignantly emotional reunion.

Victoria wanted to hear everything that had happened to them during her four-year absence, and she listened intently, not sparing herself recriminations for the difficulties her daughters had suffered because of her actions.

The conversation only became a trifle awkward, however, when Victoria brought up the subject of their futures. "Lord Danvers tells me that none of you are eager to marry." She glanced at each of them, but her gaze lingered longest on Arabella. "I know I am to blame for your disgust of matrimony."

Arabella managed a wry smile. "It was not solely your doing, Mama. I think Papa bears some responsibility as well."

"I suppose your father played a large role. But I set a terrible example for you girls to follow. Still, you cannot ruin your futures because of what we did."

Arabella's smile faded. She had already come to that realization. She couldn't make crucial decisions about her future based solely on what had happened in her parents' past, or in her own.

Before she could reply, Victoria leaned forward in her chair, her expression intent. "I grievously regret the foolish choices I made, Arabella, but you have always been wiser and stronger than I. You needn't let my circumstances prejudice your feelings about love and marriage to your detriment."

Perhaps she *was* stronger than her mother, Arabella reflected, but she wasn't so certain she was wiser. She had let fear rule her life for too long. But no more.

"You cannot judge all relationships by what happened between me and your father," Victoria insisted. "Simply because we had a terrible marriage doesn't mean that good ones are not possible."

"I realize that, Mama." She had already come to that conclusion herself.

"You *can* find love and happiness in marriage. I did at long last. It took me years to comprehend what a good man Henri is. Years to find true love when it was right under my nose the whole time. Perhaps true love is right under your nose as well."

She looked at her mother keenly. "What are you saying, Mama?"

"That you have already found a good man, Arabella. Lord Danvers went to significant trouble on your behalf. He must care for you a great deal to go to such lengths. Otherwise he would never have made so determined an effort to help us reconcile."

Indeed, Arabella reflected, Marcus had gone well beyond his obligations as her guardian, particularly when he had already agreed last week to relinquish the position as a result of their wager.

If she had wanted proof that he cared about her, she need look no further, Arabella knew. But did it mean he truly loved her as he claimed? She desperately hoped so.

"I think he does care for me," Arabella murmured.

Victoria nodded. "And he seems to be nothing like your father. Can you imagine Charles putting himself out for anyone like that?"

No, she couldn't imagine such a thing. Marcus was far, far different from her father.

Roslyn spoke up just then, her tone solemn. "Do *you* care for Lord Danvers, Arabella?"

She hesitated only a moment. "Very much." She sent Lily an apologetic glance. "I vowed I wouldn't let myself fall in love with him, but in the end, I discovered I never had any choice."

Lily regarded her solemnly, clearly troubled by her admission, but Roslyn smiled. "I only want you to be happy, Arabella. If you love him, that is all that matters."

Lily, however, didn't agree. "That is not all that matters, Belle. You loved Underwood, and look how much he hurt you. I can't bear to see you make the same mistake again."

"I know," Arabella said fondly. "But Marcus says he loves me."

"Underwood claimed he loved you, but he didn't. How can you be certain the earl is telling the truth?"

Arabella gave a light shrug. "I cannot be certain, so I will just have to trust him."

Lily still wasn't convinced. "If you marry him, he could make you miserable like Papa did Mama."

"I am willing to risk it."

In truth, she could do nothing else. She fervently wanted the kind of soul-deep love that Tess had spoken about. The kind her mother had found in her second marriage. She thought—hoped—she could have that love with Marcus. But even if he didn't love her, without a doubt, her life would be unbearably empty without him. She had learned that painful lesson during this past week.

"Lily . . ." Arabella began, wondering how she could explain her feelings. Finally, she merely smiled. "I intend to marry Marcus because I don't want to live without him. It is as simple as that."

The anxious look in Lily's eyes wavered, then faded. "If that is what you truly want . . ."

"It is. I want it with all my heart."

"Thank heavens," Victoria murmured.

Arabella met her mother's smiling gaze, then took a deep breath as she felt her bravado wavering a measure.

Marrying Marcus might not be so simple as she had made it sound. After their acrimonious parting, he might very well wish her in Hades. She had angered him profoundly by not trusting him enough to believe his declaration of love, and angered him still further by rejecting his offer of marriage so adamantly.

But she would convince him to forgive her, Arabella vowed, even if she had to grovel. She would start by admitting that he had won their wager. She would make him understand that she had come to her senses. And if Marcus loved her half as much as she loved him, he wouldn't let her stubborn blindness stand in the way of their happiness together.

Chapter Eighteen

❦

*How does one grovel properly? I think I owe it to
Marcus for frustrating him so.*

—Arabella to Fanny

"What in blazes has come over you, Marcus?" Heath
demanded after nearly being skewered by a flurry of
angry thrusts during their Monday-morning fencing
session at Marcus's London town house.

Halting his ferocious attack, Marcus lowered his
foil and stood breathing heavily.

From the sidelines, Drew stepped forward. "Why
don't you call it a morning, old man? You are bloody
dangerous with that blade."

Marcus raked a hand through his hair. "My apologies, Heath. I should not have taken my frustrations
out on you."

"How good of you to realize it," Heath drawled before adding more seriously, "I wish to hell you would
find a cure for your ailment. You have been acting like
a wounded wolf ever since you returned to London."

"I know." His mood had been foul since parting
from Arabella, despite his fiendishly intense bid to
work off his frustrations.

"Why don't you simply throw Miss Loring over
your shoulder and carry her off somewhere?" Heath

suggested. "If you had a month alone with her, surely you could convince her to accept your suit."

That idea had merit, Marcus thought before shaking his head with sardonic humor. "I haven't quite reached the point of resorting to barbarism."

"Well, you need to do something, old fellow, before you accidently exterminate us. You would regret it, I'm certain."

"I expect I would." Biting back a rueful grin, Marcus withdrew to the sidelines as Drew took the floor with Heath to resume fencing practice.

He would settle for abduction if he had to, Marcus knew, tossing his rapier on a table. He damned sure wasn't willing to admit permanent defeat in his courtship of Arabella. In fact, he was devising a new plan. His solicitors had drawn up the legal documents granting her and her sisters independence from his guardianship, but he hadn't sent them yet, since he was still determining how to use them to his best advantage.

Meanwhile, he was letting his temper cool. He had wanted to throttle Arabella last week when she refused to believe his declaration of love. He'd never made that startling confession to any woman before, and having it thrown back in his teeth along with his proposal had made his blood boil.

He still felt the urge to return to Danvers Hall and shake Arabella out of her stubborn blindness. She was making a grievous mistake, letting her past ruin her future. She would miss him, he had no doubt. Just as he missed the devil out of her—

The distant rap of the front door knocker intruded on Marcus's dark thoughts, but knowing his butler would answer it, he paid little attention until the sound of a familiar feminine voice followed. Marcus felt his stomach muscles clench. *Arabella.*

He suspected she had come to demand her emancipation but moved closer to the door, the better to hear.

Hobbs's forbidding voice floated down the corridor. "His lordship is otherwise engaged at present, Miss Loring."

"Ah, yes, I can tell he is fencing again. But I believe he will receive me."

There was a notable pause while Hobbs likely debated his chances of turning her away. Evidently he realized the futility of it. "If you will wait here, Miss Loring, I will inquire if his lordship is receiving at present."

"We needn't stand on such ceremony, Hobbs . . . isn't it?" Arabella asked, her tone charming.

"Yes, madam, the name is Hobbs."

"Well, Hobbs, you clearly do not approve of my calling at a bachelor's residence, and under ordinary circumstances I would agree with you. I assure you, I am usually *quite* proper. But in this instance, I have urgent business with Lord Danvers. And since he is my guardian, the infraction is not so very egregious, is it now?"

"Perhaps not," the butler answered, stiff with resistance.

"Then you will allow me to see him?"

"Very well, Miss Loring, if you insist . . . you may follow me."

"Oh, you needn't trouble yourself. I can find my way." Her footsteps sounded on the marble entrance hall, then hesitated. "Hobbs?" she called. Marcus could picture her speaking over her shoulder. "You are to be admired for protecting your master's privacy. I will make certain he knows of your devotion."

"Thank you, miss," the butler replied, clearly exasperated.

A moment later Arabella appeared in the doorway. Although Marcus had braced himself, he felt his heart jolt at the welcome sight of her. As she paused to survey the room, heat and hunger stabbed through him. Then her gaze locked on him, and the hunger worsened.

Her expression was intensely focused, her gray eyes searching. After another heartbeat, though, she gave him a smile of such sweetness, such utter brilliance, that he felt dazed.

Arabella was the first to tear her gaze away and seek out his friends' attention. The marquess and duke had halted their practice in order to observe her.

She turned her bright smile on the two noblemen as she advanced into the room. "My lords, I hope you will forgive me for interrupting your fencing session yet again. You must think me very vexing."

His grace, the Duke of Arden, lifted an eyebrow. "You do seem to be making a habit of intruding on our practice, Miss Loring."

But the Marquess of Claybourne's response was

more congenial. His eyes gleaming, Claybourne gave her a roguish smile. "It doesn't follow that the intrusion must be unwelcome. It is indeed a pleasure to see you."

She glanced at Marcus briefly. "Would you mind terribly if I steal his lordship away for a few moments?"

The duke answered her. "You may speak to him here, Miss Loring. We were nearly finished anyway."

Arabella was glad that the imperious duke seemed prepared to leave, for he was obviously not delighted she had come. She doubted she would be able to win over his opinion any time soon, even if she tried. Moving to the table, the duke returned his foil to its case and, after offering her a polite bow, strode from the salon. The marquess shrugged and followed suit but flashed her a charming grin as he passed.

Alone with Marcus, Arabella turned slowly to face him. He had said not a single word thus far, and she couldn't tell if that was an ominous sign or a propitious one. She only knew how she felt upon seeing him again: sheer happiness. That, and yearning. She wanted to fling herself into his arms. Wanted to press ardent kisses all over his dear, handsome face . . .

If she hadn't already realized the depths of her love for Marcus, being with him again after enduring a wretched week of despondency would have clarified her feelings.

She was keenly aware, however, that Marcus did not look happy to see her. Arabella gazed at him in uncertain silence, conscious of her thudding heartbeat brought on by a sudden case of trepidation. He was watching her soberly—not at all the welcome she had hoped for.

"So, sweeting, to what do I owe the honor of your visit this time?"

Arabella's heart sank at his impassive tone. Hesitantly, she stepped forward. "For one thing, I wished to thank you for seeking out my mother in France and bringing her home. You went to a great deal of trouble on our behalf, Marcus, and you have my gratitude, as well as that of my sisters."

His broad shoulders lifted in a shrug. "Your gratitude is unnecessary. I merely did my duty as your guardian—which doubtless is your real concern. If you're here to discover the status of your emancipation, you can set your mind at ease. The proper documents granting your independence have been prepared and only require my signature."

She managed a smile. "Thank you, but that is not my chief reason for coming."

"Then what is?"

"Actually . . . I am here to accept your proposal of marriage."

The silence that met her declaration was profound. Several heartbeats passed before Marcus's eyes narrowed. "Did you find yourself with child, Arabella?"

Her own eyes widening, she felt a flush heat her cheeks. "No, I am not with child. My . . . courses came last week. But according to Fanny, the likelihood of my conceiving is small, since you and I were only together a few nights."

Marcus's expression remained infuriatingly enigmatic. "Sometimes it takes but once for a man's seed to take root. And that would explain your willingness to accept my offer now when you refused so adamantly barely a week ago."

"Well, that is not why I changed my mind about marrying you." Arabella eyed him with misgiving. "I thought you would be pleased by my surrender."

"It depends wholly on the reason." Marcus crossed his arms over his chest, his stance the picture of resistance. "I told you, Arabella, I am not interested in a marriage of convenience."

"Neither am I. I want a love match, just as you do."

"Is that so?"

Feeling suddenly vulnerable, she clasped her hands together. "Yes. You were right, Marcus. I was acting out of fear. I was afraid to have my heart broken again, so afraid that I wouldn't risk loving you. But in the end I couldn't help myself."

Some emotion flickered in his blue eyes but she couldn't read it. "So you are saying you love me."

"Yes . . . I love you."

He gave her a skeptical look while his arms remained firmly crossed. "Why should I believe you? Perhaps you've mistaken your feelings."

Arabella shook her head, torn between exasperation and fear. Apparently Marcus wouldn't readily forgive her for rejecting him so soundly, but it frightened her to think he didn't care at all about her change of heart. "No, I have not mistaken my feelings. I love you, Marcus."

"You will have to convince me."

The words were a challenge and sounded more like the Marcus of old.

She offered him a nervous smile. "What must I do to convince you? I am willing to grovel, if you wish me to."

When a glimmer of amusement finally lit his blue eyes, Arabella sucked in a sharp breath of hope.

"I think perhaps some amount of groveling is in order," Marcus remarked. "After all the torment you put me through, you deserve to suffer a little."

"I *have* suffered," Arabella replied emphatically. "I felt utterly wretched from the moment you left. I missed you unbearably." When he showed no further sign of yielding, she realized she would have to make him believe that she truly loved him. Her voice lowered to an imploring murmur when she continued. "Marcus, once you were gone, there was this great void in my life . . . in my heart." Her fist closed over her breastbone. "I felt *empty* without you. I can't bear to live like that the rest of my life. I don't *want* to live without you. It *is* love I feel for you, Marcus," she insisted, repeating the same words he had said to her a week ago.

When he didn't reply, Arabella searched his face. "You said you feel the same way. You said you love me."

He cocked an eyebrow. "That was last week. Perhaps I've lost interest by now."

She swallowed. "Perhaps you have. But I want to be your wife, even if you don't love me."

It seemed, however, that he still wouldn't relent. "I'm afraid that isn't good enough."

"What . . . do you mean?"

"I want your trust, Arabella, as well as your love."

"I do trust you, Marcus."

"Enough to believe me when I say I will remain faithful to you to the end of our days?" His eyes held hers intently as he waited for her answer.

"Yes." She regarded him solemnly, understanding what he was asking. "You are not my father."

When his expression softened with something resembling satisfaction, her heart at last started beating again in a more normal rhythm.

"I'm glad you realize it, angel." He uncrossed his arms and strolled toward her. "Then I suppose I could consider marrying you."

If not for the hint of laughter in his eyes, she would have been alarmed. But Marcus was provoking her on purpose, she knew. Relief coursing through her, she let herself smile. "You could *consider* it? What the devil do you mean? You have been after me to marry you for weeks now."

"But I see no reason to rush now that you have finally capitulated."

Her own eyes glimmering with faint amusement, Arabella placed her hands on her hips. "I think perhaps I have groveled enough."

"I'm not so certain. I rather like this humble side of you."

"You don't want a humble wife, you said so."

"True, I don't. But I would be wise to hold out for better terms."

"So now you want to negotiate the terms of our marriage?"

"What if I do?"

Arabella's gaze settled on the rapiers the noblemen had used for their fencing session. Moving over to the table, she picked up a foil, then advanced toward Marcus. "You should know better than to leave weapons lying around when you are deliberately provoking me." She prodded his chest lightly with the tip. "You had best answer me now, Marcus. Will you marry me or not? I warn you, I may do you bodily harm if you refuse."

Laughing, he caught her wrist and pulled the rapier from her grasp, then wrapped a strong arm around her waist and drew her close, against his warm, hard body. "Ah, sweetheart," he said with delight, "you never fail to enchant me."

"Do I?" Arabella asked, smiling mistily up at him.

"You know damn well you do. Everything about you enchants me. I love the fire flashing in your eyes. I love the fire you make me feel. I love *you*, Arabella."

"But will you wed me?"

He considered her for another endless moment while she held her breath. "Yes, I will . . . but first I have something to give you."

"What is it?"

"Come with me."

Surprising her, Marcus released Arabella only to take her hand and draw her from the salon. She found herself being ushered down the corridor and across the entrance hall, where Hobbs stood ready to assist her departure. The butler pretended not to notice his lordship's odd behavior as Marcus, still carrying the foil, led her into a large room that looked to be his study. Going to a massive desk, he set down the rapier, then fished out a sheaf of papers and handed them to Arabella.

"These are the documents modifying your guardianship?" she asked.

"No."

"Then what are they?"

"Read for yourself."

Arabella's gaze scanned down the first page, then returned to the top to scrutinize the lofty legal language more slowly. As she turned the succeeding pages, recognition dawned on her. Marcus had purchased the deed to the Freemantle Academy from Winifred and had signed it over to *her*.

Tears springing to her eyes, Arabella looked up at him in awe. "You bought our academy for me?"

"Yes—and before you take my head off, it isn't charity. In the first place, you've worked damned hard for this. And in the second, I hoped to give the school to you as a wedding gift."

"Thank you, Marcus," she said softly. "I will cherish this."

Setting the papers down on the desk, she stepped closer. Smiling warmly, she reached up and threaded her arms around his neck. "Did I tell you how very much I love you?"

"You did. But I want to hear you tell me again. I won't ever tire of hearing it."

"I love you dearly, Marcus."

His expression turned smugly satisfied. "I know. You couldn't help yourself."

Arabella felt laughter bubbling up inside her. Marcus had known she would come to love him. He had understood her better than she understood herself. "You are very confident, my arrogant lord."

His bright blue gaze was amused, tender, loving. "Only now, darling. Ten minutes ago I wasn't nearly so sanguine."

"I do love you, Marcus. I love you wildly, madly. I always will."

"The feeling is mutual." He chuckled. "I admit I never intended to lose my heart to you, Belle. You intrigued me from the first. I wanted you in my bed from the moment you threatened me with my foil. But I never thought I would feel this kind of love for anyone."

"Truly?"

"Truly." He bent his head to press a light kiss on her lips. "I never expected to be so fortunate, either, Arabella. I found the woman who is my ideal match, the perfect challenge for me."

Her heart rejoiced at his declaration. "Thank you, Marcus."

"For what?"

"For not giving up. For giving me reason to risk loving again. For opening my heart."

His thumb came up to stroke her cheek. "I'll never

break your heart, Arabella. You have my solemn promise on that. I will never forsake you. I'll never stop loving you, no matter what happens in our future."

She closed her eyes for a moment. "I feared I might have lost you through my own obstinacy."

Marcus grasped her chin lightly, forcing her to look at him. "Never. Your wits have gone begging if you thought I would ever be content to let you go. I was only regrouping and planning my new campaign strategy."

Arabella laughed, her heart spilling over with love and desire. "And I was planning mine. I told my mother I intended to come here today and confess how much I love you. I was prepared to make you a new wager if you no longer wanted to marry me, but she didn't think it would be necessary."

"So she approves?"

"Yes. Mama is eager to see us wed. You clearly charmed her, just as you do every female you meet."

"Not every female. I had the devil of a time charming you, not to mention your sisters. What do they have to say about our union?"

Arabella's smile turned even softer. "Roslyn is happy for me and Lily is hopeful. I convinced them I couldn't live without you."

In response, Marcus gave her a kiss of such intimacy, such warmth and sweetness, that her knees went weak. To her surprise and disappointment, though, he broke off suddenly. Going to the study door, he turned the key, locking them inside.

"What are you doing?" Arabella asked curiously as he returned to stand before her.

"Exploring how deeply we feel for each other."

Heat flooded through her at the sensual look he was giving her, and her heart began to throb, thick slow beats. He untied the ribbons of her bonnet and set it aside, then unfastened the buttons of her spencer and slid it off her shoulders. Beneath, she wore an elegant gown of sky blue muslin.

When he drew her over to a plush leather sofa, Arabella realized Marcus intended to indulge in a passionate bout of lovemaking. "Your butler will be scandalized," she said with a mischievous smile. "Hobbs and I did not begin on the best footing, and if I am to become mistress here, perhaps I ought not offend his sense of propriety any further."

Marcus's grin was tolerant as he sank down onto the sofa. "Hobbs will have to become accustomed to us being private together. When you are my wife, I intend to spend a great deal of time behind locked doors with you. Don't worry—I won't dishevel your gown or your hair just now. But this may be the last chance I have to make love to you for some time, and I won't let it go to waste."

Arabella put up no argument. She didn't stand a chance of refusing Marcus anyway. Not when he was bent on seduction. Not when he was so irresistible. She allowed him to pull her down onto his lap and immediately twined her arms around his neck. He obsessed her, tantalized her, drove her mad with wanting him.

He took advantage of her compliance by nibbling at the soft skin below her earlobe.

"You know," she murmured, her voice suddenly

husky and thick, "when it comes to propriety, you set a terrible example as my guardian."

"True, but it hardly matters, since I am abdicating my role as guardian. From this moment forward, I'm concerned solely with my role as lover and husband."

Marcus nipped at her neck, his breath sending a warm shiver of pleasure down her spine, while his hand roved downward over the skirts of her gown. Finding the hem, his fingers glided up her bare thigh to cup the moist, feminine folds of her woman's mound.

Arabella felt the insistent swell of her own desire and arched against his magical hand, yet she didn't want the pleasure to be hers alone. "Marcus . . . you needn't wait. I am more than ready for you."

"So you are." He lifted his head, a lazy heated smile curving his mouth. "But I mean to torment you a little as punishment for driving me to distraction this past week."

"I should have known."

His fingers stroked the sleek flesh between her parted thighs, fondling her sex in a lush assault on her senses. When he slid one finger deep inside her, finding her wet with wanting, her inner muscles shuddered around him.

Gasping with pleasure, Arabella clutched at his arm. "That is quite enough torment."

"I disagree. If it were enough, you would be begging me to stop."

"I won't beg. . . ."

"We shall see, love."

He bent his head, muffling the rest of her words with searing kisses, while his hand, seductive as his voice, continued playing maddening games with her ready flesh.

He caressed her until she was aching with need, until she was light-headed and liquid with arousal, plying her with deft, skillful touches, punctuating his kisses with heated pulses of his tongue. When she felt his probing fingers slowly thrust inside her again, it kindled a soft cry from her throat.

"Hush, no screaming," Marcus admonished. "You don't want to scandalize Hobbs, remember?"

"I don't know if I can manage."

Almost whimpering, she buried her face in his throat as he went on working his tormenting magic. Soon she was shivering and trembling, yet though it was blissful, it wasn't entirely satisfying. Arabella wanted Marcus filling her, wanted him joined to her intimately, wanted him soothing the empty ache his absence had created. Even more, she wanted him feeling the love that shimmered inside her so deeply she thought she might burst with it.

"Marcus, please . . . take me," she pleaded finally.

"Are you begging me yet?"

"Yes . . . whatever you want."

His husky chuckle rasped in her ear, yet he evidently had had enough torment also, for he gathered Arabella in his arms and slid off the sofa with her. Lowering her to the Aubusson carpet, he laid her back, watching her with hot-bright eyes as he made short work of the front placket of his breeches. Easing over her then, he fitted his body to hers and sank his weight into the cradle of her thighs.

He cherished her mouth with kisses as his hard length slowly filled her. With a sob of pure pleasure, Arabella wrapped her arms tightly around him and drew Marcus close, welcoming his possession. Her chest ached with love for him; all of her senses were heightened by love. When he sank in all the way, the rapture was almost too much to bear. She let her head fall back and her eyelids fall shut.

"No, open your beautiful eyes, angel. I want to watch the expression on your face when you come for me."

Arabella obeyed, gazing up at Marcus dazedly. She knew he was seeing love and passion in her eyes, for she recognized the same emotions in his. Joy and triumph and sheer sensuality blazed in his face as he surged into her, his movements slow and passionate as he began a rhythm as timeless as man and woman, the rhythm of love.

Arabella responded with all her heart, and it wasn't long before their pleasure built into a firestorm, then exploded in a fiery blaze of lightning bolts. Marcus drank in her sobs of ecstasy as he joined her in the stunning tempest.

Afterward, she lay cupped into his body, breathless, sated, joy whispering through her. When at last he eased away to lie beside her, she opened her eyes to find Marcus still watching her tenderly. She sighed with perfect contentment and offered him a drowsy, teasing smile. "I've known for some time that you were a marvelous lover, but I think you will make a marvelous husband also."

His own smile was devastatingly irresistible. "I've been trying to convince you of that for weeks now. How gratifying to know I finally succeeded."

She reached up to trace his sensual mouth with her fingertip. "I am very glad you won our wager, but you will not always win, you know," Arabella murmured.

"I wouldn't want to always win. It's doing battle with you that adds a delectable spice to life. As long as you love me, I can deal with losing to you every now and then."

"I do love you, Marcus, more than I can say, but since we are negotiating terms of our marriage . . ."

He raised an eyebrow. "Are we still negotiating?"

"Yes, on one issue, I think we must."

"I would rather make love to you again."

When he leaned forward to take her mouth, Arabella pressed her fingers to his lips. "This is serious, Marcus."

Instantly he sobered. "Very well, you have my full attention, sweetheart."

"I want to continue managing the academy."

"I see no reason why you cannot, as long as you make time for our wedding and a wedding trip afterward."

Arabella smiled in relief. She had worried about Marcus's response, yet she should have known he would be amenable to letting her continue her avocation.

"I should have ample time for a wedding after school lets out in two weeks," she replied. "The summer term begins in mid-June, and since most of our pupils will be going home, I won't be teaching any classes. Jane Caruthers will handle the majority of the work."

"Then we shouldn't have a problem. It will be at least a month before we can hold the ceremony. We could be married by special license, but I prefer to have the banns called. I don't want it to seem as if we are rushing." He kissed the tip of her nose. "And I want a large wedding. We can be married in the Chiswick church and invite several hundred guests."

Her look turned dubious. "I doubt the church is large enough."

"Then we'll invite half the ton to a wedding breakfast at Danvers Hall afterward. I intend to put my countess on display, since it will help pave your acceptance into society."

Arabella nodded, seeing the wisdom of his plan. An invitation to celebrate the nuptials of the Earl and Countess of Danvers would go far in winning over even her haughtiest detractors. Yet that was as far as she wanted to acquiesce to the high-browed notions of society.

"I would like my mother to attend our wedding and any succeeding festivities," Arabella said, knowing that the scandalous former Lady Loring would likely be shunned by the ton's highest sticklers. "And Fanny Irwin as well. Fanny may be a renowned Cyprian, but she is a dear friend and I won't turn my back on her simply because I am marrying an earl."

"Certainly they may attend. And my sister Eleanor would doubtless enjoy helping with plans for a breakfast. As for our wedding trip, I want to take you to my family seat in Devonshire for a few weeks. The Hall will afford us too little privacy with your sisters present. I want you all to myself for a while."

Arabella's smile was soft with pleasure. "I would like that." Remembering the duke and marquess, however, she glanced at the closed door. "Do you think your two friends will come to accept me as your wife?"

"Yes, of course. They will eventually grow to love you. Meanwhile, they'll be infinitely glad that we finally came to a resolution. I nearly took off Heath's head this morning during our fencing practice because I was seething with frustration."

"His grace won't be overjoyed about our marriage."

"Drew is just cynical about love because he's never experienced it before. Heath is more adventurous, so he's more willing to concede that I might love you witless. But he doesn't want to see me turned into a tame milksop. I think he worries that you will lead me around by my bridle."

Arabella laughed. "I don't intend to bridle you, any more than I intend to wear a bridle."

"Which is exactly how it should be between us."

As Marcus gazed down at her, the passion she saw in the endless blue depths dazzled her, but it was the love shining there that made her heart sing. Then he kissed her again and made her heart race as he reached up to pull the pins from her hair.

"I thought you didn't intend to dishevel my hair," Arabella murmured.

"I changed my mind." His slow, very male smile held the wonderfully wicked charm that had won her heart during his admittedly unwanted courtship. "If I can't have you again until a full month from now, then I mean to make the most of our time here together, Hobbs or no Hobbs."

She laughed again, her breath whispering against his lips as she gave herself up to Marcus's incredible passion.

Epilogue

❦

*How glad I am that Marcus wagered for my heart
and won. I wish you could find the same bliss in love,
Fanny.*

—Arabella to Fanny

*I have never met the man who could make me blissful
in love. But I am overjoyed for you, dear Arabella. I
will dance at your wedding, if you are not afraid that
I will scandalize the company.*

—Fanny to Arabella

Danvers Hall, June 1817

When Arabella sank into a chair and sighed happily,
Roslyn smiled with love and satisfaction. "You made
an exquisite bride today, dearest. Being in love becomes you."

"You do look positively beautiful, Belle," Lily seconded.

The three of them were ensconced in Lily's bedchamber, taking the opportunity to say a private farewell. It
was nearing midnight and the wedding breakfast and
ball were almost over, so the sisters had slipped away
from the throng of guests to go abovestairs for a moment.

Lily was putting her nightclothes and a few personal
items into a bandbox, since she and Roslyn meant to

stay with Tess tonight to allow the newlyweds privacy for their wedding night.

"Thank you," Arabella replied to the compliments, glancing down at the stunning wedding dress her sisters had helped her don this morning. "I *feel* beautiful in this confection."

Her empire-waist gown of ivory silk was delicately embroidered with gold thread at the bodice and hem, and the rich fabric matched the creamy roses and gold ribbons she wore twined in her fair hair.

Her sisters, too, looked beautiful, garbed in pale rose-hued silk gowns, Arabella thought with pride.

She was very glad for this time alone with Roslyn and Lilian after the frenetic activity of the past few weeks. Not only had the renovations to the Hall required finishing, but the sheer size of the wedding celebrations had proved a challenge. A skilled hostess, Roslyn had taken on the task of arranging the enormous wedding breakfast and ball, supervising the army of servants who had prepared frantically for days.

"And thank you for your tremendous efforts, Roslyn," Arabella said. "Everything turned out perfectly."

Roslyn smiled. "My efforts were not so exceptional."

"Indeed they were."

Lily broke in. "They most certainly were. I could never have managed so many details so flawlessly, Rose. I never would have had the patience even to *try*."

"I thought the ceremony was lovely also," Roslyn said, casting an amused glance at their youngest sister. "I think even Lily enjoyed it."

Lily wrinkled her nose but laughed. "Surprisingly, I did."

The ceremony had been held at the Chiswick church in the company of friends and family. As for the groom, Marcus had driven directly from London to the church this morning, along with his sister, Eleanor, his aunt, Lady Beldon, and his two friends, the Duke of Arden and the Marquess of Claybourne. The bridal party had arrived soon after, and the festivities had begun at Danvers Hall immediately following the marriage service.

"It was good to have Mama here," Roslyn added softly.

"Yes," Lily replied. "We owe the earl a huge debt of thanks for arranging for Mama to come home."

Arabella fully agreed, feeling a glow of gratitude for what Marcus had done to unite them with their mother.

Lady Freemantle had helped also, taking Victoria and her French husband under her wing these past few weeks. It warmed Arabella's heart that Mama was gradually being accepted by many of their neighbors who wished to remain in the Earl of Danvers's good graces, even if the former Lady Loring *was* considered something of a scarlet woman.

Their neighbors had been required to swallow an even bigger affront today, Arabella reflected with a mischievous spark of humor, since the notorious Fanny Irwin had attended both the nuptials and the festivities afterward. Roslyn and Lily had kept Fanny close company so she wouldn't feel ostracized, but it was clear the gentlemen present were fascinated by the celebrated courtesan, enough to keep her dancing the entire night.

Fanny had departed for London a few minutes ago, and Tess planned to leave the ball shortly. Lily meant to accompany Tess home now, but Roslyn would remain until the last guests left, to confer with the Simpkins about putting the Hall to rights on the morrow.

Arabella gave a sigh of weary contentment. The entire day had seemed a pleasant whirl, but thankfully it was nearly over. In the morning, she and Marcus would embark on a monthlong wedding trip. They planned to tour Scotland and the Lake District in northern England, then spend time at the Pierce baronial family seat in Devonshire so Arabella could become acquainted with his estate and tenants there before returning to Danvers Hall.

Arabella eagerly anticipated both the journey and her wedding night with Marcus, since they'd had very little chance for intimacy or passion during the past month. The thought of finally sharing a nuptial bed with her new husband brought a private smile to her lips.

Lily evidently saw it, for she observed cheerfully, "I concede I was wrong to oppose your union with Marcus, Arabella. I have no doubts now that he will treat you as you deserve. It's obvious he loves you—and that you love him. I vow you are actually *glowing* with happiness."

Arabella smiled serenely. "That doesn't surprise me. I never dreamed I could be this happy, Lily. I only wish you could feel half as much happiness."

Lily laughed. "Well, I most certainly will not find it in marriage. If you have daughters, I will be content to play spinster aunt and teach them manners and deportment."

Meeting Roslyn's amused eyes, Arabella shook her head wryly. Lilian excelled at any kind of physical activity—riding and driving, archery, and dancing in particular—but manners and deportment were *not* her forte.

Both Lily and Roslyn would take on larger roles at the academy from now on. Arabella felt considerable relief, knowing the endeavor would continue to prosper. Not only would the school provide better futures for dozens of young lower-class girls, teaching them to become true ladies, but it would provide Lily and Roslyn satisfying occupations and independence, allowing them to continue earning their livings— although being penniless was no longer a concern after the generous settlement Marcus had made them.

Because he had also drastically improved their social status, Roslyn could now consider her own matrimonial prospects. Lily had no such desire. Even seeing Arabella's newfound happiness was not enough to make Lily question her refusal to surrender her cherished freedom to a husband.

"Marriage may not suit you, Lily," Arabella agreed with a fond glance.

Lily gave an unladylike snort. "I wish you would remind Winifred of that fact. Her attempts at matchmaking are driving me to distraction."

"Matchmaking?"

"She is plotting the taming and capture of Marcus's two friends. She claims they are in need of wives, and this evening she practically twisted their arms to coerce them to dance with Roslyn and me."

Arabella couldn't help but smile. Winifred would have difficulty ensnaring the two extremely eligible noblemen for her sisters or anyone else. The Duke of Arden and the Marquess of Claybourne were the bane of the ton's marriage-minded mamas, even more elusive than Marcus.

"Winifred has singled me out for Lord Claybourne," Lily complained in disgust. "It is utterly mortifying to be paraded before him like a prize heifer at a fair."

Roslyn couldn't resist teasing Lily a little. "Yet he *is* exceedingly handsome, in addition to being enormously wealthy and titled."

"Oh, he is attractive enough," Lily muttered. "But he is too arrogant for his own good, expecting me to fall swooning at his feet."

Arabella raised an eyebrow. "Is *that* why you decided to leave the ball early? To avoid any further association with the marquess?"

Lily actually blushed. "Yes. I swear, I have never met a more *persistent* man. He is well beyond my abilities to deal with."

When Roslyn couldn't suppress her laughter, Lily cast her a scowling glance. "You may find my dilemma amusing, dearest sister, but you should have a care for yourself. Winifred will try to arrange a match for you with Arden next, for she said as much."

"I am not worried," Roslyn said calmly. "I have no interest whatsoever in marrying Arden."

The unusual note of conviction in her voice surprised Arabella. "But you met him only this morning. Can you really judge him on so short an acquaintance?"

Roslyn hesitated. "To be truthful, I met the duke before today."

Arabella gave her a measuring glance, while Lily asked, "When?"

"A fortnight ago," Roslyn admitted, "when I attended the masquerade ball with Fanny. His grace didn't know who I was, since I wore a mask and refused to tell him my name."

"Rose, you never said you met him!" Lily exclaimed. "So what happened?"

An attractive flush rose to her cheeks. "Let us just say that I was not eager to further the acquaintance, even if he was."

Like Lily, Arabella was highly curious to learn what had occurred between Roslyn and the Duke of Arden, but she knew there was no point in pressing the issue. Roslyn's interests lay elsewhere, since she had a tendre for their neighbor, the Earl of Haviland. Fortunately Lord Haviland had attended the wedding celebrations today, so Roslyn was able to spend significant time in his company. Her determination to marry only for love necessitated that both parties actually have the opportunity to fall in love, so it behooved her to make good use of every encounter.

But rather than discuss her views on love and

marriage, Roslyn promptly changed the subject. "Arabella, we had best go. Marcus will be waiting for you."

At that reminder, Arabella rose to her feet and warmly embraced her sisters. Tears stung her eyes a little as they said their farewells. This was the symbolic end of their girlhood together, and she would miss the love and camaraderie they had shared. For so long it had been the three of them against the world.

And yet now she had Marcus. At the prospect of beginning her new life with him, Arabella felt her heart fill with excitement and eager anticipation.

When she went downstairs in search of him, she found Marcus emerging from his study. Her heart swelled even further at the tender look he gave her.

"There you are, love," he said. "I wondered where you had gone."

"I was saying good-bye to my sisters."

"I just had a similar council with my friends." Marcus glanced back at the study door. "Drew and Heath are still in my study, drinking my best store of brandy and mourning the loss of my bachelorhood."

Arabella regarded him curiously. "Are you mourning the loss?"

"Not in the slightest." He chuckled.

"What is so amusing?"

"Realizing how much I have changed in the past two months. I once thought matrimony was a sinister word, but no longer. Come, let us find our remaining guests and encourage them to leave. I want you all to myself for our wedding night."

It was nearly two hours later, however, before Marcus got his wish. As the final carriages pulled away, Simpkin shut the front door and discreetly disappeared from the entrance hall, leaving the earl and his new countess to themselves.

"Shall we?" Marcus asked, offering her his hand to escort her upstairs.

"Yes," Arabella replied, smiling serenely as she slipped her hand in his.

He interlaced their fingers as they mounted the stairs and negotiated the corridor to the lord's apartments. A soft glow of lamplight greeted them as they entered his bedchamber, while the covers on the massive bed had been turned down invitingly.

Marcus closed the door behind them, shutting them inside.

"Alone at last," he murmured huskily, drawing Arabella into his embrace. "I thought this day would never arrive."

"I know," she said fervently although her gray eyes danced with love and laughter. "You should be proud of yourself, my lord. You succeeded in winning our wager, just as you predicted."

"Oh, I am. And I am impatient for our wedding night to begin."

Arabella slid her hands up his chest and began to untie his cravat, her smile seductive and mischievous. "We celebrated our wedding night weeks ago, if you recall."

His blood heated dangerously at that alluring smile. "Not formally. We weren't wed then." His gaze trapped hers. "But now we are. Now you are mine," Marcus added softly.

"Yes," Arabella agreed just as softly. "And you are mine."

He saw so much tender emotion in her eyes that his heart turned over. "I'll never let you go, wife."

"Wife . . . I like the sound of that, husband."

"So do I."

They undressed each other slowly, taking the time to kiss and caress frequently. When they were both naked, his gaze locked with hers.

"No regrets?" Marcus asked.

"None whatsoever. I know our marriage will be blissfully happy."

"I intend to do my damnedest to make it so."

"I have no doubts." She stepped into the circle of his waiting arms, her eyes radiant with love as she gazed back at him.

The sight made his breath catch and his heart thud. He had never expected to feel anything so powerful, so deep, for any woman. But he had no doubts, either, that his feelings for Arabella would last a lifetime. The love inside him was painfully strong; hunger and desire a sweet ache.

"So," Arabella remarked teasingly, reaching up to twine her arms around his neck, "do you intend to show me what a marvelous husband and lover you are? I seem to remember you boasting about your amorous skills more than once."

The words were an unmistakable challenge, one that Marcus couldn't resist.

With a low laugh, he caught Arabella's hand and pressed a tender kiss to her fingers, a solemn promise of loyalty and love. Then he led her to their marriage bed and drew her down, eager to begin their future together.

Read on to catch a sneak peek at the next
seductive novel in the Courtship Wars

To Bed a Beauty

by Nicole Jordan

London, June 1817, The Masked Ball

Roslyn reached up to press her fingers against her
temple. Her head was beginning to throb under the
weight of her wig and bonnet, and the suffocating
mask was rubbing a raw spot on her left cheek.

At least she could mitigate some of her suffering by
removing the offending bonnet and mask.

Roslyn untied the ribbons beneath her chin and slid
the bonnet off, then loosened the strings of her mask
and drew it down. As the cool night air fanned her
face, she gave a sigh of relief . . . until a low, masculine voice spoke behind her.

"So this is where you are hiding yourself."

Gasping in startlement, Roslyn whirled and promptly
dropped her bonnet when she recognized the tall, im-
posing nobleman standing there. His broad, domino-
clad shoulders filled the narrow embrasure, while his

amber hair glinted more silver than gold in the moonlight.

Alarmed to see the duke, she fumbled to replace her mask, hoping he hadn't been afforded a clear glimpse of her face. "How you startled me . . ." she exclaimed too breathlessly as she finished tying the strings.

"Forgive me. It was the least of my intentions—to discomfit a beautiful woman."

Roslyn's gaze narrowed through her mask. His tone was mild, languid even. If he was attempting to flatter her, he wasn't making much effort. But perhaps he was merely playing an expected game, spouting compliments he thought she wished to hear.

There was nothing languid about the warm glance that raked over her figure, however. Instead his eyes showed pure male interest—and had the deplorable effect of making her pulse race.

"I am Arden."

"I know who you are, your grace," Roslyn said rather crossly. He was Andrew Moncrief, Duke of Arden, known as "Drew" to his intimates. And she had seldom been less pleased to see anyone in her life.

His eyebrow lifted at her tone. "Regrettably, I do not know *you*, my lovely Incognita. I would have sought an introduction, but you fled the moment you spied me. And Fanny suddenly made herself scarce before I could even discover your name."

Having no valid defense, Roslyn remained mute. When the duke stepped forward and bent to retrieve her dropped bonnet from the balcony floor, she would have retreated except that the railing was at her back.

Trapped, she was forced to endure his scrutiny. He stood watching her in speculation, holding the ribbons in his long fingers.

Roslyn stared back, unable to help herself. It was too dark to be certain, but she thought his eyes were green. A deep, vibrant green. And this close, his lean, aristocratic features were even more sensually compelling than at a distance. His nearness, as well, had a devastating effect on her composure.

He spoke before she could gain control of her whirling thoughts. "I congratulate you, sweeting. Your ploy worked."

"My ploy?" she repeated, puzzled.

"You hoped I would pursue you here, and you succeeded. I was intrigued enough to follow you."

He thought she had purposely lured him here to the alcove? "It was no ploy, your grace. I found the ballroom overly warm and came here for a respite."

One corner of his mouth twisted sardonically. "How convenient that you chose a location so well equipped for an assignation," he said, nodding at the chaise longue behind him. Before she could protest, he went on. "You must be new to London. I would certainly have remembered had I seen you before now."

Roslyn hid her wince of dismay. She hoped his memory was not so keen when she encountered him at her sister's wedding in a fortnight. "Yes, I am new to London. But I promise you, I did not lure you here for an assignation."

And she had no intention, either, of prolonging this

unwanted encounter. Murmuring a polite "thank you," Roslyn retrieved her bonnet from his grasp and tried to slip past him.

The duke, however, reached out to curl his fingers lightly around her wrist. "One might think you are actually eager to avoid me."

"One might."

"Why?" His tone held surprise and genuine curiosity.

"I dislike the way you are inspecting me, as if I am merchandise to be purchased."

"I stand corrected." His lips curved in a rueful smile that was slow, sensual. "I don't think of you as merchandise, I assure you."

It was impossible to ignore that captivating male smile, and Roslyn suddenly understood why females pursued Arden in droves. "Then you will pray excuse me," she murmured, her voice more uneven than she would have liked.

Pointedly, she glanced down at his imprisoning grasp, yet he didn't release her. "Are you currently taken?"

She blinked. "Taken?"

"Do you have a protector yet?"

He was asking if she was currently employed as a lightskirt, Roslyn realized. She considered saying yes, but then she would have to come up with a name for her nonexistent patron, and Arden would very likely see through her lie. "No, I have no protector."

"Then why don't you simply name your price? I dislike haggling."

She stared up at him. "Are you asking me to be your . . . *mistress?*"

His smile turned bland. "Unless you have another proposition in mind? Yes, I am asking you to be my mistress, darling."

Roslyn knew her jaw had dropped inelegantly, but she couldn't help it. It shocked her a little that he would offer such an intimate position to a perfect stranger. "We are complete strangers, your grace. You know nothing about me."

"I know enough to find you lovely and desirable. What more is necessary?"

"I could be a vicious harpy, for all you know."

"I am willing to risk it. A thousand pounds a year during pleasure. Half that should we decide to part ways sooner."

When Roslyn remained gaping with astonishment, he cocked his head and nodded briefly, as if coming to a decision. "Very well, two thousand. And of course I will pay all your expenses . . . a house and carriage plus an allowance for clothing and jewels."

Roslyn couldn't help being amused. It seemed an outrageous sum to offer an untried courtesan, although she knew Fanny made several times that amount. "How can you be certain I am worth it?"

Appreciative laughter lit his eyes as he gave a casual shrug. "Your beauty is alluring enough to satisfy my discriminating tastes. Anything else you need to know I can teach you."

Roslyn's own amusement faded as anger pricked her. Arden had unwittingly struck a raw nerve. He couldn't know that her beauty—or more precisely, being coveted solely for her physical attributes—was a painfully sore point with her.

She also realized it was ridiculous to resent his quite generous proposition, since she was here tonight pretending to be a Cyprian. But after the other shameful offers she had already received over the past four years, she couldn't respond with equanimity.

"I believe the proper response is to thank you for your generous offer, your grace," she said coldly, withdrawing her wrist from his grasp, "but I must decline."

His eyebrow shot up at her wintry tone. "It is common practice to feign reluctance in order to increase your price, but you will find that I dislike coyness."

Roslyn bristled. "I do not *have* a price, nor am I trying to be coy. I simply have no desire to have you for my lover—despite your vaunted reputation."

His eyes narrowed. "Did Fanny say something to give you a fear of me?"

"No."

"If you need to assure yourself of my qualifications, I would be happy to demonstrate."

"I don't need a demonstration. I don't doubt your expertise in the least."

"Then perhaps we should test *your* skills." Before she could do more than draw a breath, he stepped even closer and cupped her face in his hands. "Kiss me, love, and show me your charms."

His bold gesture caught her completely off guard. Roslyn went rigid with dismay as the duke bent his head and captured her mouth with his.

It was a startling kiss, not only because of its unexpectedness but because of the effect it had on her entire body. His lips moved over hers in a sensual exploration that was tender and arousing and wildly exciting.

She had been kissed before, but nothing whatsoever like this. Her skin suddenly felt covered in heat, as if she were standing too close to a fire.

Her heart was pounding when he finally shifted his caresses away from her mouth. His lips brushed fleetingly along her jaw to her ear, where they lingered. "You taste like innocence," he murmured, his voice surprisingly husky. "It is a charming act, but entirely unnecessary."

"It is no act," Roslyn replied shakily. "I am not experienced."

He drew back enough to study her, his gaze skeptical. "I much prefer honesty."

Roslyn stiffened. "You don't believe me?" she asked in a warning tone.

He reached up with his fingertips to trace her lips beneath her mask. "Let us say I am willing to be convinced. Come here, my sweet. . . ."

He bent to her once more and kissed her again, this time more passionately. Alarmed by her own response, Roslyn tried to retreat, but Arden pulled her fully against his body, letting her feel the hardness of him, the vitality.

Stunned by his devastating sensuality, Roslyn whimpered, amazed that she could be so aroused by a man's embrace. When finally he broke off the kiss and raised his head, she looked up at him in an unfocused daze.

His smile was rueful. "I confess . . . most women don't have this powerful an effect on me. You feel it, too, Beauty, don't deny it."

It was true, she had never in her life experienced anything like it—this lightning bolt of attraction that sparked between them. This devastating heat and desire. This yearning.

Not that she would ever admit it to *him*.

Struggling to regain a semblance of composure, Roslyn cleared her throat.

"Indeed?" she managed to say with a blithe laugh. "Your arrogance is astonishing, your grace."

It was obviously not the response he expected, and Roslyn pressed her point. "Your vanity is vastly overinflated if you think I am eager to leap into your bed."

The slow, charming smile he gave her was impossibly wicked, impossibly seductive . . . and sensual enough to bewitch a saint. "A bed isn't necessary. We can make use of the chaise longue behind us." He waved in the general direction of the alcove. "And at the same time we can remedy the fact that we are strangers."

"I have no desire to become better acquainted with you."

"Perhaps I can change your mind."

He raised his hand, his warm fingers tracing a path from the hollow of her throat to the swells of her breasts, which thrust prominently upward in her shepherdess costume.

"Your grace . . ." Roslyn began in protest, but he stole any further words away with another kiss, claiming her mouth with tender possessiveness. When he cradled her silk-clad breast in his palm, the brazen shock of it rendered her immobile. She wore no corset beneath her low-cut bodice, so she could feel the heated pressure of his caress through the fragile fabric.

A rush of excitement swept her senses; fire radiated from the hand that held her throbbing breast and from his lips that were plying hers with such expert skill.

His mouth continued to hold hers effortlessly as he stroked the bare skin above her bodice with his fingers, dipping down into the valley between her breasts. Then his hand curled over the low neckline and lightly tugged, sending the mounds spilling out of her gown.

Roslyn gasped as the cool night air brushed her exposed flesh, but she couldn't manage a word of rebuke, not even when the duke's sensual kisses ended and he drew back.

His eyes darkened as he gazed down at her nakedness, surveying the ripe firmness crested with dusky nipples.

Her breathing suspended, Roslyn remained speechless as with his thumbs he traced slow circles around the hardened peaks. A low moan was dredged from her throat while the ribbons of her bonnet slipped through her nerveless fingers.

At her response, he took the weight of her breasts in his hands and tugged the nipples to taut attention with lingering caresses, pinching lightly with his fingers, soothing with his thumbs.

Roslyn pulled in a deep, shuddering breath, finding it impossible to move. His masterful hands knew just how to arouse, to excite, to delight.

"Your grace," she finally repeated in a shaken voice.

"Hush, let me pleasure you."